SUTTON

THE BILLIONAIRES OF WHISPERS

BOOK 5

SAMANTHA SKYE

Copyright © 2025 by Samantha Skye / Handsome Henry Publishing

EBOOK ISBN: 978-1-923258-30-3

PAPERBACK ISBN: 978-1-923258-31-0

ALT PAPERBACK ISBN: 978-1-923258-32-7

Cover Design: Angela Haddon

Editor: Nice Girl Naughty Edits

Proofreading: Kimberly Dawn

Cover Photography: CJC Photography

Cover Model: Jered Youngblood

1

NIKKI - THE DINER GIRL

It's quiet, the calm before the storm of the afternoon rush.

"Nikki, can you put on a fresh pot?" My boss, Rochelle, doesn't look at me as she walks past, wiping the counter on her way, before she steps into the back to check on the kitchen. She's a multitasker specialist, always on the go.

Working at Delish Diner in the small town of Whispers wasn't a dream of mine. But in the dead of night, when I needed to run, it was the only place that sounded familiar.

"Fresh coffee coming up." My moves are habitual, even as my attention keeps flicking to the door. Having been here for months now, I know how to brew coffee, how to balance multiple dishes as I serve, how to wipe a counter so it's spotless, all while doing it with a smile on my face. The skills of which I never collected from my childhood home. The one with nannies, chefs, and housekeepers.

"I'm here." James pushes through the door, and my shoulders lower instantly.

"Hey, kiddo. I've got a cupcake with your name on it."

Being away from him all day has my anxiety skyrocketing. But he needs an education, and with me working the day shift so I can be with him at night, it leaves homeschooling out of the question.

"Chocolate?" He jumps up onto the stool at the end of the counter, his usual spot, away from the door, hidden by other patrons. His heavy bag hits the floor, full of books, as usual. As he grins at me, my heart expands. He smiles more now than he ever has, further cementing that we made the right choice in coming here.

"Nothing beats it." I slide the small plate with the chocolatey goodness across the counter to him, along with a glass of milk, and both are gone within a minute. I always ask Rochelle to take the cost of the daily cupcake from my wage, but she never does. She looks after me better than I deserve. The two of us are so familiar with each other now, we move around this diner in unison, picking up each other's orders, cleaning up each other's tables.

"Hungry today, my boy?" Rochelle walks back out from the kitchen, a tray of warm baked goods in her hands like she knows exactly what we're both thinking. The smell of freshly baked chocolate chip cookies is enough to have my own stomach twisting with a craving.

"I skipped lunch," James tells her, and my head snaps to him, my frown instant.

"What do you mean, you skipped lunch?" Truth be told, his lunch isn't much. A peanut butter and jelly sandwich, an apple from the small tree we have in our yard at the cottage, and if we're lucky, maybe a small granola bar when I work a few extra hours or my tips allow it. But regardless, he needs to eat. He's a growing boy.

He shrugs. "I wasn't hungry." He doesn't meet my eyes, so I know he's lying. It's hard being the new kid. Trying to make friends without getting too close. But as he pulls his books from his bag to start his homework, I leave him be. He's a good kid, and I don't want to put too much pressure on him. As I grab a dishcloth and clean up his crumbs, I hear the familiar small screech of the back door opening, and my breath hitches, the air around me changing.

"Oh, I was wondering when he would turn up today," Rochelle murmurs from beside me.

Sutton Silvers. Hollywood heartthrob and billionaire celebrity sneaks into the diner from the back door nearly every day as of recently. The only customer Rochelle allows to do so. His head is lowered, his baseball hat pulled down to cover most of his face, but you can't miss his tall stature, commanding presence, or the way he looks in his fitted t-shirt and jeans. *God, he looks good.*

"Can you look after him today? I've got to get the chicken pies out of the oven."

We're under strict instructions from Rochelle not to tell anyone Sutton's here. Not to broadcast it to friends or put it out on social media. None of that's hard for me. I know what it takes to stay hidden, and my lips are sealed. He slides into the last booth at the back of the diner, the one that's fast becoming his personal space.

"I'll handle it."

The front door chimes as I walk toward him, and I look over my shoulder, seeing a group of young men, probably in their early twenties and close to my age. They come to the diner a few times a month, from Williamstown, I'm told. They never tip, always leer at me, and leave a very bad taste in my mouth with every encounter.

"I'll get them." Rochelle is quick. A no-nonsense woman, she marches over to take their orders, and I grin, thankful she gives me the easier customer.

"Hey, Sutton. Your usual?" I don't bother writing it down, but I bring my notepad and pen with me anyway because I need something to do with my hands. They sweat every time I talk to him.

He looks up at me, his deep brown eyes connecting with mine, and doesn't say anything for a moment.

"Coffee would be great."

Nodding, I don't ask questions. I already know how he likes it.

"Does Rochelle have any of those chicken pies?" he asks before I walk away.

After being hungry all day, now is the time my stomach rumbles.

His eyes shoot down to my stomach, then flick back to my face. Shit. I was hoping he wouldn't hear that. Mouth opening to say something, he closes it quickly and takes a deep breath, like he's holding in his words.

I clear my throat. "Just fresh out of the oven, actually."

"I'll take one of those too." He glances past me at James, before his attention comes back to me. My hands grip tightly to my notepad, my protective instincts kicking in.

"Both are coming right up." Turning quickly, I march back to the counter to get his order in. The man makes me nervous. Not because he's a famous movie star; if anything, that fact repels me. But there's something about him. Something that intrigues me... just a little.

"Nikki, why do some buildings stay standing in earthquakes, but others fall apart?" James asks me as he chews the end of his pencil. I grab the fresh pot of coffee and my service cloth.

"It's all about structure and flexibility. The best buildings have designs that absorb shock, things like reinforced steel frames or base isolators that let them move with the ground instead of fighting it." The information rolls off my tongue easily. MIT was hard, but I graduated, right before we escaped in the dead of night, taking a Greyhound bus with our hats pulled low and all our possessions in a small duffel.

"So why don't they make every building like that?" His follow-up question gives me pause.

"Money, mostly. Safety costs. They build fast and cheap, without thinking about the consequences."

"What's with all the questions, kiddo?" Rochelle moves around quickly as more people stream in, and I know I need to get back to work.

"We're going to visit the sheriff's office tomorrow on a field trip. I want to be prepared with questions. Our topic is disaster relief."

Swallowing hard, I try not to show any emotion. Not that visiting the sheriff is bad. He comes in here a lot, and I've met him many times. He's Rochelle's husband, the two of them almost inseparable. But if anyone were going to try to find us, I have a feeling the local sheriff would be the first person to be notified.

Swallowing down that concern, I agree with him. "It's good to be prepared."

James looks at me as I walk away, his smile slipping, giving me a little nod. He knows. We've talked about it at length.

"One hot coffee..." I stand at Sutton's table and pour him a fresh cup.

"Your kid asks good questions."

I stop mid pour. James and I weren't talking loudly, but with no one here to talk to, Sutton is probably attuned to the conversations around him. James is here every day after school, doing his homework and reading books, sitting at the end of the counter for an hour until I finish my shift.

Sutton has seen him around multiple times but never commented until now.

This is new. Sutton normally doesn't talk much, doesn't look up or around. He's staying with his brother, but rumors have it that he's building a house here. Liking the privacy a small town like Whispers brings. For weeks, I've served him, and we've barely said two words to each other. But I know his eyes follow me wherever I go. I can feel him watching me. Caught him a few times too.

"He's smart," I say simply, placing the coffee in front of him.

He looks back at James and then me again. "He looks like you."

My heart thuds harder as the fear of people knowing too much creeps in. One of the first things we did when we left Manhattan was dye our hair. My usual blond tresses are now black. The upkeep is one that boxed dye ensures I do almost monthly. James grew his hair, looking less polished than he did when attending one of the most expensive private schools in New York. Again, I color it, trying anything and everything to keep our real identities hidden. So far, no one's come looking, although I know there are missing person posters everywhere in the city. Here, in Whispers, is a world away from all that.

"He would hate to hear you say that." I make light of it as a small grin comes to my face. It's the truth; James would hate to be compared to a girl.

"Shouldn't be. It's a compliment."

My smile stalls as my eyes meet his. The air around us thickens. Taking a breath, I reinforce my shield.

"Let me just go get your pie." I ignore his statement and walk briskly back to the counter. I haven't had many genuine compliments in my life. Instead, many merely tokens, off-the-cuff remarks that are said without even looking at me. That's what happens when people want to get to know your father rather than you. They use you to get to him, using a cloud of contrived bullshit to cover their real agendas.

"Can I just grab a small chicken pie for Sutton?" I ask as I approach the counter. They smell amazing as Rochelle pushes the hot little potpies from the tray into the large display dish.

"Sure, honey." The roar of my stomach has her pausing. "Sounds like you need one too?" She looks at me in a way that a mother might look at their daughter. Knowingly. "Did you eat today?"

Her eyebrows pinch when I don't respond. No, I haven't eaten. I took my lunch break and sat in the park down near the school, eating an apple that was so old I should've stewed it. I also skipped breakfast, giving James the last bagel, which I'm now thankful for because he skipped lunch.

"Of course," I lie. My fake smile is wide, but my stomach betrays me once again.

She clicks her tongue, a move my own mother used to do, giving me a sense of warmth that's been absent for too long.

"Go give Sutton his pie, and I'll put one on a plate for you and one for James."

"No, Rochelle, we're fine—"

She interrupts me quickly, frowning, giving me her don't-mess-with-me face. "The afternoon rush is about to start, and I don't need you fainting on me." Her voice is matter of fact, and I suck in a sharp breath. I know what she's doing. She acts tough, but she's a big softy underneath. I'm glad I met her; her heart is pure gold.

But I hate handouts. I'm the last person who deserves

them. Yet she's right. I don't want to faint, not here. Not now. So I deliver Sutton his pie and walk back to sit with James, the two of us eating quickly. With my stomach now settled, I get started on my last hour here, relieved I don't need to scrounge up something for dinner tonight.

2

———

SUTTON SILVERS

I've been hiding out in Whispers for what feels like a while now.

I arrived in town under the cover of darkness, hiding from the barrage of media that now comes with being one of Hollywood's most sought-after leading men.

The town's nice enough, quaint, quiet, but I haven't seen much of it. Just the view from the roads leading to the diner and the inside of my brother Sawyer's house, where I've been holed up, cycling through old TV shows and pretending I have something resembling a routine.

But I love it.

I've already purchased a block of land, and I'm drawing up plans for my own little slice of paradise as a place to come to when I need to get away from LA. It's ideal, up the back of Billionaire Boulevard; I have the woods at my door, and I've already started hiking around to get the lay of the land. Hiking has become a new interest of mine, but it's one I don't do regularly, afraid of being discovered, even in the forest.

"What are you doing?"

Sawyer walks in, pushing through the afternoon crowd, his usual polished suit on full display. Now the local lawyer in town, his city suits remain, having him look completely out of place. Noah's balanced on his hip like it's second nature now. My older brother has changed since meeting his girl Annabelle and her two boys, for the better, and I couldn't love him any more than I do. He treats those boys like his own, and I don't mind having two new nephews around. Keeps my days interesting.

I give Noah a small fist bump before stabbing my fork into my pie. "Getting a late lunch."

"If you keep coming here, someone's bound to spot you."

I hold back my annoyance. It's not the first time he's given me this warning. "Rochelle lets me in the back entrance, and this booth is reserved just for me. I'll get cabin fever staying at your house all day and all night."

At the mention of her name, Rochelle barely looks up, just nods, like we have some secret understanding. It's a quiet agreement that lets me keep slipping through her doors, unnoticed. It's nice of her to do when she barely knows me.

My only other outing is Whiteman's Distillery, drinking and talking with Sawyer, the owners, Connor and Tanner, along with my best friend from LA and new Whispers resident, Hudson. The meetup is now a highlight of my week. They're a group of friends I didn't know I needed, yet have filled my time with laughs, business conversations, and plenty of outstanding whiskey to keep me company.

Sawyer sighs, shifting Noah higher on his hip as he slides into the seat across from me. "You can't hide out forever."

"Yes, I can." Noah shuffles on his lap, giving me a grin, one that tells me he's up to no good as he grabs Sawyer's tie.

"But you need to start thinking about your next steps."

"That would be a hell of a lot easier if the media would ease off." I bite out the words. I love acting and the movie business, but along with that comes a high profile, gossip, and overwhelming media interest. I take most of it as it comes and don't get too caught up in it. But after my last movie was a box office hit, both here and overseas, the media scrutiny became intense. Fans got crazier, my life completely invaded. So I came to hide here with my brother.

"They seem to be getting worse," Sawyer acknowledges, and he's right. I thought slipping out of LA and laying low for a while would help it all die down. But it seems to have had the opposite effect. I hear there's now big money for a shot of me. Paparazzi are keen to break the story about where Sutton Silvers is hiding, what he's been doing, and with whom. Thank God for Whispers.

Whiskey flows through here like water. With it, a tight-knit community that doesn't waver in its support of their own. Led by Tanner and Connor Whiteman, billionaire owners of Whiteman's Whiskey, this town is currently my safe haven, and I couldn't have picked a better place.

"Have you talked to Bobby lately?" Sawyer's distracted as he peels the wrapper off one of Rochelle's cookies.

I nod. "He's working on something." I watch Noah closely as he grips Sawyer's tie, the end of it dangling in his little hand.

Sawyer snorts. "The only thing Bobby ever works on is deals for himself."

"He's fine." I wave him off.

"I've never liked him."

"You've made that abundantly clear." Bobby has been my manager for years, and he and Sawyer clash like true enemies. But Bobby picked me up the minute I landed in

LA, spotting me at a café, seeing something in me that I didn't yet see in myself. He sent me to auditions that afternoon, and I wouldn't be where I am today without him. Even so, he's an asshole. With roles now coming to me a little easier, deals are done with Sawyer, my legally astute brother looking over every one of them. Bobby has no other clients, his roster completely thinned out, and I don't think he's a fan of having anyone else involved in my finances or business dealings. The fame and money have gone to his head. He isn't the same man he once was.

"It could be time for you to part ways." We've had this discussion a few times over the last year or so. At first, I dismissed it completely. Primarily because I was on location filming, which meant I had to focus and keep my profile clean for movie promotion. I didn't need the media attention it would bring to drop my manager of over ten years.

"The problem is, I need to replace him, and I can't do that while hiding out. Besides, I'm not working on anything at the moment." Although, Bobby still calls most days. Sometimes, I answer, but most often not. He's been trying to pitch different movies to me, but I'm enjoying the break from the business more than I thought.

The space between me and LA has done me good. I get to spend time with my brother and his family, being the uncle I never thought I would be. It's made me think about my future, how dating models and actresses in LA isn't really my vibe anymore. That jumping from movie set to movie set is getting tiring now that I've hit the heights of movie fame, and the need to strive has now abated. It's made me think about moving in a different direction. Both in my career and in my life.

"Yeah, well, the media still has a new story on you every day."

My eyes narrow in question at my brother. I haven't been watching the gossip sites. I didn't want to bring the mental load to my new surroundings. But by the look of his face, maybe I should be.

"Anything I should be worried about?"

"Apparently, you love the color blue today." Sawyer rolls his eyes, a bad habit he has.

It's true; my favorite color is blue, but that's just one of the things everyone already knows about me. So I let that "news" roll off my shoulders.

As I scoop the last piece of pie into my mouth, Sawyer looks at his cell, not paying much attention. I keep silent yet grin as Noah dunks the end of Sawyer's tie into my now-cold black coffee. I love this new nephew of mine, giving my brother a run for his money, just like I used to when I was younger.

When I give him a wink, Noah giggles, and I watch the dark liquid start to slowly creep up the soft blue fabric of Sawyer's designer tie. That should ruffle his feathers.

"Shhh." Noah shushes me a little too loudly and gets Sawyer's attention.

"Noah, what in the world... I have no idea why you have such a fascination with my ties, but I've lost about fifty of them now," Sawyer mumbles as he grabs a napkin and starts dabbing. While he's busy, Noah grabs Sawyer's cookie and finishes it, his mission now complete. Smart kid. He strategized, knew what his endgame was, and found a way to get it. Kudos to him.

"He's got you wrapped around his finger." A year ago, if anyone had told me that Sawyer would be here in Whispers, with a kid on his lap, not fussing about a ruined designer tie, I would've called them insane. Yet here we both are. Sitting at the small-town diner, eating pie and cookies.

Looking around, I spot Nikki, the young waitress I noticed the minute I walked into this diner. Who I've been coming back to see almost daily. She moves around this place like she's trying not to be noticed, scurrying from one table to the next, turning them over, serving, cleaning up, and getting everyone what they need. She must feel my gaze on her, because she lifts her eyes, looking straight at me before she drops her head quickly. I never seem to be able to get her to meet my eyes for more than a few seconds.

"You're looking at her again." Sawyer's eyes burn into me.

"Was not." My answer isn't proving a strong case as I continue to watch her. It's hard not to. In jeans that look painted on, her ass perky to perfection. Her long, almost jet-black hair contrasting with her stunning blue eyes. But it's more than her looks. It's the way she holds herself, the way she smiles at everyone, the way she waits on tenterhooks for her son to walk in the door after school.

"Now's not the time to be looking at women, Sutton." God, if only he knew I've been looking at her since I arrived.

I pivot the subject. "She's young to have a kid, don't you think?"

Sawyer's girl Annabelle is young, had her children in her late teens, early twenties, but that's still older than what I think Nikki is. James must be at least ten, and Nikki, I'm guessing, is in her early twenties, at most. It's obviously possible, but hell, she must've had him young. Fifteen, maybe, and that doesn't bode well. She would've been a child herself.

There's something about her, though. I clocked the East Coast accent almost immediately. Like a posh upper-class tone that makes me wonder where she's from. Her nails are neatly painted soft pink. Her silky hair is well maintained. Her skin is flawless—not a freckle, not a scar, not a blemish to be seen. She wouldn't be out of place in Manhattan. Yet she's here, serving coffees in small-town Whispers. It has me intrigued.

"Agree. But it isn't our business." Sawyer looks at me closely, but I pay him little attention.

I watch her finish her shift, my jaw tight as her son James packs up his books. He's here every day too, doing his homework at the end of the counter. There's a lot of love between them. Nikki tucks a loose strand of hair behind her ear as she moves them both toward the back exit. Just before she walks out, her head turns, her eyes meeting mine again, and for an instant, we get locked in a stare, before she slides through the door, and then they're gone.

"Where do they walk to?" I ask out loud. I never see her drive; they're always walking everywhere.

Rochelle, wiping down the counter nearby, barely glances up to answer me. "Home."

"How far?"

She swipes at the counter harder than necessary. "A long way."

I frown at that. "Her car broken?"

Rochelle stops wiping, looking at me like I've said something ridiculous. "She doesn't have one."

I swivel in my seat as my jaw nearly drops. "You're joking."

"Not everyone can afford these things, Sutton. And while I pay my staff fairly, she isn't a billionaire like you."

Her tone is sharp, but there's something else beneath it, something pointed.

"That girl has a history, one she hasn't shared with me. But I can tell she's got secrets."

I don't respond, because I already knew that.

Sawyer gives me another look of his that tells me to quit

it. "Don't go looking. Nikki isn't someone you have fun with and then forget once you're gone."

With a smirk, I shake my head. "I don't know what you're talking about."

He doesn't believe me, and he shouldn't. It's been a long time since I touched a woman, and I sure as hell am noticing Nikki.

"Speaking of new faces, you might want to finish up." Rochelle's voice has me immediately on edge.

I glance up just in time to see a guy scanning the diner, someone unfamiliar, but familiar enough. The kind of guy who doesn't belong here but is pretending he does.

A journalist.

Fuck.

Pulling my baseball hat down, I quickly slide out of the booth, grateful the group of men at the front are making asses of themselves to take his attention. I toss Sawyer a quick goodbye, Rochelle a small nod, and move toward the back exit.

I step outside just in time to catch sight of Nikki and James walking away, their pace steady, their shoulders drawn inward like they don't want to be seen. My eyes don't leave them until they disappear down the street, their figures slipping into the shadows of the back roads.

I'm not the only one hiding out in Whispers, that's for sure.

3

NIKKI

I move to fill Bob's coffee, where he, Peter the local taxi, and Tim from the toy store down the street sit, chatting about farm life, before I wipe down the counter and refill the cups of the other few patrons nearby. It's quiet today, apart from the rowdy guys who are back again. The ones who stand too close to me when I pass by and who look at me longer than they should. I don't like them. But they're paying customers and never seem to bother anyone else, so I keep quiet. Not wanting to make a fuss, I serve them quickly, leaving them to come back to the safety of the counter.

I may be moving around, doing the usual things, but I feel his eyes on me the entire time. I felt it the moment he walked in. He's here earlier than usual today. Slinking in through the back door and sitting in his usual spot, no one interrupting him, hat pulled low in his signature style.

I wonder why he comes here. Why sit in a diner for hours almost every day? I mean, the chicken pie Rochelle makes is good, but not that good. I'm about to go and see if he needs anything, Rochelle serving him initially, but the chimes ring on the door, and the noise of the diner simmers to a low murmur.

Looking up, I understand why. A stranger. Slicked-back hair, fake-tanned skin, white teeth so blinding I almost laugh. Almost. My experienced city eye spots Botox, a chin implant, maybe some fillers around the jaw and cheeks. This guy has had work done, and the way he walks toward me, his smile wide like a game show host, I know there's only one reason he's here.

Sutton.

I don't dare look in Sutton's direction. But I know he can't move and run out the back door like he usually would. The diner is too quiet, and the movement would have this guy looking straight at him. Giving him away instantly. With Rochelle in the kitchen, this one is now up to me.

"Hi there." His voice razzle dazzles. Yep, Hollywood, for sure.

"Hi. What can I get you?" My fake country accent is terrible, and I wonder briefly why my heart is racing. It isn't my identity being given away.

"I'm actually looking for someone. Wondering if you can help?" He pulls some papers from his pocket, unfolding them. "Have you seen this man?"

I look down at the paper, a full page of Sutton's face staring back at me. He looks good. In a suit, from a red carpet, with a beautiful brunette on his arm. I mean, I see him most days, but with his hat lowered and his face guarded, I haven't really experienced Sutton with a full-blown smile, standing confidently in all his glory. And now, I'm glad I haven't, because his smile would melt even the most stoic woman. I swallow hard, taking in his sparkling eyes, his chiseled jaw, and movie-star good looks.

"I don't recognize him. Is he a friend of yours or some-thin'?" I act completely stupid. Of course, anyone who's anyone knows who Sutton Silvers is. He's on the side of buses and billboards all around the country.

The guy scoffs at me, and I feign confusion.

"This is Sutton Silvers." His voice has lowered, full of condensation.

I tilt my head. "Sutton who?"

Bob coughs into his coffee nearby, which almost has my lips twitching. The whole diner is watching us at this point. You could hear a pin drop.

"Silvers. Hollywood heartthrob. Billionaire movie star. His brother runs the law firm just across the road."

With my lips pursed in a thinking expression, I make a show of glancing at Sawyer's office across the street before I look back at the photo of Sutton and shake my head.

But then, I light up with a gasp. "Oh, I remember him!"

"You do?" His hopes are up, the anticipation of finding the man who doesn't want to be found.

"Yeah, my friend Jodie has a sister Sarah whose neighbor Sally said that she's going to marry him one day." I grin at him, his face now one of disbelief.

"But have you seen him? Here in the diner or around town with his brother?" he presses.

"Our local lawyer is never here. Jodie tries to take him cakes every day, you know, trying to get to know him." I wink at him like we are part of an inside joke. "But he's mostly in New York. His office is barely open." I nod across the street, proving my case. Sawyer's legal office is closed, or at least it looks that way. He's probably there or working from home, but he's always in Whispers. Hardly ever leaves now that he's settled down with Annabelle.

"Are you *sure* you haven't seen Sutton?" he asks one last time, but I feel his energy wane.

"Believe me, if a guy like that was here in Whispers, I would be all over him like a poison ivy rash. You know Jodie said that he probably kisses so good it makes a girl's toes curl." I let out a giggle for good measure. It's easy to act stupid. And men just believe it. If only he knew I graduated on the Dean's List from MIT, know three languages, and vacationed in the Swiss Alps as a kid.

"Well... you and most of the women in this country." He huffs with a smirk. "Fuck. Looks like the tip-off was bad. Glad I spent all day traveling here for nothing." Pushing off the counter, he walks out without so much as a thank you. We all hold our breath, watching him get back into his blacked-out SUV and making his way out of town.

It's only then that the few people in here start to laugh heartily.

"Who the hell is Jodie?" Bob asks, chuckling.

"You heard her, she's Sarah's sister," Tim adds, and the three men start cackling and shaking their heads at me, and I can't help but grin. There's been a few journalists come in who I've had to throw off the scent, but never has Sutton been right here when I've done it.

When I look at him, his gaze on me is intense, so with a racing heart, I walk over with the fresh pot of coffee to offer a refill.

"Thanks for that," he says quietly.

"Rochelle told me that you need to remain unseen... I know what that's like." As soon as the words leave my lips, I seize. He watches me closely, and I feel like a deer in headlights. I'm saying too much, obviously getting too relaxed. But he doesn't ask anything further, and for that, I'm grateful. So far, James and I have hidden in Whispers with success; I don't need to blow our cover.

"Sooo all over him like a poison ivy rash?" He lifts his

cup to his lips, and I notice the ends curl up a little as he takes a sip. He's trying not to laugh.

I cringe, even as I chuckle lightly. "I had to improvise."

"You're good at it. Ever had a poison ivy rash before?" His smile is small, a little cheeky, and I think my stomach flips into itself.

"Never. Also never had my toes curl, but..." Shit, my cheeks flush immediately, and the smile he had disappears as his mouth parts slightly.

"Sounds like your friend Jodie knows what she's talking about." He clears his throat, and I want to die. He knows there's no Jodie, so he's letting me off easy. I can't talk. I'm equal parts mortified that I just admitted that and terrified that I opened myself up too much.

"I should go. You've probably done enough fibbing for me for one day." As he stands, I watch him come to full height right next to me. He's tall, just like his brother and all the other men around here. But I've never stood beside him before, and now that I am, I notice I only come up to his chest. I was born with the short gene. I've hated it most of my life. I was always the shortest in the class. Always an outcast, especially around all the socialites in Manhattan who would come to my father's events. They were all models, rake thin and comically tall. Legs for days, hair long, thick, and fake. Then there was me. All five-foot-nothing, strawberry-blond hair, and a brain bigger than my boobs.

I swallow as I look up for what feels like minutes, my eyes trailing up his chest, over his well-defined broad shoulders, across his clenched jaw until I see his eyes searching mine from under his hat. Damn. They're the same deep brown ones from the photo.

"Well, acting isn't really my strong suit," I whisper as we stand chest to chest. My feet are rooted to the spot, and I have no idea what's wrong with me. He looks at me like he wants to kiss me, and for just a moment, I wonder what that would be like.

"Could've fooled me. That accent was… interesting."

My lips quirk.

"Have a good night, Nikki." Without another word, he brushes past me, his cologne leaving a trace of leather and spice that I breathe in as he slinks out the back door like the ghost he is. Taking a deep breath, I try to settle myself. I haven't been that close to a man in a long time and never one who makes me feel like this. Shaking my head, dislodging the thoughts, I turn to clean up his table, grabbing his cup and napkin before I see he left me a tip. Grabbing the cash, I pause. Because it isn't the usual few dollars the others drop around here. It's a hundred-dollar bill. Benjamin looks up at me with his thin-lipped smile, and my teeth grind.

I pocket it quickly, looking around, spotting a guy from the group of men watching me. But from his gaze, I get the shivers, not the feeling of warmth that I do from Sutton. Lowering my eyes, I quickly clean up and walk out the back door with my shoulders up around my neck and smoke coming from my ears.

4

SUTTON

I stride to my truck, equal parts amused at what I just witnessed and fucking turned on. My jeans are tight, and my heart races. She was phenomenal. Didn't miss a beat, completely in control, confident, and it was hard to keep my eyes off her. More so than usual.

Of course I have my brother in my corner, and Rochelle does a great job of turning journalists away, but I've never been in the diner to see Nikki do it. The fact that she did it so convincingly, when I was merely a few feet away, makes me want to scoop her up and take her home. Living in Hollywood, it's full of phony people, all trying to suck the life out of you to further their own agenda. Over time, that's become clearer and it's made me a little wary. But Nikki had my back, asking for nothing in return. Her morals and her authenticity are refreshing as hell.

"Wait!" Her voice stops me mid-stride, and I turn quickly, seeing her run after me. Hair flowing in the breeze, her cheeks are a little flushed, and I swallow roughly. I see beautiful women in LA and on my travels all the time. Hell, I spend weekends in Cabo with models and actresses every chance I get. But never has one taken my breath away like Nikki does.

"This must've fallen from your pocket or something." She pushes her hand out, passing back the hundred I left for her on the table.

"It didn't. It's your tip." I pocket my hands so she can't shove the bill back into them.

Looking at the cash and then back at me, she questions, "Tip?"

"Yeah. The tip." I probably sound arrogant. I always tip well, but I've never left Nikki that much before.

"But it's a hundred dollars!" Like she's both confused and shocked, her face crumples.

"I know." Sure, it's a lot for just a cup of coffee, but she deserves it.

"But it's too much." Her jaw is tight, so it seems she's not happy about it. Dare I say, this little pocket rocket has pride that runs deep. Anyone else would take the money and keep moving, for fear it was a mistake and not wanting to give it up. Yet another thing that's remarkable about this woman.

"No, it's not. This town is keeping me hidden; *you're* keeping me hidden. You just put on a hell of a performance that's over and above what Rochelle pays you to do. So, it's fair compensation. Keep it."

"I can't keep it!" She's incredulous, and I really want to grin.

"Why not?"

"It's a hundred dollars!" she yells, even though we're right near each other. I like being this close to her. From here, I can smell her fresh floral scent, the one that I now dream about. There's something about her energy that I can't get enough of. It gives me renewed life. Like I'm discovering something new.

I nod in understanding. "I know, Nikki."

Her shoulders lower in what I think is defeat. She needs it, and we both know it. I lean toward her, my head lowering to her ear.

"Indulge me... just this once." My voice vibrates across her skin, and it takes all my strength to back away, to not take a deep breath of her scent. Her eyes are wide as she looks up at me, her mouth open, her lips plump. Damn, she's beautiful. The things I want to do to that mouth are now running through my mind rapidly, like a movie. But, not wanting to push it any more, I force my feet to move and jump in the truck.

I'm using Annabelle's truck today, given the need to constantly change the vehicles I drive to ensure anonymity. Not able to keep my eyes off her for any longer, I start it up and look at Nikki from the window. She's standing in the same spot, watching me. I give her a nod, and I see her take a deep breath before she pockets the cash and walks inside, my eyes not leaving her until the door closes behind her frame. After Rochelle mentioned her situation the other day, the grin is fast to my face, now knowing she has some extra money this week.

A hundred dollars is nothing to me. My bank balance is high, my needs low, and my investments are strong. But if I don't do some type of work soon, I'm going to be stalking the poor girl more than I already am. With that thought in my mind, I hit the road and turn left instead of right.

Distillery Drive is five minutes away, and I have tunnel vision all the way there.

Bobby's been calling me about all kinds of projects, and I don't want to do any of them. They have large dollars attached, but they aren't really me. Commercials that air in Asia, movies that lean on love stories rather than action. All great jobs, but none that I want. None that fit me or my brand that I've spent over a decade building. Bobby's thinking of his own pocket. Money changes people, and Sawyer and I have been lucky to have a humble upbringing so we know the importance of keeping grounded. Bobby? He combusts just at the smell of a wad.

I pull into the Whiteman's Whiskey Distillery parking lot and stride inside, eager to get this dream of mine happening.

"Can I help you?" the receptionist at the distillery office asks. I quickly look at her name badge.

"Hi, Stephanie. Is Connor or Tanner available?"

Her cheeks tint in recognition and she starts to stammer. It's common. I don't get frustrated. People handle fame differently, but I'm just a normal person.

"Sutton?" I turn at the sound of my name, seeing Tanner walking down the hall toward me.

"Tanner." Reaching out, I shake his hand. We've only just started to get to know each other, but he and my brother are close.

"Come down. Connor's in his office." I follow Tanner, looking around as I do. They have a great business here. The walls are lined with photos and information about their whiskey, their family history, and the town. A lot of effort has gone into the storytelling; it's captivating and exactly what I want. Storytelling is why I got into the business I did. I used to sit at home and watch old movies. It's still a passion of mine when I have the time.

"Connor." Tanner barks his son's name as we walk into his office, and Connor looks at me with a wide grin.

"Silvers. Good to see you," he says, walking over to me and shaking my hand.

"Thought I'd drop by."

"Aren't you trying to lay low?" Tanner questions as we all take a seat in the small lounge.

"Well, if I'm going to be the face of your latest release, I better get my first taste of it." Confident? Absolutely. But when I want something, I go after it. It's how I made my entire career.

"Why should you be the face of our whiskey?"

This is an idea I've toyed with for years. Whenever we've been in the same room, I've always joked about being the face of their brand. Not only because I love their whiskey, but because I love what they represent. Family. Connection. Heritage. Now having been here in Whispers for a while, I can understand it even more. Up until now, Tanner and Connor have both had large profiles, but I know that's not what they love to do. Me, my face is already everywhere, so what's one more place?

"Because I'm in hiding. I'm elusive. I'm a *Shadow Gentleman*." They look at me in slight awe.

"What's a shadow gentleman?" Connor asks as Tanner looks on, intrigued, and I feel like I'm coming alive inside as I think about it.

"A Shadow Gentleman is a man of undeniable refinement and intrigue. He carries an air of mystery, perhaps due to a hidden past, concealed identity, or the deliberate choice to remain in the background while still influencing the world around him. He commands attention without seeking it. He's polished, perceptive, and quietly powerful. Whether he's evading detection, orchestrating events from the shadows, or simply existing in a space between elegance and secrecy, he remains someone people notice, but rarely truly know."

Connor smiles. "Have you ever worked in marketing?"

"Never." My answer's quick as I feel the bud of possibility blooming.

"We have a new batch. It's a bit different." I can tell Tanner's considering this.

"How so?" I ask.

"I charred the barrels before I aged it. Then coated them with our honey. Giving it a smokey, caramelized edge to it that we've never had before."

Excitement buzzes through me as I nod, loving the sound of that.

"Shadow Gentleman. A whiskey with quiet power and undeniable allure."

They both look at me.

"Shit, that's good." Connor throws his pen down on his desk like it's already a done deal.

"Damn, I like it." Tanner rubs his chin in thought.

"You do know if we position this right, it's going to go crazy." Connor looks at me seriously.

"I know." I can already see it. Me staying here, working with them in secret. Filming commercials around Whispers, shoots for magazines, social media. Then me coming out as being in Whispers when it first launches, it's going to be a media frenzy.

"I can see it," Tanner adds, relaxing back in his seat.

"It'll work well with our global expansion proposals with Grant Holdings."

My eyebrows rise at Connor's statement. I knew they were expanding, but Grant Holdings is big. I've met the Grant brothers a few times. They've been at the same restaurants I frequent, their money giving them access to a global field of people like no other.

"I know Tyler," I tell them, and Connor looks at me sharply.

"Of course you do." He shakes his head, grinning. Seemingly, his plans are all coming together.

"We could film the commercials here on-site and in town. A photoshoot in your barrel rooms, aging rooms." I haven't auditioned or pitched myself in a long time. It feels refreshing, like I'm taking charge of my career all by myself without Bobby and his bias. I've missed that control.

"Sounds like you're planning to stick around in Whispers a bit longer? Sawyer told me you purchased a block of land and are working with Griffin on a place." Tanner smiles, clearly proud to add me to the list of residents in his town.

I shrug. "Whispers is nice. Private. Secure. Quiet. A good place for someone like me to come and hide once in a while. I like it here. The whiskey is good too."

Connor chuckles, lifting an eyebrow. "We've never partnered with a celebrity, never wanted celebrity endorsement."

"I was thinking I might fall into the friend category..."

Tanner smirks, one that his son quickly matches. "I think we have a deal, Sutton. Shall we toast?"

Jumping up from his seat, Connor walks straight to the small bar in his office and pours three glasses. And just like that, a new marketing campaign is born, and I have a job. One I pitched and booked myself. Sawyer can do the negotiation and paperwork. I'll keep Bobby none the wiser.

5

———

NIKKI

There's something about the end of the week that makes me feel a little lighter. Whether it's because I don't work weekends and can now stay at home with James, in our own cottage in the middle of nowhere, just doing our own thing, away from prying eyes. Or whether it's because James and I get to explore the forest, learning about the animals, digging around in the garden, or just keeping things simple. Probably both.

"Nikki, take the leftover lasagna from today." Rochelle's already walking toward me with the plastic container holding almost a week's worth of food.

"Rochelle!" I rear back, surprised. She does this sometimes. I've never spoken to her about our circumstances. I've never asked for food or help from anyone. Even though I probably should at this point. Dad froze all my trust funds, and I'm almost out of the money I saved for our escape, which means I'm barely keeping James and me fed. But when my family has so much money that they could feed a small country, I feel conflicted, almost shameful.

Call it women's intuition, but Rochelle seems to know

things aren't normal with James and me. Hell, most of the town thinks he's my son. Given I'm only twenty-three and he's ten, I would've been way too young to have a baby. It happens. It's not impossible, but it isn't my story.

"It's going into the bin unless you take it." She shoves the container in my hand and walks away before I can say another word. Tears sting my eyes. Sure, I made some good tips this week, and certainly Sutton's hundred dollars put us in a good position to buy some food and things we need that we haven't had for a while. But this container will feed us for days.

"Yum, I love her lasagna," James whispers, and I can almost see the drool running down his chin. I give him a close-lipped smile, resigned to accept the food. For him. Everything I do is for him.

"Let's go. My feet are killing me, so it's going to take forever to walk home tonight." We grab our things and walk out the back. We're both tired, after a big day for him at school and work for me even longer.

"We need to start on my school project this weekend," James reminds me as we step out the back door of Delish, beginning the walk home. Just under two miles away sits our small run-down cottage, the one I use most of my saved cash for every month and silently thank fate for spotting on the Whispers community noticeboard, the moment the owner put up the small ad.

"What's it on again?" I throw my bag over my shoulder, then help him with his heavy backpack. He's diligent and his dedication to his schoolwork is unrivaled. Like me, we're both studious. It was ingrained in us both from a young age. While Mom was a little more free-flowing, Dad was strict. Mom had us outside in the garden, learning by doing. Dad buried our heads in books, having had us pegged for positions in his oil company since birth. He made it clear to us how important grades were, that we needed to be successful to work at the firm, and luckily, it's an area that James and I both succeed in. Yet the vision our father had for us, it's not the vision we want for ourselves.

"I need to do a biography on a well-known person."

"Who did you choose?" My lips purse as I try to think what person a ten-year-old should base their project on.

"I haven't decided. But I need to research."

"We can walk to the library tomorrow; it's open in the morning." It's another long walk back to town, but we don't have internet at home and my cell phone is an old one that barely works. I can't risk anyone tracking us digitally or finding us in any way, so whenever I need to do any online searching, I do it at the library.

"Hey!" There's a shout from behind us, and I swivel around quickly. I spot the group of men who come into the diner a few times per month. The ones who are usually rude, who offer me unwelcome advances and are generally just horrible.

"Can I help you?" My diner manners are hard to ignore as I shuffle James behind me. It's comical; at ten, he's almost as tall as I am.

"What you got there." One of them nods to my bag.

"Nothing." I frown, wondering what they want.

"I'll be the judge." His hand whips forward so quickly I almost miss it.

"Hey!" I shout as he pulls my bag from my arm, and I grip on to it just as tight. But with the container of food in one hand, I'm left outmuscled.

"Give it up, darlin'. I saw the tip you got today."

I grit my teeth. Nothing good comes from money. Everything bad has happened in my life because of it.

"Let go!" I feel James edge away from me and back toward the door of the diner, I assume to get help. My heart pounds powerfully, stomach twisting at what these men might do.

"Not so quick, little guy." One of the other men grabs James around the upper arms, holding him still, and that's when I release my grip.

My handbag is now being rifled through, and I turn and grab James, ripping him from the guy's arms as they swarm my bag like a pack of seagulls after a hot fry at the beach. Seems like I'm not the only one around here in need of cash.

"Give it back," I bite out but give them space. I have no idea what they're capable of, and here, in the small private parking lot behind the diner, no one can hear us. The only things here are the large garbage bins and now my bag strewn all over the ground. They pay me little attention as they throw my sweater to the side, then my small makeup case that holds my lip gloss and tampons scatters. My little notepad and pen go flying. I pass James the container of food. If everything else goes, at least we can still eat for the week.

"I said, give it back!" I step toward them as I yell, not liking the way they're throwing my things around. I have no idea where my confidence comes from, but my anger at this situation is taking over my nerves.

"Shut it!" a guy barks back before his fist flies and connects with my cheek. I stumble, almost falling, but James balances me. It's hard enough to leave me shocked, my cheek throbbing and my hair clip dropping from my hair.

"Nikki!" James gasps as I lean on him, my ears ringing. I've never been hit before. There were plenty of threats, hard grabs, pushes, my stepmother Maribel has slapped me a few times, but I've never had a fist to my face. With my head pounding and the taste of blood in my mouth, I can now tick that off my list.

"Now shut up!" The guy stomps his foot, and I feel my world turn. Because underneath his boot is my hair clip. The one my mother gave me when I was a child, the one thing that I took with me when we ran. It's the last reminder I have of her, and while the guys continue to rifle through my bag, my heart shatters.

"No!" I cry, my voice weak, my eyes glued to the ground. The clip is broken in three places, the sparkling rhinestones glittering among the gravel.

"Shit, why'd you hit her, man?" one of the crew says, stepping away from my bag like he doesn't want anything to do with it anymore as I clutch my face, the pain exploding in my cheek.

"Got it." Another one pulls the small wad of cash from my bag, throwing everything else on the ground. All my tips from today. The money that needs to see James and me through most of the week with food, supplies, rent, and bills.

"Thanks, beautiful." He gives me a wink before they walk off without a care in the world.

"Nikki!" James looks at me with wide, teary eyes, and I take in a breath. I feel my cheek burning up, so I wiggle my jaw back and forth. It's throbbing but not broken.

"I'm okay. It'll just be sore for a few days."

"You sure?" James doesn't look convinced, so I give him a small smile, one I regret immediately as the throbbing pulses through my cheek, up to my eye.

"I'm sure. Come on, let's get home." Bending over, I grab my things, shoving them back into my bag, trying my best not to cry. I can't. I need to be strong. I need to keep it together for James.

"But they broke your clip... the one from Mom." He

picks up the pieces, one by one. It was a jeweled clip that had hand-painted bees on it. Mom used to say she was the big one and the other two were James and me. It was because she loved gardening and said that a garden without bees is like a song without a melody; let them hum, and the earth will thrive. She's where I got my love for the environment and passion for sustainability. Passing the broken glass and jewels to me, I wrap them in a tissue and pocket it. The shattered pieces reflect my shattered heart. It's only a clip. But it was her clip.

"Who were they?" He looks over his shoulder, watching them all get in a truck. My eyes canvass the area to see if anyone nearby saw what happened. But it's empty, as I expected. No one besides Rochelle, Sutton, and I come through the back way, and now only James and I stand here. I should take us into the diner. Get some ice. Ensure James is all okay. But I don't want to bring that issue to Rochelle. She does so much for us already; she doesn't need to know that I've had an altercation with some of her customers.

"Just some guys. Let's try to stay clear of them from now on." With my bag now recovered, we begin to walk.

"What are we going to do?" James' voice is quiet, but I hear the fear. The uncertainty.

Once Mom died, our family died too. Dad threw himself into work, was barely home. So my brother and I grieved together. But soon after, Dad met Maribel, and things changed. While I was away at college, James' life spiraled, and our father was too busy to notice. Now, as we disappear into the background, his young, beautiful wife, who's also the devil in disguise, is celebrating our absence.

"We'll do what we always do. We carry on."

He looks up at me and smiles, but that drops immediately as he says, "You're going to have a black eye tomorrow."

He's right. And we don't have an ice pack or anything. When I get home, I'll have to dunk my head in some cold water for a while, because I already feel it swelling.

"Yeah, well, I never said running away was going to be easy." The words are more for my benefit than James'.

"It's already better than what it was," he adds. Maribel was awful to us both, but James took the brunt of it. While I know Dad is canvassing the countryside looking for us, he's blind to the fact that his new wife is the entire reason we're running in the first place.

Whispers is better, by a long shot.

6

———

SUTTON

I push my way through the back door and slip to my booth. *My booth*. There's no reserved sign. There's nothing blocking others from sitting here. But every day when I come, it's vacant, waiting for me.

My eyes immediately find Nikki as she moves around the counter, filling coffee cups. Like the stalker I am, I watch her for a moment. She has her hair down today, which is unusual, since it's always up. She usually wears it in this cute clip that has bees on it. Three of them. I know because I've counted. It's a little quirky and always catches my eye. Probably because I'm highly allergic, so bees are something I notice. But today, her hair is flowing in soft waves around her face, just past her shoulders, and I'm almost breathless at how beautiful she is.

"Fuck." I rub my eyes, obsessing over a woman I barely know.

When she spots me, I tilt my head, confused. She looks different, but I can't pinpoint why. It's more than the hair. Her face is beautiful, as always, yet slightly unfamiliar. As she walks toward me, my eyes stay on her, searching, and then I balk.

"What's that on your face?" My anger is instant. It always has been since I was a kid. I'm surprised I haven't been in more fistfights in LA since I've been there. Although, I only get upset when something happens to people I care about, and in LA, people generally only care for themselves.

As a kid, it was always about protecting my mom. But now, as I look at Nikki, I see she has a black eye, and that instinct rises to the surface in a brand-new way. Her skin is soft blue and a little swollen, her hair covering it mostly. I knew something was amiss.

"It's nothing." She fills my cup with hot coffee without me even asking.

"It sure doesn't look like nothing." My shoulders are tight, my jaw clenched as I stand. I haven't felt like this in a long time, but a burning rage fills me and runs rapidly through my limbs, so strongly that I need to move.

"I said it's nothing." Her voice is a mere whisper, and she won't meet my eyes. I fist my hands before I lift one, brushing her hair from her face gently, getting a full view that has me murderous. She looks at me, wide-eyed. I haven't touched her before, but now that my hand brushes over her skin, I know she's as delicate as she looks.

"What happened?" I pull in a sharp breath to calm myself. The urge to hit someone pulses through my bones.

"Sutton." Her eyes hold a combination of fear and fire, a combustible mix, but hearing my name from her sweet lips nearly has me buckling.

"What happened?" I grit out again, my hand still in her silky hair. The diner is busy, but everyone is too into their own conversations to worry about ours. Which is a good thing, because I'm going to keep asking until she tells me.

All the other fuckers needing their caffeine fix can wait. She must see the commitment in my eyes because she relents.

"I fell."

"This isn't a fall." My response is immediate. I see the pattern on her skin. A hand did this. She takes a deep breath, her resolve falling to the wayside.

"Fine. I got mugged." She puts the coffeepot on the table and looks at me with exasperation.

"Mugged? In Whispers?" I'm in disbelief. Sure, there's petty crime everywhere. But here? In *Whispers*?

"Yeah, out of all the places, it happens to me here. They... saw the tip you left me." Her words have a resigned feeling to them. I don't like it. I see the kindness in her eyes. I see the love she has for her boy. As I look at her, I register what she said.

"It's my fault?" My eyes widen, anger now aimed at myself.

"It isn't your fault." She shakes her head, looking around quickly. I move my hand, gliding it across her jaw and gripping her chin lightly. The way her hair falls back, I notice up close that it's a little lighter at the roots, so she isn't naturally dark. As I tilt her face up to mine, her lips part in surprise, and I drink her in. The way her lips are plump, her neck curves, her eyes gazing up into mine.

"Who was it?" I demand as softly as I can.

"I don't know." She's lying.

I lift an eyebrow and press on. "Give me a name."

"I don't know their names."

"Their? More than one?" Fuck, did she get completely ambushed?

"About four of them. Those same guys who come in here. You know, they always sit at the front." Her eyes flick to my hand, like she might be uneasy, and I pull it away.

"What did the sheriff say?" I assume he was here. Someone saw it. Helped her.

"I... I didn't report it."

"But who helped you?" I'm confused, wondering why whomever came to her aid didn't call the police.

"No one. I can take care of myself. I put cold water on it, then dreamed of peanut butter cups because eating them always makes me feel better." The stubbornness in her expression tells me she can, but the bruise on her cheek tells a different story.

"You need to report it." I'm too commanding, almost towering over her, but my protective instincts are pinging off the charts.

"They're customers. I don't want to bring negativity to Rochelle or the diner."

Shaking my head, I frown. "Rochelle would be the first person to kick them out for touching you. You should report it."

"Not happening." She scoffs at me like I'm being unreasonable.

"Why not?" I squint, confused as to why a young woman wouldn't. Especially since Rochelle is married to the sheriff.

"For the same reason you can't do or say anything about it either."

I stall. Her words make me pause briefly, confirming she's running or hiding from something or someone too.

"Oh, I'll fucking do something about it," I mutter gruffly.

"What? So you'll go and get the bad guys, and as soon as you do, they'll talk. If they don't already know who you are, then they will the moment you show your face. I don't need eyeballs on me and neither do you." Grabbing the coffeepot, she walks away, and I stand frozen to the spot, feeling bereft from her absence before I slump into the booth.

She's right, of course, but that doesn't make me any less angry. I think about calling Jackson from my security team. He and his team are on vacation right now, with me here, not needing them in Whispers. I could have them scouring this town to find the men within a few hours, and then I'd show these guys exactly what happens if they go near Nikki again.

But that would blow my cover. As soon as anyone in my security team moves, they'll be followed and they sure as hell would look out of place here in Whispers. The reason I've been so successful at not being noticed is because I'm on my own; I blend into the background.

I'm intrigued by her words. *She doesn't need eyeballs on her.* The mystery around this woman thickens, and while I appreciate the need for privacy, I sure do want to know more about her.

Frustration nips at my shoulders from not jumping in my truck and driving around town to look for them. I think I know the guys she's talking about. I see them in here. Nice as pie to Rochelle, but as soon as Rochelle is out of sight, they carry on. But she's right. They'd have no problem blowing my cover. Not only would they go straight to the media, making up some lies, no doubt, but if I'm found, it'll ruin the entire concept of the surprise release I'm doing with White-man's. The aim being that the launch coincides with me outing myself, creating the perfect media storm to promote the new whiskey. The one they're already pulling together, with photoshoots happening next week and commercials being filmed not long after.

I grip the coffee cup so hard I'm amazed it doesn't shatter in my hand. I won't go looking for them, but if they step in my path, I'm not sure I'll be able to stop myself. I grew up in a single mom household and I saw the struggles she had. I don't remember my dad, but for a while, there were different men who would come and go. I unfortunately saw my mom with bruises a few times. She always thought Sawyer and I were too young to remember. But I remember. I remember her trying to cover them with makeup. I remember seeing her cheek tinted blue just like Nikki's.

I'm still seething as my cell vibrates, and I pull it out of my pocket. Bobby. His timing is fucking impeccable. I decide to answer him today, for no other reason than to try to get my mind on other things.

"Bobby," I murmur quietly. There isn't anyone around who can hear me. The locals who are here are all people I see frequently, who keep my secret and leave me be.

"Sutton! My man, how are you?" I hear him driving. No doubt with the roof of his convertible down, the LA sun beating down. The wind in the background gives it away.

"What's up?" Taking a breath, I feel my shoulders lower slightly.

"Are you coming back soon? I have so many things lined up, it's insane. I can have you scheduled well into next year. The dollars are adding up each and every day, my man!" I'm not his man, and I hate it when he calls me that. We're not best friends at a frat house, sitting around a keg.

"Not for a while, Bobby." I keep my guard up, knowing I can't tell him anything. The minute he knows where I am, he'll turn up on my doorstep. That little thought brings my mind to Griffin. The country's best builder, who works out of Whispers for the most part. Sawyer introduced me, and now we're working on the plans for my new home.

It may be a snap decision, but I fell in love with this town the minute they kept my presence a secret. You can't pay for that kind of loyalty. I know I'm on borrowed time, but the fact that I've been here for a while now and that hasn't been leaked to the media is unheard of. Clooney has his mansion in Como, surrounded by the lake so no one can reach him. I'm building mine right here in Whispers because the town is my security. In fact, I'll be right next door to Sawyer, because what are family for if you can't live next door? And the only job I've had lately is being his babysitter. Kevin and Noah are my two best friends.

"What do you mean, man! You need to get back here. The studios are calling me every day. I have so many scripts on my desk, I can barely see it, and the international models all come in next week for the big lingerie show they do all year... if you know what I mean."

Yeah, I know what he means. Once upon a time, I would be up for all that. Jumping from movie set to movie set, working my ass off, early mornings and long days before I would take off on my private jet for a week, sit on a beach somewhere, with a tall glamorous model with legs for days. They were all nice girls, but none of them were really my type. We were both there for a good time, not a long time, and our endgame was always the same. Be flirty on the beach together, paparazzi can get their shots as we became a hot topic for a few weeks, keeping our stars rising before the next movie started. It was great to increase my profile, but it left me feeling empty. It kept me busy but taught me that everyone's after me for something, and that something wasn't the real me.

"Not anytime soon. I'm enjoying the downtime."

I hear him scoff before he collects himself.

"You wait too long, my man, and no one will want you when you come back." His words are spoken with humor, but they're meant to sting. And once upon a time, they would've. But I'm older now; I know better. I've been in this game a long time, too long probably. Now in my late thirties, I need something new, something fresh.

"Yeah, I'll take my chances." While I know any publicity is good publicity, I also know that a person or brand can become oversaturated. Me being away a little while has already sent the industry into a meltdown. When they find me, it's going to explode.

"Why don't you tell me where you are? I can come see you, talk to you, show you what's on offer?"

I look up and spot Nikki by my side. I haven't asked her to, but she delivers one of Rochelle's delicious chicken pies, sliding it in front of me with a genuine smile, and I soak it up. I eat these almost every day. They're delicious. The pie is steamy hot, smells amazing, as does Nikki. Her floral aroma fills my senses, making me feel like I'm on solid ground for the first time in a long time.

I notice she brushes her hair back around her ear, the thick, glossy tendrils falling again almost immediately before she retreats. I watch her go. Her looks are what captured me from the first moment I saw her, but our snippets of conversation are what keep me coming back. What I really need to do, though, is get my head out of my ass and start concentrating on things other than her. My life is crazy and trying to get to know someone and dragging them into my world is not fair to them.

"Sutton? Sutton? Are you there?" Bobby's annoying voice jolts me from my daydreaming.

"Not just yet, Bobby. I'm not ready." I end the call, throwing my cell on the table and grabbing my fork. Looking up, I spot Nikki again. She gives me her little smile, and Bobby becomes a distant memory.

The best way to a man's heart is through his stomach. And now I'm hungry, for more than just chicken pie.

7

———

NIKKI

Sutton's eyes have been on me for my entire shift. He was on his phone for a while, then accepted a delivery from the local drugstore, but has remained in his booth all afternoon.

It has me on edge. The two of us can't be seen together. If he gets found out, I can't get photographed as a bystander. While he's well known, my face is one that would be familiar, too, and I don't want my location to be revealed. I'm safe here for the time being; I know that. But both James and I have had our faces on the news for a time as the search for us continues.

Yet I would be lying if I said I wanted Sutton gone, because even though we barely know each other, I feel a connection. Maybe it's because we're both on the run, in hiding, and this town is our safety net. We have that in common.

It's also been a long time since I took any interest in the opposite sex. While there were a few guys who asked me out in college, aside from quick flings that never lasted, I spent most of my downtime trying to get to James. Weekends when he was locked up in his room, Maribel at one function or another, my dad working or away. Someone had to ensure he was safe, away from Maribel's hands that tried to make his life unbearable. Ironic, really, that in all that time I snuck back home, I never saw my dad. Not even once.

"More coffee?" I ask, approaching him.

"Why does coffee taste worse when it sits too long?"

"Oxidation. The acids break down, changing the pH balance, which makes it bitter." My answer is too quick, out before I can shut my mouth.

Sutton looks at me with a gaze that's a mix of surprise, admiration, and confusion. "There's no way normal people just know that."

I feel a little caught out. Clearly, I need to watch what I say a little more. I'm becoming too comfortable around him. This is why I always keep my distance from people. Swallowing roughly, I shrug, acting like it's no big deal before I go to pour him another cup, but he stops me.

"I've got so much caffeine in my veins I'm vibrating." His grin is wide, and I snort a laugh. My hand comes to my face immediately, my cheeks heating. I hate laughing. I'm one of those snorters. I've been like this my entire life. At school, I was picked on, people called me "porky" every time I laughed. But my mom loved it. She used to tell me that when I laughed, the whole world lit up. The two of us were always in fits of laughter together. We had a good time. I haven't laughed much since she died.

"Was that a snort?" His expression brightens, like I just made his day.

"No." I brush him off, pretending I don't know what he's talking about.

"Oh no, I think that was a laugh-snort."

I quirk an eyebrow. "A laugh-snort?"

"Yeah, they're the best kind of laughs." His eyes dance in delight as he watches me. Taking a deep breath, the humor settles, my chest warming.

Getting the attention off me, I ask, "If there's too much coffee in your veins, why are you here all day, then?" I hold up the hot pot of coffee, intrigued why he's still here.

"I'll leave when you leave."

My breath catches. "What?"

"I'm making sure you finish and get home okay."

I start to shake my head as my heartbeat quickens. I'm apprehensive, yet butterflies dance in my stomach, leaving my emotions all over the place.

"You don't have to do that."

"I'm here!" James pushes through the door, beelining right for me. "How's your face?" he asks as he basically slams into me and hugs me tightly.

"I'm fine. All good." I give him a wide smile of reassurance. Looking at Sutton, I see he's smiling at James, and I decide to introduce them formally, Sutton aware of who he is anyway.

"James, this is Sutton."

"Hey, buddy." Sutton offers his fist, and James taps it with his own in a boy code I don't understand. The chime of the door sounds again, and I see a few others filing in after school, signaling the afternoon rush.

"Hang on," I tell James, moving around him and greeting the new customers.

As people order, more walk in. It's getting busy, and I run around, filling cups, taking orders, delivering food and back again. Rochelle and I move in tandem, ensuring everyone has what they need, and it isn't until it starts to slow that I take a breath. The clock says I worked a half hour of overtime, and I know by the time we walk home, James is going to be starving. I thank God for the last pieces of leftover lasagna from Rochelle that's still in my fridge.

My eyes flick around the diner for him. He isn't in his usual spot at the end of the counter and as I look around, I spot him sitting at the booth in the back. James is sitting opposite Sutton, the two of them with their heads together, and my heart almost stops. I pause what I'm doing and watch them. James looks so happy, and Sutton's grin is wide. He looks good with a smile. I bite the inside of my cheeks, knowing that Sutton Silvers looks good in anything.

"Now look who's staring," Rochelle teases as she approaches my side, taking in the two of them.

"I'm just making sure James is behaving. Not annoying the customers."

She looks at me like she doesn't believe a word of that.

"James is a good kid; he's always welcome here anytime, and he doesn't bother anyone. But I don't think you're just looking at James…"

I feel my cheeks heat and lift my hand to touch them before I wince, the black eye and bruised cheek I'd forgotten about still sore at the touch.

"Did you put ice on that?" she asks with a pinched brow.

I told Rochelle I fell. Unlike Sutton, she didn't dispute my claim.

"Yes. Of course."

Her lips thin. Damn her and her all-knowing maternal instinct. Maybe the fact that she's married to the local sheriff helps her spot a liar, but I swear she knows the minute I tell a small fib.

"Fine. No, I didn't have an ice pack; I just ran it under cool water for a bit."

"You'll take one home today from the freezer out back."

"That's not necessary."

"What if James falls and needs it?"

I sigh. She knows exactly what button of mine to press.

"Rochelle…" I start to dispute, not wanting to be that girl, always taking and never giving.

"And you've almost worked an entire hour over today, so I'll add that to your weekly."

When I open my mouth to push back on that, too, she cuts me off.

"I'm not taking no for an answer, Nikki. You're my best waitress. Here every day. Work every minute allocated. I'm grateful to have you."

"Rochelle, that's my job." I've always had a strong work ethic, that's why I did so well at school. My study schedule was rigorous. A lot of good that's done me so far. I could've walked straight from college into a well-paying job on the East Coast, but my last name carries weight, and with a few calls from my father's office, I was booted from every job I ever applied for. Including working at a small café. It was hopeless. Dad wanted me to take over his legacy and was doing anything he could to get me to work in the business, blind to the fact that it isn't what I want.

He drills for oil, and I believe in climate change. He has no issues with destroying people's homes, communities, or the animal habitat to buy a parcel of land to excavate. Whereas I want to have a sustainable life and leave no footprint. He'll do anything to get his hands on that liquid gold, and I prefer to leave nature alone and bask in her elements. So while I could've been well on my way to an amazing career, my father put a stop to it. He couldn't have his daughter rising through the ranks as a successful environmental engineer with a passion for climate change, while he was digging up the ground, making a mess of everything. It would've made headline news; it would've had his shareholders nervous.

"Well, think of it all as a bonus for good work, then." And with that, Rochelle walks to the kitchen to get the ice pack and my paycheck. I'm also the only waitress who asks for cash payment, something that she doesn't mind offering. With my bank accounts almost empty and me not wanting to identify myself to open another one, I use cash for everything.

As she pushes through the double doors, I wipe down the counter, putting away what little needs to be done. My feet ache. My face throbs. But none of it keeps my eyes from drifting to the booth at the back, to Sutton.

The way he held my cheek earlier, the way he looked into my eyes, ready to burn the world down for my bruises left me a little speechless. I've never had that before. Someone who had my back. Someone who was angry for me, someone who cares. But I need to stay away from him. I can't entertain getting close to anyone; it's just not right. James and I hope to stay here in Whispers, but if things change, then we need to be on the move. So no friendships, no quiet conversations, no misplaced trust. And James, he shouldn't get close either.

But then I see James smile again, pulling Sutton's attention, the two of them bent over a book on Benjamin Franklin. Sutton listens, nodding, helping him with something he doesn't understand.

And just like that, I know.

Whatever this is, whatever's going on, it's already too late. Because Sutton Silvers is starting to infiltrate my thoughts, and those thoughts are not just of friendship.

8

SUTTON

My ass is sore from sitting here for so damn long. I got here hours ago. But I'm not leaving until she does.

"It says here he had a pet mouse that he trained to do tricks…" James' face scrunches in thought. He's a smart kid. Puts me to shame. I was never studious, all those brain cells went to my brother. Me, I'm creative and think off the cuff. I like movies and music, not textbooks or literature.

"So… your dad around?" I wince at my poor attempt at finding out more about his mom.

"No." He doesn't seem too upset about that fact, so I continue.

"I didn't grow up with a dad either," I admit, trying to connect with him.

"Was your dad angry all the time too?" His eyebrows rise expectantly, and I frown.

"I didn't really know him. My mom looked after me, though. She was the best." I love my mom. I wish I could see her more, but in the current climate, her retirement village is being harassed by paparazzi too. Leaving me no choice but to stay away for the time being. But I have a security team keeping her and her retirement friends safe, and I have plans to bring her here to Whispers when I can. Although now, any move she makes, she'll be followed, so I need to be careful.

"Nikki looks after me too."

I tilt my head. I know kids these days are more relaxed, not as formal with how they address their parents, but I'm surprised he calls his mom by her first name.

"How do you like school?"

He shrugs. "Eh. It's fine."

"Got lots of friends?"

"Kind of. I'm still the new kid."

I nod in understanding. School is hard. I hated it.

"When did you start?" I wonder how long they've been here. I already know they're not locals.

"A few months ago." James doesn't give me much. I get it; our trust hasn't formed yet.

"Where did you move from?" His eyes finally meet mine before he looks at Nikki, then back at me.

Quietly, he admits, "I'm not allowed to say."

"That's okay. You don't have to tell me. You don't have to tell me anything you don't want to."

James looks at me, and for a moment, I think he might talk, but his lips remain closed. Further cementing the fact that they're on the run.

"Okay, it's home time." Nikki steps toward us like a fresh morning breeze, although she looks tired as hell.

"Thanks for your help, Sutton." There it is again. Like Nikki, James has a hint of a posh accent that comes out a little more prevalent in Nikki when she's tired and not trying to hide it. Old money.

"Anytime, buddy." I stand with him, my ass now completely numb, a big session at the gym needed.

"I'm sorry if he was taking too much of your time." Nikki looks up at me sweetly, and her bruise shines like only a black eye can.

"I liked the company. Come on, let's get you home." I grab my bag that was delivered from the drugstore and start to walk with her out the back door.

"Um, home?"

"At a guess, I'm assuming you just worked a twelve-hour shift on your feet with a black eye that's probably thumping across your head about now. James has had a full day at school and an hour of homework already. So I can drop you off at home today." We let the back door close behind us, my truck all black and shiny waiting for us in the lot.

"Oh, I don't want to impose." Ever polite, her jaw works overtime. She hates taking things from people. I notice the look on her face whenever Rochelle offers her food or the little extras.

"I have the time," I tell her easily.

She waves me off. "No, that's really not necessary. We can walk."

"I know, but the truck will be quicker. Look at him." I nod toward James, who's already yawning, and see her face fall. Her shoulders a little too.

"Come on." I take her bag and then James' backpack and walk to the truck. I'm not used to driving a truck of this size. Back home in LA, I had either a driver or my sports car. Yet another thing that I'm enjoying here in Whispers—the freedom to drive.

"In you get, buddy." I don't even bother waiting to see if James can climb up in the back because he can't; it's too high up. So I grab his waist and lift him up, sitting him in the seat, and he smiles. Putting on his seatbelt, I close the door.

"Your turn." I open the front passenger door.

"I got it." She's quick, stepping in front of me, grabbing on to the handles and pulling herself up. She gets halfway and slips a little, but I catch her.

She squeals as her ass falls straight into my hold. "Whoa!"

"I've got you." My words are a mere whisper straight to her ear, my lips almost teasing the flesh of her neck where she's leaning against my chest. She takes a sharp breath in, and I have no idea how I'm remaining gentlemanly when her peachy ass is right in my palms. But I do. I lift her slowly the rest of the way, placing her in the seat before she looks at me.

"Thank you." Her cheeks are pink again. The color is fast becoming one of my favorites. I don't know what the hell I'm doing. Sawyer's right. I can't entertain the idea of a woman, for a good time or a long time. My life's a mess. I'm in hiding, and I have no idea what my next steps are beyond the Whiteman's Whiskey launch and building a base here. But as her lips turn up a little at the sides, my body melts, and just like that, I'm back to not caring what I should be doing and focusing on what I want to. I close the door and run around the truck, eager to get back to her.

Driving out of the small parking lot, I turn in the direction I've seen her walking, having no idea where I'm going.

"It's just a mile down here." I whip my head around to her with a frown.

"You guys walk a mile every day?"

"Three, actually. One and a half in the morning, then the same back at night."

"That's a good walk." Fuck, I had no idea it was that far.

If you're doing it for exercise, it's probably great, but out here, walking on the side of the road, with backpacks after a long day at work and school, I can't imagine that's easy.

"Well, I don't go to the gym anymore, so it's my daily exercise." She rubs her temples, and I know I was right earlier when I mentioned her head must be thumping.

"Got pain relief at home?" I murmur to her quietly, not wanting James to worry about her.

"Sure." Her voice sounds too upbeat, and I know she's lying. The little fibs roll off her tongue like oil touching water.

"It's just up here." She points out the windshield and I see a small dirt road up ahead.

"You can drop us off here at the end of the road." Like hell I can. I can't see any homes around here, nothing but the thick dense forest.

"I'll take you up." I turn in and continue to drive. She looks at me in question, and I notice her hand gripping on to the door handle so hard her knuckles are white. But she stays quiet.

"We're at the end of the road."

I can feel her unease, hear her hesitance. I could tell her she's in safe hands, that she doesn't need to worry, but that's a conclusion she needs to come to herself. I'll prove myself to her. I haven't had to do that in a long time, but I will.

Not being a local, I have no idea where we are or who owns this land. I see a small cottage up ahead and slow down as I approach. I'm not sure if it's scary as fuck or like a fairy tale. On a bright sunny day, this would be extremely tranquil. I can envision butterflies dancing around and birds singing. But at night, who knows what animals are out here? The cottage looks quaint but old, and as Rochelle mentioned, I don't see any vehicles around. But there's a small garden of flowers, some lawn that's cleared at the front, and what looks to be a large apple tree standing in the center.

I pull to a stop and James opens the door, jumping out. "Thanks, Sutton," he singsongs, grabbing his backpack before running inside.

"Here." I grab the small bag from the drugstore and hand it to her. "I got this for you."

Lips pursed, she looks into the bag, and then her eyes widen in surprise. It's just a bottle of pain relief, an ice pack, some antiseptic cream and Arnica, plus a few bags of peanut butter cups to make her feel better. But she looks at it like it's a pot of gold or something. Without a word, I jump out of the truck and walk around her side.

I take in a deep breath, the cool afternoon air fresh. James has turned on a light inside as I open her door, just as she turns to get out, and I meet her, eye to eye. I grit my teeth, the blue of her skin still making my shoulders tense.

"You alright out here?" My hands are placed on either side of the door, effectively keeping her in place.

She nods slowly. "Mm-hmm. We're fine."

"You got anyone to call if you're not?" I know she doesn't. Rochelle, maybe. But that would be it. Considering Rochelle is married to the sheriff, there's probably no better person to have in your corner.

She shakes her head, a small hint of vulnerability cloaking her face. "We've got no one else. It's just us."

"Put your number in." I hand her my phone, and she looks at me with more hesitance, taking a deep breath. "I won't let anyone have your number. I won't tell anyone you live here. But I will text you so you have mine in case you need anything."

After another pause, she moves to take my cell, putting in her number.

"You and Rochelle are the only two people that know my number." Her eyes meet mine in a silent pact. Trust. She's trusting me to keep it that way, and I nod quickly in understanding.

"Here." I grab her waist, lifting her from the truck, her small size making it easy, and place her on her feet right in front of me. She looks up, her hair falling away, her eyes searching mine.

"Thanks, Sutton." It's not the words, but the way she says them that has my chest burning. I feel it. I feel her gratitude, her genuine nature. People say sweet things to me all the time. But I know they never mean them. They're just words. They throw them around, telling me what they think I want to hear. What they think will get them what they want.

Nikki doesn't want anything. In fact, she's the total opposite and probably doesn't want me around. I'm a global movie star, my face familiar, privacy not something I have, and while many people want in on that lifestyle, I know Nikki isn't one of them. That's what I like about her the most. The simple things impress her. The real me. Not the movie star me. I have a feeling she's seen all the same bullshit I have.

"Anytime." I absentmindedly brush my fingers across her blue-tinted skin once more, carefully, still not over the fact that some asshole decided to take her money and put their hands on her. "Better get inside before James finds a mouse."

Head tilting, she looks at me like I have three heads.

"Benjamin Franklin had a pet mouse he trained," I explain, and she releases a breath of relief, then shakes her head and smiles.

"Benjamin Franklin also thought taking 'air baths'—basically sitting around naked—was good for his health. I think I'd take the mouse over that." She steps away from me, walking up to her house. I watch her the entire way, my mind now on seeing her in an air bath, and I know I'm too far gone.

I should've listened to Sawyer and kept my distance, because now that we're friends, there's no way I can turn back.

9

———

NIKKI

James and I walk through the library. It's quiet, no one's here. Being a Saturday, most people are watching sports or out doing things. The swelling around my eye has completely gone, so now I'm just left with a small bruise, the Arnica Sutton gave me helping immensely.

"Sutton was nice yesterday," James comments as we move down the rows of books, flicking through some before we move to the next.

"I saw you guys chatting at the diner yesterday. What were you talking about?" I was going to ask him last night, but by the time we both shoveled in some lasagna and had showers, he was out like a light.

"Just stuff. He helped me a little with my project."

I smile. "That's nice of him."

"Yeah. He asked about... us." Now he has my full attention.

"Asked what, exactly?" I'm cautious. Not because I fear Sutton, but because I fear everyone.

"Just asked about my dad. He thinks you're my mom." James rolls his eyes, knowing that's what most people think.

I nod, then ask, "Did you tell him the truth?"

"No. I stayed quiet, just like you've told me to. He said his dad was bad growing up too."

Sutton opening up to James is nice, as is helping him with his homework, but I'm still scared for us to get too close. He isn't the only one. I see Rochelle watching me too, her husband, the sheriff, is always looking at us when he comes into the diner as well. At least their looks are compassionate, not looks of callousness.

"Good. He can work out that you're my brother in his own time. We don't need to go filling in the blanks. Not with him, not with anybody." I pause as we walk toward the magazine section, because there, on the stand, is Sutton's image staring right at me.

"Look." James grabs it, the magazine next to it, and the one next to that, all with him on the cover. The photos are from a red carpet. A beautiful woman on his arm, her grin as wide as his. He looks different, almost too polished, too airbrushed and nothing like the guy I serve in the diner every day. Nothing like the man who touched my cheek like I was the most delicate and most important person in that moment.

"Yep, he's a real-life movie star." It all feels so surreal. In my former life, I met some important people. Chairman of boards, dignitaries, senior professors, all who were at our various galas and balls that my father and his company held every year. There were also celebrities, athletes, movie stars like Sutton. Dad would probably love to have Sutton in his inner circle. That thought gives me pause, wondering if they've already met.

"I think we can trust him, Nikki." James is a good judge of character. He picked up on how awful Maribel was the minute Dad introduced us. She proved him right in every way.

"Maybe. Time will tell." I need proof. I can no longer just make assumptions that people are genuine, nice, decent humans. If our own stepmother can't be that, then I hesitate to think a Hollywood movie star is.

"He watches you, you know." James is also observant.

My heart beats just a little faster. "I know."

"I think he likes you."

I look at him pointedly. "He's just a friend."

"Yeah, but you've never had a boyfriend. Not that I met anyway. Why don't you—"

I cut him off. "I think we need more Benjamin Franklin and less Sutton Silvers this morning, don't you?"

He rolls his eyes at me again. He might be younger than me, yet with his height and maturity, he comes across as older sometimes. But I need to stop the conversation. Boyfriend? Sutton? Those two things just don't go together. Sure, he's hiding, just like we are. But for him, it's temporary. He'll go back to LA in a few months, maybe even weeks, and jump into the spotlight again, a gorgeous model on his arm no doubt, flashing his smile to everyone he meets, just like what's on the cover of these magazines. Me? Hiding is permanent, and the plight of it all feels insurmountable.

"Fine. Let's go to the history section." Once he puts the magazine back on the shelf, we walk to the other side of the library. I wander after him, feeling Sutton's eyes on me from the magazine shelf the entire way. James is right; he does watch me. Every day. And he didn't need to drive us home yesterday, but he did. When he passed me the bag from the drugstore, I couldn't believe it. Not only had he thought of everything I needed, but when I saw a few bags of peanut butter cups, I almost cried. Not because they're the only treat I love, and I haven't indulged in them for months, but because he listened. I mentioned it to him in passing, and he remembered.

He also didn't need to give me his number. I was hesitant, not wanting to give anyone our number, but last night, when I sat with my thoughts, I realized that he gave me his too. A Hollywood megastar handed me his number. He trusts me, and now maybe I need to trust him.

"I just want to look through this one." James grabs a book about our founding fathers and takes a seat at the small lounge nearby. He flicks through a few pages, coming to a halt when he spots the chapter on Benjamin Franklin.

As he does, I find my cell in my bag. I hardly use it. It's so the school or Rochelle can contact me, mainly. My thumb brushes over the screen. This is probably a really bad idea, but I take a photo of the magazine rack, my stomach swirling as I put together a text.

> Even the library has you all over their shelves.

Before I can talk myself out of it, I send the text quickly and immediately cringe. God, it feels like forever since I texted a man. But I need to start trusting someone. I need to have someone in my corner.

I look at the screen, seeing no bubbles or indication that he's seen it. The stupid message stays unread, and I throw my cell back in my bag, remorse for sending it already sinking into my shoulders.

"I'll just go look at the noticeboard." Stepping away from

James, I walk to the far wall, coming face-to-face with the large community noticeboard that's been like a lifeline for us. This board is where I found our cottage. It's also where I learned about the diner needing a waitress and found some free secondhand furniture and items for our home. It's my good luck board.

"Hey, Nikki."

Looking up, I see Daisy, a new local resident, who moved here not long ago. Always bright and bubbly, her boyfriend owns the luxury whiskey distillery in town, the Whiteman men well known and central figures around here. They're both nice guys, although I don't speak to them much. I keep my head low, my presence small, not wanting any attention.

"Hi, Daisy." I shuffle back as she pins something to the board.

She turns to me and smiles. "I'm starting a new class, if you're interested?"

I look at the paper she pinned. A new community yoga class at her studio down the street.

"Oh, um, I can't. I have work during the day and have James after school." I swallow my disappointment. I used to do yoga, all through high school and college. It was the only thing that kept me sane. I really miss it.

"It's at night, so bring James. Kids love yoga, and even if he doesn't, he can always sit in my office and read or play games."

James would probably hate yoga but would actually love the peace and quiet of a studio where he can escape with a good book. I look back at the paper and bite my lip. It doesn't have the price on it. My rule of thumb in life is, if you have to ask, you can't afford it.

"I don't think I can do it."

"Are you sure? It's free. It's a community night," she tells me softly, like she already knows my inner thoughts.

My brow pinches. "Community night?"

"Yeah, one night a week, open for all, no cost to anyone. I'm trying to talk Rochelle into coming. I think it would do her good to stretch out her back."

That makes me smile. It would do her good.

"I do miss it." My voice is low, like I'm talking to myself, but Daisy catches it, and her face lights up.

"You've done yoga before?"

Shit. I said too much.

"Not much. Just a little in college." I try to wave it off.

"Oh, what college did you go to?"

Shit. Shit. Shit. I'm getting too relaxed around here.

"Just a small college," I say simply, not offering more information.

Her face falters, and I feel bad. It's a stupid response. Obviously, my college has a name. But I can't give it. The silence around us turns awkward, and I inwardly break a little.

"Oh... well... I'm always looking for yoga buddies..." Her voice lifts at the end, sounding hopeful, and I know better than most what it's like to move to a small town and have no friends. Daisy has friends, but I'm sure she'd like more. She's about my age, super friendly, and we seem to get along whenever we talk.

"Maybe I can come this week?" I'm tentative. I don't want to promise her; I'll probably chicken out on the day. But I do love yoga, and while walking home in the dark isn't my idea of a good time, especially after getting mugged, Whispers is generally quiet, so I don't fear it like I probably should.

"I'll save you a mat. I can't wait. See you then!" She has an extra spring in her step as she walks out.

"Bye!" I shout after her as James walks up.

"Nikki, look." He points to the noticeboard, and I read the paper. *Bikes free to a good home.*

Giddy, I grab the paper, knowing that will cut our commute in half. "Oooh, looks like we've just found some transport."

10

SUTTON

I push out the last set, my bench press done, sweat running down my body, yet my mind still not exhausted. Ripping my singlet from my frame, I wipe my face before throwing it on the floor. My mind is full of one thing and one thing only. *Her.*

Nikki doesn't work today, and I've been here in Sawyer's gym all morning, wondering what she does on the weekends. Does she sleep in? Does she garden? Does she make a big breakfast? Does she walk to town?

"Told you he'd be in here." My brother's voice filters in from the doorway, and I look up, seeing him walk in with Tanner and Griffin. He isn't wrong. Aside from my daily visits to the diner, the next place I spend most of my time is the gym. I work out every day. Both strength and stamina. I run for an hour, and then I lift heavy for another hour. Usually, I also swim and steam, my body put through its paces for at least four hours a day. I was buff before, but all this work is really getting my physique toned. Besides, I need to work off all the chicken pies I eat at the diner.

"Boys. Come for a session?" My comment is a flyaway

because none of them are dressed for the gym. Sawyer is in his signature suit, one that looks completely odd in this small town. Tanner stands tall and proud in his jeans and shirt, Griffin dressed similarly by his side.

"Are you getting your body ready for the shoots?" Tanner looks at me with a lifted eyebrow, and I flex my bicep. I'm happy that I'm in prime condition to be the face of his latest release.

"I don't need to get ready. I'm always ready." It's true. If LA has taught me anything, it's that a healthy body is what's constantly needed. You never know when the next offer will land, and you never know what the role will entail, and after Nikki got mugged this week, I want my muscles ready for that takedown as well.

"I'm here going over the new accommodation build at the distillery, so thought I'd drop by to chat with you to finalize your plans and get started," Griffin says, holding some paperwork. He and I are new friends, having only met a few weeks ago. As soon as I told my brother I bought a plot of land next to his, he immediately called Griffin.

"I can't believe you're moving here." Sawyer shakes his head, but his smile is wide.

"Well, maybe not to live permanently, but I might base myself out of Whispers, at least for a while." I have no idea what my future is going to be like. I've lived in LA for my entire career. I have a penthouse in New York right next to Sawyer, too, as well as a house in Hawaii, a lodge in Colorado, and even have a loft in Paris. My investment in real estate is in depth.

"Believe me, you won't find anywhere better than Whispers." Tanner grins, happy to have a global celebrity in his town.

"You should fund a tourism commercial," I quip, because his love for this town is well known.

"Want to star in it?" He looks at me seriously, and I frown. I hadn't thought about that, but it could be yet another project for me to consider.

"First the whiskey and now Whispers. God, I'm so sick of seeing your face," my brother says as only a brother can.

I shrug, chuckling. "Better looking than yours."

"I love a bit of sibling rivalry. Does that mean your place is going to be bigger than this one?" Griffin grins with a waggle of his eyebrows. Known for his luxury builds, Griffin likes doing new and different things. Which comes with people with money. He charges well, but his portfolio is detailed and seemingly endless.

"I have low skin in the game. I just need something secure, with a theater room, a pool, a gym, a few bedrooms, an office, maybe a tennis court..."

"That's a yes, then," Tanner cuts in, making me laugh.

"I just need the basics."

Sawyer joins in. "Do you need a secret entrance for all your models to come and go unseen?"

I look at him sharply. Once upon a time, I may have thought about that. But now it leaves a bad taste in my mouth.

"No models," I grit out, thinking about the one person I'd like to visit me and how she's probably the last person who would.

"Alright, well, I'm also getting started on mine next week, so I'll finalize the plans for you, and we can get it sorted quickly. I'll put two teams here. One on each house, making it a fast build; they can work on both sites, in tandem, around the clock. Deliveries will be structured, cutting the usual time frame in half." I see Griffin mentally calculating his to-do list. This is why he's the country's best builder. He works fast, has the best teams, and is always two steps ahead.

"Glad you're gonna make a home here, even if it's not your only one. There really is no better place to be." Tanner's smirk reeks of *I told you so*. Again, his love for this town is unmatched.

But what he says reminds me of something. "Speaking of that..." I frown as soon as I say it, wondering if I should bring this up.

"What's going on?" Sawyer's already on guard, obviously knowing my uneasy look.

I clear my throat. "Well, did you know that Nikki got mugged?"

Tanner's head rears back, eyes widening in a way I haven't seen from him. "*Mugged?*"

"What happened?" Sawyer asks, his tone taking on an edge, already in detective mode.

"A journalist came in the other day, and she put on a great act. It was pretty funny, actually." I can't help but smile, remembering her bad country accent and how the journalist believed it immediately.

"So the journalist mugged her?" Griffin needs to stick to building. I mentally note never to be his partner in a murder mystery game.

"No, I gave her a tip. A hundred. To say thanks."

All three pairs of eyes stare right at me in silence before Tanner breaks it.

"Mighty generous," he murmurs.

"Whatever. Anyway, some guys saw it and followed her when her shift ended. They jumped her and James at the back of the diner on their way home."

"What the hell?" Tanner is ropeable, nearly barking his outrage.

"What did the sheriff say?" Griffin frowns.

My lips purse, knowing this won't go over well. "That's the thing... No sheriff."

"No sheriff?" he pushes.

"Yeah, Nikki keeps to herself," I add, looking at Griffin, and I see the moment it registers.

"She has secrets," Tanner says with a pinched expression, rubbing his chin like he's coming up with a plan.

"Have you had anything like this happen around town before?" I ask him.

"No. No petty crime. Sure, the local kids can be a bit troublesome at times, but they're all usually okay and certainly wouldn't hurt someone deliberately like that."

My brother looks concerned. "Is Nikki alright?"

"Yeah. I drove her home last night. I didn't want her walking." I swallow the fury building inside me, hating that she won't feel safe now. Glancing at the bench, I wonder if I can push out a few more, needing to expel this frustration from my body.

"You drove her home?" Sawyer confirms.

I nod mindlessly. "Yeah. Did you know she walks over three miles per day?"

"She's up the back of town, in the middle of the pines, isn't she?" Of course Tanner would know.

I nearly shiver. "In the middle of the fucking serial killer forest, you mean? The ones so dense, I don't think you would hear anyone scream?"

He raises an eyebrow at me.

"Slightly dramatic, but yes, those would be the ones."

"She's an adult, Sutton. She chose to live there." My brother, as usual, tries to be the voice of reason.

"Yeaaaah, I'm not sure it was a choice."

"Me neither," Tanner agrees, and we have a silent conversation with our eyes.

He's just as worried as I am. But his perspective is ensuring everyone in his town is safe and happy. Me, I just want Nikki to be safe and happy. Maybe even safe and happy with me.

"We'll keep an eye out. I'll tell Connor and Hudson too. I assume Rochelle knows, which means the sheriff will find out?" Tanner adds, and I feel somewhat better that others now know and will be on the lookout in case it happens to anyone else.

"Yeah, I guess." I should ask Nikki, but I don't want to push her. But if I saw her face, then so did Rochelle and she's a smart woman. She would know something isn't right.

"Let's go for a walk, check out the site, and talk more about what you want. Sounds like security needs to be a priority for you. These two assholes can stay here and talk business." Griffin nods to Sawyer and Tanner, who are already talking about Gertie's Soaps, the small brand that has just exploded, all thanks to a strategic business deal from Sawyer and some perfectly timed celebrity endorsement from me on my social media.

At the thought of social media, I grab my cell from where I left it on the floor near my towel and internally curse when I see a message from Nikki. Shit, I missed it. But I grin. She sent me a text, with an image of my face on some magazines.

Even the library has you all over their shelves.

I'm a literary genius.

I'm quick with my response. Keeping it light, fun, hoping to make her smile. I also like knowing more about her, that she goes to the library on her days off.

> They say you're in the Maldives with a
> model.

> Just goes to show you can't believe a word
> they're saying.

> If they only knew you hang out at a small-
> town diner all day.

> I like the scenery there better.

> So do I…

She sends an image with the last text, one of the Whispers landscape. The scenery is amazing on the back roads that lead to her place. But while the landscape is beautiful, there's something else that catches my eye.

> You got bikes?

> Toy store was giving them away. We saw a
> notice on the community noticeboard.
> James loves it.

She's fucking resourceful, and while I prefer she has a car, bikes are better than nothing.

"Ahhhh, Sutton?" Griffin prods, and I look up from my phone, seeing the three men staring at me. My wide grin falters a little, as they have that "gotcha" smirk on their faces.

"Alright, let's go." Reluctantly, I pocket my cell. Probably better, since she needs to concentrate on the road anyway.

"I also want a library," I tell Griffin as we start to walk out of the gym and make our way over to the vacant plot of land next door. "A big one."

He chuckles. "Of course you do."

"You don't even fucking read!" Sawyer yells from behind me, and I hear Tanner laugh in response.

Yeah, life in Whispers is feeling better and better with every passing minute.

It kind of makes me want to stay more permanently.

11

NIKKI

With our hair now marinading in black dye, James and I sit together, watching the TV, eating our homemade spaghetti, the one amazing dish I can make.

I love cooking. I'm just not great at it. Years of having all meals prepared by a private chef will do that to you.

"Oh, look. It's Dad!" James blurts, and my eyes snap to the TV that's showing the nightly news.

"Turn it up." I sit forward, my heart in my throat as James increases the volume.

"Titan Holdings, the US-based oil conglomerate, wrapped up its annual shareholder meeting earlier today, reporting strong financials and steady year-on-year growth. Company executives highlighted strategic expansions in shale operations and refining capabilities, attributing their performance to resilient market demand and cost efficiency. Investors reacted positively to the company's long-term outlook, with Titan's share price edging higher following the announcement.

"Owner and CEO Colin Titan described the fiscal year as 'a

turning point' for Titan Holdings, signaling plans for increased investment in domestic infrastructure. Although his face is still solemn, as his personal life continues to weigh heavy on him. Missing now for over three months, there's no news on his two children and their whereabouts. In what many are describing a serious turn of events, he's also spearheaded a new department within Titan Holdings, one which reinvests into the environment, inspired by his daughter's passion for sustainability. It's said that for every acre of land purchased for drilling, he's also buying an acre of land for reforestation. Thereby balancing his impact on the environment, aiming for net zero. The move has caused a ripple through his competitors, further showcasing how he and Titan Energy are at the forefront and leaders in this space."

My breath hitches in disbelief. It was an idea I mentioned when he was pushing me to work with him. I suggested offsetting the business footprint, knowing that he wasn't ever going to stop drilling. I can't believe he's put it in action. The recording shows Dad walking out of his New York high-rise office and getting into his waiting car, moving past the cameras quickly, head down, focused. He looks older than I remember, with dark circles around his eyes, thinner than before, and my heart hurts for him. I miss him, but I'm scared to go home. James and I both sit in silence, glued to the screen, as a reporter chases my dad from his building to his waiting car.

"Mr. Titan, any update for shareholders on new oil drills?"

My dad stops, and I still. He never stops. He never takes questions like this. He looks at the reporter and then looks straight at the camera.

"Kids, if you see this, please come home. I miss you."

As he stares at us unknowingly through the TV, my eyes are glued to his, emotion rising to the surface.

"Should we call him?" James whispers, the two of us unmoving.

"I don't know... Maribel warned us," I remind him, and his shoulders slump.

Maribel and my dad had a secret wedding in Vegas, a month after meeting. It is the most reckless thing he's ever done. James and I knew nothing about her until we saw it all play out in the media. Afterward, I laughed, thinking it was a joke.

Turns out, it wasn't. That's when things really started going downhill.

"I miss him. The old him." My brother looks at me, sadness in his gaze reflecting mine.

"Me too." Looking back at the TV, I search for anything more of my father. Of the man who used to laugh and joke and smile. The one who used to bring me peanut butter cups every Friday after work. That all stopped when Mom died and got worse when Maribel arrived on the scene.

Maribel wanted our father to hate us. Blaming us for anything and everything, and it worked. I thought it was jealousy. Some women are just insecure; they want their man to focus solely on them, one hundred percent of the time. I'm sure us kids were an inconvenience.

But it was more than that. She wanted his money, and the longer she was around, the more I came to see it. A lot of our family money is tied up in the business, in trusts, in banks. But mostly, in inheritance, left to James and me. And she knew that.

So she wanted us gone. Out of the picture. Wanted Dad and his money all to herself. Well, she got her wish.

"Do we need to move again?" James looks torn as he asks the dreaded question. We both love it here. We're literally in the middle of nowhere, surrounded by kind people who allow us to just be. James gets to continue his education, and I can work a cash job and bring in some money, all the while spending time on little side projects that I love. I have no endgame; I'm just taking it day by day.

"No. We're safe. No one is looking for us here."

He nods as I feel my heart break. My younger brother with black dye in his hair, living life like no ten-year-old should.

But he's safe from the hands of Maribel, and that's all that matters.

WITH THE COTTAGE QUIET, my brother sound asleep, and the smell of hair dye still faint in my nose, I sit in the darkness of my room, my phone heavy in my hands. I've been sitting here, rolling it in my palm since I came to bed. The vision of Dad hasn't left my mind since the news came on earlier.

I miss him. We both do. Seeing him not look himself, his shoulders slumped, dark circles under his eyes—broken— it shattered something inside me that I've been trying to hold together. Hearing that he's started an environmental team gives me hope. Hope that he can change his views, that maybe, just maybe, I was the catalyst for it.

I swallow roughly, and with my heart pounding, I dial his number. The ringing in my ear is thunderously loud as I wait for him to pick up. I feel like I'm about to break out of my skin.

"Hello?" I hear a voice and end the call immediately. I'm breathless, even though I haven't moved.

"Stupid," I hiss at myself, then look at the time. Almost

midnight. I thought it was late enough. I thought it was safe. It wasn't. The voice at the other end wasn't my father's. It was Maribel's.

"Straight home?" James asks as we grab our bikes where they're parked at the library. We spent some time here, researching for his project, and I scoured the non-fiction area to read up on apple trees. I've decided to propagate the lonely apple tree in our yard. I've never grafted a tree before, and while it will take a while to grow, what a great way to sustainably harvest our own food right on our doorstep. Now the late morning is warmer, and I don't want to go straight home. I look at my brother, knowing what I'm about to say might surprise him.

"Should we go watch the school baseball team?"

His face lights up immediately. It's unusual for us. We keep a low profile, don't go out much, but he needs to cement his friendships. Seeing the kids outside of school is one of the ways in which he can do that.

"Are you sure?" His voice is high with anticipation. He's never done it before. Here in Whispers or back at home.

Smiling, I shrug. "Sure, we'll ride around the back, park the bikes, and watch for a little bit. Then we can cut through the forest and ride home."

"Yes. Let's do it." He almost jumps in excitement.

It's a nice ride in the sun and takes us no time to get to the school grounds, where we pull up and park our bikes before walking down toward the pitch.

"We're batting!" he says eagerly, and I look around. There's a small group of parents huddled together, watching the game, and then a playground where other kids are playing. Something catches my eye as I'm turning back to the game. I see a man standing back away from the crowd, underneath some tall pines, his stature familiar.

"Is that Sutton?" James asks, and as we get closer, I spot the familiar hat.

"Why don't you go hang in the playground and watch, and I'll go say hi," I suggest, knowing he needs a bit of freedom, and without needing any more encouragement, he races off.

I walk down to where Sutton is standing, head lowered and hands in the pockets of his jacket, obviously trying to remain inconspicuous as he watches one of his nephews play baseball.

"Hey, you," I say softly.

He looks up, startled, then his mouth curves into a wide grin, the surprise and happiness at seeing me instant, making me feel warm all over.

"Hey. Where'd you come from?"

"James and I just finished at the library. It was too nice of a morning just to go home. I know he needs more friends and closer connections, so I thought coming here for a bit might help."

At that, we both look over at the playground and see James running around with a few other kids.

Smiling, he nods. "Looks like it was the right call."

Seeing James laugh and play, my shoulders lower.

"Your eye is looking better." His gaze moves over me, like he's checking for any other injuries.

"Yep, I'm brand new."

"Your hair's darker?" he observes, and I run my hand over my long hair.

"Yeah. It needed to be freshened up." I hide any sadness I have from making my blond tresses darker with a fake grin. "Got to hide those grays," I lie through my teeth. Noticing James running around, I take the opportunity to change the subject.

"Odd, he usually only runs that fast when Rochelle's cupcakes are up for grabs."

"Food must be a universal motivator. My nephew, Kevin, demanded pancakes before the game, half a stack minimum."

I laugh lightly, loving seeing this casual side of Sutton.

"Sounds like he knows where to find the good stuff. Let me guess... you're the indulgent uncle with questionable boundaries?" I raise an eyebrow in jest, but my grin is genuine.

Sutton makes an act of clutching pearls at his neck. "Ouch. I prefer 'supportive with flair.' Though I think James just tried a backflip in the playground, so you might be the one raising a daredevil."

"Daredevils we are not." I shake my head, looking down at the playground again, wondering how I feel so at ease with the man next to me.

"Oh, Kevin is up."

My head whips to the field as Sutton stands taller, looking intently at the game. I can tell he wants to cheer, but he can't, not wanting to draw attention to himself.

"He looks confident," I say, hoping that one day James can maybe join a team like that.

"He's a great little player. Sawyer is part owner of The Mets, so he's had a few clinics with the pros and learned a few things."

"I haven't been to a game since my dad had season tickets right behind home plate. The ones with the valet and the private sushi chef. Spoiled me for stadium peanuts forever." As soon as the last word leaves my lips, I slap my hand over my mouth. Sutton looks at me quickly; meanwhile, we both miss Kevin's hit as the ball flies over the field and he gets a home run. The only way we can tell is from all the shouts of excitement we can hear from the crowd.

"Season tickets, eh?" he says with lifted eyebrows. My heart is pounding so hard I feel sick. "Don't worry. I won't tell anybody." Even when Sutton winks at me, I'm still frozen, shock taking over me as my hands start to shake.

"Hey, hey." Shaking his head, he speaks with a gentle tone, his brow now furrowed. "I mean it. Your secrets are not mine to share." He reaches for my hand, removing it from my face. Bringing it down to my side, he holds it in his, not letting me go. My shortness of breath is now not just due to shock, but also the heat that travels through my body at the feeling of his touch.

"Sorry." I clear my throat, wondering what the hell is wrong with me. I should've cycled straight home. Of course the one time I deviate from our usual plan, things get messy.

Sutton still doesn't let go of my hand. Not yet. His thumb brushes the inside of my wrist once, his touch barely there, and I melt a little. It feels nice. Too nice. The kind of feeling you get when you want more. It's been a long time since I felt the touch of a man like this.

A whistle blows from the field, and we both turn, grateful for the distraction. Kevin's coach is waving him over, while James has collapsed into a giggling pile of dirt with two other boys.

"You know, if you ever want a fresh start that isn't just a new hair color... I'm good at disappearing. Could give you a few tips."

I raise my eyebrow. "Disappearing's easy. It's the reappearing that's hard."

"Maybe the trick isn't hiding. Maybe it's finding the right person to show up for."

I think about that statement long after the game ends. Feeling them to my core as a flutter builds in my chest. When Sutton finally lets go of my hand, I don't just miss his touch, but the unspoken support I felt in his grip.

12

SUTTON

I grab one of Sawyer's cushions and slap Kevin across the head with it.

"Got you!" I yell as little Noah jumps on me, the two kids now pushing me to the ground, bruising my kidneys in the process. This kind of rough and tumble I haven't done for years, but it's almost a daily occurrence in this house since I arrived. The kids love it, as do I.

"We've got you!" Kevin says proudly, sitting on my chest, pinning my arms to the floor and little Noah sits behind him on my stomach, making me slightly regret the extra set of sit-ups I did after baseball today.

"Kevin, do you know James, the new kid at school?" I ask, thinking about how James is new and needs more friends.

"Yeah. We're in the same class."

"Are you friends?"

"Kind of. He doesn't play baseball, though." He shrugs.

"Maybe you need to teach him?" I wonder if my nephew could take him under his wing and build his friend circle a little.

At that, his face pinches, unsure. "I mean, he's always reading..."

"Maybe he's just waiting for a friend to invite him to play? Must be hard being the new kid."

I see Kevin's mind ticking over.

"Yeah, okay. I'll ask him on Monday," Kevin says, just as little Noah grabs a cushion and slaps me in the head.

"What in the world is going on in here?" Sawyer walks in and berates us all. "Seriously, this place is a mess."

With a groan, I roll my eyes. "You heard him, let's clean up." I lift up quickly, causing the two kids to spill from my frame, giggling all the way until they crash on the floor and the three of us tidy up.

"Seriously. You're a bigger kid than them." Sawyer looks at me, rolling his eyes right back.

"Hey! It's my first time having nephews. I'm banking this time I have with them before I go back," I tell him honestly, a heavy feeling twisting in my gut when I think about leaving Whispers and going back to LA.

"Boys, go wash your hands and get ready for dinner." The two boys wander down the hall at Sawyer's command, and I look at my hand. The one that held on to Nikki when she clearly said too much to me this morning. I haven't washed it. Her soft hand felt too delicate in my own.

"I was talking to Mom earlier," Sawyer starts as we take a seat on the sofa.

"She alright? I was thinking we could fly her up here, spend some time with her. But I know she'll be followed." I scrub my chin, hating that I can't see my mom because the fucking media are hounding everyone I know.

"You know Mom. She loves life down in Florida. It's hard to get ahold of her. She's always playing bowls, cooking, having drinks with her friends. Her social life is better than mine." Sawyer huffs a laugh, and I grin. He isn't wrong. Mom has a great group of friends.

"I'm thinking of putting in a cottage on my land. Somewhere she can stay when she comes. It gives her some privacy while also being close to us."

"Good idea. The kids could be a handful for her, so she might need the space. Although winter isn't too far away, so I don't think she'll like the weather." At that, we both look out the window, noticing the gray clouds rolling in. This morning, it was beautiful. The sun turned out just as Nikki arrived, warming up my day without even knowing it. Now without her, the clouds are back, the weather outside looking cold.

"Hopefully, there are still a few more weeks left of okay weather so I can do some more hiking. There's a bit of a path at the back of my new block I want to explore."

"How much longer you planning to stay?" my brother asks, looking at me with interest. When I first got here, I didn't really have a time frame in mind. I just needed a break. Now, as I settle into the community, and with the new Whiteman's Whiskey partnership in the process, I'll be here for longer.

"I need to lay low until the launch of The Shadow Gentleman. Me outing myself at the launch is one of the key drivers to catapult the new line and have everyone frothing to grab a bottle. Plus, I'm liking this town and its people." Or should I say, *person*. Nikki is constantly on my mind, so much so, it's startling.

My brother frowns but nods along with my idea of a plan.

"You look stressed," I comment, and he scoffs.

"This is how I always look."

"Permanently stressed?"

"I just need my virtual assistant to get up to speed and things will settle down."

My brother works hard. Too hard if you ask me.

"Why don't you hire a local?"

Sawyer looks at me like I have rocks in my head. "There's no one here in Whispers who would work."

"What about Nikki?" I suggest.

His eyes bore into mine.

"I already approached her about it," he mutters, and now I'm intrigued.

I quirk an eyebrow. "Oh yeah? And?"

"And... she rejected me."

I cough out a laugh.

"Rejected you?" It's obvious that she needs a day job, with James to look after at night, and I would've thought that working with Sawyer would mean more money for her than working with Rochelle at the diner.

"It's never happened to me before." I can tell my brother's ego is bruised just from his tight expression.

"Why wouldn't she accept?" I ask quietly, almost to myself.

"I asked her a few weeks before you turned up. Saw how she seemed quick to learn and knew about admin and computers a bit. I have no idea why she declined the opportunity; most people I talk to would die to work for my firm."

"You've lost your shine," I tease him, even though I'm left with more questions than answers.

He sighs. "She's a hard one to get to know."

"She keeps things close to her chest," I admit, thinking about our chat today, the way she let a little more about herself slip than she intended. I'm eager to get to know her. I sometimes find I want to call her just to hear her voice. But I have to tame myself.

"Well, Rochelle did say she has a history."

"She needs a car. Why wouldn't she take the job if she obviously needs the cash?"

"Maybe she has a record. You can't really work for a law firm if you have a record." Sawyer watches me at that statement, and my face contorts, knowing that woman doesn't have a bad bone in her body.

I'm already shaking my head in denial. "There's no way."

"I guess time will tell. You know as well as I do that all secrets come out eventually." Sawyer stands, throws a cushion at me, and walks out. Leaving me sinking deeper into the silence, knowing that I'm not going to let anything hurt her.

Not on my watch.

13

NIKKI

"You know, the sheriff and I have been talking…" Rochelle starts, looking at me from where she's icing a cake.

Wiping down the counter, I look up at her, waiting.

"And we were wondering if perhaps you and James wanted to come over for dinner one night a week. You know, have some company."

I swallow past a sudden lump in my throat, keeping my hands busy by putting on a fresh batch of coffee. I really want to say yes. Sometimes, the cottage is deathly quiet at night. But I can't risk it.

"Oh, that sounds lovely, but you know I try to get James to do his homework and have an early night to be ready for school again the next day." I sink into the horrible feeling of lying to her and rejecting her offer.

"Well, we can always do the weekend? Think about it, honey. I sure do worry about the two of you all the way out in the forest." She pauses and looks at me meaningfully, and I give her a forced closed-lip grin.

"I'll think about it." That's the best answer I have, at least for right now. The door chimes, and I turn, getting back into work mode. I see a new face, a middle-aged man, and grab the fresh pot of coffee to meet him at the counter.

"Good afternoon. Coffee?" I ask as he takes a seat right in front of me.

He nods. "That would be nice." He's a stranger, but he seems pleasant enough and doesn't look like a journalist.

"Would you like something to eat? We have the specials here, and we're well known for our amazing chicken pies."

He grins, chuckling to himself.

"My stomach's been rumbling for the entire drive here, so a pie sounds delightful."

"Coming right up." I move quickly, grabbing a fresh pie and getting his meal sorted.

As I come back to the counter, I ask, "Where did you drive from?" It's an attempt to make polite conversation but also to find out more about him. If it turns out he's a journalist here for Sutton, then it's best I know before Sutton turns up.

"Oh, I'm retired. The wife and I are currently on a trip across the country. She's shopping in Williamstown for the day, and I wanted to visit the distillery. She's not really into whiskey, but I don't mind the odd sip here and there."

I smile. He's harmless, and my shoulders lower almost immediately.

"Well, it's the best whiskey in the country, so you made a good choice."

I've tried Whiteman's before. On my twenty-first birthday, my father sat me down, and we shared a glass together. It's his favorite whiskey, and he bought a special bottle at a charity gala a few years ago just for the occasion. I remember the night like it was yesterday. It was one of the rare occasions he seemed happy after Mom died. We sat for hours, reminiscing about my life and the last few years. That's why James and I landed here. The name of this small town was familiar and held the last loving memories before everything changed.

"It's a beautiful town. Have you lived here long?"

I wipe down the nearby counter before my eyes shoot to the clock, knowing James will be here soon.

"All my life. Grew up here not far from the distillery." I lie through my teeth, but he smiles and nods, not caring for anything different.

"My wife tells me that small towns are quaint but hold a lot of secrets." He chuckles.

"Sounds like she watches too many crime shows." I grin just as the door chimes, and James walks in, looking chipper.

"Good day?" I ask as I get him a glass of milk, and Rochelle slides him a small plate with a cupcake.

"The best day!" he says before taking a big bite.

"Oh yeah? Why so good?" I smile at his excitement.

"Kevin from my class asked me to play baseball with them at lunchtime today. It was awesome!" His eyes alight, and I laugh.

"Really? That's amazing!" My eyes water, seeing his genuine happiness. I know Kevin is Sutton's nephew, so I wonder if Sutton had anything to do with this. Thinking he probably did has my heart swelling in size for the man who continues to surprise me.

"Yeah, well, I sucked at it. But they showed me how to throw and how to bat and asked me to play with them again tomorrow." He isn't too sporty, but he hasn't had a lot of friends before, so he'd probably do anything to be included.

"Maybe we can try to find some equipment and practice at home." We can check the community noticeboard to see if there's any garage sales advertised or if the toy store has any sports equipment they're giving away.

"I'm going to start running around the apple tree. I gotta practice my slides."

My eyebrows rise as I chuckle. "Slides?" This is a new side of my brother and one that's been missing for a while.

He nods. "Yeah, when you slide along the ground to get to home base safely."

"They call it a dirt dive," the older gentleman at the counter says, and I look at him, forgetting momentarily he was there.

"A dirt dive?" I ask with curiosity.

He wipes his mouth with his napkin. "The kids dive into the dirt and slide all the way to home base to prevent from getting out."

"A dirt dive…" I nod, already thinking about how I'm going to have to do some heavy-duty washing of his clothes to get dirt stains out.

"Thank you, my dear, for the pie." The older guys stands with a kind smile, throwing a few bills onto the counter.

"You're very welcome. Enjoy the whiskey," I tell him as he steps out of the diner.

"Who was that?" James asks as I clean up the counter, thankful for the small tip.

"Oh, just a tourist. Seemed like a nice guy." I shrug as Rochelle comes out.

"Did I hear that you played baseball today?" She beams at James, who's back to grinning so wide it almost splits his face. He replays his day to Rochelle, who looks just as excited as we are about it all.

"You know, I'm sure the sheriff has some old balls, bats, and gloves lying around in the shed at home, gathering dust. I'll bring them in. Can't have our newest baseball player without some gear!" she says, walking around the diner like a proud parent herself. My chest warms at her generosity.

Then she calls out over her shoulder, "And have another cupcake, honey. You need to build your strength." She sends my brother a wink, and James dives for another cupcake as I chuckle, loving this small town even more.

14

SUTTON

Sitting in my booth, I sip my coffee as the chime on the door rings out. I look at my watch, noting he's right on time. James walks in with his backpack full, but today instead of going to the counter like he usually does, he comes to my booth.

"Hey, Sutton, are you any good at math?" He gives me a look of hope, and I grimace.

"I'm shit at math. But take a seat, and we'll work it out together." I shuffle over, and he sits beside me, opening his bag and grabbing his books. I try to tame my grin. The kid is coming around to me... Now I just need his mom to do the same.

James opens his books in front of us both, having complete tunnel vision on his studies.

"James, honey. I think you should come up to the counter." Nikki's voice has me looking up. She sounds hesitant.

I give her a shake of my head. "He's fine." And damn, so is she. Her uniform fits her small frame just right. Her hair is tied back up today, her bee clip long gone, and I wonder why she doesn't wear it anymore.

"But you're in the middle of…"

"I got math homework," James tells her.

"He's got math homework," I repeat, and she gives me an unsure look. Grinning, I wait for her to melt for me, just a little.

"It's fine, I promise. I got it." I scruff James' hair, making him laugh.

"Okay." She smiles softly, and I almost fucking beam at her. She's giving me an inch. Bit by bit, she's opening up a little, and I sit up taller, taking her trust seriously. I've never worked this hard for someone before. Usually, people gravitate toward me naturally; I've never had to put in effort. It's new and exciting as hell.

As she walks away, I watch her for a moment, getting busy, doing all the daily tasks I notice she does before closing time. Cleaning the counters, rubbish removal. She always sorts the recyclables into separate bins, taking great care and attention to put the glass and plastics aside from the general waste. The diner is the place to be and is open late, but every day before she ends her shift, she makes the whole place a little cleaner than how she found it. I like that about her. She takes pride in her environment, looks after people, including Rochelle, ensuring things are done for her so that she doesn't have to worry about it later at lockup time.

The few conversations we've had, it's clear that she's intelligent. Her voice, her mannerisms, the way she holds herself. She isn't a country girl. She's worldly, and I have a feeling she's all city. How she ended up here, where she knows no one, with a little boy who looks just as smart as she is, I have no idea.

Bringing my attention back to James, I ask, "Sooo, how are the bikes?"

"They're so cool, and we get around so much quicker. They only had pink ones, though..." His face scrunches up. I noticed both bikes out back when I pulled up today.

"They didn't have any boys' bikes?"

"They were old stock at the toy store. But we take what we can get."

Huh. I look at him, seeing him swallow his pride for his mom.

"How old are you?" My eyes narrow in on him, trying to work out the age logistics here.

"Ten."

"How old's your mom?"

His brow pinches as he looks at me. "Nikki is twenty-three." There he goes with calling her Nikki again.

"Twenty-three?" I hum, a small frown on my face.

James looks toward Nikki, deep remorse taking over his expression.

"She's not my mom," he admits quietly.

I still. "Oh?"

"She's my sister."

A whoosh of relief flies through me so damn quickly I'm glad I'm sitting down.

James looks at me firmly. "Just... don't tell anyone."

"Your secrets are safe with me." And they are. There's a reason they don't want people in their business, and who am I to start telling everyone I know?

"How's that math homework going?"

Nikki moves past the booth quickly, her arms full of plates and bowls, heading to the kitchen, clearly reminding James he has work to do. James looks down at his books and my eyes remain glued to her.

His sister. This whole town has pegged her as a teen mom. A young mom struggling, running from someone, probably a horrible ex or something. But she isn't; she's looking after her brother. She could be anywhere, having the time of her life, but she's here, in Whispers, with him. I don't know their story, but deep admiration fills me. I know what that's like. Sawyer looked after me as a kid. With no dad and a mom who worked long hours, Sawyer and I were left to ourselves a lot, and he was my safe space. Still is. My respect for her grows.

"If you cut a pizza into eight pieces and ate two of them, how many are left and what is it in a fraction?"

I look down at his expectant face, his book open, his pencil ready to go.

"None, because I would eat the whole box."

James' eyes widen. "You eat a whole pizza?"

"Oh yeah. I love me some pepperoni."

"It's been a long time since I had a pizza. Pepperoni is the best." His face drops a little as memories seem to swirl for him.

"Hmmm... now I feel like pizza."

"It's raining," I hear someone in the diner comment, and I look out the window, seeing a few drops coming down. If it's starting to rain, there's no way they're cycling home tonight. No matter how pink and shiny their new bikes are.

"So school is going good?" I wonder how he's doing with making friends.

"I'm going to play baseball now." His eyes grow big, and he can't contain his grin, one which I match.

"Really? My nephew Kevin have anything to do with that?"

"Yeah. Him and Harvey are really great. They asked me to play at lunchtime, and we now play every day." The words rush out fast, but I still notice how well he pronounces every syllable. Just like his sister.

"Well, that's good. You'll be beating them all in no time." I scruff his hair, the movement happening so naturally I don't even register it. But then I look at his hair, the jet-black just barely starting to show a slim strip of lighter hair at the roots, and I suck in a deep breath.

"Are you two chatting or homeworking over here?" Rochelle comes up, hands on her hips, looking at us accusingly.

"We're working..." James says sweetly. He's definitely a charmer.

She grins and shakes her head. I think the love she has for Nikki and James is probably bigger than the moon.

As the rain comes down a little harder, and with James counting out on his fingers, Rochelle's about to leave when I ask, "Hey, Rochelle, any chance I could order two pepperoni pizzas to take away?"

The twinkle in her eye says she knows they're not both for me.

"Sure thing, movie star." She nods before heading to the kitchen, and I get back to helping James.

Dinner is on me tonight.

15

NIKKI

I rush around as I always do at the end of my shift, making sure things are put away and the counter is sparkling so Rochelle has an easier time locking up. I don't have to, but I know she appreciates it. It was one of the things my mom instilled in me. Always leave things how you would like them to be left for you.

"Here they are." Rochelle comes through the kitchen and my mouth immediately waters. Sutton ordered two pizzas to take away, and my stomach growls just smelling them. I'm going home to a dinner of canned meat and peas, which sounds as appetizing as eating my own arm. "There's that stomach again, girl..."

I try to brush it off. "I'll be eating soon enough. You don't need to worry." I feel a strong connection to Rochelle. When Mom died, we had no one until Maribel turned up. Since that relationship didn't work, I've been hesitant to lean on any other mother figure, but Rochelle is kind, warm, and loving. The kind of woman any child would want for a mother.

She nods, albeit reluctantly. "How are those bikes working out for you?"

"Oh, they're great. Might be one of our best finds yet."

"That noticeboard is your lucky board, I would say." She grins wide as I smile in agreement, but then my stomach rumbles again, catching her attention.

"I'm fine." I put my hand up to stop her offering me food again.

"Are you, though? Are you okay, darlin'?" Her voice is laced with concern, and I swallow. She looks at me knowingly. I could tell her. I could tell her all about my life, my father, my mother, how we ran away. But I swallow any words that threaten to escape.

"Yeah, Rochelle. I am. Everything will be okay," I tell her with as much assurance as I can muster. Her frown is immediate, seeing right through me, so I ask, "Do you need me to do anything else before I leave?"

"No, darlin', you always do too much. Go, take that boy home and settle in for the night. It's just started to rain again." I look out the window, seeing the heavy drops landing against the glass and my shoulders sink. James and I are going to get wet, but at least we have our bikes now.

"Ready to go, buddy?" I deliver Sutton's pizzas to his table and get James to pack up.

"Where're your bikes?" Sutton looks at me as he stands. This man at full height gives me butterflies every time. Today more so than ever, in his blue jeans that fit him too well and his white t-shirt that shows exactly how much time he spends in the gym. I don't know how it's possible, but he seems bigger and bigger every week. My eyes do a quick once-over as my heart rate escalates. As I look back up at him, he's watching me. Shit. I never check out guys. A few guys in college, maybe, but that feels like a lifetime ago.

Dating hasn't been on my mind for a long time. I guess the fight for survival does that to a person.

But now, in this quaint town, in the family-friendly diner, where life has felt more secure, the woman in me starts to bloom. Sutton's lips quirk, and my cheeks heat. I feel his hand then, his fingers touching mine by our sides. Our hands hidden between us, no one else can see, but a few of his fingers curl around a few of mine, and for a split second, I forget to breathe.

"Out back. Why?" I answer his question about a full minute late. James struggles with his bag, and I break our hold to help him out.

"You can't ride home in the rain. I'll put them in the back of my truck and give you a lift."

I freeze a little, not expecting it. "Ahhh... you don't have to do that."

Sutton gives me a grin that doesn't contain the usual sympathetic look most people offer.

"I know."

"No, I mean, we can ride home." I follow him out the back door and immediately come to a stop. The rain is a complete downpour, not just a little sprinkle.

"You're not riding home in this. Stay here and hold the pizzas so they don't get wet." He moves to where the bikes are parked, picking up James' in one hand and mine in the other and my mouth hangs open. His white t-shirt is almost immediately see-through, arms bulging from the weight of the bikes and his shoulders strong. I've never seen his movies, but I've seen the posters. They may be airbrushed, but his muscles are all his. "James, jump in the back, it's unlocked."

James runs out before I can stop him, and I stand under cover, holding the two hot pizzas that continue to make my stomach cave in on itself as I watch this all unravel. Sutton grabs him and lifts him up and inside before going back to the bikes, lifting them into the back, all the while getting completely soaked.

"Let me help." I start to move, feeling bad that I'm not doing anything.

"You stay right there." His voice stops me in my tracks, and I look up, seeing him striding toward me. All tall, dark, and handsome. His face and hair are wet, droplets of water running down him.

"You're a bit wet..." Is that my voice? I sound like a harlot as Sutton's smile turns into a seductive smirk, and I think I almost trip.

"Hmmmm, you will be too in a minute. Let's go." He grabs the pizzas, and we both run to his truck before I can think too hard about what he said. He has the door open for me in a flash, and as I pull myself up, he gives the pizzas to James, before coming back to me, ensuring I'm inside and closing the door. Chivalry didn't die like I thought it did.

I wipe the water droplets from my brow, trying to pull myself together, my body hot and thrumming while my clothes are a damp and cold contrast.

"This pizza smells sooooo good..." James murmurs from the back, just as Sutton jumps into the truck.

"Everyone alright?" He looks from me to James and back again. His hair hangs over his forehead a little, droplets falling from the ends. The water from his scalp runs down his temple, but he doesn't seem to notice. Before I think about it, my hand shoots out, brushing the water from his brow before it hits his eyes.

We both still. The action catches us off guard, and I snatch my hand back like I've been burned.

My heart thuds in my ears. "Sorry."

"It's alright." His smirk is in full effect. "I kinda like your hands on me."

I want to die. I want my hot cheeks to ignite me into a raging ball of fire and end it all right here. We look at each other, the tension thick, and I swallow, needing to dampen my dry throat. I have no idea what's gotten into me today. But after a few weeks of him watching me from afar, his kind gestures, his help with James, I'm starting to see that this man is much more than just a movie star in hiding.

"The pizza's getting cold!" James interrupts us from the back, and we both chuckle, the tension relieved for now. As Sutton starts the truck, I look down his body again, seeing just how transparent his shirt is up close and just how big his muscles are. It's not helping my flush.

I look away, my gaze straight ahead at the parking lot as I tell him, "You didn't need to do this, you know."

His fingers reach over to my chin, and he lifts my gaze to meet his, my cheeks turning redder at being caught out. *Again.*

"I like your eyes on me like that, Tinker Bell, but right now, we need to get you home and fed." His grin is wicked, and as if on cue, my traitorous stomach rumbles so loud it can be heard from the next county.

But what he said distracts me from that embarrassment. "Tinker Bell?"

He drives us out of the diner and onto the road. Going slow in the rain.

"Tiny. Cute. Spirited, Enchanting. Pretty fitting if you ask me."

He has a nickname for me? I lose my breath before my brain starts working again. "You know, the name *Tinker Bell* comes from the old English term *tinker*, referring to a metalworker who repaired pots and kettles." I internally cringe. I have no idea why I'm even talking at this point.

Sutton barks out a laugh. "I like when you do that."

"Do what?" I ask, biting the inside of my lip.

"Spout out those quirky, intelligent facts about things." He looks from the road to me quickly, smiling.

"I don't *spout* things."

"Yeah, you do. You told me all about old coffee the other day."

I think about what he's referring to. The little tokens of facts usually fly out so quickly, I barely register them anymore.

"They're just little tidbits," I murmur.

"Okay, well, tell me something about rain?" he says playfully. I shouldn't lean into it. Just like I shouldn't smile when I see him or miss him when I don't.

"Raindrops aren't tear-shaped. They're more like hamburger buns due to air resistance."

James groans. "Now I feel like hamburgers."

Laughing lightly, Sutton asks me, "How do you know all these things?"

"Nikki's the smartest person I know," James' voice pipes up from the back, and I sink into my seat, zipping my lips. I clearly can't be trusted with my body or my voice around this man. But I find myself grinning as I wrap my arms around my legs and cuddle into the warm, luxurious heated seat of his truck.

It's nice to feel a little more like me.

16

SUTTON

I'm in awe. She's hella smart. Like, really smart. And it's such a fucking turn-on. There's no doubt she went to a university somewhere; that type of knowledge and brain power doesn't just show up in anyone. I swear I learn more from her than I do anyone else. I could probably learn more from her than I did in school. On the days when I turned up anyway.

She cuddles up on the seat next to me, making herself smaller than she is. Which is crazy, given how little she is. All of five-foot-nothing, like a little Tinker Bell, and I feel like an ogre beside her. I turned on the heated seats, and I think she's enjoying that. It isn't too cold, but we're all wet, and I still feel water running down my cheeks and back. Damn, when she touched my face a moment ago, I could've sworn I felt my heart stop. It's never done that before. I've never felt that with another woman, especially from such a simple touch.

"Hungry?" If the sounds from her stomach are any indication, I'd guess she is.

"A little," she says softly.

"I wasn't sure what you liked on your pizza, so I just got pepperoni."

"What?" She sits up a little, her eyes a mix of confusion.

"It's James' fault. He started talking about pizza slices in math homework tonight, and I can't eat two pizzas myself." It's a lie; I can. I could down those suckers easily.

A shout of excitement from the back seat has me chuckling. "Yes! Thanks, Sutton."

As I turn down their dirt road, the forest covers us. With the rain clouds thick in the sky, the journey is even scarier than last time. No birds singing, no sunlight filtering through. Just rain, clouds, and the dark forest. It's spooky as hell.

She's quiet, clearly in her head. Is it a bad idea? Probably. I should be keeping my distance, but I can't. I should be planning my re-emergence into LA, looking at which project Bobby has lined up, figure out what I want to do with my future. But none of that holds my interest like she does. I've watched her for weeks, spoken to her almost daily, and now, as I edge toward her home for the second time, I know no one else comes here and the fact that she's letting me in speaks volumes.

She isn't scared of me, but she's hesitant. I get it. I'm a lot. My name is well known, my face even more so. I have people trying to find me, and I'm on the cover of magazines. She wants quiet, doesn't want to be found. She doesn't want to be seen.

But I see her. Innocent, beautiful, enticing. Not caring who I am, even though she knows exactly what my fame level is. Never once has she or James asked for a photo or an autograph like the rest of the town has. She could probably get me to sign something and sell it online to make money —she needs it. But she doesn't. She's never treated me any differently than the usual patrons who come to the diner and I like that. She likes me for me, and I like her for her.

"I'm starving." James opens his door the minute I pull up to their cottage, and with his bag on his back and the pizzas in his hands, he jumps from the truck and runs through the rain and inside. Nikki laughs, her face lighting up seeing him happy.

I turn to her. "He's a great kid."

"He really is. Thank you, Sutton. Really, thank you." She's watching me, and I notice a thread of wet hair stuck to her face. Lifting my hand, I brush it away, caressing her skin, trailing my finger down her jaw. She swallows audibly, the movement of her neck smooth and delicate just like the rest of her.

"Anytime." I mean it, even though my voice sounds like gravel. My gaze hits hers, then moves to her lips and back again. Fuck, I want to kiss her.

"You know... Hawaiian pizza was actually invented in Canada by a Greek chef," she whispers, her eyes darting from my lips to my eyes and back again, following the same movement mine just made. Wanting my lips closer to hers, I lean forward, just a little. God, the things I could do to this woman.

"Really? I didn't know that." There she goes again with her random facts that are fast becoming like an aphrodisiac to me.

"It's said that—"

"Are you coming? I'm staaaaarrvvvving!"

We pull back, startled, hearing James yell over the rain. I spot him at the front door, looking right at us, and I huff a laugh.

"Let me get your door." Before she can reply, I open my door, running in the rain around to her side, needing the water to cool me down before I lift her out. She squeals a little at the cold rain thrashing down on us, her hands holding on to my shoulders tight.

"It's cold!" She shrieks with laughter before I hear her snort that has me grinning. Makes me smile every fucking time.

"And wet." I put her on her feet in front of me, but I don't move my hands; they feel permanently connected to her waist. Her hands don't drop from me either as we both stand there, rain pelting down, her hair and mine now almost plastered to our faces.

My smile falters as my gaze turns hungry. I look down at her, seeing her eyes sparkle up into mine, small water droplets on the ends of her long lashes. Her breathing escalates as her fingers slide up to the back of my neck. Her hands on my body are everything. I watch a rain droplet glide down her cheek before it curves toward her mouth. It trickles over her top lip, before it slowly slips over her bottom. The sight is the last tease I need, especially when her fingers dig into my neck and her breathing grows faster.

"Fuck it." I step forward, my lips colliding with hers immediately.

I feel her stiffen in my hands for a millisecond before her body melts into my hold. Wrapping my hands around her waist, I pull her body tight against mine as hers thread into the hair at my nape. I groan as my tongue lashes hers, relishing her breathy moan in response. Sliding my hands down her back, I cup her ass and lift her to me, her legs automatically circling my waist as I lean us against the side of the seat, her door still open, the interior of the car now also wet.

As I kiss her hard, she gives as good as she gets. Her lips are warm and soft, her hands running over my shoulders, making me feel like a wanted man. I've kissed a lot of women. Too many, probably. But never in the rain. I've never been this needy for them and never taken them as furiously as I'm kissing Nikki right now. I should be embarrassed by how much I want her.

"Come on!" James yells again, and we both pull apart quickly, panting. I almost forgot he was there waiting for us.

"Shit." We look up, and I say a silent prayer that he can't really see us, the open truck door blocking his view.

"Sorry…" She drops her legs quickly, and I step back, giving her room.

"Nothing to be sorry about, Tinker Bell. I'd do that again in a heartbeat." I push her wet hair off her face again, just so I can cup her jaw. Preventing her from hiding from me, I tilt her face up to meet mine.

"Yeah?" she breathes out like she doesn't yet believe me.

"Yeah," I confirm. That was one hell of a taste and my appetite for her isn't wavering.

A dazed smile shines up at me. "Me too." And then she ducks under my arm and sprints inside, making me laugh.

Still chuckling, I grab the bikes, placing them under the cover of the porch on the side of the house, feeling like I'm on cloud fucking nine. I run back to the truck, getting a sweater I have in the back before looking around quickly, seeing nothing, no one. All the lights are on inside, and as I step up to her front door, immediate warmth and a welcoming feeling hits me. I wasn't sure what I was expecting from the outside, since this little cottage is old, and the inside, it isn't much better, but she has made it nice. I spot a small sofa and an armchair, a little side table, and a larger table, where James is getting the pizzas organized. It's small, could do with some rugs or other fixtures, but it's cozy.

"Here." Nikki passes me a towel as I kick off my boots by the door, where hers and James' both sit. "I'm gonna get the fireplace going."

I watch her as I scrub my hair, again looking at the kindling, pushing it around, moving it just right for it to light up, before putting on a small log. There's something about open fires. The way the light flickers around the room or the way the crackle hits my ears immediately lowering my shoulders.

I'm still watching her as she stands and walks back to where I am. Something about me has her balking.

"What?" I look down at myself to where her eyes burn into my chest and see my white t-shirt soaked through and completely sticking to my body.

"Shit. Mind if I take it off?" I pull the wet material from my frame before she replies because I can't leave it on; it's like I plucked it straight out of water.

"Ummm… ohhhhh… sure." Her cheeks turn vibrant red.

Lifting it off my shoulders, I step outside to the porch and wring it out. When I come back inside, she's in the same spot, staring at me, and I grin a wicked grin. I know I look good. It may be arrogant, but I work hard on my physique every day. I'm glad she's just as attracted to me as I am to her.

I step toward her as I hear James clattering around in the kitchen, but her eyes don't move from me, and I see her swallow. I like her eyes on my body and take delight in putting my fingers to her chin and lifting her gaze to meet mine.

"Do you mind if I hang this in front of the fire to dry?"

"Mm-hmm. Sure. Here, let me." She grabs my wet t-shirt and lays it out on her small drying rack near the fire, and I towel off before I grab my sweater and pull it on. It gives me the coverage and warmth I need before I sit down to eat.

"Now can we eat?" James' patience is running thin as he nearly huffs at the end of his question. Someone's hangry for the pizza.

"Sure, honey." Nikki smiles, and we all take a seat. It smells amazing, and James dives straight in, grabbing a slice and putting it on a plate before picking up his cutlery. I pause, watching as Nikki does the same thing, the two of them placing their paper napkins across their laps delicately, their table manners better than anyone's I've seen. And it's just pizza.

They both cut into the pizza with their cutlery, taking small bites like they're eating at The Ritz or something. Nikki's eyes close, and I swear I hear her moan, the sound zinging around my body.

"Why aren't you eating?" James takes my attention from his sister.

"Better question. Why are you eating pizza with a knife and fork?" I know, of course, because these small snippets further cement to me where they come from. And it's not poverty. They have refined table manners, similar to what I've seen in Europe or when out for a fancy dinner.

"Oh." Nikki pauses, looking at James with wide eyes before looking back at me.

"Habit." She shakes her head like it's nothing before placing her utensils down and grabbing her pizza with her hand. It's clumsy, like she's never done it before. I look at James, who watches his sister, like he's trying to understand how to do it, before he follows suit and grabs the slice with his hand.

"So... much... better..." He moans as he eats the slice like he hasn't seen food in days. The sight of them both has me suppressing a laugh, happy to see them loosening up a little.

As I pick up my slice, I feel Nikki's eyes on me. My little Tinker Bell is a mystery, one I really want to unravel... with my tongue.

17

NIKKI

Grease slides down my hand, and I internally cringe. This feels odd. It's been years since I ate pizza, and I've never done it with my hands. Somewhere between the side salad and grilled fish I ate every night and the times I was locked in my room without any dinner when Maribel first arrived, I didn't get the masterclass on how to eat pizza like a normal person.

"This is amazing..." James is doing little to hide his enthusiasm, taking large bites and being messier than usual. But I smile. He's in heaven. He loves pizza; it's his favorite.

"Pretty good, huh?" Sutton speaks with a mouthful of food, and I pause, my body so attuned to the discipline we had at home, I'm almost waiting for my stepmother to slam her hand down on the table. I wait, and when nothing happens, I look at James, him already watching me with wide eyes.

"What? What did I say?" Sutton stops mid-bite.

"Nothing." I gloss over it, like I do most things as he looks at me like he's searching my soul. His eyes burn into mine, and my thoughts go to our kiss. It was *scorching*. I have no idea what came over me. I nearly climbed him like a monkey up a tree. It was like I've never been kissed before. But to be honest, I've never been kissed like *that* before. When his lips touched mine, I paused for the briefest of seconds before I kissed him back so feverishly that I think I almost blacked out.

"You keep staring at me like that, Tinker Bell, and we might have a problem," he says quietly, so only I can hear him, before I blink, coming back to myself. I pick up a second piece of pizza, pushing my thoughts aside. He's a movie star, here hiding just like I am, but with plans to go back and be in the spotlight again. Me? I want to burrow further down.

It was stupid. Shouldn't have happened. I can't kiss a movie star. I can't get close to anyone, and I certainly can't catch feelings. But it felt good. So good. It was so nice to be in someone's arms, to be held so tight like he never wanted to let me go. I dated the quarterback in college for a time. He was a nice guy, and our fathers were friends. His hugs were big and full like Sutton's. Until his hugs became suffocating, and just like everyone else in my life, he used me just to get to my father.

Dating, men, flirting, none of it was genuine. None of it was because they wanted me. Liked me. Loved me. It was all because they wanted to be the son-in-law of one of the richest men on the planet.

"Is there anything she can't cook?" Sutton leans back, clearly happy with Rochelle's pizza.

"She makes me cupcakes. They are ahhh-mazing." James licks his fingers clean. After he snarfed down three slices, dare I say he's now feeling full.

Sutton grins at my brother. "Cupcakes, mmm. I need to try those."

"Nikki, remember those cookies that Mom used to—" James stops and looks at me, horrified.

"Don't tell me your mom's a good cook too?" Sutton watches us both as the blood drains from James' face from saying too much.

"Sorry," he whispers to me, and I give him a small grin.

"It's okay." I feel bad. He's young. He has memories he wants to share, and now he's forced to keep them inside. It isn't healthy. I look at Sutton, who's watching me intently, confusion pulling at his brow. My insides swirl, but I know in my gut, I can trust him.

"Our mom used to make these chocolate chip cookies that would melt in your mouth." I smile at the memories, and James smiles too.

"Used to?" he asks.

"She died," is all I say as my eyes sting. Sutton heaves in a breath.

"Remember when she used to dunk them in milk and make chocolate milk chasers?" James smiles. I'm surprised he remembers so much. Mom died a few years ago now, just when I graduated high school and when James was about five or six.

Suddenly, a realization hits me. Sutton doesn't seem surprised that James isn't my son.

Seemingly reading my mind, James admits, "I told him earlier."

This is why he needs to sit at the counter. To remain quiet, not to talk. But I see Sutton wink at James, giving him a little support in what's now a heavier conversation than was planned. Only, I'm surprisingly okay with it.

"I'm going to go read a book. Thanks again for the pizzas, Sutton." James stands, getting himself out of this situation. He and Sutton fist-bump, and I watch him go off to his bedroom.

"Tell me about her." Sutton's voice is quieter, his gaze aimed right at me. The pizza now forgotten.

"She was my best friend. The best mom, beautiful. Friendly to everyone, not a bad bone in her body. We used to garden together. She loved bees." Even as I tear up with her on my mind, I smile.

He leans closer. "Bees?"

"Yeah, she had a hive and would go and collect honey every day, even talked to them. Said bees were one of the most intelligent living things because they looked after each other. It was something she instilled in me. To always look after James."

"I'm highly allergic. They scare me," he shares, sounding a little unnerved at the thought of being near bees.

My eyebrows rise. "Really?"

"Yeah, my face blows up like a balloon." He huffs, and I laugh, then snort.

"Sorry, I shouldn't laugh. I just can't imagine your face all swollen."

A teasing glint shines in his eyes as he grins. "Yeah, well, it's only happened a few times, but it isn't pretty."

"I love them. Makes me feel like the garden is healthy when there are bees around. I'm planning to plant some wildflowers around the apple tree outside. I want to try to promote pollination to see if it increases fruit production. You know, one-third of the world's crops depend on bees for pollination. Without them, we'd lose many fruits, vegetables, nuts, and seeds. Plus, they remind me of her."

"Is that why you have a bee hair clip?"

I look at Sutton, a frown coming to my face. "How did you know?"

His shoulders lift slightly, like it's obvious. "You wear it in your hair almost every day."

"I used to." That weight on my chest is back.

"What happened?"

"It broke when I was mugged. It was the one thing I had left of her, and now that's gone too."

Sutton's jaw tics. I stand, moving to the drawer in the kitchen and pulling out the tissue, placing it on the table. Unwrapping it, I show him the beautiful jeweled clip now broken in about three places.

"I thought about getting some superglue, but I don't think it'll work."

Sutton eyes the broken pieces before looking back at me.

"I'm sorry that happened to you." His voice is low, tender, as he looks over the broken pieces.

"It's fine. It's just rhinestones. I mean, real black diamonds are expensive, but they're also associated with strength, mystery, and boldness. In medieval Europe, they were believed to ward off evil. I probably could've used their help in this instance." I try to lighten the mood a little.

A sympathetic look changes his expression. "How did she die?"

"Car accident. About five years ago."

"And your dad?" My eyes meet his immediately, and his face hardens like my own.

"I think when she died, a little bit of him did too." I leave it at that. There's nothing else to say. That I hate that when Mom died he gave up? On life, on James, on me. That he married the first woman who threw herself at him and let her stay in the house ever since? Mom held the family together; she was our queen bee, and when she died, so did our family.

"I never really knew my dad. I remember him a little, but

I think the last time I saw him, I was probably about James' age," Sutton shares, and I wait, knowing there's more. "He wasn't nice, not to Mom or Sawyer or me. He tried to reach out to me a few years ago. Obviously, he heard I was doing well for myself and wanted to reconcile."

"Did you?" Is forgiveness something you can give a parent when they left you when you needed them the most?

"No. That part of my life is over. It was over the minute he walked out on Mom and us boys. He left us broke, hungry, struggling. That's not a man. A man looks after his family. Protects them. Loves them. Nothing else should matter but them." Sutton's words hit home so fiercely, it's like a gut punch.

Taking a deep breath, I work up the courage to ask, "Can I trust you, Sutton?" I feel that I can. I've shared more with him tonight than I have anyone else here in Whispers.

He reaches for my hand, nodding slowly with his eyes never straying from mine. "Can I trust you, Nikki?" My words come back to me, and that's how I know I can. We both have things to lose in this.

Our hands stay intertwined among the pizza boxes and plates, the fire illuminating us both in a golden light, the quiet among the forest surrounding us.

"Your secrets are safe with me, Tinker Bell." He lifts my hand to his mouth, kissing it gently, and little by little, my guard lowers and my walls come down.

18

SUTTON

I t has rained all night. After sitting around the table with Nikki once we finished dinner, I helped her clean up and left her the moment I saw her stifling a yawn. And me? I fell asleep as soon as my head hit the pillow. My sleep here in Whispers is so good. Deep. Rejuvenating. This small town is proving to be good for more than I first thought.

I find that I'm no longer in a rush. To leave. To live. My pace has slowed. I appreciate the small things. I appreciate Nikki. Her smile. Her snort-laughs. The way she knows things about everything. The way she kisses. Especially the way she kisses... Now the idea of leaving Whispers doesn't feel like the right move anymore. The thought is sobering. My life is in LA. My work, too. But family, friends, connections, Nikki... they're all here.

I scrub my face as I sit on the sofa, laptop on, staring at the screen, where a video about beekeeping plays.

After being stung as a kid, I blew up like a balloon. Had to be raced to the hospital. My allergy to them was severe. Then one time in the Hollywood Hills, I had another sting.

It wasn't as violent, but my lips still blew up to the size of tires. As I read now, allergies are something that can be outgrown. I wonder if I've outgrown it. I look outside. Probably not a theory I should try when on my own.

That's why I've lived in cities all my life. As much as I love nature, it isn't really my friend. I grew up in New York, now based in LA, so bees haven't been a big concern in those concrete jungles.

I scroll through more information, searching for allergies until my eyes hook on an article about venom immunotherapy. Frowning, I read through the first two lines and immediately grab my cell, calling Hudson. He's my best friend from LA who moved back to Whispers with his son and is, conveniently for me, now the local doctor here.

"What?" he answers. We don't need niceties; I know he loves me.

"Venom immunotherapy."

"What about it?" he asks with curiosity.

"I want it."

"What?" Now there's confusion in his tone.

"I want to try venom immunotherapy."

"Okaaay. Why is that?"

I sigh. "I'm allergic to bees, remember?"

"Oh, I remember." He chuckles. "I still have the photo of you on my phone, waiting for the perfect time to use it against you."

"You wouldn't." I can't believe he still has that. The one from LA, with my lips bloated and my face so swollen, my eyes closed. I'm sure the gossip pages would love to get their hands on it. The headline would probably say something about me getting cosmetic surgery rather than having a bee sting. But they never let the truth get in the way of a good story.

"Of course I would." I smile. I've missed him.

"So, can you do it?" I'm keen to get started. Nikki loves bees. Bees are important to her. And since bees could kill me, I need to fix this issue now.

"Why? Got a movie coming up in Australia or something?"

My brow pinches at that. "Does Australia have bees?"

"Sure. Every deadly animal comes from there."

"No. Not going there." Thank God. That sounds terrible.

"Well, why?"

"Can't you just let me trial it?"

"Sure, let me just ring bee headquarters at the hospital and book you in."

Exasperation has me groaning. "Hudson."

"Sutton," he mocks.

"Fuck. Fine. I want to get over my allergic reaction and the internet says that this is ninety-eight percent effective."

"You're right. It is. But why now? Why do you all of a sudden want to be free of your bee allergy?"

"Why not? I've lived in a concrete jungle all my life, but now I'm in Whispers and Whispers has bees." I haven't seen any, but I'm sure they're around.

He hums. "True... Just seems a bit sudden."

I ignore his hidden questioning. "Can we start today?"

"Sure. We keep stock of it all here for emergencies. It'll be good to stick a needle in you."

Shit. I didn't think that through. "Needle?" I fucking hate needles too.

"Yeah. How else do you think the venom goes into your body?" Hudson chuckles. He's such an asshole. "Oh, this is going to be fun."

~

"On a scale from one to ten, how bad does it look?"

Hudson looks down at me, the grin on his face telling me it's bad. My lips feel fat and full, my throat scratchy and my eyes watery.

Without answering, he pulls out his phone. "Say cheese…"

"Asshole," I grumble.

"Well, you still have an allergy to bees. You look like you've had too much lip filler, cheek filler, and no sleep for over a month."

"Fuck. When does it wear off?"

"Should calm down in an hour or so. Here." Hudson passes me an ice pack that I press to my face. I look at the clock on the wall, seeing it's midafternoon. For the first time in weeks, I'm not going to make it to the diner. I can't go there looking like this.

"So, you want to tell me the real reason you're doing this?"

I eyeball my best friend. He's caught me in a vulnerable state.

Taking a deep breath, I relent. "Fine. You know Nikki from the diner?"

"Fuck, is this over a girl?"

"Listen, mister, I won't take no for an answer and send my girl hundreds of gifts, including live butterflies. She has a thing for bees. They are important to her."

Hudson fell fast and hard for Lacy. Something I'm starting to understand more and more.

"So what? You're going through all this to be a beekeeper for her or something?" He looks at me like I'm crazy.

"Maybe." I shrug, kind of liking the idea of making my own honey. Maybe I can sell jars of it on that noticeboard Nikki mentioned.

Trying to figure me out, his eyes search my face. "Aren't you going to go back to LA?"

"Maybe I'll stick around. It worked out okay for you here."

His eyebrows shoot up. "I have family here. I grew up here. It's good for Harvey to be here."

"I have family here too. I have two new nephews to get to know."

"Whispers is not Hollywood, Sutton." He sounds like my brother. I'm not sure why they both think I'm so tied to LA. I mean, sure, I've lived there for most of my life and have loved the lifestyle. But the older I get, the less of it I want.

"Maybe that's what I want."

"Is it?" he asks me, more seriously now.

I think about his question, wondering if I could really leave my career and LA behind. I've built my brand there, have networks and contacts there. But maybe those aren't even necessary anymore.

"Maybe."

"It's a big move. Especially for a woman."

My eyes flick back to him, but I remain silent. There are many things in Whispers that keep me connected. Friends, family, peace, and privacy. But Nikki is new, and I shouldn't be making big decisions based on a woman I've just met, only kissed once, and who I don't even truly know who she is.

"Yeah. But I feel like it's the right one." I feel it in my soul. He looks surprised but nods. He knows. He practically did the same thing with his girl Lacy.

My cell rings, and I pull it out, my eyes watering so bad I can hardly see the screen.

"Bobby," I murmur to Hudson, and he rolls his eyes. He's not a fan of Bobby either.

"Hey, Bobby," I answer, my voice normal, even though my lips hardly move.

"Sutton, my man!" I cringe, hating it. My shoulders tense immediately.

"What's up?" I want to get to the point. I'm already cursing that I even answered his call.

"There's a lot going on, a lot of balls in the air. I need to talk to you. I need a face-to-face." What would he think if he saw my actual face right now?

"We can chat now. Over the phone is fine."

"But I need to know where you are."

"Why?" I don't know why I no longer trust my manager. But I don't.

"What do you mean, why? I'm your manager, and I've let you go off for over a month now, but it's time to come back now, man. You've had your little break, time to get back to it. Soooo...?"

I suppress a sigh. "Soooo what?"

"So I need to know where you are."

"No, you don't. I'm having time away. I told you that."

"Well, you're not in New York."

"How do you know?"

"The paps are eager to find you, and I heard the price on a photo of you is up around half a million."

Half a million. Fuck. Frustrated, I scrub my swollen face. They're vultures.

"I can't protect you if I don't know where you are."

"No one has found me yet. So I think I'm doing a good job of protecting myself, Bobby."

"They will. It's only a matter of time." His words sound like a threat, so much so, Hudson looks at me with a frown.

"I have so many new projects for you, man. So much for us to talk about."

I roll my eyes. "I'm working on something." I throw him a bone so he can lay off me for a bit.

He jumps right on it. "What? What deals are you doing?"

"Just something." I'm not telling him. Contractually, I can't. The Whiteman's Whiskey launch is firmly confidential. A small team knows; they're all flying in next week to get filming done.

"Why are you being so sketchy?"

"I'm not being sketchy. I'm just having a go at doing something close to my heart."

I think about Nikki, looking at the clock again, thankful that the rain stopped for her ride home and feeling bad that I missed her today.

"Get your ass back here. I've lined up a movie." I know exactly what he's lined up. I've seen the gossip. I've heard the rumors. And while it has potential to be a blockbuster, it isn't what I want to do.

"Not yet."

"It's a multimillion-dollar deal!" I know he thinks I'm crazy. Hell, most people probably think I am.

"I gotta go, Bobby." I hang up, not wanting to entertain him any further. When he calls back immediately, I shut off my phone.

"Never liked him," Hudson murmurs.

"You and Sawyer both."

"He's a snake. He's out for himself. Not you."

Sawyer has been telling me for years that Bobby wasn't the best person to associate with. But he was the first guy to take me on when I landed in LA, and we built an empire together. Made each other wealthy beyond measure. I invested everything I earned, had Sawyer making smart business decisions for me. Bobby splashes his cash around, on fast cars, opulent dinners, a different woman on his arm every night. I thought that was what I wanted. I thought that meant I'd made it. But right now, lying on a hospital bed with a swollen face and looking at my best friend, I know none of that was real.

This is real. Whispers is real. Nikki is real.

And I want real from now on.

19
______

NIKKI

As I get dinner ready, I wonder where Sutton was today. It's the first day he hasn't been in, and while I know he can come and go however he likes, I hope he's okay.

"Where was Sutton today?" James asks. Clearly, I'm not the only one who noticed his absence.

"I'm not sure. But I guess he had other things to do." I plate up some of the leftover chicken pies Rochelle gave us earlier. I have almost a whole tray of them.

We're both starving because I ended up taking him to the free yoga class Daisy runs after work tonight. I feel more limber than I have in a long time. As he eats, I look at my phone, and as if I conjured him, the screen lights up with a message from Sutton.

Sorry I didn't make it to the diner today.

It was a little quieter without you.

Does that mean you missed me?

I grin, my stomach fluttering.

> It means that we had leftover pie that we're now enjoying for dinner.

> Damn, I miss that pie.

> You have it every day! How can you miss it?

I laugh out loud, then snort, and my brother rolls his eyes as he continues to dig in.

> I see you every day but still miss you.

I pause as my heart thuds harder.

> As much as you miss the pie?

It's tongue in cheek, but I'm interested in what he has to say.

> You already know the answer, Tinker. I miss you all day, every day.

Putting my phone down, I take a deep breath and see my brother watching me so I grab my plate and sit down to eat my pie.

"I'm hungry tonight." I almost moan when Rochelle's pie hits my tongue. She's an expert in the kitchen. She could manufacture these and sell them countrywide and make a killing.

"You know, I think these are my favorite," James grabs his napkin and wipes his mouth. His table manners are better than most kids his age.

"I think she adds extra butter to the pastry," I murmur, knowing these pies go straight to my hips.

"You know what Chef Luc always says, *la meilleure recette, c'est quand tu mets du beurre deux fois!* The best recipe is when you add butter twice."

We both laugh together. These lighthearted moments are coming in more and more the longer we stay in Whispers.

His grin falters slightly a moment later. "I miss Chef Luc."

I sigh but nod. "Yeah, me too."

Chef Luc was our family's personal chef, a man who was the head chef in our household since we were kids. He was the one person who was always there when we got home from school when we were younger, the person who made us our favorite meals when Mom died. And he's the one person who looked out for James when I was asked to leave. He heard and saw more than most in that house.

"Remember when he made you eat snails!" James is back to laughing. This is what we do most nights. Sit around and reminisce about our former life. We had a good time before Mom died.

"Yeah. That feels like so long ago now..." I finish my pie in silence, both lost in our own thoughts of what was and what will be.

"I'm going to go work on my school project," James says, clearing his plate.

"Need a hand?" I offer as I clean the table, liking the crackle of the fire that embraces the cottage in warmth that's much needed tonight.

"Nah. I'm just going to do some reading." He saunters off to his room, and I lean against the kitchen cupboard, watching him go. It's a Friday night. Before my life took a turn, Friday nights were usually spent hanging out with friends, attending dinners, maybe going to the movies. Now, it's about survival.

With the cottage tidy, I head to my room, sit on the floor, and lift the loose floorboard, looking at the duffel bag I have hidden underneath before I lean in and pull it out.

I check this every week. Unzipping it, I look through the stash of clothes for James and me. The small stash of cash I have ready for emergencies, our passports, and identifying documents that I won't use but need to have.

This is our go-bag. The one thing I'll grab if we need to leave in a hurry. Whispers has been good to us, but I'm under no illusion that somewhere, somehow, we'll be found. It isn't a matter of if, but when.

I grab the photo I have in the bag. It's one taken the afternoon before Mom died. All four of us, Mom, Dad, my brother, and I. We looked so happy. Dad is making a funny face, Mom is laughing, James in a fit of giggles, and I'm looking at all of them with a big smile on my face.

We were happy once.

My brother and I grew up with heavy expectations from our father. He loved us, but he had a plan for our future. When Mom died, he changed. He wasn't around as much. He wasn't himself. But it wasn't until I said no to working in the business that we really started to clash. When I first told him I wasn't interested in working in the oil business, he laughed. When he encouraged me to do a summer internship during my last year of college, I turned him down. He ignored my pleas until I didn't turn up, leaving him embarrassed in front of his staff.

He was angry and threatened to take away my trust fund, not expecting me to shrug and say okay. Sure, I grew up with money. But I was a quick learner; my college degree was almost done, and I was optimistic for the future, one that I would forge myself. I get my tenacity from my mom.

While Dad instilled obedience, my mom gave us the love of freedom. Freedom to choose what we want to do with our lives, which is why I want to use my environmental engineering degree for good, for sustainability and environmentalism instead of assessing new oil spots and which land holdings to buy to decimate.

So, unable to change my mind, Dad followed through. He froze my funds and then ensured no one in Manhattan would hire me. So while I finished college on a high, made the dean's list and had the world at my feet, soon after, I had no money, no job prospects, and then Maribel really sunk her teeth in.

"You checking the bag?" James' voice is quiet as he stands near the doorway. I gasp in surprise, so locked in my own memories I didn't hear him.

"Yeah." I shove the photo back in the bag and zip it all up, pushing the bag back into the floor cavity and placing the floorboard on top, securing my hiding spot.

"Do you think Maribel would really do it?" He steps into my room, and we both take a seat on the edge of my bed.

I release a heavy breath. "At first, no. But now... yeah. I think she would."

"She really hates us, huh?" He's a little melancholy, so I reach over and pull him close. He needs to know he's loved. We lost Mom, we lost Dad, and Maribel almost made us lose each other.

"Yeah. She's just... selfish."

Maribel hated us the minute she moved in. While Dad worked long hours, she managed the house, managed my brother. And he suffered. I tried talking to Dad, but he wouldn't hear it, blinded by his new beautiful wife, thinking that I was just a troublesome child, one who wouldn't work in his business and now wouldn't approve of his new wife.

Tensions ran high, until Maribel suggested to him that I learn some hard truths by kicking me out of the house. So that's what he did. Leaving James all alone. Losing his mother and then his sister, having no one to look out for him and no one who cared.

"We could go to the police?"

I shake my head. We have this same conversation almost weekly.

"You know we can't."

The evil stepmother Maribel took her role to the extreme. Locking my brother in his room when he was home, school the only place she would allow him to go. I was prohibited from coming home to see him. She kept him isolated as she flaunted her newfound wealth, not just around town, but with the many male *friends* who happened to stop by when Dad was out of town.

So, I snuck into the house as often as I could to check on him, but as his mental and physical health deteriorated, I knew I had to do something. Maribel had made it clear that she was getting rid of us. She wanted us gone, and sometimes I wondered if she wanted us both dead. She hated us enough.

Then one night, as I was sneaking into the house, she caught me in the hallway. I froze; my heart literally stopped beating.

There was no point fighting, since I had no evidence of her mistreatment. It was still going to be her word against mine, and I knew Dad wouldn't believe me. He still wasn't even taking my calls.

So that night, we made a deal.

James and I had to leave.

If we didn't? If I went to Dad? James would be shipped off to a private military boarding school in Virginia. She showed me the flyers; she had already started talking to Dad about it. He wasn't keen, but we both knew Maribel would get her way eventually. Especially now that she caught me sneaking back in.

James would be broken. The kind, sweet, introverted boy would be sent away to live a life that was isolating, disciplined, strict, and harsh, one that I know would have detrimental effects and harm him deeply. With me in the city, living on friend's sofa, trying to get any job I could, I wouldn't be able to save him from that. I wouldn't have a hope.

Then she dangled another threat. That she would ruin my father. That if we didn't disappear and leave him, our home, and our lives, she would start spreading rumors. Talk to the media about Dad, start spreading misinformation about his business tactics. I know better than most that the media doesn't need the truth for a good story. All it would take is the slightest scandal to ruin my father's business and everything he worked so hard for. As much as we clash, he's still my father, and I couldn't let that happen.

So, she made me an offer. To leave that night with James and to never come back. I needed to get us out safely because I truly didn't know exactly what she was capable of, and I knew if I fought her that within a day, things would go from bad to worse. With our bags packed, I grabbed all the cash I had, and we fled, taking a bus in the middle of the night here to Whispers.

The decision saved us. Saved James. But it still haunts me every single day.

20

SUTTON

I walk around my plot of land, my face back to normal and my lips now able to suck a straw. The immunotherapy wasn't too bad, and with any luck, with a few more treatments, my reaction to bees will be minimal.

"So, the living space will go here, facing north. The view is spectacular."

I follow Griffin's gaze. He's right; you can see most of the town from up here. Rolling hills, my privacy still protected, but I'm elevated enough that only drones would be able to get pictures of me. The media uses drones all the time, but out here, someone will spot them and probably shoot them down. That thought makes me grin.

Sawyer and Annabelle's place is right next door, but next door is still more than a hundred yards away. His place is surrounded by a high steel fence combined with large green hedges. But we both agreed to cut out a walkway, so that I can walk over to him and he to me at any time.

"I want to put in a guesthouse out back, over on the side near Sawyer's. For my mom or my security team." My mom's welcome to stay with me anytime she wants, and I'll have more than enough room. But maybe having her own permanent place to stay might suit her better.

"We can make it work. You have one of the bigger plots on Billionaire Boulevard. Hudson and Huxley's ranch down the road is the biggest, and Tanner's is about the same size as yours. So you have plenty of room."

"What about yours?" I know he has a plot here; the fact that we're all neighbors is nice.

"Mine is a good size, but I chose seclusion. I'm a little more hidden. I don't have the views."

I quirk an eyebrow. "Do you need privacy?"

He's a builder. Out of all of us who live up here, I'm the one the media stalks.

"I like to be left alone. Don't like a lot of people, prefer my own space."

I can see that about him. A little grumpy, set in his ways.

"You got a girlfriend? A wife?" I know he doesn't, but I want to see his reaction.

"Nope. I travel too much. I don't have the time to invest. Kids give me hives."

I huff a laugh. At least he's honest.

"So, where's the pool?" Griffin pulls out the plans, and we get a feel for the space. He's done an amazing job. I now understand why he's the most sought-after builder in the country.

"Pool, large deck, hot tub, sauna are all along here. Entrance to your gym will be here, and the tennis court over here. We could probably fit in a helipad here if you want it?"

I look at the drawings, imagining it all. Is it too much? Probably.

"Let's do that. What about this space?" I spot an area that's clear of any dwellings.

"Gardens. Unless you want something else?"

"Can your landscaper put something in for me?"

"My landscaper can do anything."

"Beehives."

"Beehives?" Griffin looks at me like I've lost my mind. Maybe I have. Is it suicide? Death by stinger? Will my brother write that on my gravestone? *Died by a stinger because he had a stupid crush on the diner girl.*

I nod. "Just one or two."

Griffin thinks for a moment. "What if we put a full vegetable patch, hives, fruit orchards, that kind of thing could work? We can build a little cottage shed. Somewhere you can store all the equipment. The bees could then utilize the garden to pollinate, and you'd get a nice garden honey, then."

There's that word "pollinate." Nikki mentioned it the other day. Am I the only person who doesn't know this shit?

"Yeah, bees are apparently important for gardens…" I say, thinking about it all.

"They are. I have a client out in Southern California who talks about them all the time. Apparently, they're dying all too quickly, which isn't a good thing."

"Really? I had no idea."

"Yeah, well, they have that Save the Bees charity now. Sounds all a bit peculiar, but it's probably warranted." Griffin moves around the block, but what he says piques my interest. A Save the Bees charity? I need to look that up.

"A cottage shed would actually be nice. We could match the building design to the guesthouse. Put some flowers around, make it a welcoming spot. You could have an open firepit, chairs, somewhere to sit in the evenings, away from the main house."

"Do it." I nod eagerly as I follow him around, and he chuckles. "What's so funny?"

"I never really thought an action movie star would be into cottages and gardens, that's all."

"Can't be fighting crime all the time." Making movies, building my celebrity is all I've ever known. Outside of that, I have no hobbies. I'm not sure what else I'm good at or what else makes me tick.

"I used to love watching movies as a kid... Don't really get the time for them anymore."

"What do you do outside of work?" Maybe Griffin has a cool hobby I could try.

"Oh, I started working young. Had to make something of myself. I put my head down, and I haven't pulled it back up since." He's so successful, and starting something from nothing takes time, commitment, focus.

"Surely, you do other things? Do you read? Do you hike?" I press, wanting to know more.

"Don't really have the time..."

"Well, I've learned you need to make time, so feel free to jump on the bee bandwagon, you know, since we're going to be neighbors and all." I change the tone of the conversation, and he huffs a laugh.

"Right, like I need to be chased by bees. I gotta run. Call you with the updates. Frame will start going up tomorrow, and it'll be quick from there on. My teams work around the clock, and they're fast."

"Thanks, Griff." I shake his hand and watch him walk to his truck.

I wave goodbye, then walk around the plot slowly, wondering briefly if I've lost my damn mind. I think about LA; my house there is undeniably amazing, but there's no yard. I'm up in the hills, but my view isn't this incredible, and my neighbors are assholes. So is Sawyer, but at least I'm related to him.

The more I think about it, the more foreign LA feels and the more comfortable Whispers does. I don't know why, but thinking about LA has my chest tightening. I feel stressed and don't have a strong desire to go back. Not for good anyway. Here in Whispers, I kind of like the sanctuary of it. The gardens, the trees, nature.

But what does that all mean?

Maybe I can live here and fly in and out for filming. Lots of people do it. Hell, Sawyer still flies to New York often, and Connor and his girl Daisy fly to New York every month as well. Although if I move here more permanently, I know that'll bring a lot of people to town. Tanner might like it. It'll bring more business to the distillery and to the local shops. Journalists, fans, celebrity spotters will all come. It's not a totally bad thing.

It's fucking crazy, but I feel like it's the right decision.

With a renewed sense of purpose and my shoulders lower than they have been for a while, I pause, looking up at the clouds moving overhead. Another shower threatens sometime soon, no doubt, but I think I have time for a quick hike. It's something I couldn't do in LA because of all the fans and media who would follow my every move. But out here, I'm trying my hand at it. I see an opening in the pines and walk over, looking at the fields to the woods nearby. Trying to get my bearings. I have no idea where they lead, but I won't go far. The last thing I need is to get lost before it rains.

Striding through the trees, it feels good to move my body. My gym sessions are great, but there's something about walking and discovering new things, breathing in fresh air and letting nature lead the way. I get lost in my thoughts, hiking up a small hill, surrounded by the forest. Spotting a large log overturned, I take a seat.

Looking around, I get that same contradiction as I did at Nikki's the other night. Not sure whether the forest is welcoming or a frightening place to be. I wonder who owns this land. I like being here in nature, in solitude. Alone with my thoughts, the fresh breeze, the silence. There's no one around, and I didn't ask Sawyer if there are bears in Whispers. Something I probably should've asked. That's all I need. To be mauled by a fucking bear.

Then I feel it. A fat hamburger raindrop hits me from above, and I look up, not able to see much as the cloud cover rolls in and the trees block any sunlight.

"Shit." I jump up from my tranquil spot and start speed-walking. The pines seem different than when I came through before, and after about a hundred yards, I realize I've walked in the wrong direction.

I stride to my left, wondering what way I came, the woods now all looking the same, nothing distinct showing me the way home. I'm starting to understand that being lost in the fucking woods is now a clear possibility. I grab my cell but have no service. It shouldn't be a surprise, since the forest is dense and I'm in the middle of fucking nowhere. In my haste to turn, I trip. The soil is wet from all the recent rain, my leg sliding. A tree branch catches my shin, scraping it.

"Fuck!" Frustration nips at my shoulders as I lean over to grab my stinging shin before my foot gives way on the slippery soil again. I'm falling fast, straight down a small ravine. Sliding like a fucking kid on a playground slide, I land hard on my ass, about fifteen feet from my track above me, the drop not one I can climb.

"Motherfucker..." My teeth clench, angry, frustrated, and

hoping like hell I don't spot a bee out here. Looking around, nothing is familiar. I have no idea where I am and no idea what direction to walk in. I grab my cell again and curse when I see I broke it in the fall. It's now completely useless. This is why I don't do nature. What the hell was I thinking? With no cell service and no one knowing where I am, I push off the mud and grass and try to stand on my injured foot.

"Ahh, dammit." My foot isn't broken, but it's starting to bruise already. I limp a few steps, trying to warm it up, the pain still shooting through my ankle, but it's bearable. If only Hollywood could see me now.

I step along an opening in the trees before I see a small track. Thinking it must lead somewhere, I limp along, all the while the rain falls, the sky darkens, and I question how much more of an idiot I could be. No one knows where I am. At least Griffin would give them a time and day, although he's probably already on his jet, flying to his next job, working while he travels.

As the forest gets darker, I spot a little light up ahead. So I hobble a little quicker as the rain falls a little faster, hoping like hell that someone is there.

21

NIKKI

The rain won't let up. It's been like this for days. And while snuggling in front of the fire with a good book is my idea of paradise, James and I are going a little crazy not spending some time outside.

At the moment, my free time is taken up by trying to build a small wind turbine, something I can wire into a battery, giving us electricity if we need it in case the power cuts out. Out here, surrounded by forest, is the last place I want to be without power. I thought on windy days I would test it on the hill nearby, see if I could find a spare battery from Bob at the hardware store and connect it all. I love playing around like this. Seeing what I can make from what would otherwise be discarded items and using it for something like clean energy. Can you imagine what the world would be like if we reused items to create amazing things like this? So far, it's looking good, but all this rain puts a damper on it.

"I'm just going to run outside and move my turbine under the porch," I tell James, whose head is stuck in a book near the fire.

"Need help?"

"I got it." I don't bother with a jacket as I run outside. Getting to the turbine I left on the far side of the lawn, I look at how best to grab it quickly without damaging it. I bend down and start to lift, before I drop it quickly, hearing a noise that has me freezing in place. My heart thuds as fear creeps up my spine. I look quickly back to the cottage, seeing no one. Nothing. I wonder if I imagined it as I glance around, seeing nothing but trees. The cloud cover makes it too dark to see anyone else.

"Hey! Anyone there?" I shout, backing away from the turbine.

I think it was a man's voice. I swallow the quickly rising panic that's consuming me and look around for a weapon, spotting a tree branch at my feet and lowering myself slowly to grab it before I turn.

And when I do, my breath catches all over again at who's stepping out from the tree line.

"Sutton?"

"Are you planning on killing me with that stick, Tinker Bell, or just bruising my ego some more?" His grin is wicked and full of happiness. Relieved, I drop the stick immediately.

Seeing him limping, I rush to his side. "What happened?"

"I was out hiking... Fell down a ravine."

That surprises me. "You hike?"

"Clearly not very well. I went once in the last few weeks, fell then too. It's probably a hobby that I'm not equipped for, but I do like it."

I roll my lips to hold back a chuckle. "So, what? Action heroes are clumsy?"

He waves that off playfully. "Action heroes are awesome.

What's that?" He nods toward the turbine, the one that's starting to move in the small breeze that's picked up. I examine it before looking right and left, the breeze coming through here nicely, something I hadn't noticed before.

"I'm trying to build a wind turbine." The words are out before I even think. I'm too excited to see it all moving as it should.

"Wind turbine?" he asks with a tilt of his head.

I internally cringe. I'm getting way too comfortable around him, but I relent.

"I'm passionate about sustainability. I wanted to see if I could put something together, using the junk I found around our place."

"Looks like it works?" Sutton's eyes are wide as he takes in the turning turbine. "What's it going to charge?"

"I'm thinking a battery. I just need to find one and connect it."

"That's cool, Tinker Bell." He looks down at me before we start to move a little, and he winces as we walk toward the cottage. I see his jeans are a little ripped, and there's blood on one leg. Thank God I have a first aid kit, so at least I might be able to help.

"Let's get you inside." I duck under his arm to assist him, and he laughs.

"This is cute, you helping me."

"Someone has to. You clearly can't walk." Unfortunately, I provide next to no support, our height difference comical.

"Want to give me a piggyback?" he teases. At least he hasn't lost his sense of humor.

We hop up the steps together and push through the door.

"James, can you get me some towels and the first aid kit?" I call out to my brother.

"Sutton!" James pops out from around the corner, looking worried as soon as he sees us.

Sutton smiles to reassure him. "Hey, buddy. I'm fine. Just took a little tumble."

James runs to the cupboard, grabbing the things I need as I get Sutton to the armchair.

With a sigh, he slumps into the chair, tired but happy to be off his leg. I pull up a small stool and lift his leg gently, placing it on the cushion.

"What's it look like? Am I going to lose my leg? Do we have to amputate?"

I can't help my smile, snorting a quiet laugh. His ankle is a little blue, so that ice pack from Rochelle will help. The cut on his leg? I've seen James with bigger grazes from school.

"I think you'll survive," I tell him, my eyes meeting his. He's already looking at me with a grin quirking his lips.

"What were you doing walking in the woods anyway?" I step over to the kitchen, grabbing the ice pack from the freezer as James passes him a towel to dry off.

"Went for a quick hike to clear my mind. I was walking on my plot, working on the building plan."

My eyebrows rise. I haven't traveled around Whispers much. Here to the diner and library and back mostly. But I've heard the locals all talk about different places. Billionaire Boulevard is the road that leads up the mountains. That's where all the large, luxurious ranches are, the homes that would ordinarily house people like my dad and his friends if small-town living was his thing.

"I had no idea it was that close." I shimmy up his jeans to give me access to his shin.

"Maybe I should build a path..." he says almost mindlessly, like he's deep in thought, as I get to work cleaning his leg.

But I'm curious. "Path?"

"Yeah, a path leading me here, so next time I come for a visit, I won't fall."

My heart beats a little faster. I pause what I'm doing and look at him.

"Visit?" I ask on a breath.

"Yeah, since we're neighbors and all." His grin is wicked.

"You're moving here permanently?"

"What, do you think I would build a place and not move into it?"

My mind is a whirl as I place the ice pack on his ankle. Neighbors? Sutton is moving here? We sit in the quiet for a moment as James runs to the bathroom to grab me another towel. My back is saturated.

"Lots of celebrities do," I admit, because I'm sure movie stars have homes all over the world they barely use. Clearing my throat, I change the subject. "You want me to warm up your chicken pie?"

Since Sutton didn't come in yesterday, Rochelle gave James and me a few pies that were leftover. I was planning on cooking them again tonight for dinner.

"Seriously?" His eyes alight like I just offered him the world, not a day-old potpie. "How can I say no to that— Ouch!"

He flinches as I pat antiseptic on his ankle before I blow on it a little to relieve the sting.

"Sorry…" I place his ankle on my knee and put the ice pack back on. He looks almost as good as new, leaning his head against the back of the chair.

"Hmmmm, chicken pie, your hands on my skin, and this warm fire is making me feel a certain way…" His words trail off, and then I notice that I have one hand gently cupping his ankle while the other holds the ice to his skin, my fingers caressing the spot. The move happened so naturally, I didn't even realize.

"What way is that?" My voice is a mere whisper, and he looks me dead in the eye.

There's no hesitation in his response. "Like I never want to leave."

I swallow roughly as our gazes lock, the fire crackling in the background and the rain now pounding the roof.

Is it bad that I never want him to leave either?

22

———

SUTTON

I'm warm. My belly is full, my leg all better, yet I'm on edge, because a ten-year-old is sweeping me up in a game of poker.

"Full house," James says, placing his cards on the table.

Chuckling, I throw my cards down. "You're a shark!" How the hell does this kid know how to play poker so well?

"He's good." Nikki nods, her expression gleaming with pride from where she stands in the kitchen doorway, watching.

"How did you get so good?" I'm in awe. If he keeps playing, he'll rule Vegas for sure.

"I was stuck in my room a lot, so I played cards to pass the time." He shrugs like it's no big deal.

These two are so unique. I still haven't gotten to the bottom of why she's building a fucking wind turbine out of junk, but the fact that she is, that's astounding. How does anyone know how to do that?

"Yeah, when I'm stuck in my room, I just watch TV."

Looking glum, he admits, "I wasn't allowed." Again,

another piece of their life falls from his lips, and I pocket the information away for later.

"Looks like you gained an amazing skill through it, though. I just wasted my brain watching TV and movies."

"No, you didn't." Nikki steps over to us, frowning at me. "All those hours of TV are probably what got you so interested in acting. You were studying the craft, watching how others did it. You used Social Learning Theory."

"Social what?" As usual, I have no idea what she's talking about, and I could hang on to every word she speaks.

"It's a concept in psychology, emphasizing that people learn through observation, imitation, and modeling." Her words come to me with warmth. There she goes again, spouting these highly intellectual facts like she's asking me to pass the butter.

"Sawyer just told me I was wasting my time." I think back to those days when his head was always in a book, studying for exams or tests, trying hard to get his law degree. Me? I was laid out on the sofa, a bowl of potato chips balanced on my chest, watching whatever TV show or movie was on at the time.

"Everyone learns differently. I bet Sawyer is probably a cognitive learner. Someone who absorbs and processes information through reading and thinking."

She's right. He is. But I never knew there were other ways. I just felt like the dumb brother. For most of my life, people have told me that my looks would only get me so far. Well, so far, they led me to Hollywood to be a global movie star, and right now, they've led me to her.

"Social Learning Theory..." I murmur, wanting to remember it. "How do you learn?"

"Good question. I'm probably like Sawyer. I was pretty studious at school. Always had my head in a book."

"Like you," I tell James, and he nods. They're both textbook fiends.

James yawns, and I look at my watch. It's getting late.

"I'm going to bed," James says, giving his sister a hug, and I offer my fist.

"Night, Sutton." He fist-bumps me, then wanders down the small hall, and I hear his door close.

Turning to Nikki, I smile. "He's a good kid."

She gives me a small smile in return. She's not telling me everything; I can feel it. But I don't expect her to. Considering they could be anyone, though, I feel extremely comfortable here, in her home, in her presence.

"I love him. I would put my life down for his." There's something about the way she says those words that makes me think that might be a choice she has to make in the future. I don't like it one bit.

"Is that something you need to consider?"

She bites the inside of her lip. "I hope not."

Well, that doesn't leave me feeling any more settled.

"Sawyer thinks you might have a record."

Her eyes widen. "Like, a criminal record?"

When I nod, she laughs, and then snorts, making me grin. "Not yet," she teases.

"His bruised ego for rejecting his job had him thinking all kinds of things, I'm sure." I watch her, waiting to see how much she'll tell me.

"I need a cash job. I can't be traceable. Rochelle provides that. And I want to be close to the school... I don't ever want to be away from James."

I pull in a sharp breath. She's doing all this for that kid. She herself is an adult, so she can go anywhere, do anything she wants. But she won't leave him.

"My turn to ask some questions..."

Surprised, I nod. "Sure."

"What's a global movie star hiding from that he's here in Whispers, sitting in my little garden cottage on an old timber chair?"

That has me sighing. "Well, starting tomorrow, I'm working on a top secret project with Tanner and Connor at the distillery."

"But that isn't what brought you here was it?"

I forgot how smart she was.

"No, it wasn't." Taking a deep breath, I clear my throat. "The media was getting increasingly intense in LA. It made it almost impossible to stay there. Weird things kept happening…"

"What kind of weird things?"

I can't help but wince before sharing. "I got home from a trip I took to Cabo and found a young girl naked in my bed."

Her eyebrows rise. "Is that a common theme among movie stars?"

"Nope. This one was underage. Not sure how she got in, and not sure why. I had my security team with me who dealt with it, but now I can't even walk into my own home without them completing a thorough sweep. It's creepy. Doesn't feel like my safe place anymore."

"Your house?" she asks softly.

"LA." As I speak it, the truth hits me. LA isn't home anymore. It's not the sanctuary I need now. And it hasn't been for a long time.

She nods like she understands. "I guess fans can be crazy."

I frown in thought. "I went out for dinner a few nights before I landed here in Whispers. My driver hit a young man. We were going slow, just pulling out from the curb, but this guy got up, smiled, waved, and walked off like nothing happened. The next day, it was all over the media that he ended up in the hospital with a broken leg and my name was plastered everywhere for all the wrong reasons."

Her smile falters a little. "Coincidence?" She's smart; I should've known she would come to the same conclusion as I did.

"Maybe. Maybe not." I shrug. I have no idea if my fans are just too fanatical, or if someone is deliberately trying to drag my name through the mud. But a hit-and-run and spending alone time with an underage girl are crimes, and I don't want to be pinned for something I didn't do.

"So we're both in hiding..." she concludes, though we already knew that.

"Here at this little cottage..." I whisper.

"In Whispers..."

The fact that we're both in the same circumstance has us feeling more connected than I have with anyone else. I have her back and I know she has mine. A low rumble of thunder rolls through the sky outside, and I know I should probably go.

"I'll text Sawyer to come get me." I don't want to. I want to stay here with her all night. But she has to be up early tomorrow for work, and she already looks tired.

"Here." She passes me her phone, since mine is broken from the fall. I send him a quick text before passing her cell back.

"I'll make sure he deletes your number," I tell her.

"Thank you. But I'm okay with Sawyer having my number. I trust you. I trust him by association."

My heart swirls at that. "I'll never break your trust."

She swallows, biting her lip as my eyes canvass her body, appreciating every inch of her.

"I should pack up." As she stands, leaning over me to

scrape together all the playing cards, my hands move before I think.

"Come here..." My voice cracks a little as I grab her waist, turning her to face me. I hear her sharp intake of breath as I sit forward. Her low height in comparison to my large frame puts her not too much taller as I sit at her side. I glide my hands up her curves and back down again, getting a feel for her as her hands land on my forearms.

"Sutton?" Her eyes search mine, full of heat, as her body leans toward me a little more.

"You're pretty fucking amazing, Tinker Bell."

She's tentative, but as her hands trail up my arms and settle on my neck, it's like she's telling me I'm safe in her arms too. This is what I need. Maybe I just need another taste of her, another touch. Maybe this infatuation I seem to have developed is all in my head. Maybe one night with her and it'll be all out of my system...

"You're not too bad yourself." Her voice becomes even quieter, if that's possible, like she's too scared to say what she really thinks. Not because she's shy, but if I could hazard a guess, it's because she's running from someone who's told her she can't be the person she is. I lower my hands to her ass and down one of her thighs, lifting her leg from behind her knee so she straddles me, before she lowers onto my lap.

She relaxes against me, and I grip under her knees to slide her body up my thighs until her hips hit mine. That's one benefit of our size difference; I can put her anywhere I want to. She swallows, her neck right in my line of sight. My dick pulses right underneath her, and her hips shift in response.

"That's a little better," I hum, looking up at her.

"What now?" Her question holds many meanings. What

now for right now? What now, as in what the hell are we doing? What now, as in, where's this going?

"Right now... right now, I want your lips on mine." The words barely leave my lips before I'm claiming hers. With a sigh, her hands delve into my hair, and I pull her flush against me, our mouths searching each other's before I delve my tongue inside. It felt good to kiss her in the rain the other day. It feels fucking fantastic to taste her right now. My whole body melts completely when she's in my arms, my stress and worries leaving me instantly.

The fire crackles, the rain hasn't let up, and the cottage is quiet, James no doubt reading or already asleep. Her body starts to move in my hold, her hips grinding, and I drop my hands to her lower back, my palms almost cupping the top of her ass as I push her into me over and over. Her back curves, her chest hitting mine, and God, I want her so badly it almost hurts. My cock's so hard, there's no way she can't feel me.

"Jesus, you're fucking perfect..." I grit out, my lips leaving hers as I trail them down her neck and take in her floral aroma, the fresh, innocent smell hitting my senses and making my hands grip on to her tighter. It's light, not over-powering, just feminine and flirty. Kind of like her. My lips peck and kiss her skin, and she pulls her hair around her neck to the other slide, leaving me nothing but her bare neck and shoulder.

She pants, "Far from it..."

"Not from where I'm sitting. And let me tell you, I've got the best seat in the house." I lift my face, taking her lips with mine again, because I can't fucking stop. My hands continue to push and pull her ass across my lap. Fuck, it's been a long time since I dry-humped a woman, but that's exactly what we're doing.

I'm usually more suave than this. Take women on dates, a nice restaurant, a bottle of wine. I'm in a suit, them in a little black dress that while sexy is boringly the same each and every time. Small talk happens that doesn't really lead into any robust or inspiring conversations, doesn't tell me anything about them. None of them are interested in me outside of the movie business. I then take them home, where they drape themselves over me, barely wearing a thing, maybe some expensive lace underwear or something. They usually have on too much makeup, which mixes when we kiss, tasting horrible.

But this... right now with Nikki... I'm hungry. I'm enamored. It feels organic, feels like real life and not a movie set. I'm engulfed by her, and I don't want to stop.

"We're going to break this chair," she says into our kiss, grinding her hips down harder.

"Fuck the chair," I say on an exhale.

"I thought you were trying to fuck me..."

Her unexpected forwardness has me groaning, pulling back slightly to look at her. "If James wasn't right down the hall, believe me, I would be."

A seductive smile pulls at her kiss-swollen lips. "You would? How? Tell me." Fuck, I'm hard. Her breathy pants are faster now, her hips not slowing. I feel like a horny teenager and a man who's totally smitten all rolled into one.

"I'd pick you up, rip your jeans open, and take you against the wall." It's in my vision now, and the only thing keeping me sitting is the deck of cards on the table reminding me of the little boy who was just here.

She moans softly. "Then what?"

"Then I would carry you to the floor in front of the fire, put your head down, pull your pretty ass up, and fuck you from behind. I'd slide in and out of your pussy so good..."

"Shit... Oh..." Her voice quivers, and I feel her fingers digging into my shoulders. Oh, hell yeah, she's going to come.

"But I wouldn't stop there..."

"No?" She can barely get the word out, and I feel my balls tightening. I'm going to come in my pants.

"Oh no... Then, my little Tinker Bell," I grit out, my teeth grinding, trying to hold on. She pulls me against her, my head buried in her chest, and I suck her nipple through her shirt, biting teasing kisses along her breast.

Her breath catches. "That feels... so good..." She's so fucking close.

"Then I'd have you riding me like this, taking what you want, my cock buried so deep you feel me for days... God, I want to fuck you." I grab on to her ass so roughly, I know she'll bruise. The way her jeans-clad hips rub against my own will be in my dreams for fucking eternity. We're both going to be chafed, but I don't really care.

"Ohmygod. Shit... Yessssss..." It happens. Her body locks before trembling, her hips thrusting wildly, and she comes on a silent cry of my name. "Sutton!"

"Fuuuuck," I blurt out before biting my bottom lip, sealing my mouth shut as I come hard. I hold on to her tight as my release coats the inside of my briefs, burying my head in her chest. She shivers with one last aftershock of her orgasm, grabbing on to me just as tight.

We're both panting, our bodies sealed to each other, and I can hear her heart thudding fast, my own matching her speed.

"Well... apparently, I'm an auditory learner as well."

I grin against her, hearing the lightness to her voice. She has a way with words. She likes when I talk dirty to her, and I need to remember that.

Pulling back, I look at her, searching her face for any indication of embarrassment or regret and see none.

My smile is wide. "That was fucking hot."

"It was." She grins back at me. "But we have a slight problem now." She looks down, referencing the issue I now have with my jeans. The wet patch is growing by the second, seeping through my briefs. "I found some men's overalls in one of the cupboards out back. Probably from the owner when he comes to clean up the place. I can grab them for you?"

"Probably a good idea," I say, seeing headlights flash outside from Sawyer's arrival.

I get changed and kiss her good night, making my brother wait a solid ten minutes because my lips don't want to leave hers.

23

NIKKI

I tighten my grip on the steering wheel. It's been a while since I've driven a car, and it's the first time I'm driving this little van that Rochelle uses for deliveries. When I arrived at work today to see her sneezing and coughing, I knew she wasn't going to last too long. Then when she asked me to run the deliveries today, a job she normally does, I knew then she must be feeling terrible. Because getting out and about is what she loves and what I hate. I'm so far away from the school and James, if anything should happen. Some would think that's highly unlikely— blame me for having anxiety or something, call me a helicopter parent, but I need to be ready for anything.

Pulling up to a parking spot near the main entrance to the distillery, I sit in the van and look out. My chest burns. The logo of Whiteman's Whiskey stands out, large and proud, on the building, reminding me of the whiskey bottle that Dad shared with me on my twenty-first birthday. I shake my head, trying to dislodge the emotions coming to the surface.

I've never been here before, and it's nicer than I imagined. Big, tall trees line the parking area, and the buildings are new yet have a rustic feel to them, almost blending in with nature. Their gardens are amazing, too—green, colorful, lush. It looks like you could spend a spa day here as well as enjoy a liquor tasting. While I know Tanner and Connor Whiteman are wealthy and well liked, I wasn't expecting a whiskey distillery to be so picturesque.

Jumping out, I round the back of the van, grabbing the two large trays I have ready to go. I need to close my eyes and take a deep breath as I close the door, because there's chafing on the inside of my legs that burns with every movement. Even so, a grin comes to my face. What Sutton and I did was completely and utterly insane, but so good in the best possible way.

Walking inside, I spot generators and cables everywhere, spotlights on out back, and if I didn't know any better, it looks like a movie set.

"Hey, Stephanie." I smile as I greet the receptionist.

"Hi, Nikki. They're about to break for lunch, so they'll be wanting those sandwiches down in the end room. Along this hall and last turn on your right."

I nod, the trays starting to feel heavy in my arms, and with only Stephanie's directions on my mind, I make my way down the hall. People stride past me, commotion in every room I pass. I have no idea what's going on, but I find it fascinating.

As I get toward the end of the hall, I look into one of the rooms and stop short. Because standing there, in a designer suit that looks like it was made just for him, is the very same man I dry-humped last night. There are lights and cameras everywhere. He's next to the bar, bottles and glassware propped perfectly, the lighting just right. I watch as Sutton pours whiskey into a glass, a dazzling Rolex watch sparkling on his wrist before he brings the glass to his lips and sips. A camera whirls around him, taking a close up of the way his neck moves when he swallows, how his large hand grips the crystal glass with ease. I swallow in unison with him, my mouth feeling dry. It's hot, captivating, and so on brand for a whiskey company, it's genius. It's not how I usually see him. No, this is Sutton Silvers, the movie star, not Sutton the clumsy hiker, who walks around with his hat pulled low, who stalks me at the diner. I vaguely remember him mentioning he had a job at the distillery, but I had no idea it was all this.

"Cut," I hear someone yell as a few people clap, the noise startlingly me to gasp. Sutton looks right at me, my breath catching all over again as he grins and gives me a wink. I offer him a small smile as my cheeks heat, then continue down the hall on wobbly legs, not wanting to interrupt his work. I see the last door on the right and turn, walking in and almost slamming the trays down, relieved to have them out of my hands.

"Rough night?"

His deep voice sends a shiver down my spine, landing between my legs. Looking up, I see Sutton's blazing eyes burning into me. His grin is wicked, and I can't help the smile that comes to my lips. He steps forward, eyes locked on mine, still in his suit, full of confidence, and slides a hand around my waist, pulling me to him.

"Something like that." My hands land on his forearms as he leans down, taking my lips in his so tenderly I feel my knees almost buckle.

"Mmmmm... I needed that," he says gruffly, like he's holding himself back. Last night was fun, sexy, flirtatious. But you never really know what the next move is after a night like that. A man like Sutton has women falling over themselves to get to him. He's used to women who are beautiful, polished, and sexy. Not ones who dry-hump him into oblivion. God, even now, my cheeks heat at the memory.

"You did?" I ask breathily.

"I haven't stopped thinking about last night, Tinker Bell, and seeing you now, kissing you, just makes me feel better."

My stomach swooping is interrupted as a throat clears behind him, and I pull back, startled, seeing Tanner Whiteman is standing right next to him.

"Oh." My eyes widen, my flush now traveling all over my body with embarrassment. But Sutton doesn't move, not worried that Tanner just caught us together.

"This a private party, or can I get a sandwich?" Tanner gives Sutton a shit-eating grin, and Sutton smirks at him, pulling me into his side protectively.

"Oh... they're here!" I internally cringe, but Sutton's thumb brushes against my lower back, easing my nerves.

"Good, the crew are starving." Tanner smiles my way like I saved the day.

"Filming something?" I ask.

"Something." Sutton's eyes haven't left me as he nods, not giving much away.

Before my brain can stop me, I tell them, "With all that power draw, you may be exceeding the amperage rating of your circuit breakers."

Tanner's eyebrows shoot to his hairline, and Sutton's grin widens. Meanwhile, I mentally scold myself for opening my mouth.

"Explain." Tanner moves his body to face me completely, giving me his full attention.

"Oh... I just... well... usually, that's the case on most film sets," I say quietly.

Sutton looks at me with intrigue. "Been on a film set before?"

I bite my tongue and remain quiet, not answering. I've been around them. Not a lot, but my dad has been interviewed before; the media followed him a bit, more so when Mom died.

"What do you suggest? I don't want an OH&S problem," Tanner asks. He's a big man and pretty intimidating, although one of the nicest guys I've met.

"Um, you just need to redistribute the load across multiple circuits to prevent tripping." It's an easy fix. I assume they have the people here to do it.

Tanner looks at me like he's trying to figure me out. "Okay..."

"But with all this land out here, I'm surprised you're dirty." I huff before I gasp, my eyes widening, and I slam my hand over my mouth. *Why can't I just shut up?!*

"Sorry. I didn't mean... I just... I don't mean to say *you're* dirty. I just mean dirty *energy*." Heat blooms across my cheeks as Sutton throws his head back and laughs.

"God, I love these facts..." Sutton says quietly next to me. Tanner looks at him, then back to me. His brow furrows a little before a small smile comes to his face.

"I'm listening," Tanner prods.

"I should probably just go..."

"Tell me what you think. Might as well, you've already started." He crosses his arms over his chest and watches me, and I look up at Sutton for encouragement.

His proud expression never wavers. "Tell him, Tinker bell."

I clear my throat. "The wind runs west to southwest out here most of the time, which is in line with the gardens I just saw out front. I mean, I've never been here before, not sure what else is out there or out back, but you could harvest it."

"Harvest it?" Tanner clarifies.

"The wind." It's simple, really. What's he not understanding?

"What about solar? I'm currently looking at covering the roof with panels."

"There's not enough sun," I explain easily.

"I had a team come in to consult last week. They were adamant that solar was the best option."

That sparks my interest. "Which team?"

Tanner's eyes narrow. "SunVault Strategies."

I laugh before I snort and then gasp with another layer of embarrassment. Fuck my life.

"And I love that little snort too..." Sutton shakes his head, smiling like he's won the lottery, his hand never leaving my back, but Tanner eyes me suspiciously and takes a step forward, startling me. I feel my heart racing beneath my ribs, nerves dancing, but he's only grabbing a sandwich.

"Step back from her." Sutton's voice is immediate, sensing my unease as he stands at full height, stepping forward a little. Tanner stops immediately with a quirked eyebrow, taking a step back.

"I apologize. I didn't realize I was. I'm just interested in the topic, since it's something I'm looking to invest in."

Now it's my turn to be surprised. Tanner Whiteman just apologized. To me. Sutton stood up for me, protecting me. What the hell is going on in my life lately?

"Continue." Sutton allows me the time and space to gather my thoughts.

"SunVault only offers solar, so of course they would pitch that. But Whispers has more wind here than daylight hours. Plus, wind can be generated day or night, doubling your capacity. You have the space to run a few turbines. I don't know the whiskey business, but it's possible to run this place on one hundred percent renewable energy, and possibly be the only distillery that does so." Once I get talking about my favorite topic, it's hard to stop.

Tanner rubs his chin in thought. "That was my plan. I like reusing what we've already got. I don't like creating a bigger footprint than needed. I just thought solar would be better."

"The environment doesn't lie. You just need to listen to it." As if on cue, a wail of wind brushes past the window.

"You should see the wind turbine she's making at home. It's awesome," Sutton tells him, and my gaze snaps up to his. Again, there's pride in his voice. This man really sees *me*.

"You make turbines?" Tanner asks.

I shrug it off. "Just a hobby."

"A hobby? Wind turbines?" Tanner's eyebrows are sky-high in surprise. I wring my hands together, not wanting to go on another ramble. I really need to leave and get out of this conversation.

"Some people knit, some people run, I like sustain-ability."

"Have views on waste recycling?" he asks.

"Some, yes." I'm not offering any more. I need to go.

"Want a job?"

I still. Did he just offer me a job? I'm too startled to speak, so he continues.

"Come on board here at the distillery. Be our sustain-ability officer. I'm not sure yet what that will involve, other than overseeing the distillery to be completely renewable, but you seem to know what you're talking about. We'll work it out as we go. Where did you go to college?"

I let myself feel excited for just a moment. Getting paid

to do something I spent years at college studying and have a passion for is what I really want. It's on the tip of my tongue to say yes, to scream it. But reality crashes down on me in an instant. Sutton watches me closely, and I notice his shoulders slump the moment he knows I'm going to decline.

"I'm sorry. I can't." Shaking my head, I brush past them both. "I need to go." Then I bolt down the hall and back to Rochelle's van.

This is why I don't do deliveries.

24

SUTTON

"Tell me what I'm missing?" Tanner looks at me, my eyes still glued to the doorway she just fled through. I'm itching to follow her, but I know she needs space, and I need to get back to set in a minute.

"She's a private person." I shrug, not telling him a thing. Her secrets are safe with me. She's safe with me. Hell, just feeling her go rigid the moment Tanner stepped forward had me so on guard, I felt like a pit bull. I know Tanner wouldn't hurt her; I knew he wasn't a threat, but my instincts kicked in, and there was no way he was getting closer to her.

"She's smart, confident, talks like a city girl but hides out in the country..." Tanner trails off, a contemplative look pinching his expression.

"She's very smart. I could listen to her for hours."

At that, Tanner looks at me and raises an eyebrow. "Seems like you two are close?"

Shit. If he only knew I came in my jeans last night like a fucking teenager. I thought a little taste of her might have me more settled, but all it did was make me want more. More touching, more kissing, more of her.

"We're spending time together. I like her."

"Hmmmm. I bet you are." Tanner gives me a small grin, one that I can't stop from forming on my face either.

My brother walks in a moment later, asking, "Hey, what happened with Nikki? I just saw her bolt out of here like she was on fire." He's been here all day, watching the shoot. We kicked everything off at five this morning. Grabbed some footage of Tanner and Connor walking through the morning mist, starting their day. I did a photoshoot in the aging rooms before I went in front of the camera just now to shoot the first part of the commercial, in my suit, with a whiskey, acting like the billionaire everyone wants to be.

"Tanner offered her a job."

"No shit. She declined you too?" Head reared back, Sawyer looks at Tanner, and I watch with interest. Both of these men have had their ego bruised by the woman I can't stop thinking about. But it does concern me. Sawyer's job, I could understand. Who the hell wants to work in law? But here at Whiteman's, a sustainability job? It sounds right up her alley.

"Why? Did she decline you?" Tanner asks.

"Yeah. Something's going on with her. She must have a record." Sawyer's words have my shoulders tightening.

"She doesn't have a fucking record," I grit out, wanting him to drop that line of thought.

"How do you know?" Sawyer's eyes pin me in place.

"I asked her. She said she doesn't, and I believe her." She wouldn't hurt a fly.

"Sure your views on her are not... clouded?" Tanner's tentative with his words, I'll give him that, but he still has a big, shit-eating grin on his face. One I match.

With a shake of my head, I dismiss him. "No idea what you're talking about."

"Does this have anything to do with the fact I picked you up from her house last night in a delightful pair of overalls?" my brother teases. Those overalls were bad. I looked fucking ridiculous, but it was worth it.

"Overalls?" Tanner looks perplexed before he grins, putting two and two together.

"Fuck the both you." I can't help it when my mouth turns up at the sides.

"Protective of her too, hmm? You've been watching her and hanging out with her at the diner for a while now. Is this getting serious?" Sawyer's playful grin changes to a gaze full of caution, and I wonder how I tell them that it kind of is. At least for me. I can't stop thinking about this girl.

"Hey. Why didn't I get invited to this meeting?" Connor walks in, saving me from having to answer as he grabs a sandwich from the tray, shoving it in his mouth.

"I offered Nikki a job," Tanner tells him.

Connor lifts an eyebrow, talking through his mouthful. "A job?"

"She declined," Sawyer adds with amusement, his ego not so bruised now, knowing he's not the only one she turned down.

"Technically, she didn't accept or decline..." I can see the wheels turning in Tanner's head.

"She's running from something, that girl." Connor grabs another sandwich half, and if we don't start eating soon, they'll be all gone.

"Do you really trust her?" My brother's words penetrate deep as he turns to me.

"With my life," I say without any hesitation.

"Then so do we." Tanner's statement is firm before he walks out the door, Connor following.

Sawyer's eyes are still on me, and I can feel his interrogation isn't over yet. "Are you sure about her, Sutton? I mean, let's be serious. This isn't like you. You never get attached to women. You have a different one every week, but you never catch feelings."

"I can't stop fucking thinking about her," I admit to him, and he looks a little surprised.

"Maybe it's just Whispers. Being here, not working, not having anything else to do but pine over a cute girl you've met?"

My head is already shaking. "That's not it."

"Maybe it's because she's forbidden. No one really knows her, and she has you intrigued? Like a puzzle you want to put together?"

"Nope." I'm armed with the truth, and my brother's eyes narrow.

"What is it, then? What is it about her that has you coming home in overalls, smiling every time you see her?"

"She doesn't like Sutton Silvers."

That has his brow pinching. "What?"

"She doesn't like my name. Doesn't like my job. Doesn't want the limelight, doesn't want to be associated with me and my celebrity at all. Doesn't want my money. Isn't with me to grow her social media following—hell, I doubt she even has social media. She just likes me for me. Do you know how refreshing that is?"

Understanding washes over his face as he nods.

"I do." He's talking about Annabelle. The woman he managed to sweep off her feet who didn't care about his money or his status.

"Do you know what she's running from?" His concern is now back in full force. "I won't say a word."

"No. I have no idea. But it isn't good. I think she's from money. She has her own status she's hiding from."

He nods resolutely. "Then we keep her hidden, and we'll be ready to help her when she asks." Sawyer slaps my shoulder, giving me his approval. Not that I needed it, but I do appreciate it, nonetheless.

"Can you babysit on Friday night?" he asks, catching me off guard.

Given that I'm currently living in a wing of his massive mansion, he already knows he has a built-in babysitter.

"Sure, where are you going?"

"I just want to take Annabelle out to the bar. A break from the boys."

That gives me an idea. "I might see if Nikki and James want to come over to hang out."

"Fine. Just clean up the mess you make this time." His parting words have me chuckling, already wishing it was the weekend.

I hear the call to get back to set, and I quickly shoot her a text.

> Sandwiches are almost as good as the
> chicken pies.

I keep it lighthearted. I know she was taken aback by the job offer and she might have a wall up because of it.

> I made them myself.

I huff, surprised.

> They just went up to number one food
> source in my book.

> Chocolate is the number one food source.
> Everyone knows that. Specifically peanut
> butter cups.

"Sutton, we're ready for you," Lacy, the marketing manager here at the distillery and Hudson's girl, pops her head around the door.

"Coming." I pocket my cell, and my smile doesn't dissipate all afternoon.

WITH THE WHITEMAN'S shoot taking a few days, I haven't seen Nikki since she walked in carrying trays of sandwiches and spouting her smart facts to Tanner before rejecting his job offer. Now, as I step through the back door of the diner and slide into my booth, it feels like coming home.

I look up from under the brim of my hat, catching her eye from where she is across the room. Her grin is immediate, and her eyes sparkle at seeing me.

"Good to see you too, Tinker Bell." God, I've missed her.

Not even a minute later, she's approaching me, her little notepad in hand. "Hey there." My mouth waters just from looking at her.

"You're a sight for sore eyes..." I reach out my hand and rub it up and down her thigh inconspicuously, blowing out a breath I didn't know I was holding. The tense feelings from working long days, ignoring Bobby's incessant calls, and having Griffin's team already on-site, the slab to my place poured and framing already in progress, starts to dissipate just from being in her presence. I see Rochelle eyeing the move; that old woman is smart as a tack and doesn't miss a thing. But I don't remove my hand. I keep it on her, liking being close to her again.

Leaning into me slightly, she asks, "Did you finish up your shoot?"

"All done. It's still a secret project, though. A few edits

and things need to happen, but we're all proud of it. It's going to be amazing when it releases."

"I'm so happy for you." Her words are genuine, as is her bright smile.

"Do you guys have plans tonight?" I ask her.

She shakes her head, eyes on mine. "No. Nothing."

"How about after work, I take you home to change, and then you come over to my place to hang tonight?"

She looks hesitant to leave her safe haven of the cottage in the woods. "I'm not sure..."

"Sawyer and Annabelle are going out. I need to babysit my nephews, and I was thinking maybe James would like to spend some time with Kevin, you know, outside of school." Nerves dance around me, wondering if she'll agree.

"He's been loving playing baseball with them all..."

"The boys can all watch a movie or something, and we can have dinner..." My voice trails off as I squeeze her leg, because I know exactly what I want to be eating tonight, and it isn't fucking dinner.

The grin that pulls at her lips is sexy as fuck. "Dinner?"

"Mm-hmm, then dessert." My words are laced with innuendo, and I watch in delight as pink tints her cheeks.

She nods, speaking almost shyly. "That sounds... good..."

I nod right back, slowly, my eyes on hers. "It will be very good."

"Okay," she says with more confidence than I was expecting. When she smiles, I bite back my groan. I'm so fucking needy for her, it's almost embarrassing.

"Okay?" I confirm, not believing she said yes.

"Yeah. Sounds like fun."

I already know it's going to be downright electric. So electric, she won't need her fucking turbine to charge any battery. I feel a warmth rush over me, knowing that she's trusting me. She's counting on me to keep her and her brother close, keep their secrets hidden and look after them. And I will. I also know that she'll never go anywhere without her brother, so if I want her in my bed, then he needs to come and sleep over too. Thank God Sawyer's house is big. Kids down at one end, adults up the other.

As she clears her throat in question, I realize I got lost in my head for a minute.

"Pies are fresh out of the oven." She looks at me expectantly, biting her bottom lip, making me want to stand and suck it from her mouth.

"You're a woman after my own heart, Tinker Bell." I might as well just open my chest, take out the beating organ, and pass it right to her at this point. Sawyer's right; I've never been this smitten for anyone. I'm clearly losing my mind here in this small town.

"Coming right up." She walks away with a little more pep in her step, and I smile to myself.

I want her. She wants me. If only life were that simple.

25

NIKKI

"What will we do?" James asks from the back seat of Sutton's truck, sounding confused yet excited.

"Hang out, eat pizza, watch movies. Oh, and I got a hell of a lot of chocolate," Sutton tells him, looking at me quickly with a cheeky grin. "You know, since it's the number one food choice." He winks, and I smile as we drive to our cottage to get changed and freshened up before heading to his place.

To be honest, I was so happy to finally see Sutton today that I accepted his invitation without thinking too hard about it. I probably need to check myself.

It's hard around him, though. I tried to keep my distance. I tried not to feel connected, get close, talk too much. But he feels like a safe space. He has as much to lose as I do in regard to our privacy, and the fact that I have a permanent smile on my face whenever he's around, like I've never had before, makes me feel good. For the first time in months, I'm throwing caution to the wind and just going with it.

"Do I need to pack anything? What do we take?" James

wants to go, but having never really hung out with friends before, it's all new to him. Poor kid was locked up tight in his room after school, night after night. His weekends were all spent at home too, either in his room or, on the odd occasion when our wicked stepmother wasn't home, he was downstairs, talking to Chef Luc in the kitchen. Because of this, James can now make the best *Croque Monsieur* I've ever eaten.

"Just bring yourself. I have everything we need." Sutton parks his truck, and James is out before he even turns it off.

"I'm changing!" he yells, running inside, making us chuckle.

"Man, if I knew he'd be this excited, I would've arranged a playdate earlier," Sutton says playfully.

"First time jitters, I think." I grab my bag, opening my door, and Sutton runs around to help me out.

"What do you mean, first time?" He's frowning, looking down at me, where he just planted my feet. His hands don't leave my waist. They haven't left me all afternoon, actually. The minute we walked out of the diner, his hand grabbed mine. In the truck on the drive here, he still held it, resting my hand in his lap.

"He's never hung out with friends like this before."

"Never? Never gone to play catch or watch a movie or sleep over?" He looks stricken. It would almost be funny if it wasn't so sad.

"Never. I guess he wants to make a good first impression."

Sutton watches me quietly before his hand lifts to cup my jaw. "Are you two running from someone who locked him up?"

I inhale sharply as his thumb brushes across my cheek

to soothe me. It seems I don't need to say anything; he already knows. He's more observant than most.

"Something like that," I whisper, and the line between his eyebrows deepens as he nods.

"They lock you up as well, Tinker Bell?" His jaw tics with his question, his body tense. My chest heats at the intensity. He looks ready to go to war for me.

"Not exactly..." I blow out a breath, thinking about it all. I have secrets, ones I'm not ready to share just yet.

"You're a good sister," he says softly. My eyes get a little glassy, because I'm trying really hard to be exactly that. "He's lucky to have you."

A lone tear falls at his words, the pressure, the buildup, the acknowledgment all striking hard.

He leans forward then, placing his lips on my cheek, kissing my tear and down the wet trail until his lips find mine.

As he curls his arm around my waist and pulls me tight to him, my feet barely stay on the ground. I sink into his hold, kissing him back, this tender side new and full of emotion. Our lips move against each other slowly, deliberately, my heart racing, because he completely takes my breath away.

He pulls back a bit, the two of us a little breathless, his forehead meeting mine.

"Mmmm, I like kissing you." Every time he grins, it's contagious.

"I like kissing you too." I feel the blush on my cheeks.

"I... ahhh... I got you something." He's acting a little coy, somewhat shy all of a sudden as he scrubs the back of his head. Leaning into the truck, he grabs a small box that I didn't see before. "Here."

"A gift?" I look up at him, surprised. The box is simple enough. Black, nondescript.

Nodding, he looks hesitant, and my heart thuds harder as I start to open it. Inside is a black velvet box, the kind that, in my experience, usually houses jewelry.

"Sutton?" I look back up at him, unsure what's happening here.

"Come on. Open it," he encourages, but he still looks nervous.

As soon as I open the box, it's like the earth tilts beneath my feet. Because there, sitting in the box, is the most beautiful bee clip. Just like my broken one, but sparkling and new.

"I know how much your clip means to you. It's the last thing you have of your mom. I used to look at it in your hair every day when I came to the diner. I almost had it memorized. So, I had my jeweler create a new one, replacing the gemstones with real diamonds and strengthening the clip with platinum. Now you have genuine yellow and black diamonds to ward off those evil spirits you talked about." He's watching me closely, and I think I'm about to pass out. Real diamonds. The cost of this would have been exorbitant. But that isn't what sets my chest on fire. It's the fact that he memorized my clip. The fact that he had it made, knowing it was special to me. The tears I had moments ago are back with a vengeance.

"Oh my God..." My voice is almost nonexistent. I still have the broken pieces inside, but they are so damaged, there's no way to repair it. I'm just keeping them for sentimental value at this point.

"I was hoping this would bring you comfort, like she's back with you, and now you can wear your bee clip again every day."

Tears fall rapidly down my cheeks as I stare up at him.

"Sutton, I have no words... You shouldn't have... I mean, I can't..."

He shakes his head, reaching up to cup my face so my eyes stay on his. "I wanted to. I know it means something to you. You mean something to me too, Tinker Bell..." Something shifts between us. It's deep, emotional, and I'm almost powerless to stop it, even if I wanted to.

"Thank you." It doesn't feel like enough. "Thank you so much, Sutton." I can barely get the words out around the tears that fall thick and fast. Sutton's thumbs brush over my cheeks, wiping away each and every one of them.

"What do you say we go inside, put that in a safe spot, and pack you an overnight bag? You guys are sleeping over tonight, because I can guarantee that there's going to be a chocolate hangover."

That makes me laugh. "Oh gosh, how much did you buy?" I pretend to groan, but I'm actually really excited. His hands drop from my face and run down to my waist, keeping me close.

"Let's just say, if I got the chocolate from Willy Wonka himself, then I would have about twenty golden tickets." He gives me a sheepish look, and I laugh some more.

"You're suuure you want us to sleep over?" I smile as I ask, because the way he's now looking at me, I already know the answer.

"Your brother needs a sleepover experience," he says quickly, and I zip my lips. He does. He really does. "And I need you in my bed." His tone drops, as does his head as he rests his forehead against mine.

"Oh?" I'm already short of breath. God, I'm such a hussy for him. Like he knows exactly what I'm thinking, his eyes turn molten.

"Buuut, if you prefer not to, then that's okay too. We can

take this as slow as we need to," he assures me sweetly, pressing a kiss on my forehead and pulling away slightly to look at me.

"I want it." I say the words so fast, his wicked grin widens.

"Sorry, I didn't quite catch that?" He knows exactly what I said. I take a deep breath, trying to center myself as I run my hands up his arms and cup the back of his head.

"I said… I will go pack my bag… although I don't think I have any clean pajamas for this sleepover." I bite my smile as I tease him, and he groans as his hands flex against my waist.

"You're killing me, Tinker Bell. But I mean it. I'll go as slow as you need. We don't need to rush anything," he reiterates, and I appreciate it. But while my history with men is limited and mediocre at best, I'm all in.

"I don't need slow, Sutton. I just need you."

Smiling, like that's the best thing he's ever heard, he kisses my forehead again and holds me close. With the bee clip firmly in my hand and feeling safe in Sutton's arms, I can't help but think my mom might just be looking down on me.

Telling me everything is going to be alright.

JAMES and I should be in awe. Should be amazed by this mansion up on Billionaire Boulevard, but we're not. It looks like the homes we used to visit when we were kids. Like the one we grew up in. Like the prison we escaped.

Sawyer and Annabelle left to go out as soon as we got here, and we've all been watching movies since.

"That was the best." Kevin stretches out as the movie

ends. I look at my brother, and his grin can't be contained, even though he's looking a little tired. He's had the best time, running around, eating junk food, making him and Kevin firm friends. But I know they'll both be asleep the minute their heads hit their pillows.

"Right. Bedtime." Sutton jumps from the sofa, full of energy. In fact, his knee has been bouncing for the entire time we've been here. He's jittery, and I wonder what's going on with him tonight.

"What? No!" Kevin whines, little Noah already asleep, Sutton putting him to bed hours ago.

"Yep, it's late." He promptly turns off the TV, and I look at my watch. It's close to ten. Not early, but maybe a little late for kids having a sleepover.

"We went to bed much later than this last time you babysat us." Kevin stands up, crossing his arms over his chest.

"Maybe. But don't you two want to go into your room, sneak candy in, talk about sports?"

Kevin thinks that over, and James watches the interaction with interest.

"Can we take the chocolate?" he asks as Sutton starts switching off the lights.

Sutton nods. "As much as you want."

"Marshmallows?"

"No worries." Sutton picks up the cushions, cleaning up the space, not even listening, and I smile.

"Sour Patches?"

"Uh-huh. Fine."

"Yes!" Kevin fists the air and grabs James' hand, pulling him into the kitchen, where I hear them raiding the cupboards and laughing.

I let out a giggle and small snort that has Sutton pausing and looking straight at me.

"What?"

"He has you wrapped around his little finger." It's sweet.

"No, he doesn't."

My brow pinches. "You just gave him everything he wanted."

"Not for him. For me."

I frown, still not understanding. Together, we walk to the kitchen to see what they're up to.

Looking at me, he leans in close to whisper, "I just want those little fuckers to get to bed so I can take you to mine." Then he strides forward like a good uncle, helping the boys get their goods, ensuring they have full bottles of water as I watch it all unfold with a swooping stomach.

I lean against the kitchen table, spotting a newspaper, recognizing the masthead as one from the East Coast. It's the business section, and I know I shouldn't, but I can't help but flick through it. Sure enough, my father's hard-set face stares back at me, so I read some of the article.

In a move that has sparked euphoria among environmental advocates, The Titan Family Corporation has acquired 10,000 acres of protected wetlands in Louisiana, aiming to secure it from development for future generations. The purchase, valued at $500 million, is one of the first investments from Titan since the announcement of his new environmental department, showing exactly how serious he is about helping the environment and offsetting his lucrative crude extractions around the world.

I swallow hard, looking at the image of my father. He doesn't look like himself. Again, older than I remember, yet still doing big deals, even though he has no one to take over his legacy.

"You alright there, Tinker Bell?"

I look up quickly, seeing Sutton watching me with concern. The boys are nowhere to be seen, but I hear them down the hall in Kevin's room.

"Fine. Why?" I fake the smile, trying to shake off the emotions that pulse through me.

"You're ripping the page."

I follow his line of sight down to my hand that's gripping the newspaper so hard the page has crumpled.

"Oh." Pulling back immediately, I wipe my hands on my thighs, trying to get my head on straight.

"Come on. The boys are in bed, safe and happy." Sutton takes my hand gently in his, and we stop to say good night to the kids before he pulls me down the hallway. It's dark, but I can make out the luxurious light fittings, the artwork on the walls, the tall ceilings, the marble floors.

As he opens the door to his suite at the end of the hall, we step inside, the carpet lush, the bed huge, and his hand comes up to cup my face, tilting my eyes to meet his. There's heat in his gaze as his thumb brushes across my lips.

"Let me help you forget whatever's in that beautiful brain of yours, at least for a little while."

His lips press against mine, and I'm ready to forget it all.

26

SUTTON

I see the fear and hurt laced in her gaze, but as my lips connect with hers, her body relents, and I hold her tight. I want to soak up all her fears. I want to protect her, but with no idea what from, I'm searching for a faceless villain.

I've been itching to have her to myself for the entire night. I could barely concentrate on the movie, my hand running up and down her thigh as we sat on the sofa, wanting to rip the jeans off her legs and taste her instead of the salty popcorn I was stuck shoving into my mouth instead.

I kiss down her neck, relishing her light moan, her shoulders lowering as her hands run up my back. With her body melting like butter in my hold, I grin against her skin.

"Why are you smiling?" Her head has fallen back, her eyes closed, and I kiss back up her neck to her ear to answer her.

"Just happy..." It's the truth. I can't remember a time when I felt so good about everything. When she grins right back, I return the question.

"Why are you smiling?" My hands smooth up and down her torso, her curves, loving the feeling of having her here with me. In my arms.

"Just happy..." she whispers.

And that's how I know I have her focus. When I saw her clenching the newspaper, she wasn't with me, her mind clearly on something else and that something else left sadness in her eyes. Now, they sparkle, right in my direction.

Slowly, I grab the hem of her top and draw it up and off her frame, leaving her encased in her bra. White. Fresh. Innocent. But there's nothing innocent about what we're going to do. I want her naked, bouncing on me. My balls are so blue from waiting weeks for her, I'm not sure I can wait much longer. But I will. For her.

"Tell me what you're going to do to me?" She steps closer, lifting her mouth to meet mine. She instigates the kiss, one so featherlight that I swear she's teasing me on purpose.

"I'm going to get you naked, kiss every inch of your beautiful body, and then I'm going to fuck you all night long." Okay, maybe I'm not as slow and steady as I want to be, but having her right in front of me like this is testing my willpower. At my response, I swear I can hear her heart hammering in her chest, so I pull back to look at her. Did I go too far? Have I scared her off? I stand in front of her, remaining firm, waiting as her mouth turns up, and she gives me a saucy grin as her hand reaches for my belt.

"What are you waiting for?" is all she says before I slam my mouth back onto hers. It's game on.

I swallow her moans as my hands hit the waistband of her jeans, making quick work of them, her kicking them off just as fast. My hands find her perky ass, and I lift her up easily. As her legs wrap around me, I take two steps forward, pushing her back against the wall.

"God, I've been waiting for this for so long," I moan against her skin as I grind into her, wanting her to feel how hard I am. What she does to me.

"You know what Aristotle said…" She's already breathless as she fists my top, trying to lift it from my frame. I lean back, grabbing it from the back of my neck and helping her rip it off.

"Tell me, Tinker." I grin, barely pulling my lips from hers. Her words are my aphrodisiac, our movement becoming quicker as her hands dive into the hair at the nape of my neck.

"Patience is bitter, but its fruit is sweet," she pants, her head lolling back against the wall as I grab her bra straps, pulling them down her shoulders, wanting her tits in my mouth.

"Oh, your fruit is very fucking sweet, baby," I grit out as her breasts spill from her bra cups, and I lower my head, taking a nipple into my mouth. As I do, her hips grind against me, and my cock weeps. I nearly whimper. And that's when I know I'm in trouble with this woman.

We are feverish, hands exploring, mouths smashing, hips grinding, wanting more. I can feel the heat between her legs every time she moves against me, and with each needy moan crawling up her throat, I'm edging toward desperate.

"I can't wait. I'm going to fuck you right here against the wall," I growl as the two of us unbutton my jeans, and I shove them down. I'm so fucking hard, I can't even think. Getting her naked, having her scream my name, making her come over and over and over again, those thoughts are taking up the forefront of my mind.

"Please, I need it," she begs as her feet push down my

underwear, and my hand finds her center. She whimpers when I rub her there, feeling how damp her panties are.

"Fuck, you're so wet," I push her underwear to the side, wanting to touch her bare skin, and when I find her clit, her body convulses in my grip.

"Oh my God... yes..." Her words rush out with relief, nails digging into my shoulders.

"That's it, baby... Fuck, your pussy is ready for me, isn't she?"

An eager nod is her response before I find her mouth, our tongues tangling, my body pushing hers against the wall harder because I'm almost raging. I circle her clit over and over, and her hips grind on my hands, taking what she needs.

"Yes... Sutton... yeeeees..." she says breathily against my lips, shivering against my touch like she's already on the verge of coming.

"Are you on birth control?" I grit out, barely hanging on.

"Yes. Implant," she moans.

I have condoms. The responsible thing to do would be to stop what we're doing, walk to the bathroom, grab a rubber, and put it on, but instead, I find myself saying, "I'm clean."

"Me too."

"Holy shit." I kiss her with a passion that I don't even recognize. I haven't gone bare with a woman in many years. The last few years, I've played the field, met and spent time with a lot of women, but I never had sex without a condom. Never trusting them fully. I read too many horror stories of pregnancies and being baby trapped to risk it.

"Please... please... I want you inside me, Sutton." She's begging me again, and it's the sweetest fucking sound. I can't deny her a thing, so without another word, I rip her panties away and slide inside her in one quick, deep thrust that has her gasping.

"Fuuuuuckkkk," I groan, both of us stilling as her eyes roll to the back of her head. She feels good. Like, really damn good.

"Yes," she breathes out and moves her hips on my length, her head falling forward to rest on my shoulder. I let her go at her pace for a moment, savoring the feeling of her surrounding me. As she gets used to my size, she sucks in another sharp breath, gripping tighter on to my shoulders, eyes meeting mine. "Fuck me, please."

Goddammit. She's perfect. "That's it, baby..." I clench my jaw as I slide slowly in and out, warming us up, and it feels fucking fantastic.

"Harder," she pants as her head falls back again, and she gives me a sexy-as-sin grin. I smile before giving her exactly that. I slam into her over and over, her pretty breasts bouncing, her mouth dropping open as her hips grind into me just as fast. She looks magnificent.

I can feel every inch I'm giving her. "You like that?"

"Yes... God, yes..." Her hands move to cup my face, pulling me to her, our kiss bruising, but my thrusts don't slow. I can't get enough. My need grows, my chase of her, of our high, too much.

What's this girl doing to me?

"Do you know how long I've been dreaming about this?" My honesty whips out of me as my hand finds her clit, making her shiver. "Thinking about taking you, having you in my bed, trailing kisses down your beautiful body..."

"Don't stop..." she mewls, and I'm not planning on stopping. Circling her clit, I thrust in deeper and hold myself there, feeling her pulse around me.

"Oh, baby, the night is just beginning."

She begs again, and I hear in her voice that she's close. Fuck, so am I. The way her body jolts with every thrust, the way her hips move, her back arches. I've never been with a woman of her small stature; the power I feel in being able to lift her and put her anywhere I want is making me feel like a caveman.

"You feel me sliding in and out, you feel what you do to me? You make me so hard… so fucking hard, baby."

"Sutton…" she warns, body trembling.

"Your pussy is weeping for me… throbbing…"

"Yes… yes…" She can barely talk, but I know she likes my words. Her body tells me on its own.

"Are you going to come for me, Tinker Bell?" My thrusts hit her right where she needs me as she remains pinned against the wall. "Be a good girl and come on my cock."

Her eyes fly open and meet mine, and as we stare at each other, she lets go with a cry. I'm in awe at the sight. She's the most beautiful woman in the world as she shudders, her pussy fluttering, tears of pleasure glossing her eyes as she kisses me messily.

And that's all I need to come inside her with a suppressed roar.

27

———

NIKKI

Rain pelts down outside, but I don't hear the roof leak, the wind as it rattles windows, or the creaks of the old cottage. Instead, I'm snuggled in tight to a Hollywood movie star in his bed, which, at a guess, is made up with fine Egyptian cotton and maybe even some cashmere.

"Where did you grow up?" His fingers run up and down my bare arm, my back flush with his chest. We showered and fell into bed, him pulling me close immediately. Now, as the moonlight filters through the crack in the curtain, we're up late, talking.

"Manhattan," I whisper the truth, no longer scared to share it with him.

He huffs a laugh against my bare shoulder. "I grew up in the Bronx."

"No way?" It's probably a fact I should've known, but unlike most girls my age, celebrities were never my thing, and I don't spend my time looking at gossip news or social media. I prefer a good book instead.

"We were practically neighbors." His lips brush my skin, pecking kisses, not able to stop touching me.

"I've never been to the Bronx."

His kisses stop abruptly. "Never?"

I shake my head slightly. "Nope."

"Like not even for a Sunday afternoon stroll?"

"No. We had a house in Connecticut. Mom, James, and I used to stay there most of the time. School and other commitments were in the city, and then we'd rush back to the home and gardens we all loved so much." I remember it all like it was yesterday.

"So you loved nature as a kid, then?" He smiles against my skin. I like this. We're a tangle of naked limbs, his hands not leaving my body. I feel safer here in his arms than I've felt in forever.

"I guess. I took after my mom."

"Was it something you studied at college?" His fingers draw small circles across my shoulder.

"It's my passion. I love working the garden, growing herbs, vegetables, fruits. I like building things that compliment nature, not take from it." I refrain from mentioning my father is the opposite, in almost every way.

"I see that. I watch you go through the rubbish at the diner, sorting it into recyclables."

I love that he noticed that. "I've done that since I was a kid," I tell him, huffing a laugh.

"I think the fact that you can make your own turbine is insane... It's good that you have something you're passionate about."

"I guess it's a little odd. I mean, most girls my age are shopping, out dancing, maybe traveling the world. And here's me—"

He cuts me off. "Smart. Sexy. Genuine. You are ahead of

them by leaps and bounds. You're beautiful. The most beautiful woman I've ever met."

I turn my head a little, looking back at him, my heart stuttering.

"Both inside and out." His nose nudges mine, and our lips meet briefly as his hand slides down to my hip.

"What about you? Have you always acted?"

"Struggled a bit initially. Left school. I wasn't studious; Sawyer got all the brains. Rolled around, working blue collar jobs for a while until I moved to LA."

"That takes courage."

"Or desperation. I could see Sawyer making it, and I wanted to make something of myself too."

I nod in understanding. "Well, I think you succeeded, although…"

"Although what?" he asks curiously.

I squint, not wanting to tell him, but knowing I should.

"Okay, truth time. I've never actually seen any of your movies." I squeeze my eyes shut, waiting, before Sutton barks out a laugh. I feel bad for a moment, but they aren't really the kinds of movies I watch. All those action films were never my idea of fun, but I can appreciate that they take time, dedication, and commitment to make.

"Maybe you can watch me in the Whiteman's commercials. That'll be a way to get you to watch me onscreen."

Puzzle pieces click together as I turn my head a little to look at him, seeing him gazing at me adoringly. "Is that what you're doing out at the distillery?"

"Well, it's top secret. But yes, I'm the new face of their latest release. Filmed a few commercials, did a photoshoot. It's been great, actually."

"If you enjoy it so much, you should do more of it." I'm sure movies are the cream of the crop for actors, but he might as well be doing something he enjoys; otherwise, what's the point of it all?

"Yeah... I came here for a break. I didn't think I would be gone from LA this long. But there's been a lot of good that's happened here."

I want to know more, so I ask softly, "Like what?"

"Well, the project with Whiteman's is what I've always wanted. I've been trying to collaborate with them for a while, and timing wise, it never worked until now. I like the idea of being connected to a brand; it has longevity, and Whiteman's Whiskey is something that I could promote long term. I also get to spend time with my brother, which I'm grateful for, because we're usually so busy. The time we do spend together is never long enough. Now he also has an instant family, which I love being a part of, and then... there's you."

My cheeks heat a little for getting a mention. "Me?" I almost hold my breath.

"Yeah. I kinda like hiding out in Whispers with you."

"I kinda like hiding out in Whispers with you too." I haven't been this honest with another man in my life. It's equal parts terrifying and liberating. Which is what has me saying something that's been on my mind more and more. "But I can't go back to my life, Sutton. And eventually, you will."

I trust Sutton and I'm having fun. But that's all it can be. A friend when I needed one. A rest stop. Somewhere I can just let go for a little while. Be the young, free woman I should be. But he'll eventually go back to LA, to his movie sets and his models. Me, I'll be at the diner, just the girl who served him coffee once upon a time.

"I'm not in a hurry to leave. I feel more at home here than I have anywhere."

I swallow roughly, not answering. I don't want my heart broken.

"But you... you should definitely take Tanner's offer." I shake my head again.

"I can't." If all the stars aligned, then staying in this small town and working in the field I love would be a dream. Away from the pollution of the city. Away from my father's shadow. With my brother safe to be the boy he needs to be. But I know the minute I start a career working on my passion that my father will notice. My name will start discussions, and eventually, the wind will pick it up and take it straight to Dad.

I also know that he won't have my back. Any pleas I had fell on deaf ears. Having his daughter work in the complete opposition of his corporation would bring reputational damage. We both can't succeed. Not in his world. But that isn't what scares me. What scares me is that he will take James back.

"Why? Tell me why, Tinker Bell." Sutton moves then, lifting to hover above me, his elbows resting on either side of my head, our eyes locked. His body is hot, heavy, and hard against my thighs, and my legs widen, letting him settle between them.

I bite the inside of my lip, my nerves a mess but my body craving more of him. "It's complicated."

"Things that are worth it always are..." He leans down, his lips brushing mine as he slides inside me, taking my breath as we devour each other again.

28

NIKKI

The startling ringing of Sutton's phone wakes me as he peels from my side, reaching over to his bedside table to grab it.

"Fuck. What?" he grumbles into his cell before he looks at me through tired eyes, the blanket moving and showcasing my naked torso, easily taking his attention.

"Good morning..." he murmurs to me, looking lust drunk and completely ignoring whoever is on the other end of the call. His eyes look hungry, and I'm not sure how; we had each other three more times last night. But my grin is instant as I suppress a giggle.

"Morning," I whisper as my lips kiss up his bare chest to his neck, the guy on the other end of the call talking so loudly I can hear him.

"Who was that?" the man barks, and I pull back to raise an eyebrow to Sutton, who just gives me a cheeky smirk.

"None of your business." Sutton kisses me wholly when I meet his lips.

"Like hell it is. Where are you?" The man barks again as Sutton takes his turn to explore me, trailing down my body, his lips touching every inch of my bare skin, from my jaw to my neck, across my shoulders. I melt for him every time, my skin pebbling in anticipation.

"What do you want, Bobby? It's too fucking early for your calls."

I bite my bottom lip as Sutton reaches my breasts. I've never been big-chested. I hated that fact growing up. I didn't really need a bra until I was older, and now my B-cup is average.

When his tongue circles my nipple, I stretch out, tingles rippling across my skin as I arch into him a little. His other hand smooths lower, curving around my back, holding me to his mouth. It's still dark out, the sun barely up, the two of us in a mess of blankets and sheets from a night of exploring.

"If you answered my fucking calls any other time, I wouldn't have to call you so early," the man says, and even though the phone isn't against my ear, his anger comes through clear as day.

"What do you want?" Sutton repeats himself as he moves down my stomach, his lips caressing my skin the whole way to his destination. As he hits my pelvic bone, I suck in a sharp breath. Looking up at me, he gives me a wink.

"What I want is for you to come back to LA. I've locked you in for a movie. You start in a week."

My breath hitches in my chest at hearing the news. Does that mean Sutton is leaving now? Is this guy his manager or something, and now that he has a deal lined up, my fairy tale in Whispers is already over? But Sutton's lips edge deliciously close to my core, and I push my head back into the pillow, the teasing sensation overwhelming me and any worrying thoughts.

"No movies. Not interested." Sutton ends the call

abruptly, throwing his phone across the room, and I hear a thud on the floor where it lands, just as his lips suction fully onto my clit and I see stars.

"Yeeesss." Moaning, I roll my hips against his mouth. I can't remember the last time a man went down on me. Probably some drunken college night that isn't worth remembering.

"You taste so good." His hands grip around the backs of my thighs, tilting my hips, bringing me closer to him and pulling me wider at the same time. I bite my bottom lip to keep quiet as he nibbles and licks, devouring me like he can't get enough. My hands shoot up, and I grip on to the pillow around my head as my hips start to move in earnest against his face.

"You do that so well," I say through another moan. "Shit, right there." I don't even recognize my own voice with the way he has me panting with every flick and swirl his tongue makes.

I feel my orgasm closing in on me quickly, and I have no idea how I'm going to function today. The lack of sleep, combined with the muscle soreness, I could probably rest for days.

"Fuck my face, baby... That's it." His lips don't leave me as his words, hot and rumbly, caress my skin. And if I thought I was wanton a moment ago; I wasn't. At his comment, I unleash any inhibitions, rolling against his face with abandon, dropping my hand to his head to grip on to his hair. The world could end right now and I wouldn't know it.

He groans with satisfaction, and the vibration has me tensing all over.

"Sutton!" I almost hiccup, my orgasm taking me by

surprise. He doesn't stop, keeps his lips on me through every wave of my release like I'm his favorite meal.

As I come down from heaven, I'm panting, my body shivering in aftershocks, and he kisses me a little more tenderly, his hands squeezing and massaging my ass.

"Mmmmmm, well, good morning to you too..." I say cheekily, knowing that I probably need to get up and showered before the boys wake and then head to the library before making our way home.

"It's a very fucking good morning..." He kisses back up my body, and I have never felt sexier.

Waking up a little more, I hum as I stretch. "This bed is so comfortable."

"And you look so good in it." He grins at me.

"Someone woke up on the right side of the bed?" I tease.

"Any side of the bed is a good side, as long as you're in it." His comment takes my breath away.

"I like being with you too," I whisper honestly, his eyes never leaving mine.

He lowers his head again, kissing my neck and shoulders. "Hmmmm... not sure I want to let you leave..."

"I'm not sure I want you to, either." But I will be leaving soon, and before I do, I have to ask, "Sooo... that guy?"

"My manager."

I nod. Thought as much.

"He has a movie for you? Does that mean—"

"I'm not going anywhere. I'm right where I want to be."

"Oh yeah?" I can't help smiling as he leans on me, his warm hands connecting with my own and our fingers entwining together.

"Yeah. I don't know if I told you, but I kinda met someone..."

I roll my lips, feeling giddy.

"Well, she must be a catch. You're a Hollywood movie star, after all," I say playfully, but he's taken on a more serious look in his eyes.

"She's fucking amazing. And I'm completely smitten."

I swallow, feeling truly happy for the first time in a really long time.

"I think she's totally smitten as well." His smile he shines down on me has butterflies going wild in my belly.

"Yeah?"

"Yeah. She's a goner..." I laugh lightly at the giddiness on his face, then snort, and Sutton laughs right along with me. Dropping his head, his lips touch mine briefly before we reluctantly get up, shower, and start the day.

I LOOK AROUND, seeing it quiet.

"You shouldn't be here," I whisper to Sutton, his hat pulled down low as we walk through the library.

"Why not?"

"Because someone will recognize you. This isn't Delish; Rochelle isn't here to save you."

"Yeah, but you will. Besides, no one's looking for me here, surrounded by books on gardening and nature..." He picks up a book, one on beekeeping, and flicks through the pages. Odd, considering he's allergic. I look at the few in my hands that I picked up to try to learn more about grafting apple trees and pollination, still wondering where I can get some wildflower seeds.

"Okay, all done." James heads back over to us, his library books now all returned.

"Wow, did you know you can get stingless bees?" Sutton

glances up from his book, wide-eyed, and I smile at his clear surprise.

"Where are they found?" I ask, having not heard of them before, and he lowers his head to continue reading.

"Australia, Asia... Not here." He sounds a little miffed at that, before putting the book on a small new pile James has collected, obviously wanting to bring it home.

"I'm just going to look at the noticeboard real quick." I stride over to the board to start my weekly examination. James comes to my side, looking carefully as Sutton approaches my other side.

"What are you looking for?" Sutton asks.

"Anything and everything. I need some parts for the turbine... I also want to find some wildflower seeds to plant around the apple tree. This board has been my lifesaver since we arrived. It's where I found the cottage, my job, and the bikes." My eyes narrow in on one notice. "Bingo."

"What is it?" James looks over my shoulder to see the piece of paper I grabbed.

"Peter, the local taxi driver, is having a garage sale, and if anyone would have a spare battery, surely he will." I feel confident. If he doesn't have what I'm looking for, I'm sure he'll have some other things I'd find useful.

"Yes! Look." My brother points, and I look back at the board.

I give my brother a deadpan expression. "We're not getting a cat, James."

He huffs. "Why not? I always wanted one."

"Because we don't have the time or money for one."

"Sutton, tell her we can get a cat," James says to Sutton, who looks at him seriously before he looks at me.

"She's the boss," is all he says, and my brother sulks before wandering off to look at more books.

Sutton watches him before he leans into me, his lips against my ear as he whispers, "I only like one pussy anyway, and it isn't for fucking sale."

Goosebumps line my skin, even as I chuckle. "We need to go!" I say quickly before I combust right there in the library.

"Your chariot awaits." He swings his arm out ahead of us, and me and my reddened cheeks walk ahead, with him and James following. The two of them giggle at something, having playful banter, and all the while, I'm unable to remove my smile.

29

SUTTON

I frown, looking at my laptop screen. The timelines on my build are efficient, but I want it completed faster.

"What are you doing?" Annabelle and Sawyer step into the kitchen, where I'm perched at the counter. The kids are settled for the night, and I grab my whiskey, the new Shadow Gentleman, taking a sip.

"Working."

Sawyer huffs a laugh.

"What are you really doing?" He grabs a glass and joins me with the whiskey as Annabelle makes a hot drink.

"Offering Griffin more money to work faster."

Sawyer pauses, his glass touching his lips before he lowers it to ask, "Faster? Are you in a rush to move out of here?"

"Just want my own place." I've been living here with Sawyer and Annabelle for a few months now, and I want my own space, my own things. It's time to get my own life started here in Whispers. I still feel like a visitor, and I want permanent lodgings.

"Doesn't have anything to do with Nikki?" Annabelle raises an eyebrow at me.

"It has everything to do with it." I'm honest, because if I can't be honest with my siblings, then I'm fucked.

"I can't believe that it's finally happened." Sawyer looks dumbfounded, sounds like it too.

I narrow my eyes. "What?"

"That you have fallen so hard and fast for a woman? Was it love at first sight or something?"

"It's not love." The words taste bitter on my tongue. It can't be love, can it? "We're having a good time," I tell him, more for my own benefit than his.

"Sure. I know. That's all you do. A good time. Probably time you started to rein it in a bit, isn't it? I mean, Nikki is nice, and the town has accepted her and James as their own. But you're going to, what? Go back to LA? Back to your movies and your ladies and forget all about her?" His gaze homes in on me, and he couldn't be more wrong. There's no way I would forget about her. Just the thought of leaving her to go back to LA makes me feel hollow inside.

"I don't know her well, but James sure seems like a bright kid," Annabelle comments, and I smile, thinking of the kid who, like his sister, has embedded himself into my heart.

"He's smart. Just like Nikki. She knows all these facts and stats, and I don't think I've ever met anyone smarter than her." *Or more beautiful, genuine, easy to talk with.*

"Must run in the family..." Annabelle huffs before sipping her tea.

"What?" I frown, wondering what she thinks.

"Hero savior complex."

"Hero what?" Sawyer and I both ask in unison, confusion pinching our brows.

"Your brother tried to rescue me, and you might be doing the same."

"We both know you didn't need rescuing," Sawyer says, and she grins softly.

"Yeah, but you kinda tried. It was cute."

I smile, seeing her wink at my brother.

"Cute?" Sawyer gives her a look that says *seriously?*

"All I'm saying is that the two of you grew up with nothing, made something of yourselves, and now you both want to help others. Sawyer found me. Maybe you feel that way about Nikki too?"

I understand what she's saying. I do like to help others. But that's not what draws me to Nikki. The way I feel about her, the way I want to see her, spend time with her, be around her... I feel like she's the one who's rescuing me.

"You sure have been spending a lot of time at the diner. Maybe you need to cool it a bit, you know, so you don't get caught out by the media," Sawyer offers, and my shoulders tense. This might be the twentieth time he's brought this up to me.

"I'm fine at the diner," I say through a clenched jaw.

"People will find you. There's been an increase in media attention. I know you live with your head in the sand about it, but they're going to find you, and when they do, it's going to be bedlam."

He's right. I go there every day. It doesn't take a smart man to figure out where to find me if they want to. I take a long sip of whiskey, feeling the burn.

"Maybe you should go back to LA... just for a week or so. Show your face around, help to cool down the media attention."

My answer is immediate. "No." Leaving Whispers at this point in time feels like the worst decision I can make.

"You live in LA, remember? You're going to have to go back there at some point." Sawyer watches me carefully as Annabelle squeezes his arm and walks out to check on the boys.

"LA isn't where I want to be anymore."

I wait for him to say something as he exhales slowly. "We're not only talking about where you live and your life-style, but we're talking about your career here, Sutton. I know you can work from anywhere, but you know as well as I do that the minute you leave LA and the gossip dies off, your name won't be front and center for the studios anymore."

I swallow. He's right. I may still get a few parts, but not like I used to.

"It was bound to happen someday. There's always a young kid about to rise the stardom ranks and take over as the new Hollywood it guy. Maybe this way, I go out on top. On my terms. Not spending my years as a washed-up actor in the Hollywood Hills, still hanging out with women who only want me for my money."

He nods, but he's no less concerned. "That's a big decision to make. Especially over a girl."

"It's not just Nikki, although she's fast becoming a big part of it. If I'm honest, it's a decision that I've toyed with ever since I arrived here. Shit, even before, really." Taking a deep breath, I shake my head. This conversation is getting heavier and more honest than I was anticipating.

"It did get a little crazy for a while," my brother huffs out with a bit of a wince. "The girl in your bed after Cabo, the guy who you hit with your car... We're missing something; we have to be." Turning to face me fully, he asks, "Who knew you were in Cabo?"

Sawyer's my brother, and I love him. But he's also a kick-ass lawyer, so I know he's latched on to a train of thought.

"Everyone. The paps had it on the front page of every magazine that week."

"Who knew what time you would be home?" he pushes, and I have to think about this, because while I get followed all the time, there are only a handful of people who know the exact days and times of my whereabouts.

"Security team, led by Jackson, Bobby, you. The model I took with me and her people." The list is longer than I thought.

"What about the guy who you hit with your car?" He's trying to connect dots that are still too far apart to connect just yet.

"Again, security, Jackson, Bobby... Jackson was driving, and I had another security guy in the back with me. Bobby was at the restaurant, standing on the sidewalk when it happened, waiting for the valet to get his car."

"So Jackson and Bobby are the consistent people, then?"

"Uh-huh... Why? What are you thinking?" I can see it in his face, he has something he wants to say.

"I'm thinking that you have a mole on your team. Someone who's setting up these events, hoping to tarnish your name, or at least get you negative media attention."

"Why, though? There's no benefit." I'm confused as to why someone on my team would want to see me fail.

"Money. It's always about money."

That doesn't make sense. "They get paid extremely well."

"Yeah, but someone might want to bring you down so they could leverage that to either earn more, or maybe they have another client they want to rise up over you, then nega-tive media is what they would use to do that. You know what Bobby says, *any publicity is good publicity.* What about Jackson? Maybe the media is paying him to catch you out? Get some photos of you in a compromised position?"

I shake my head. There's no way. Jackson is former special ops. He's genuine, loyal, and he's been with me for years now.

"Alright. Then Bobby?" Sawyer looks at me pointedly.

"Bobby is an asshole, but he isn't one to do something like that."

He sighs heavily, like he's annoyed I won't get on the same page. "We both know he's in it for himself. Money talks with him."

"Maybe..." I'm not sure what to think. But one thing's for certain; I don't trust Bobby anymore, and once trust is gone, you can never regain it.

I look at her contraption in awe. While I pretended to help James with his homework, Nikki was outside, connecting an old car battery she picked up for her turbine.

Seeing it working brought a smile to all our faces. The simple act of creating something with your own hands is one I admire.

"Wish I could do something like that." I watch the breeze push the turbine and all the cables and wires connected to the battery.

Her frown is cute as she takes in her masterpiece. "We need to test it..."

"How do we do that?" James asks exactly what I was thinking.

"I need a power inverter."

"Where do we get one of those?" I question, and she looks at me with a sad smile.

"We don't." Her shoulders slump. "They cost a lot, and I don't think I will find one of those on the noticeboard here in Whispers." She starts packing up her tools, the experiment now apparently over.

"Bummer." James looks as disappointed as I feel.

"So that's it? You built this and are just going to stop now?" It's like finishing a movie at the climax and not getting the end scenes that bring it all together.

"That's it." She throws her tools into her small toolbox and cleans up the area.

"But that can't be it." I have no idea how she can be so calm.

She shrugs. "Unless you know anyone who has an inverter."

"I'm going inside." Her brother is clearly not interested, now that the final piece of the puzzle isn't here.

"You're a tease..." I look at her with a sigh.

"How so?" She's disappointed I can see it, even if it's not at the surface. But there's also humor in her eyes; she doesn't take these things too seriously.

"Because you sold me on a dream and are not delivering..." I murmur as she steps toward me, her hair pinned back but strands coming loose, looking like my answer to everything. Wanting to touch her, wanting to have her close, in my arms, I reach out for her immediately. If I thought one night with this woman was going to put her out of my mind, I was wrong. Very wrong. I want to spend every night with her.

"Your dream was to have electricity?" With lifted eyebrows, a grin pulls at her pretty lips.

"My dream is already turning into reality.... here in Whispers, hanging out with my dream girl... watching her make something from nothing."

She blushes, and I peck her forehead, reveling in her presence, loving spending time with her.

"Come on. Let's go for a walk. I need to step out my frustrations," I tell her, and she laughs. When I hear her little snort, I grin wide. Taking her hand, I lead her away from the cottage, this area so quiet and secure, like our own slice of hideaway heaven.

"It's so pretty out here." She gazes around, taking in the tranquil chirping of the birds and the rustle of the leaves on the large trees.

"I haven't worked out if it's beautiful or somewhere to hide a body."

Giving me an amused look, she asks, "A body?"

"These dense trees look like a serial killer forest. Even Tanner thinks so." I squeeze her hand.

"I can see that. I choose to go with something beautiful, though."

I've noticed that about her. No matter what gets thrown her way, she always has a silver lining.

With dusk now approaching, we aren't too far from the cottage when I spot a familiar-looking tree fallen up ahead.

"Let's take a seat." Pulling her down with me, the two of us take in the peaceful surroundings. I see some familiarity and look where I think my place is, the rough path that I took the other day. My new place is closer to her cottage than I first realized, and a smile comes to my face at the thought.

"You know, forests like this one store massive amounts of carbon, but seventy percent of it is hidden underground in the soil rather than in the trees themselves."

My grin widens. "I didn't know that. Is that because of all the bodies buried there? They break down and distribute all that carbon."

She snorts a laugh. "Well, I don't know how many bodies are buried out here…"

"Hopefully none."

"I like it out here." She sighs, looking up at the trees, leaning her head against my shoulder, and I hold her tight. There're no cameras, no phones, no people shouting, no timeline, no requirements other than just *being*. I get to have her with me, touch her how I want to, not worried about paparazzi or what articles are going to show up tomorrow.

"Me too. Is it private land?"

"Not sure. I pay an older guy rent in cash every week. He comes into the diner, knows Rochelle, a longtime resident. I think he owns it all."

I wonder what his plans are for all this space, ideas of my own forming.

"My new place is just through there." I point up the small hill, and she takes it in.

"I think this fallen log is about the halfway point between our two places. Maybe we could put something here. Mark it as ours?" The breeze rustles through the trees, moving her hair with it, and something in my chest tightens. It's like I have an angel in my arms.

Biting her bottom lip, she looks around, unaware of my state of awe. "What can we use?"

"Why not your turbine? The wind comes through the break in the trees over there. When I fell, I broke my phone, so maybe we can have our own little security box, too?"

"Security box?" She's smiling, intrigued. I feel like a kid coming up with a random idea like this, but it's exciting. I want to have something that's just ours. Something we make together.

"Have your turbine charge a satellite phone, so if I ever get lost again, I'll just call you to come save me."

Her whole face lights up. "That is both a great idea and totally insane, but I love it."

I bet in her previous life she was an inventor. She seems to love putting things together and creating new weird and wonderful contraptions.

"It can be our own call box, but instead of being found along a highway, it's found here, in serial killer forest."

She giggles, then tells me, "Call boxes on highways are charged using solar panels."

"We'll just use your turbine. Charge it with the wind."

I know as soon as I leave her, I'm going home to order a satellite phone and the inverter she needs. Then I'll build a box. I frown, thinking about it. I have no idea how to do that or what to use, but Griffin can help me.

She nods, giddiness radiating from her. "Sounds practical."

"That way, no matter what, you can call me, and I can call you."

Her smile falters, the heat in her gaze igniting me. Our eyes don't waver, a myriad of feelings filtering through our minds. I know if she ever lost her phone, it would be a big issue to get another one. This way, she would have access to one. She would also have access to electricity, be merely a hundred yards from my place, where she's welcome anytime and, hopefully, that means she'll never feel alone again.

"Thank you, Sutton." Her voice is a mere whisper, and her words float over to me and embed into my heart.

I swallow. "For what, Tinker Bell?"

"For just being you."

I pull her tighter against me, sealing her lips to mine, and I swear, I never want to let her go.

30

NIKKI

I'm sweating. That's how unfit I am.

"That's it, everyone. Good work tonight!" Daisy says, her own cheeks pink, but at least she doesn't resemble a tomato like me.

I grab my bottle of water and my sweater, getting organized to leave.

"How did you do, Nikki?"

Daisy's perky voice has me swiveling around, surprised.

"I feel so good," I tell her honestly.

Her genuine smile widens.

"You were amazing. It's clear that you've done it regularly before."

My smile falters, but I catch it quickly. I did love yoga. I would do it most mornings. I did it every morning back when life felt safe, before survival became my priority.

"A few of us are going over to the diner for a drink. Do you want to join us?" Daisy looks at me expectantly. My eyes sweep the room to see who's left, spotting Rochelle, of course, and Tina from the toy store. Evelyn, who I know owns the local home decor store, is also here and a few other people I don't know as well.

"Oh, thanks, but I need to get home to James."

"Of course." She frowns. "Is he home alone?" Her concern would be warranted if it was accurate.

He and Sutton spent the last hour together. It took Sutton a while to encourage me to come to yoga again. Having tried it a few weeks ago, I fell back in love with it, but it's hard for me to put myself out there and trust that things will be okay. With Sutton around so much, the boys dropped me here at the start of my class and then went to his place to watch movies. "Sutton's watching him," I admit, knowing this might trigger more questions.

We start walking out together, the cool night air a little brisk on my cheeks.

"Sutton... as in Sutton Silvers?" Daisy's eyes twinkle.

"Ahhh, yeah." I can't help the warmth that hits my cheeks.

"Connor mentioned that you two were a couple. I love Connor with all my heart, but Sutton Silvers... *phew*." Fanning herself, she laughs.

A couple? Sutton's been talking about us? My mouth dries as I take in Daisy's words. I feel something for Sutton, and those feelings grow by the second. I try daily to pull myself back. I know getting close is a bad idea, but like being on a diet and craving chocolate cake, I can't stop. He makes me feel alive, wanted, heard, and sometimes, that terrifies me more than the past I'm running from.

"He has that effect on people," is all I say, summoning a light laugh.

Daisy's joking, of course, but I'm starting to understand what Sutton's life must be like. Having people gush over you who don't really know you. What are they gushing for? A fictional character that he portrays on camera?

"He's a great guy, from what I'd heard. He's been so professional on set at the distillery, too. Connor's really excited for the launch of this new batch they're all working on."

That has me smiling. "I know Sutton is excited as well."

Like I conjured him, I hear a truck pull up next to me, windows so dark, making it difficult at night to see anyone inside.

He jumps out, wearing jeans and a t-shirt, his baseball hat still in place, even though it's nighttime.

"Ladies." He nods in greeting, and I feel my stomach flip-flop as Daisy's cheeks grow a little pinker.

"Right on time." I grin up at him, his eyes solely on me. There could be anyone around, and he wouldn't notice.

"Your chariot awaits." Leaning back, he opens the passenger door for me.

"A man after my own heart, that one," Tina murmurs to me as she and Rochelle walk past, going to the diner across the road. Rochelle gives me a little grin that tells me she knows exactly what's going on between us.

"Thanks for tonight, Daisy. I'll see you next week."

"See you then!" Daisy steps back inside to lock up her studio, and I turn, looking straight at Sutton, who's watching me intently.

"Did you do your stretches?" He raises an eyebrow at me, a small, mischievous grin dancing on his face. As I step up to get into the truck, he helps me, his hands lingering just long enough to spark something warm in my chest, something dangerously familiar that travels lower.

"Yes…" I say cautiously, wondering what he has planned.

"Good. Now you're all mine." He shuts the door quickly

and runs around to the driver's side. I look into the back seat, where my brother sits, heat filling my cheeks at what he might've heard, but then I balk. Because in the back seat is my brother, with large noise-canceling headphones on and a brand-new tablet in his hands.

"Um, what's that?" I ask Sutton as soon as he's sitting beside me.

When he sees my quirked eyebrow, he looks back at James before looking back at me, clearing his throat. "I got that for him today."

I can't be mad at his thoughtfulness. It's no use trying to stop him anyway. "Thank you. I know he'll love it, but you didn't have to."

"It's a twofold gift."

"Twofold?" I ask.

Sutton reaches over and grabs my hand. I feel his warmth as he looks at me intently. "I don't know why you're hiding or who you're running from. But I need you safe. I have no idea what's happening between us other than I really love being with you, and every time I think about danger coming to you, I could burn the world down." His grip tightens just slightly, like he's holding himself back.

"So, in the interest of keeping the world whole, I set up a secure account, one that will only be traced to Sawyer, not to me, not to you. I also installed some security software. So you can track me, and I can track you, in case you need me. In case you need help at any point. There's an emergency call button. It calls me, Sawyer, Rochelle, Tanner, then the sheriff in that order. As long as this is all okay with you, of course."

I can barely breathe. I'm frozen with emotion, in equal parts shock and gratitude. When we left my father's place in the dead of night, I took nothing. Nothing that could trace us. I had enough cash to see us through for the first month or so, for travel and food and accommodation. The last of which I used to lease the cottage for the first month, Rochelle's job came along just in the nick of time.

Sure, I got a new cell phone. One that doesn't have the internet, hopeful that it couldn't be tracked. But Sutton has just given us a lifeline that I could never supply. Something in my chest tightens. It's not fear, but trust. And it hits me just how much of that I've lost over the years.

"I... I can't believe you did all this." My eyes fill with tears, and Sutton's hand lifts, cupping my cheek before he grabs my chin and tilts my face up so I'm looking at him.

"I also thought the noise-canceling headphones might come in handy..." Sutton gives me a not-so-subtle look, lightening the mood, and I chuckle, even as a tear trails down my cheek.

"Hmmmm, might be something my brother needs on nights like tonight," I say playfully.

"Oh...?" Sutton acts all coy. "What's happening tonight?" He mocks confusion.

"Well, I think I'll need help getting out of this activewear..." I reach over, resting my hand on his thigh, loving how his jaw clenches.

Swallowing roughly, he nods. "I could probably help with that."

"Maybe my underwear too..." I whisper as I move my hand up his thigh, my brother completely oblivious in the back seat.

"Hmmm, Tinker Bell..." he growls in a warning, my hand sliding right up to his groin with a teasing brush before pulling away.

"Yes, Sutton?" I look at him innocently.

"Are you saying you want me naked in your bed tonight?

Because if not, your hand on my dick is not the right message to be sending a man." He grins, lifting both eyebrows, and I can't tame my smile.

Nodding slowly, I whisper, "Mm-hmm. That's exactly what I'm saying."

"Let's go!" Sutton starts the truck like we're running from a fire, breaking the tension, and a loud laugh bursts from my lips.

When I look back at James, he gives me a big smile and a thumbs-up, like it's the best day of his life. My eyes drop to the movie on his screen, seeing Sutton's latest project, and without knowing for certain, I assume Sutton's downloaded his entire back catalog to keep my brother busy until well into tomorrow.

31

SUTTON

We got back to the cottage and James basically ignored us both and went straight to his room, lying on his bed with his head and eyes focused on the movie he just started. When I gave him his own earphones and tablet, it was a purely selfish move on my part. But the way his eyes lit up, it was like he never received such a gift before. It made me equal parts elated and sad. I have no idea what they've both been through, but I know it isn't good.

I wasn't lying to her earlier. I want her to be safe. Both of them. With no security team here, I had to improvise, knowing that she wants to remain hidden in her little cottage in the forest. I also don't want to be without her for one more night, and with the cottage so small, James is bound to hear things he shouldn't.

So noise-canceling headphones and a loud movie, it is.

"He loves it." Nikki grins as she locks up the place. "He's probably going to be your biggest fan after watching all those movies."

"I was kinda hoping that might be your spot…" I walk

closer, taking her in. She looks good, all flexible, blissed out, and in tight yoga gear that I can't wait to peel off.

"You want me to be your number one fan?" Her head tilts in this cute way when she asks questions. Like she's teasing but also testing the waters.

"No." I shake my head. "I want to be your number one."

Her smile falters for just a second, just long enough for me to catch the flicker of surprise in her eyes. She wasn't expecting me to say that.

"That's a bold statement." There's no challenge in her voice, just curiosity. Dare I say, hope.

"I mean it." I dip my head, voice softer now, more certain. "Whatever this is... whatever we are... I want it to be real."

Her eyes search mine. "Really?"

"It feels very fucking real to me, Tinker..." I settle my hands around her waist, waiting for her response. My heart feels like it's going to thump right out of my chest. I haven't put my feelings on the line like this before. I need a fucking glass of Whiteman's Whiskey just to tame the swirl of my stomach.

"It feels real for me too," she says with her eyes on mine, and I can't stop my smile forming. "But I'm scared..." And the tremble in her body emphasizes that fear. All I want is to take that feeling away and replace it with comfort. She needs to know how serious I am.

"I want us to be exclusive. I want to be with you and you me."

She takes a big breath, exhaling. "Exclusive?" She looks like she can't believe the words we're speaking.

"Nikki, I want you to be all mine." I feel like I might have a heart attack.

"I already am..." Her honesty lashes across my chest like

a whip, leaving me breathless. I'm motionless for a second before I breathe out my surprise and pull her close, my lips crashing onto hers in an instant.

She falls into me with a moan, and I'm already lifting her off the floor, throwing her over my shoulder.

"Sutton!" she squeals as I hold her over my shoulder and walk down the hall to her room. Smiling at her laughter, I kick the door closed before tossing her onto the bed, then something catches my eye.

"What's that?" I still, seeing the floorboard up in her room, instantly on alert. When I glance at the window, it's shut.

"Oh, shit." She jumps off the bed and rushes to the floor, and I follow.

"I just have my go-bag here," she says, stuffing what looks like a small duffel down under the floorboards, before replacing the board, making it look like it was never missing.

"Go-bag?" I don't like the sound of that. I sit on the floor beside her as she sighs.

"I have a bag with some clothes, cash, a few things ready, just in case."

"In case of what?" I already know what she's going to say, and I hate it.

"In case we need to run again." She looks at me with a pinched brow, and I want to smooth her worries away. While I'm thankful she's opening up, I have no idea how to rein in my protective anger that bubbles.

"Is that likely? That you'll have to flee that quickly that you need a go-bag?"

She blows out a breath. "I hope not, but it eases my mind that I'm prepared."

I nod, taking it all in as I grab her hand, my fingers gripping on to her tight.

"You run to me, okay?"

"Sutton..." She's already shaking her head.

"No. I mean it. You run to me." I've just told her how much she means to me, and I already feel her falling through my grasp. I hate it.

She gives me a soft, "Okay."

I'm not sure if she means it or if she says it to appease me, so I grip her chin and move her eyes to meet mine. "Promise me, Tinker."

Lifting her hand, she cups my jaw, her thumb brushing over my cheek. "I promise." And then she leans in, sealing her word with a kiss so tender I almost crumble. I slide my arm around her waist and pull her close, her body moving with ease.

"I've never wanted a woman the way I want you..." I speak against her lips before deepening the kiss, our moves now quickening, our need evident. I want to show her. I want to show her what she means to me, and my body is itching to be with her.

"I think those noise-canceling headphones were a really good idea." She giggles, making me smile, and I stand us up. Placing her on the bed, I lift my top from my frame, and she makes quick work of hers as well.

"I have a lot of good ideas," I tease her as she sits up on her knees, and our bodies collide, heat and passion swirling.

I lay her back on the bed, the mattress the most uncomfortable thing I've ever been on, but I care very little about that right now. I can't help as my hands roam over her curves, ensuring I touch every part of her, every inch I want marked as mine.

"You do? Tell me one..." Her hands are on my jeans, unbuttoning them as I pull at her bra, getting her clothes off her beautiful body now my number one task. Her cheeks are flushed pink, and I can't help but look at her, amazed that I met someone so undeniably beautiful and smart and kind.

"Coming to the diner when I first arrived in Whispers was my first brilliant idea." I kick off my jeans, then pull her yoga pants straight off her legs. She smiles up at me as I dive back to her, nuzzling her neck, kissing her skin, my hands exploring her nakedness.

"I agree." Her body arches into me, her bed squeaking with the movements.

"Coming in every day to watch you work was the next good idea." I kiss down her neck, palming her breasts before moving down her torso, trailing my lips across her skin as she moans breathily.

"Yes..."

I look up at her as I kiss across her hip bone, my final destination almost in sight. Eyes closed, her head tilts back, hair flowing over her pillow, looking like my dreams.

"Kissing you... touching you... talking with you..." I peck kisses across her soft skin as she writhes in my hold, needy for more, my hands palming her ass, not wanting to waste a second of being in this moment with her.

"Hmmmm... you're teasing me..." She has a slight grin on her face, and I bask in it. How she's relaxed as I rest here in between her legs, her sweet pussy right in my face. She trusts me, lying before me, all open and beautiful, her center glistening.

"Mm-hmm. I might be. Maybe that's another one of my good ideas..." My lips trail more kisses to the inside of her thighs, her soft, tender skin delicate against my lips as she shivers. I want my lips brandishing her body like no man has ever done before. My cock is throbbing, hard against the mattress, and I might be teasing her, but I'm killing myself in the process.

Her hands fall to my head, digging into my hair, and I growl as I lift my hands, entwining my fingers with hers, keeping us connected by her side as I slide my lips up.

"Kissing your beautiful pussy until you scream is one of the best ideas I've had yet." I put my lips on her center and look up at her briefly, seeing her bite her bottom lip as her legs fall wider, and I suck on her clit, a groan leaving me instantly. She tastes just as sweet as she is.

"Yes..." she whispers. We're quiet, her door firmly shut, but God, I want her to unravel on my tongue. I bury myself. Licking and circling her clit, her body grinding against my face with every swipe.

Our hands grip on to each other, like we are each other's lifeline, as I taste everything she's offering. When her body arches a little, the bed squeaks again, but my movements quicken as I can feel her quivering, knowing how worked up she is.

I like this. Getting to know her body as well as her mind. Having her at my mercy, having her hands clasping on to mine.

"Oh God, Sutton... That feels so good." Her words make my already hard dick thicker, and I grind my hips against the mattress, needing some reprieve while I devour her. I worship her, just like she deserves, and just like I've wanted to since the moment I saw her beautiful face.

"Take what you need, baby. Smother me with this pretty pussy," I say against her wetness, my tongue stroking through her opening with every word. Her nipples peak as her hips move faster.

"Yes... yes..." she whimpers.

I hum, loving this with her, every minute I get to spend

with her. Knowing that I'm in deep, that there's no way I can go back to my life as it was.

"Sutton!" she whisper-screams as I suck hard on her clit. She detonates, her hands gripping mine like they're in a vise, pussy fluttering against my mouth, and I keep going, licking at her like the decadent dessert she is until her body softens and her moans turn to pants. She's fucking phenomenal.

Pressing a soft kiss to her thigh, I relish the fact that I'm the man who brought her such pleasure.

I slide back up her body, and with each movement, the bed continues to squeak. She giggles before snorting, her expression like sunshine.

"It's not funny." I bite her breast playfully, circling my tongue over her nipple, and she squirms. God, I could die happy right now.

"It kinda is." She looks at me with glassy eyes, tinted cheeks, and a grin that has me slamming my lips onto hers. I kiss her hard, pushing my hips against hers, my hardness so close to where it wants to be. Her hands lower down my body, reaching for me, and the bed squeaks again.

"That's it." I jump up, and she giggles heartily.

But then I tell her, "On your knees," as I stand at the side of the bed.

Her eyes snap up to mine. "What?"

"You keep giggling like that and you're going to startle your brother, so on your knees, Tinker Bell. You need my cock in your mouth to keep you quiet."

Biting her lip, her gaze like pure seduction, she slides off the bed and gets on her knees on the floor in front of me.

"What will keep *you* quiet?" she sasses with an eyebrow raised, just before she leans forward and takes me in her mouth.

As I slide into her warm, wet mouth, I release a husky groan. I'm in heaven. She's my heaven. This little cottage is our secret hideaway, and I grit my teeth so as not to make a noise. She's right; it's harder than I thought.

I look down at the vision she is. Naked, her hair flowing down her back, cheeks flushed, my cock sliding in and out of her mouth so perfectly.

"Mmmmm... Now you're quiet, Tinker. You look so good on your knees for me."

I watch as my words start to take effect, her hand skimming her breasts and down her stomach to her center. My ab muscles tighten as she works me over eagerly, taking me deeper.

"You suck my dick so well, baby. Your lips wrap around me perfectly."

She mewls, the noise vibrating down my cock, straight to my balls. I sink my hands into her hair, gripping it, holding it up off her head as her body arches, showing off her curvy ass. The view of her is phenomenal.

"Are you touching yourself? Touching your pretty pussy while I fuck your beautiful face..." My jaw tightens, my orgasm close as my hips start to move.

Her own hips move as she moans, her hand rubbing her clit with vigor.

"Fuck... open wide, baby. Let me feel that throat," I grit out as I slide into her again and again. Her body shakes, lips tensing around my length as she whimpers. I know the moment she comes because her jaw relaxes, and I let go, coming down her throat.

"Fuuuck..." Biting down hard, I hold back my roar of euphoria as she swallows everything I have to give.

With a coy smile, she relaxes back on her heels, and I

slide from her lips before I bend down and grab her, throw her on the bed, and dive back into her pussy.

"Sutton..." she pants.

"One more, baby... One more for me," I tell her as I suck hard on her clit, and her back arches, already on the edge and sensitive.

"I can't..." she whimpers, the lie falling from her lips as her hands grip the sheets beside her.

"Your pussy is telling me a different story." My words push into her skin before I circle and stroke her clit with my tongue, gripping her ass and pulling her to me. Her hips move against my face, grinding as she moans my name, ready to crumble. God, I've never wanted a woman as much as I do her, and to have her open to me like this is equal parts pleasure and pain.

"Shit. Oh my God. Ooooh..." She's surprised as her orgasm approaches for a third time, hitting her powerfully. "Sutt—" she starts to yell, and I lift my hand, slapping it across her mouth just as she screams into my palm, thrashing under me. Her beauty is unrivaled. As I continue placing gentle kisses on her core, her body turns to liquid. Understandably, she's spent after an hour of yoga and then multiple orgasms. She kisses my palm, her touch tender, sensual, like no one has ever handled me before. I remove my hand from her breathless face as I kiss up her body, the bed squeaking as I move and I lie next to her and pull her close.

"Wow... that was..."

"I know... it was." I hold her tight, her small body curling into mine. The rain has started up again, the cool Whispers night now in full effect. I feel her body relax, her breathing calm, and within moments, she's asleep.

Listening to the sound of nature around us, I strum my

fingers gently up and down her bare arm, and my mind drifts back to the bag underneath her floor.

I need to get my security team briefed. I need to get things organized. I need to do something. Because here in the dark of the night, in the middle of serial killer forest, I know, without a doubt, I'm done for.

She is the girl for me, and no one is going to take her away.

32

NIKKI

Life in Whispers is becoming normal. As normal as being on the run can be.

I work, James goes to school, then Sutton brings us home most days, our weekends now filled with more than just quiet days at home. James teaches Sutton poker while I tinker. I get to enjoy spending nights wrapped up in the arms of my lover. The one slowly embedding himself into my chest so tight I know it's going to be hard to let him go.

Despite the constant fight-or-flight my body remains in most of the time, I doubt my life could get any more settled than it is now.

As I wipe the counter, the lunch rush over, I wait patiently for James to finish school. When the door chimes, I look up expectantly, but instead of my brother, I see a somewhat familiar face.

"Good afternoon," I greet him with a grin. The old guy is back. He isn't a local, but I remember him.

"Hello, dear. The chicken pie was so good, I wanted to bring my wife to try it."

I look at the older lady at his side. She offers me a warm smile, one I return.

"I told you it was good. Two chicken pies?" I ask them as they take a seat at the counter.

"Yes, thank you. He's been talking about it nonstop since he had it." His wife chuckles. They're cute. I put them at maybe in their sixties, although they both look really fit. Travelers are not uncommon around here because of the distillery, but we rarely see the same people twice.

I get their pies, fresh from the kitchen, and then fill a cup of coffee for each of them. "So still in Williamstown?" I pour, remembering him saying that's where they were staying.

"Just for another few days," he says.

"We just love it here. So nice and tranquil. Have you lived here all your life?" his wife asks me.

"I have." I nod, sticking to my script.

"What a magical place to grow up in," she gushes.

"Do you still have family here?" the man asks, just as James rushes in.

"I'm starving." He throws his bag on the floor and sits at the end of the counter. Sutton's late today, but I'm sure he'll be here soon.

"Excuse me," I tell the couple, not answering their question as I move to grab James his cupcake and milk and get him settled.

"So how was school?"

"Great," he says happily.

"Did you hand in your project?" I lift my eyebrows, because he's so keen to play baseball at lunch now, I wouldn't be surprised if he forgot to hand in his Benjamin Franklin project. The one he's been working on for a while.

"Yeeees," he moans, and while for most parents and guardians, I'm sure they would find it frustrating, I'm ecstatic that he's got a good group of friends at school and acting like a young boy should.

"Where's Sutton?" We both look toward the empty booth.

"Not sure. He'll be here soon, I'm sure." I nod to him, then move around the diner, clearing other tables, seating a few new people as the afternoon rush starts.

"That was wonderful, my dear," the older lady says as I step to the counter and take their empty plates.

"It's the best pie I've ever had," I agree with her. Rochelle's chicken pies are now building somewhat of a name in these parts.

"Almost reminds me of this lovely café in Manhattan... what's it called, dear?" She looks at her husband, and I know the one she's talking about.

"Do you mean Thistle & Wren?" I ask, and they both look at me with bright grins.

"That's the one. Do you know it?" the man asks, and I immediately still. I was too relaxed. I wasn't thinking.

I swallow and clear my throat. "Oh, I've never been, but I had some people through here last month that talked about it," I tell them easily.

"Well, we better get going. So nice to meet you, my dear," the woman says as they both stand, grab their things, and leave some money on the counter.

"Enjoy the rest of your travels," I say as they walk out. With my heart beating hard and fast, I clear their section, and only a few minutes later the familiar sound of the back door catches my attention. My stress immediately lowers, knowing the man I feel so safe around is finally here.

THE SUN BEATS down as I plant my apple tree. The section I cut will hopefully take, and now all I need is the wildflowers. I stand to stretch out my back, just as I hear Sutton's truck drive slowly up to the cottage.

"Hey, you." He jumps out, walking straight to me with purpose, his lips eagerly hitting mine in greeting.

Smiling, I speak against his lips. "Hey. What a nice greeting." I lean in for another kiss, pulling back when my brother walks out from inside. "James has the deck of cards ready."

"Well... Kevin won baseball today, so Sawyer told him he could have some friends over tonight. He was hoping that James wanted to sleep over. Sawyer said he's happy to return the babysitting duties after we watched them the other week." Sutton searches my face as I take in what he's saying.

My heart stalls. It's not that I don't trust Sawyer with my brother. I mean, the house is secure, and he's a lawyer. But I'm not sure I'm ready to be apart from him. Especially when we did so much to ensure his safety.

"Oh yes! Please? Please, please, please?" My brother never begs.

"I... ah..." I feel a little lost in this decision. I know my brother wants to go, and deep down, I know he'll be safe and it'll be good for him. But my heart feels like it's going to sink down to my toes.

"I thought we might drop him off now, leave him for a few hours, and if you don't want him to sleep over, then we can go pick him back up before it gets too late."

It's late afternoon, dusk fast approaching, but I take a deep breath. I need to trust him; he just gave me the perfect compromise.

"I guess he could go for dinner and a movie and see how

it goes." I'm happy with that. I mentally note to thank Sutton for helping ease me into it.

"I'm packing my bag, just in case. I want to sleep over. Kevin's dad does these cool pancakes for breakfast that are amazing..."

James is giddy, already running back into the house to pack an overnight bag, and I breathe out any remaining fear, rolling my head on my shoulders. How in the world do moms let go of their kids when they're old enough?

"He'll be fine, you know that, right? Sawyer has gates, security, and both he and Annabelle will be home with the boys. I don't know what you're hiding from, but I've hidden with Sawyer for months, and no one has found me." Sutton's hands land on my waist as he looks down at me, concern etched into his brow.

"I know. It's just..." I can't even explain it.

"It's hard. I get it. When you love someone so deeply that you'll do anything to protect them. I understand. And I'm proud of you for letting him go, at least for a little while." He kisses my forehead, then whispers against my ear, "Sooooo, while James is with the boys, I have somewhere I thought we could go."

My eyebrows rise. "Like a date?" We haven't really been on a date.

"Mm-hmm, like a date. But one where no one will ever find us." He grins down at me, speaking in riddles, and I'm already intrigued.

I chuckle, feeling a little giddy.

"You want to grab a change of clothes?" Sutton asks, which has me tilting my head in question.

"What will I need?"

"Well, we'll be outside, so some warm clothes for later might be good."

"Okay..." It's been a long time since someone surprised me, so I'm not asking any more questions.

"Hop to it, woman." He slaps my ass, and I squeal as I run inside, packing a small bag with a sweater and jeans, having no idea where we're going.

Once we drop James off at Sawyer's, we're back on the road, but not for long. His truck pulls up to Marie's place a few minutes later. No lights are on, so I'm assuming no one's here. Marie's place is next door to the distillery on Distillery Drive. A small accommodation place that Tanner and Victoria own.

"What are we doing here? Are we allowed here?" I whisper like we're robbers, and Sutton laughs.

"Don't worry. Tanner knows we're here. Come on." He grabs our bags from the back of the truck, then comes to my door to take my hand and help me out, leading me into the fields.

"Do you know where you're going?" I look around, the sun hanging low. The afternoon glow spreads across the fields, giving an array of yellow and orange and a touch of pink to the sky. It's beautiful.

"Not a clue, but Tanner gave directions." Sutton's deep in concentration as he leads me down a dirt path.

"To where?" I stop short behind him when he stalls. As I look up, my breath catches.

"Wow..." I'm immediately mesmerized.

"Yeah. Wow." Sutton and I can only stare at the view in front of us.

"I've heard about these, but I've never seen them. Never knew where they were." I glance around the mineral springs, in awe of how breathtaking nature is. It's cool out, the steam from the water rising. There's no one else here, so it's nice and quiet, the bugs and birds slowing down for the day as it gets darker out, and the temperature perfect for spending time outside.

"Wanna go for a swim?" He looks at me cheekily as he starts to disrobe.

"But I don't have a swimsuit." I frown as he throws his t-shirt to the ground near our bags, opening his jeans and pulling them off.

"That's fine. Neither do I." He strips completely, giving me a sexy-as-sin smirk before he runs in, the water surrounding him instantly.

"Sutton!" I giggle at seeing his naked form out in the elements, looking around making sure no one else is here.

"Ohhhh, this is nice. Come on!" he yells. Feeling like a rebellious teenager, I strip down, leaving my clothes and underwear on the edge and running into the water, Sutton's eyes on me the entire way.

The water is hot, soothingly so, and as I immerse myself deeper, my muscles instantly relax.

Paddling straight toward him, I hum, "It's so warm."

"Mmmm, feels good..." he groans, reaching for me, his large hands wrapping around my waist.

"A few of the locals talk about these springs. They use them for the distillery spa now, too, I think."

We both bob in the water, my legs around his hips, droplets running down our faces and arms.

"Tanner mentioned it to me the other day, and to be honest, there isn't really any pools or beaches I can go to these days without getting photographed, so I was keen to try it." He leans his head back into the water, enjoying the moment.

"What's it like?" I watch him closely.

"What?"

"Being photographed everywhere you go?"

He blows out a breath, his hands holding me firmly. "At first, it was a novelty. I was single, working my ass off, and I needed the publicity. After a few years, it became annoying. I couldn't go anywhere without a tail. But again, I knew it was part of the business. If I wanted success, I needed the media attention. But now... I mean, I've hit the heights I always dreamed of hitting in Hollywood. There really isn't anything else I need to achieve there. The movie deals, media calls, living in LA, it all feels like something I've already conquered, you know? I no longer have the patience for it. I'm older, and I want more privacy, a calmer life."

"I understand that." I think back to my mom's funeral, where cameras were stationed outside the church, just to capture my dad's tears. And he isn't even a movie star.

"I think that's why I like it here so much. I get to just be me." His tone softens.

Running my hands into his hair, I brush it back from his forehead.

I smile, loving the look on his face when I touch him. "I like just you."

"I like just you too." Our smiles meet, turning into a slow-burning kiss. I've never felt more wanted or safer in my entire life than I do right here in his arms.

"There's no way I could kiss my girl in public like this if the media were around..." he murmurs between kisses, and I feel my body flush when he refers to me as his.

"There's no way I would want the media to capture us both naked in Mother Nature either."

His grip on me hardens, as does his cock, where I feel it nudging at my core.

"Good thing all this steam is making it hard for the bugs and birds to see exactly what we're doing under the surface..." His kisses become more demanding as his hand slips between my legs. My hold on him tightens as I move my hips, wanting friction.

"Touch me…" I pant out.

"Fuck, Tinker Bell, you're so hot." His fingers explore, and I hold him close, my arms looping around his neck as he circles my clit over and over. My heart rate spikes as he slips a finger inside, and I almost combust.

"Oh God…" I moan, grinding down on his hand. I'm lost in the sensation, the sound of the water lapping as we move, the firm hold he has on me with one hand while the other makes my eyes roll back.

"You like that?" He's hoarse as he kisses up my neck, and I let my head fall back a little as he continues to work me over, knowing my body better than anyone else ever has.

I whimper as tingles scatter from my core. "Yes, Sutton… Oh God."

"Fuck, you make me so hard. Are you going to come for me, baby?"

I hear him panting and lift my head to look at him, our foreheads pressing against each other and breathing the same air. Our lips hover close but just an inch apart.

I can barely talk as I nod, and when he circles my clit again, this time, a little quicker, my body shakes. "Yes, Sutton."

His grin is wicked as he kisses me, our bodies sealed from our lips to our hips. I pull back a little to gasp a breath, his eyes hooked on mine.

"Yes… yes… yes!" I bite my bottom lip as I moan through my orgasm, Sutton's arm around my waist tightening as his fingers continue their movements.

When I open my eyes, breathless and dazed, they meet the pink sky. It's like my own taste of heaven.

33

SUTTON

Fuck me.

I swallow hard as Nikki looks at me, her face all relaxed, completely liquid in my arms and at my mercy. Her naked body sealed against mine, I move my hand from her clit and run it up her body to cup her face, bringing her lips back to me.

I take them with mine. Hungrily. My tongue lashes hers, our bodies both now wet with water, sweat, and steam. Her hair hangs low, wet in the water, the jet-black tresses looking like they're painted onto her head.

"I want more," she moans against my lips, and if that isn't the sweetest fucking thing a man can hear...

"Yes... Fuck yes..." My hands palm her ass, and I pull and squeeze her cheeks, knowing her clit is sensitive and wanting to tease her. Giving me a seductive look, like it's not my turn to play, she leans back a little, grabbing my cock in her hand. I swear I almost come from the contact.

"You manhandling me now?" I grin, because she can touch my cock any damn day of the week.

Her lust-drunk eyes tell me I'm in serious trouble with

this girl. *My girl.* I said it earlier, and I meant it. I've never had someone in my life whom I wanted more than the air I breathe.

"You got a problem with that?" she teases, lining me up with her center, and I sink into her warmth. I grit my teeth as I feel her clench around me, holding her hips to thrust deeper.

"Yes... like that," she moans as her head falls back, and my mouth connects with her neck.

I think I've hit euphoria. The pinnacle. I've had lots of sex in my life, but right here, under the sunburnt sky, no one around, out in the open in a warm mineral spring with this woman I can't stop thinking about... Fuck, this is it. This is what life is.

"You like that?" I know she does. Her hands dig into my shoulders, her nails leaving little dents, but I don't care. All it does is remind me that this is real, she is real, and not some make-believe fairy tale I've made up.

"Yes... oh God, yes... Right there, pleeease." She lifts her head back up with a moan as I hit her G-spot, then take her lips with mine again. We move in sync, our hips grinding against each other's, and I lower my hand, finding her clit again, needing her to come one more time before I can let go.

"Shit— I-I'm c-coming," she warns almost immediately, and I knew she would. I'm starting to learn her body, what she likes, what makes her come hardest, and I know when she's sensitive from one orgasm, the second comes from her easier.

I continue to circle as I thrust, massaging that spot deep inside her every time I move, the water around us splashing a little more.

"Yeeees... Come for me again... Give me another, baby,

all over my cock," I tell her gruffly, and I feel her quiver around me as I grit my teeth.

"Sutton!" she yells with a hiccup and shudder, and I let go right along with her, sliding into her one, two, three more times before I come with a harsh exhale.

"Tinker..." My knees feel weak, her body slumping against mine and we hold on tightly to each other.

Panting, I stand with her in my arms and catch my breath. Being with her is becoming better, more comfortable yet passionate, with every passing day. Now that we have clearly taken things to the next step, I feel even more protective of her than I thought possible.

I look around the springs, listening and relishing the peacefulness. I can't hear the distinct sound of cameras shuttering. I can't see anyone hiding in the bushes, no one up on the hill. We're completely on our own, and it's the most blissful feeling I've experienced.

"I could fall asleep here..." she murmurs, and I grin as I kiss her shoulder, running my hand up and down her back.

"You can. I'll hold you. Like your own little floatation tank experience."

She laughs, and then I hear her little snort, and I grin wider.

"Do you ever wish you could just freeze a moment in time? Like this part is so good that you never want it to change?"

I swallow, because that's exactly how I feel.

"Yeah. This is pretty perfect... You're pretty perfect, Nikki," I say softly, with adoration, and her hands tighten around my neck, like she's scared I'll let her go. But I wrap mine around her waist tighter, ensuring she knows that I never will. That kind of feeling imprints on my heart, making my already protective feelings for her increase even more.

"It's... Charlotte. My name's Charlotte." Her voice is a mere whisper, her admission a gift that hits me in the chest. I swallow hard, knowing she's sharing a big piece of her secret life with me, and I'm more than happy to carry that for her.

"Charlotte." My tongue wraps around the name, getting a feel for it, and I hear her suck in a sharp breath.

"A beautiful name for a beautiful woman." Leaning forward, I place my lips on hers, holding her a little bit tighter, wanting her to know that I've got her. She hums into the kiss, and I pull back, pressing another on her forehead before pulling back to look at her.

"Your brother?" I ask.

Her smile is small but full of meaning as she shares another truth. "Preston."

I nod. Preston suits him much better.

"There's so much I need to tell you, so much that you should know—"

I cut her off, seeing the turmoil on her face. "You tell me when you're ready. I don't want to rush you. Believe me, there's nothing you can tell me that would ever scare me away."

She wants to be honest with me. It's in her nature; she's a genuine person, and I know she isn't keeping things from me maliciously. It's more about self-preservation than anything else.

I run my hands over her hair, wondering, not for the first time, what her natural color is. Her body relaxes against mine again. She feels safe with me.

"I could be an axe murderer on the run?" Her lips quirk as her eyebrows rise.

I chuckle at that. "Hmmmm... I think you would've killed me already," I murmur against her lips before I take them in mine.

"I could be a journalist, here to get the Hollywood scoop..."

I grin against her mouth. "Nope, you would've cashed your money in by now. I would be front-page news already. Can't fool me, baby."

She purses her lips playfully. "Maybe I'm just using you for your amazing... swimming skills..."

My hands squeeze her ass as she giggles. "You think I have good skills, huh?" I kiss her then, our words muffled as our lips don't part, and I feel her smile against me.

"I think you have very good skills..." Her hips move, and now it's my turn to smile.

"You're pretty perfect, Charlotte," I whisper exactly what I said before, but with her real name now, and she sinks into my hold.

As I keep us afloat, our bodies still connected, her head buried into my shoulder, my arms wrapped around her tight, I know that I'm completely and utterly in love with her. And I don't know what in the world to do about it.

Because I still don't know who she really is.

I sit in the kitchen, my brother staring at me.

"You know, I was thinking it before, with all the bees and things. But now, I'm sure of it. You've lost your damn mind."

I might be the actor in the family, but my brother got the dramatics.

"What is it that you have a problem with, exactly?"

"It's fifty acres!" He throws his hands up into the air, and I roll my eyes.

"Listen, I can't go looking for this guy. It'll probably blow my cover. But Rochelle knows him. Apparently, he comes into the diner sometimes."

"What the hell are you going to do with fifty acres of forest?"

"Nothing," I say simply.

Sawyer's eyes narrow at me, incredulous. "Nothing? You are going to buy fifty acres of forest and leave it as forest?"

"You're meant to be the smart one, Sawyer... For someone so smart, you're taking an awful long time to figure this out."

His face reddens. "Please, explain it to me..." Even though his voice is calm, he certainly is not.

"I'm buying serial killer forest, and I'm going to leave it exactly how it is."

"But *why*?" he presses, exasperated.

"Because it's at the back of my property. Because it's beautiful, tranquil. I can go for small hikes. It covers the cottage and offers privacy. Plus, wildflowers grow around there. They're important for the bees."

"Those fucking bees again. I swear, if Noah or Kevin get stung..."

"Can you find the guy and make him an offer for me, or do I need to find new legal representation?" I deadpan with a lifted eyebrow.

"I'm charging you double for this shit," he grumbles.

I grin. "I thought you lowered your price for the locals?"

"Yeah, well, you don't count. You should rename it."

"What to?" I hadn't thought of that. As creepy as it is, serial killer forest is what Charlotte and I call it, and I would like it to remain.

"*Think with His Dick Woods* sounds more fitting."

I huff a laugh, shaking my head. My brother grabs his car keys and heads into town, and I know I'll own fifty acres of trees by the end of the week.

34

CHARLOTTE TITAN

"Is that going to last in the weather?" My brother watches me from the porch as I push the pipe into the smaller one I have coming from the roof.

The sun's shining today, although the rain is still threatening. It always is, almost like a metaphor for my life.

"I hope so," I grit out as I force the two pieces together, smiling when I feel them seal. I'm trying to harvest the rainwater from the roof and put it in a small tank. I might as well, but now I just need to find a tank.

"Is Sutton coming back?"

I quickly turn to look at him, and my brow scrunches. Sutton's stayed with us almost every night for at least the last couple of weeks. Still in hiding, in my bed. He bought me a new one, so sick of the constant squeaks every time we moved. It made sense.

"At some point. He said he had to go and do a few things." I inhale a deep breath. The guilt at not telling Sutton everything continues to gnaw at me every day. I told him our names, but he hasn't connected any more dots. I need to tell him exactly who we are and why we're hiding, but I'm scared. Not of him knowing, I know he'd never turn us in to the authorities. But once I say it all out loud, it becomes real. It becomes a bigger burden, a bigger issue. The target on my head gets bigger. At the moment, no one knows. Preston and I are just small-town folk.

"I like having him around," he says softly.

I look at Preston as he sits on the porch in the sun. He's smiling, happy, relaxed, has more color in his cheeks than he ever has. He sleeps well, eats well, his studies are excellent. He's really thriving. He's never really had a strong male in his life, aside from Dad. Given that Dad hasn't been involved or around as much in the last few years, a big brother figure like Sutton is really good for him.

I smile right back. "I do too." Sutton and I haven't talked too much about what the future holds. At first, I thought he might be a bit of fun. A safe space for a while, and he was that. But now, my feelings have grown. I've completely fallen for him.

"I really like it here in Whispers..." Preston trails off, staring at me, and I stop what I'm doing to give him my full attention. "Do you think we could stay here? I've got awesome friends now. I've never had friends like this before."

I swallow. This town has wrapped us up; it really has become our home.

"I'd like to stay... but..." I shrug, because I don't know what the future holds. For any part of my life. I'm just taking each day as it comes.

His shoulders sag as he nods in understanding.

"I wonder what Sutton will think of this." I change the subject, looking at the rainwater collector I've built. It's very rustic, but it does the job. With any luck, Preston and I will always have fresh, clean water to use in addition to the water from inside that's supplied from the town.

"You can ask him. He's back." Preston grins, and I look up, seeing Sutton's truck pulling up the road toward the cottage. I can't help it. My smile is immediate too.

"Is that what you've been doing with the junk from the taxi place?" Sutton jumps out of his truck and strides over to me. There's no hesitation as he wraps his arms around me and pulls me tight, his lips hitting mine so quickly it's like he's starved. Every day is like this. During the week, he watches from his booth, brings us home, and spends the night. On the weekends, like today, he spends the day with us, helping around the cottage, hanging out with Preston, or reading a few of the library books we've brought home. He's taken a big interest in bees, which is comical, given his allergy. But it's nice he's found a subject he enjoys.

I reciprocate and hold him tight, because being without him lately is like I'm without oxygen. My need for survival is his touch, his kisses, and his attention. I loop my hands around his neck, and he lifts me from my feet, crushing me to his chest before lowering me back to the ground slowly.

"What do you think?" I ask him.

He watches me closely. "I think I want more of you, Tinker Bell..." he murmurs against my cheek so Preston can't hear. I swat him, gesturing to the pipes and bits, making him chuckle. "Just like everything you do, I think it's amazing. What is it?" He looks at my rudimental contraption, frowning in confusion.

"It's a rainwater collection system. Rain hits the roof, then flows down the slant and into the tubing here. I have a mesh layer that filters the leaves and heavy debris before the water flows along this pipe. At the end, I have some muslin cloth that filters it again."

"But then it just runs into the garden?" He looks perplexed.

"That's because I need to find a tank or some type of storage..."

"Then what will you do with the water?"

"Well, I'll probably need to test it to ensure that it's clean, but out here, there isn't a lot of pollution. So we could store it for a while. Water the garden in the hotter months, wash clothes with it, or use it in emergencies if the town water ever has issues."

He shakes his head in what seems like disbelief.

"I still don't know how you do all this stuff. You really need to take Tanner up on his offer."

I give him a smile but remain tight-lipped. His eyes flick to Preston, who's sitting, watching.

"Preston. I got something for you," he calls out before striding to his truck. Preston walks over, looking at me in question, and I shrug.

"What is it?" Preston asks.

"Electric bikes."

"*What?*" we both say in unison, eyes bugging.

"Well, Preston can't keep riding a pink bike around town. That's social suicide. And I was going to buy you a car, but I thought you might freak out over that, so I thought the electric bikes would go quicker and take less energy after a long day at work. They're good for the environment... Plus, I got myself one too so we can ride around here together," he lifts three brand-new big black bikes from the back.

I don't know much about bikes, but they look top of the line. The wheels are chunky, heavy duty, to make it easier to ride out here on the grass and dirt.

"Maybe you can charge them using your turbine?" He looks at me expectantly, and I stare, open-mouthed. He's right. I wouldn't have accepted a car. The fact that he even considered that astounds me. But it's the way he thought about the turbine charging it, the way he isn't remotely skeptical of the rainwater system, that he isn't looking at me like I'm some crazy chick here in a run-down cottage, making things with junk. He's being supportive and thoughtful with his generosity.

"No way!" Preston finally breaks free of his frozen state, in awe. As am I, but for two totally different reasons. I watch quietly as Preston slams into Sutton, hugging him, and shock soon gives way for Sutton as he pulls my little brother closer. I nearly melt.

Preston hasn't had anyone else in his corner except for me. There were a few kids at school he was friendly with, but once Mom died and I went to college, Maribel refused to take him to birthday parties or other social gatherings. Preston turned in on himself at that point. Becoming more introverted, burying his head in books, all while locked in his room. Now, as I see him hugging Sutton, I feel that Preston is stepping into his confidence. I haven't noticed it till now. Before Sutton, Preston and I were just going through the motions. The most important thing for me was survival.

"This is so cool." Preston grabs a bike that Sutton rolls over to him and jumps on, then starts riding all over the lawn haphazardly, giggling. "This is awesoooommmeeeeee!" he yells as his bike speeds past us again faster and takes off toward the forest.

"Be careful! Watch my apple tree!" I call out to him as Sutton laughs. I smile, watching him, weaving in and out among the trees. He knows the forest behind the cottage as well as I do. When we first arrived, we spent a lot of time outside.

"Thank you. You didn't have—"

"I know, baby," Sutton interrupts me softly, walking back toward me. "But it kills me when I can't bring you home after your shift. It hurts my heart that you walk or cycle every day. I need you home safe. Both of you. I need you home as fast as possible and warm in the winter. I need you to be able to get to me if I can't get to you." He swallows audibly, and anxiety of the unknown gnaws at my skin.

"Are you still going to be here in the winter?" I look up at him, my heart heavy. Winter isn't too far away. The days are getting shorter, the temperature cooler.

"I have no plans of leaving... Besides, Thanksgiving is coming up soon."

It isn't a yes, but it isn't a no. I don't push for more, purely because I know he doesn't have the answer. He might want to stay here, make a life here, but he'll be followed, hounded, and harassed by the media. What that means for me is my face plastered on websites, my name uncovered and alerting Maribel. All things I don't want.

His eyes flick to my rainwater collector, and he grins. "I like getting you things. You're so resourceful, it makes me want to match your energy." I watch him for a beat, catching the slight vulnerability sneaking through, like this is more than just a passing comment.

"You're resourceful too."

He looks at me like he doesn't believe me.

"You went to Whiteman's and talked yourself into being the face of their brand. You sneak in and out of that diner like an undercover FBI agent. You're learning new hiking skills, walking the back path and creating a trail..." I pause, watching something shift in his expression.

"You saw that, huh?" His grin is all mischief and quiet satisfaction.

He mentioned it once when he was here weeks ago, but I had forgotten about it until I went for a walk yesterday and noticed the yellow gravel trail, the way it blended effortlessly with the forest floor. It was intentional, careful... cute.

"I just want to come to you and you to me anytime we want. Our secret little passage. Our own yellow brick road."

My heart beats faster, suddenly very aware of the weight behind his words. "See. Resourceful...?"

He smiles like I just handed him something precious. "I own it."

The words come so fast, so effortlessly, like it's the most obvious thing in the world, but my brain can't process them.

I tilt my head. "Wait. What do you mean, you own it?"

"Well, after our chat in the forest, I got Sawyer to investigate. Turns out, the guy who owns all this was interested in selling. So... I made him a cash offer."

I blink a few times. He waits for my reaction, looking a little unsure.

"You bought it?" My voice is barely above a whisper.

"All of it. Most of serial killer forest, and your little cottage, too. So, you can keep your monthly lease payments. I don't want it."

At that, I think my heart actually stops before speeding up again. This isn't just a gesture. It's a declaration. I'm speechless.

"Oh, I also built something." He moves to the back of his truck, pulling out a white box as I stand, motionless, wondering what in the world is happening.

"A beehive?" Piecing together his words, I try to comprehend what I'm seeing.

"I'm putting hives at my new place, so I got an extra one without all the frames. For our call box in the trees..." His voice drops slightly as he places the box on the ground and then looks at me. He's searching for my reaction, for confirmation that I understand what he's saying.

I shake my head, perplexed. "But... you're allergic?"

"I am." He smiles.

"Sooo, why are you getting bees?"

"Because you love them and they remind you of your mom." My breath halts, tears blurring my eyes. "And not only are bees a big part of who you are and what you love, but they're also great for the environment."

My eyebrows rise at all this bee knowledge.

"Well, that's what the books tell me," he mumbles.

Biting my lip, I say nervously, "But you could get stung." It's highly likely it will happen.

"Worth it just to see you happy." The tenderness in his tone has butterflies swirling around my stomach.

I lift my hand and cup his cheek, looking deep into the eyes of the man who has embedded himself so deep into my heart and soul it disarms me.

"Sutton... I don't know what to say..." Because if I open my mouth, *"I love you"* might escape all on its own.

He grabs my hand from his jaw and slides it across to his lips, kissing my palm before lowering it, still holding on at our sides.

"I love seeing you build your life here, and I want to do that too. But I do need to know you're safe." He steps closer, enough that I feel his warmth. His other hand circles around my waist, resting on my lower back.

"And if I'm not?" I whisper.

His jaw tenses. "Then I'll do something about it." The weight of his words settles between us. Dangerous. Unwavering. A promise. "I have security, I have people, I have resources."

I shake my head, half a laugh escaping as I blink back

the burn behind my eyes. "You can't just fix everything by throwing money at it." I know Sutton is wealthy, but money isn't going to win this battle; it's what started it all in the first place.

His fingers brush my wrist, just barely. "No, but I can make sure you never have to face it alone."

I swallow roughly. "You don't know what you're taking on."

"No. But I know you're worth it. Just like those bee stings will be. As long as you're happy and with me."

My body warms as he releases my hand and I run my hands up his arms, all the way to circle his neck. Moving his other hand to my waist, he lifts me a little, holding me flush against him as I stand on tiptoes to place a kiss on his lips.

And just like that, my heart splits wide open for him. Sutton Silvers, the man I never saw coming, and the one I can't imagine ever letting go of.

"You look like the cat that got the canary this morning," Rochelle comments as I step back up to the counter, setting the coffeepot down. "Wouldn't have anything to do with that dashing movie star you've been spending time with?" She cocks an eyebrow, already knowing the answer.

"Movie star? I don't know any movie star, certainly not here in Whispers." I grin wide, and she laughs.

"Well, just be careful, darlin'. A man like that could sweep any woman off their feet."

I pause, my smile dimming. "I'm being careful."

"I know. I'm always here for you, sweetheart. The sheriff and me. You need anything, you come to us." Her look is pointed, and I nod, feeling like the world is slowly encasing me in a warm hug. First, Sutton and now, Rochelle. She's the closest to a mother figure I've had in a long time.

"Thank you, Rochelle. For everything." I give her my thanks often, but I really want her to understand that giving me this job, offering me extra food, looking out for me, it's all made such a difference.

She gives me a warm smile, and I know her door will always be open for me.

"Now, speaking of the sheriff, I need to go deliver him his lunch. That man can't make a sandwich if his life depended on it. You okay here on your own for half an hour?"

I glance around the diner, seeing it's pretty quiet. The cook went home already, and the other waitress is on her lunch break. The lunchtime rush is over, so I know I'll be fine. One person's finishing up their coffee at the counter, a few others just leaving. I look at Sutton's vacant booth. He'll turn up in the afternoon at some point.

"I'll be fine," I assure her.

She pats my arm and walks out the back with a delicious pastrami sandwich and a cookie for her husband. It's sweet that she still makes her husband lunch every day. I don't know their story, so I'm not sure if they grew up here or landed here some other way. They have no children, but the love they have for each other and this town is big enough to make everyone feel welcome.

As the back door closes behind her, I wipe down the counter and fill the coffeepots, then start to sort the trash into recyclables. It's not something Rochelle did before I arrived, but now, I separate them all, and she takes them to Williamstown for recycling, getting a nice little rebate that she can spend any way she wants.

The door chimes, bringing me out of my thoughts, and I turn with my smile, ready to greet customers. Only, my smile falters when I see who it is. The same group of men who took my bag. Subconsciously, my hand lifts to my face, the black eye they gave me now long gone.

"Hello, sugar." One of them looks at me hungrily before he gives me a wink, and along with his three friends, they slide into a booth at the front of the diner.

I swallow, my stomach twisting in knots. I'm not often at the diner alone, but on the few occasions I have been, it's been quiet and non-eventful. I already know that today is going to be different. Shivers run up my spine as I grab a few menus, and rolling my shoulders back, I walk over. The smell hits me instantly. It's like they came straight from a bar. The strong stench of liquor, and not the good kind, settles around them.

"After some lunch today?" I place the menus on the table in front of them. Then the other customer finishes up his coffee. I watch helplessly as the older man walks out, leaving me here, all alone, with these four men.

I don't have a lot of experience with unruly men. I never rode the subway, never really walked the streets outside of the Upper East Side, and even then, I always had a body-guard. We flew private and had town cars. It wasn't until Mom died and I went to college that I had more freedom while living on campus, but instead of going out dancing on weekends or shopping with friends, I was back in New York, trying to sneak into our family home to get to Preston.

"I could eat," one of them answers as he licks his lips, his legs spread wide, taking up most of the space around him. Sitting like a king holding court, he's the ringleader of this crew, as the others merely sneer and smirk.

"Specials today are the vegetable soup, a beef pot roast and, of course, Rochelle's famous chicken pie." I list off the specials like I do for every other customer. Even though my heart is hammering in my chest, the thud of it loud in my ears.

"Speaking of, where's Rochelle?" He looks behind me, his eyes darting around the diner.

"She's busy." I don't want to tell him that she isn't here. That I'm on my own. But they sit, watching me for a moment, hearing nothing. No pots banging in the back, no people talking. He knows no one else is here.

"Looks like your eye healed just fine..." His words hang in the air. The other guys look at me, and my jaw tightens.

"So what would you like?" I raise my pen and notepad again, keeping the conversation on track. The sooner they eat, the sooner they go.

"Hmmm, how 'bout you tell me what you like." His tongue dashes out to lick his bottom lip again before his hand shoots out and grabs my thigh. Jolting, I slap his hand away.

"Don't touch me," I spit out, fear almost consuming me.

His hand immediately comes back, sliding up my leg and landing on my ass. I freeze for a moment before I slap him away again.

"I said, *don't* touch me!" My voice is a mix of anger and fear. I'm terrified. With shaking hands, I try to remain confident. But right now, I'm stuck. I look out the window at the sleepy small-town Main Street, watching for someone I might know to walk past, but there's no one.

"Aw, look boys, she doesn't like everyone touching her, just the guy who usually sits in the back," he mocks me, and his friends laugh.

"Is he your boyfriend or something?" one of his friends asks.

"If you're not ordering, then I think you should leave." I try to sound professional, yet stern. I'm not sure what

Rochelle will think of me turning away paying customers; I'd hate to ruin things for her here by sending them away, but I'm in survival mode now.

"You're cute when you're angry," the leader of the group says as they all look at me like I'm their lunch. I take a deep breath, my head spinning with how to get myself out of this mess.

"You need to leave," I grit out as his hand comes back to my leg, and I try to step away, out of his reach.

"Are *you* hungry, sugar? Because I sure as hell have something for you to eat." He grabs his crotch, and his friends laugh some more. Cringing, I swallow roughly as he stands, towering over me, his hand grabbing my upper arm, just as I hear the familiar squeak of the back door opening.

Then all hell breaks loose, and my quiet, hidden life unravels.

35

SUTTON

"What's it like today?" My words sound clear, my face feeling a little swollen but nothing like previously.

"It's actually looking great." Hudson checks me over before throwing a cool pack my way. I did my immunotherapy in the morning this time, giving me plenty of time to recover so I can still make it to the diner before Charlotte's shift ends.

"That's good, right?" I put the cool pad against my lips.

"Well, it means it's working. Another few doses, and your allergy may be nearly nonexistent. You will always have to be careful, though."

"Shit, so I'm cured?" Excitement takes over my face. That would mean I could get the beehives going for Charlotte.

"With each treatment, you're getting better and better. Looking at you now, I can't even really tell that you have an allergy. So your histamine reaction has reduced rapidly."

"Good. I want to start building the hives soon."

Hudson quirks an eyebrow at me. "Soooo Nikki? Your

brother tells me you're never home anymore. Hiding out with her, I hear?"

I would beam if I could, but my lips feel too tight. It's been weeks now of being with her. I'm sure most of the town suspects that we're together, but only my closest friends really know the truth. Any and all thoughts I may have had about getting her out of my system are null and void. She's in my system. Deeply embedded. I crave her daily. Can't function without seeing her. Every afternoon, I'm at the diner, pretending to help Preston with his homework before I drive them home. I usually grab us dinner, spend the night with them, Preston going to bed, and I get to have her all to myself. That's my favorite part of my day. It's now our routine, and I don't ever want it to change.

"Yeah," I say with a smile.

"That's it? Yeah? Is Mr. Sutton Silvers, international movie star, billionaire bachelor, the man every woman wants in her bed, lost for words?" He looks at me like I've grown a second head.

At that, how I really feel tumbles from my lips. "What do you want from me? You want me to tell you that she's fucking amazing? That she's smart as well as beautiful? That I could listen to her from sunup to sundown? That I could sit at that fucking diner all day, every day, just watching her?"

"You already do that. From what I hear, Rochelle does a roaring trade on the chicken pies lately, all because you order them for lunch and dinner most nights."

"Well, they are delicious." *So is my girl*, I think, keeping that tidbit to myself.

"What are you going to do about it all, then? I mean, we all thought you would be here for a few weeks, and so far, it's been months. You're building a property here, but I thought that would just be for a yearly holiday visit. Are you, what? Planning on moving here permanently?"

Clearing my throat, I bypass his question with a simpler one of my own. "I gotta get to the diner. Want to join me?" I stand, looking at the clock, not wanting to be late.

He rolls his eyes at my distraction but relents. "Yeah, why the hell not. I need a break."

We walk out of his office, straight to my truck, settling in for the five-minute drive to the diner. Taking a breath, I decide to be honest with Hudson. I don't need to hide my intentions from him.

"I've been pushing Griffin to finish the house in record time. I want to be in it. I want her to be in it with me," I tell my friend, keeping my eyes on the road, but I can feel him looking at me in complete fascination.

"That's serious, Sutton."

"I know it is. I think she's it. I think she's the one." I feel vulnerable, but I know it deep in my core, and I have since the moment I first laid eyes on her. People talk about love at first sight. I always thought it was bullshit. But now, I know differently.

"This is Whispers, not Vegas. You can't just meet a girl and get married in a matter of months."

"I didn't say marriage..." Although, now that thought is in my brain, it's starting to grow legs.

"Yeah, alright, just be careful. Harvey is starting to become good friends with James at school, and the kid doesn't need some high-profile celebrity coming in and out of his life like a yo-yo."

I smile, my chest warming at the fact that Preston's friends group is growing. He's a kid, and running about with his friends is what kids do. Ever since he slept over, Harvey, Kevin, and Preston are a formidable trio. It's good to see.

As what he says sinks in, though, I get a bit irritated. "Why does everyone think I'm just going to pack up and go back to LA?" Pulling up outside the back door of the diner, I turn off the truck, moving in my seat to look at my best friend.

"Well, that's where you live. That's the lifestyle you lead. That's where your work is..." Hudson makes his point.

Sure, I've always been known as a bit of a joker. Led the playboy lifestyle for years, traveled with no ties and no responsibilities. But I'm different now. This life I've started to cultivate here in Whispers, it feels like it's where I'm meant to be.

"Not anymore," I tell him seriously, and his eyes narrow.

"What do you mean, not anymore?"

"I think that part of life is closing for me."

His shock is palpable as his head rears back. "What? No more movies?"

"Never say never. If the right one came along, I would consider it. But I don't want the media, the nightclubs, the models, the travel. I'm older. I've reached all my goals. I want something new. I want to settle here. I can still work periodically if I want to, but I like the lifestyle here. I like that people leave me alone, and I'm even starting to enjoy the peace of the forest."

Hudson laughs. "Sutton Silvers in nature... you really have done a complete turn."

"So what, Sawyer can move here and love it, but I can't?" With a huff, I jump out of the truck, and Hudson follows me.

"That's not what I'm saying—"

"What are you saying?" I cut him off as I push through

the back door, feeling agitated and wanting nothing more than to see my girl. Looking up and around, I smile when I spot her. But then my vision turns red.

"What the fuck."

A man has his hand on her, and the complete terror in her eyes is noticeable from across the diner.

"What? Oh, shit." Hudson tries to grab me, but I'm already on the move. I don't stop as I stride over, Charlotte stepping away just as I reach her. I have tunnel vision as I grab the guy's collar and yank him up off his feet. He's tall like me, but overweight, and by the smell of him, he drinks too much. But I don't care as I pull back my fist, launching it into his face as his three friends jump up to his defense. I haven't been in a fistfight in years. But Hudson knows I'm quick to anger in these kinds of circumstances, and as kids, Sawyer and I were always fighting with kids at school or from the neighborhood. I grew up tough and that toughness hasn't left me.

"You're going to regret fucking touching her," I spit out, knowing exactly who these guys are.

"Who the fuck are you?" he sneers through a bloody lip.

"I'm her boyfriend, asshole." I throw another punch, straight into his jaw.

"That's for breaking her bee clip," I tell him with a growl.

"Her what?" He rolls around on the ground, trying to stand, and I clench my fists, waiting for him before I hit him again.

"That's for mugging her," I bite out as he staggers back from another punch.

Shit really hits the fan as the other three men try to pull me back, one even taking a swing that I dodge. Hudson springs into action, throwing down with one of his friends beside me and shoving back another. The asshole beneath me lunges while I'm distracted, his punch connecting with my cheek and sending stars through my vision for a few seconds.

I hear the front door open, relief momentarily taking over my rage as Tanner strides across the diner to us. He doesn't have to even ask what's happening; his eyes take in the scene of four strangers who now look like they've been through the ringer, Charlotte wide-eyed and standing at a distance, and both me and Hudson seething.

With Tanner's hulking form approaching, Hudson pushes the other guy off him, one who still hasn't caught wind of there being another strong man in their midst, until he collides with the booth, eyes snapping to me and my friends standing like a brick wall before all four of them.

"She isn't worth the hassle." The asshole I punched spits blood on the floor.

"Yeah, let's get the fuck out of here," another says, his cheek and nose red from where Hudson must've hit him.

Seeing that they're now somewhat outnumbered in size and brawn, the guys start to step away, back toward the front door.

But they don't leave soon enough.

"Why do you look so familiar...?" one of the guys says, looking at me like he just won the jackpot. He probably has; I heard the media is now offering well over half a million for a photo or a sighting. "Hey, you're that movie star everyone is looking for!"

The four of them pause at the door, all with matching shit-eating grins.

"No one knows where you are, do they?" the asshole who touched Charlotte says as he smiles at me with his split lip and cut eye. My jaw tics, and I step forward to punch him again, when Charlotte grabs me.

"Sutton." Her voice sounds like a sweet melody. Calming me almost instantly. And stopping me in my tracks.

"Well, well, well... Buckle up, because they're all going to know in about five minutes," he says with a sickening laugh, and all four walk out, taking my secret haven with them.

36

CHARLOTTE

My eyes are wide. I've never seen a real fistfight before. Thank God Preston is still in school.

Spinning around, Sutton, wide-eyed, steps closer, his breathing hard. From protecting me.

"You alright? Are you hurt?" His hands land on my shoulders, hot, firm, scanning me for injuries. His jaw might be tight, but his fingers are careful, as if confirming I'm whole will bring him some peace. I swallow roughly as I look at his swelling eye, split lip, and raw knuckles.

"Shouldn't I be asking you that question?" I hate how shaky I sound.

"I don't give a shit how I am. I need to know you're okay, baby," his tone edging on desperation.

All I can do is nod before exhaling. "I'm okay."

He doesn't look like he believes me, but before he can say anything else, the door chimes as Tanner strides back inside.

"They're gone." Dragging his fingers through his hair, Tanner huffs a breath. "I called Sawyer and the sheriff."

Hudson grumbles. "What assholes."

I glance at the local doctor, who's disheveled, his shirt ruffled, his cheek slightly bruised, looking as rattled as I feel. My body trembles from the inside out as I try to regulate my breathing. One moment, fear. The next, chaos. A full-on fight. Sutton throwing punches like his life depended on it.

Tanner's gaze flicks between us all. "What happened?"

"He was touching Nikki. I lost it," Sutton murmurs.

"He touched you?" Tanner's voice sharpens, focus snapping to me.

I pull myself together, piecing my words into place. "Rochelle's with the sheriff, so I was alone. They walked in, started getting... suggestive. Then he touched me. I pushed him off, told them to leave, but he did it again, and then..." Sutton was there.

Sutton's hand slides around my waist, pulling me closer, rubbing my lower back slowly, grounding me, telling me I'm safe now. I want to believe him, but I'm too shaken up to think straight.

Only a few minutes later, Rochelle barrels through the back door, the sheriff at her heels.

"What's going on?" she rushes out, eyes wide and worried.

We rehash everything as Rochelle closes the diner for the afternoon, locking the doors being the first thing she does.

"Those boys are good for nothing... I should've kicked them out weeks ago. I could tell they were bad news. I can't believe they were the ones who mugged you." She shakes her head. When I admitted that, I could tell she was hurt I didn't tell her sooner. "We need ice." Her gaze is full of concern before disappearing into the kitchen as the sheriff stares at us all with a critical eye.

I wring my hands. They won't stop shaking.

"Come here." Sutton's voice is soft, feeling like a safe space. I don't hesitate. I go to him, slamming into his chest as he pulls me tightly to him.

"I'm fine, really. Just trying to calm down," I whisper, even though my bones still feel like they're rattling inside me.

"I know." His grip is steady, warm, rubbing long strokes up and down my back. "I'm sorry you had to deal with that. I'm sorry he touched you, and I'm sorry there was a scuffle. But when he touched you, all I saw was red."

I lift his hand, seeing it bruised, the torn skin raw across his knuckles.

"When capillaries heal, they undergo a process called angiogenesis, where new blood vessels form to replace damaged ones." The words fall out unconsciously, my brain trying to find order in the mess of everything.

"There she is." Sutton's small, swollen smile is one of pure adoration, his lips pressing against my temple.

Looking up at him, my brow pinches, hating that it's come to this. "He's going to tell the media about you."

"He will." Sutton expression is unreadable.

"What will we do?" I already know the answer. The second the news spreads, everything changes for us. Sutton pulls me against him tighter, and I want to bury my head in his chest and ignore it all.

Sutton's about to answer me when Sawyer bursts in, suit open, tie askew, like he's just run a marathon. "I came as soon as I could. What the hell happened?"

"We're outed." Sutton stands tall, all eyes on us. I'm shaking, my stomach clenching, and I wonder if I need to dash to the bathroom.

I know what I have to do. I have to let him go. But I don't want to. Panic climbs through my veins, threatening to strangle me as I glance at the wall clock. School is almost out. Can I get Preston, dash home for my go-bag, and then disappear before morning?

Sutton must hear me thinking, his hand cupping my cheek so my eyes meet his.

"Oh no. You don't get to look at me like that." His voice is rough, low, unwavering, his grip on my waist tightening to keep me from running away, and the one on my cheek, gentle yet possessive.

"Like what?" I swallow my denial, my survival instincts pinging.

"Like you're leaving me. You don't get to do that." He's firm. I frown, trying to understand what he's saying.

"Do what?"

Something in his eyes changes as he looks into mine. "You don't get to make me fall in love with you and then skip town."

Silence slams into the diner like a freight train, and my heart stops before restarting with new life. I wonder briefly if I'm going to faint as I look up at him, his eyes boring into mine.

"Shit," Hudson mutters.

Sawyer stares, open-mouthed, at his brother.

But Sutton's gaze is unyielding.

And me? I can't move. I can't speak. I'm stuck in shock. He hasn't let me go. I want to tell him that I love him too. That I feel the same. But I'm so damn scared.

Rochelle clears her throat, breaking the moment. Sutton's attention finally shifts, his hand dropping from my cheek and taking my hand.

"Sorry, Rochelle. I'll pay for cleanup, security, whatever you need once the story breaks." His voice is businesslike now, composed, like he's flipping a switch. "Tanner, the brand launch might take a hit. Hudson, I hate that you got dragged into this. You've all been incredibly kind, and I appreciate you keeping my identity hidden. I'm sorry for today and for whatever comes next."

He squeezes my hand, and bile rises in my throat.

Rochelle frowns. "Don't go apologizing for something that isn't your fault."

"The brand launch will be fine. We have contingency plans." Tanner waves it off, unaffected.

"You can hide at home," Sawyer offers. "Both of you." His gaze flicks to me, sincerity in his tone.

I'm overwhelmed by how fiercely this town protects him. Protects me. Protects us.

"I can't do that to you and Annabelle and the boys," Sutton says. "We both know Whispers will be flooded by morning. Cameras, reporters, there will be no escaping it."

"I'll get extra men, if needed," the sheriff says.

"You'll need it." Sutton doesn't sound relieved.

"We also need to be ready in case those men press charges," the sheriff adds, looking at him pointedly.

Sutton nods. "Sawyer will know where to contact me."

"Where will you go?" Sawyer asks.

Sutton exhales, thoughtful. "There's only one place that can hide us a little longer, just a week or so, until we figure out our next steps."

I frown, biting the inside of my lip. "What does that mean?"

Sutton's eyes lock on mine once more, the intensity there so unlike him. This man has my back. "Do you trust me, Tinker Bell?"

"With my life," I admit easily, because I do. His eyes soften, and a small smile pulls at his lips.

I have a feeling things are about to get crazier.

WE GOT PRESTON FROM SCHOOL, and Sutton drove us straight to the cottage, where we frantically packed enough to last a week before locking the place up tight. There was an old sign warning trespassers that Sutton put up on the front fence, the gate that has mostly remained open for us now firmly locked as well, not to mention, the shutters on every window closed. In this dreary weather, the cottage looks about as inviting as a horror movie.

Preston had questions, and I answered them all truthfully, but now, we sit in Sawyer's kitchen in thick silence. Annabelle watches us, concern flickering in her eyes as Sutton shoves clothes into a bag, his movements clipped, restless.

Sawyer grips a glass of whiskey, leaning against the counter. "Pack light. You'll be back."

Clinging to the words, I try to believe them. Whispers is the first place that's felt like home since Mom passed. But if I have to leave, I will.

"I know." Sutton's tone is flat, forced, his body tense as he yanks the zipper closed.

I reach out, my fingers wrapping around his hand. He's warm. Strong. Trembling.

"It's okay. We're okay."

His breath shudders as he turns, pulling me close, holding on like he's trying to absorb the moment.

"I'm so damn sorry." His whisper rumbles against my hair, thick with something unspoken, heavy.

I squeeze him tighter. Fighting fate feels impossible.

"The fairy tale had to end sometime."

His hold tightens. "Our fairy tale is everlasting. We'll get through this. I told you I will keep you hidden, and that's exactly what I will do."

I have to believe him. I have no other option. The last bus left Whispers an hour ago. By morning, the media will be at our doorstep.

As he's pressing a kiss to my head, Sutton's phone rings. He stiffens.

"Fuck. It's Bobby." His gaze flicks to me, then to Sawyer, before he answers it on speakerphone.

"Bobby." His greeting is blank.

"So... how's Whispers, Sutton?"

I inhale sharply, and Sutton's jaw tics.

"I don't know what you're talking about."

Grabbing his own phone from his pocket, Sawyer starts texting madly. Panic coils in my chest, twisting tighter and tighter.

"Paps got a tip-off that you're playing happy family in Whispers." Bobby's tone is smug. "You and a woman. And a young boy. Rumors are swirling that you have a secret kid."

My chest locks up as my eyes fly to Preston. This is too much for him, too adult, too unfair. But I don't hide it from him. I reach for his hand, holding it gently. None of this would've happened if I hadn't fallen for a man I never should've known.

"Fuck." Sutton scrubs his hand over his face.

"Media are already on the way. I'm jumping in a jet now. I should be there in three or four hours. About time you come out of hiding anyway. Although if the kid is fucking yours, we have a problem." Bobby laughs, like this is some game he's about to win.

"What kind of problem?" Sutton glances at Preston, nothing but love and protectiveness in his gaze.

"You're the king of women in LA. They love you because

they think you're available. A secret wife and kid tucked away in some backwards town? It's bad for business."

Sutton's nostrils flare, his voice taking on a dark edge. "Is my life a fucking joke to you, Bobby?"

"Shit. He's your love child, isn't he?" He snickers, amusement dripping from every syllable. "The media are going to have a field day."

The way he says it, like Sutton's life is nothing but a brand to be managed, I hate him for it.

And before Sutton can reply, he's saying, "My wheels are up. See you soon."

The line cuts dead. Sutton slams his phone down, running his hands through his hair, muttering curses. I move my gaze to Preston, who's looking solemn.

"We'll be alright," I try to reassure him, and he nods, but I can see that he's scared.

"If we get found, Maribel will…" he trails off.

"I know." I know what's on the line here. Sutton's appearance might make headline news, but our lives will be ruined forever.

"I need you to trust me, little man." Sutton walks over and puts his hand on Preston's shoulder, pulling him tight. When Preston crashes into his chest and holds him like he's his lifeline, I almost sob. My emotions are a wreck today.

Sawyer steps in, always solutions-first, steady as hell. "Tanner's jet is fueling. The pilot is waiting for you. Where do you need to go?"

Sutton exhales, his fingers flexing. "France."

I blink, my eyes snapping to his. "France?"

"I have friends." He watches me, seeing my panic. "They'll keep us safe."

"But I—" My heart pounds faster. "I don't have our passports."

"It'll be fine."

I frown. *Fine?*

"There's nowhere you can go without being spotted," Sawyer warns.

Annabelle squeezes my hand over the counter, her gaze soft but unwavering, trying to anchor me, woman to woman.

"There's one place..." Sutton mutters.

Sawyer goes pale.

"That's a really bad idea." His voice drops, controlled but deadly serious. "And as your legal representative, I don't want to know anything about it."

Sutton doesn't seem affected. "I need to get Charlotte and Preston away. We just need a bit more time to sort things out."

"Charlotte and Preston?" Sawyer's expression tightens, looking at me as realization clicks into place of our real names.

"I'll fill you in later. Right now, we need to go," Sutton says, and I offer Sawyer an empathetic smile.

"I still don't think France is a good idea," Sawyer mutters with a shake of his head.

"If the mob can't keep us hidden... then we have no hope," Sutton tells his brother. Unshaken. Decided.

The air thickens as my stomach falls to my feet.

Did he just say the mob?

37

SUTTON

My chest feels tight as I take the love of my life and her brother into what can only be described as an illegally funded paradise.

"Are we safe here?" she asks, her nerves lingering at the surface.

Charlotte and Preston are wide-eyed, looking out the window as the lavender-covered fields of Provence filter past. I made the call last night to Hugo, an acquaintance whom I signed some limited-edition merchandise for to give his nephew a couple of years ago. He then flew me out to do an exclusive movie premiere and a meet-and-greet at his casino here in the South of France. He always said he owed me a favor. I never thought much of it, but this is me collecting.

"They owe me," I tell her quietly.

She looks at me curiously. "Who owes you?"

"Dragonfly."

"Who's Dragonfly?" she presses, understandably. I'm just not sure how much to tell her right now. I want her to feel relaxed, and it's a toss-up if any more information will help or hinder that.

The driver, who has remained silent all this time, looks at me through the car mirror, and I swallow.

"Just some people who run a casino here." I keep my answer vague as the driver looks at me again, with a quirked eyebrow this time.

"Are they safe? I mean, are they legal?" Charlotte whispers to me, and if it wasn't such a dire situation, it would be comical. Because no, they're not.

"They're safe for us. That's what we need. We just need to buy us some time, figure out our next steps, and keep the two of you hidden."

"But what are they into? We just came into the country without showing our passport..." She's smart; her mind must be spinning about all of this.

"Best you don't know, Tinker Bell. But rest assured, there's probably nowhere safer for us to be." My hand hasn't left hers. From the moment we fled Sawyer's house in the darkness of a Whispers evening, we've been on the go. Boarding Tanner's plane, which took us to Portugal, where we switched to another private jet. Anyone would think I'm a fucking criminal mastermind on the run, not a global movie star just trying to get a little peace.

The car slows as we enter a gated compound, and we drive around manicured gardens until we pull up and stop right at the front door where Hugo Moreau, head of the French mafia, commonly known as Dragonfly, stands, his men at his sides, making him look like the mobster he is.

"Hollywood. Good to see you." He greets me by the nickname I hate, offering me his hand as I step out of his car. I don't correct him. He's a dangerous man; he can call me whatever the fuck he wants. I'm at his mercy now. He could ask me for anything, and I would have to say yes. But Charlotte's security is my number one priority. I'd do anything for her.

"Hugo." I shake his hand before ensuring Charlotte and Preston are by my side. Hugo's gaze drops to her, his head tilting with interest, and my jaw tightens.

"Thank you for offering your home," I say to bring his attention back to me, and his gaze slowly drifts to meet mine. He gives me a smile, but it's chilling. I hope I haven't made a mistake by coming here.

"I owe you. And I always honor my word." He nods. "Besides, it's not every day that my nephew's favorite movie star spends a week at my compound."

"Is he here?" I ask, trying to work out exactly who's here and who knows I am.

He shrugs. "I might fly Bean in at the end of the week to get a photo." He loves his nephew. It's the only part of him that shows any kind of emotion. Hugo Moreau is all business, hotheaded, and completely deadly.

"Maybe your son here would like a little friend?" Hugo looks at Preston, and I remain silent, not correcting him.

"*Tu aimerais avoir un petit ami pour jouer?*" he says to Preston, and I have no idea what he just said, but Preston offers a small smile.

"*Peut-être...*" Preston mumbles, and my eyebrows rise.

"*Merci de nous avoir accueillis chez vous.*"

I try to tame my smile when Charlotte speaks. I should've known they would know another language.

"You're welcome. Stay the week. I hear the media are troublesome in America. We don't have that issue here. Brigitte will manage your stay. *Au revoir.*"

Hugo nods toward a woman to his side, before slapping my shoulder and moving past us, getting in the same car that brought us here and he and his men drive away. As he does, my shoulders lower a little. There's security all around, the front gate is locked with a guard house, and the entire property is surrounded by large fencing, but the gardens are extensive.

"This way…" Brigitte says in poor English as another few guys grab our bags like we're staying in some hotel.

"Any other language you speak?" I murmur to Charlotte as we walk, my smile small, the stress of the past twenty-four hours slowly leaving me.

"A few." She looks up at me, grinning playfully as we walk inside and are shown around.

The place is magnificent. We're in the middle of nowhere, the nearest neighbor not even visible. Our bags are whisked away as Brigitte, who I assume is the house-keeper, takes us on a tour. Partway through, Charlotte speaks French to her, and she seems relieved. I guess I'm now the only one among us who has absolutely no idea what they're talking about.

"Our rooms are this way," Charlotte whispers as we walk down a hall to the far side of the compound. "We have this entire wing to ourselves."

My eyes feast on the space. High ceilings, luxurious furnishings, French doors leading out to a private pool and gardens. It doesn't feel as homey as our cottage, but it's beautiful.

"*Merci.*" Charlotte nods to Brigitte, who walks out, shutting the doors on us, and we all can finally breathe.

"You alright, buddy?"

Preston looks tired, it's been a hell of a day.

"I'm okay." He nods sleepily.

"Everything will be okay, Preston. We're safe," Charlotte says, but his face doesn't change. His expression is remorseful, with a healthy dose of fear.

"It's all my fault."

I frown at that. "None of it is your fault," I tell him adamantly, because if anyone is to blame, it's me. I'm the one the media are after. I'm the one who couldn't stay away from her, even though I know she can't go public. "Come here." Taking a seat on the large sofa, I pull him down next to me.

"Why do you think any of this is your fault?" Charlotte's concern creeps into her voice as we both look at her brother.

"Because if it wasn't for me, we wouldn't need to hide. You could've left me. You could've had a life where you didn't have to run." His glossy eyes stare straight ahead, not looking at his sister, who swoops down on her knees, right in front of where Preston sits. She grabs his hands in hers and forces him to meet her gaze.

"I would never leave you. I would never leave you there with her. Hiding here is better than what you had."

"But none of this would've happened if it wasn't for me…"

"You're right," I tell him, and Charlotte's eyes widen at me in disbelief.

"None of this would've happened. Thanks to you, I've met the love of my life. I have a cool younger brother and an amazing new home in Whispers. Thanks, Preston. Without you, I wouldn't have any of the good things in my life that I have now."

Charlotte's gaze melts, a tear trailing down her cheek that she quickly brushes away.

"You mean that?" Preston looks up at me, his eyes searching mine.

"Yeah. I mean all of it. I can't wait to hang out more, take you to ball games or museums or whatever you enjoy." I hold his gaze, and before I know what's happening, he slams into me. Charlotte's hand covers her mouth as more emotion takes over her face, and I hug her brother tight. "I always wanted a little brother," I tell him quietly. "I'm happy it gets to be you."

"Thanks, Sutton," he whispers against me.

My chest feels a little wet so I just hold him for a moment before I release him and we both wipe our eyes.

"Why don't you go and check out the bedrooms. You can take first pick," Charlotte tells him, and he gives her a smile before jumping up to go explore.

I take a deep breath, releasing it slowly, my eyes still blurry with tears. "That got heavy quickly."

"I had no idea he felt like that." She sits next to me, and I pull her to my chest.

"He's a pretty smart kid. Takes after you in that regard."

"He also got my inability to dance, my total incoordination at anything remotely rhythmic."

I grin, because she moves just fine on me; the rest doesn't matter.

Lightening the mood, I ask what I've been curious about since we stepped into this house. "So, what other languages do you speak?"

"Italian, a little German. We traveled a lot as kids. Mom wanted us to learn the cultures and languages of the places we traveled. She believed understanding a place meant understanding its people. It all stopped when she died, though."

"The only language I speak is superhero." I huff out a half laugh, a bit embarrassed. I've been everywhere—Paris, Tokyo, Rome—but I never really belonged. Never immersed myself in another culture.

Her lips curve. "Well, that's globally recognized. You may not speak another language fluently, but your language touches millions of people, Sutton. No matter the country, your movies filter into lives, both young and old."

I swallow past a sudden lump in my throat.

"Never underestimate your abilities."

My chest pulses. Even after everything I've put her through, she empowers me.

"I've never really thought about it like that."

I turn her words over in my mind, letting them settle. I've jumped from movie set to movie set, doing what Bobby told me, attending interviews, taking meetings, shaking hands, signing contracts. Living in a home Bobby picked. Driven in a car Bobby organized. Eating meals my trainer approved. Wearing the clothes my stylist chose.

"Bobby handled everything." I exhale, my fingers flexing. "I just did what was asked, never thinking about my impact, never thinking about... me."

She watches me quietly. "Your life moved pretty fast."

"Until I came to Whispers." I meet her gaze, the weight of the last twenty-four hours pressing into me.

"Until I finally put the brakes on." Not just on my career, but on everything. For the first time, I realize how little control I've had over my own life. For the first time, I feel what it's like to make my own choices and what it's like to fight for them. And in the rush of running away, hiding, protecting, falling, something inside me clicked into place.

I've spent my entire life playing roles, fitting into a mold someone else designed and moving at a schedule someone else managed.

But now? Now, I know what was missing.

The missing piece was me.

38

CHARLOTTE

I walk into the bedroom after checking on Preston, who's now out like a light, tucked into bed in the room next door.

"Is he alright?" Sutton walks out from the adjoining bathroom with nothing but a towel wrapped around his waist. The vision of him never gets old, and I smile as I think about the first time I saw his naked torso, wet at my cottage after we got stuck in the rain. That feels like a lifetime ago.

"My eyes are up here, Tinker Bell," he murmurs as his fingers touch my chin and he lifts my gaze to his.

"I just like looking at all of you." I grin as he leans down and kisses me.

"I want to do wicked, wicked things to you when you look at me like that." His voice sounds like he's parched, husky as he speaks against my lips.

"Like what?" I tease as I place my hand on his naked chest, running it down his body slowly, until I reach the roll of towel at his waist.

"Things that I can't say or do because the room is probably bugged." My smile disappears, and my hands still.

"What?" I clearly don't live in the real world. That thought didn't even enter my mind.

"We're at one of the Dragonfly compounds. They aren't going to just let a global movie star stay here without ensuring they have some type of collateral on me that they can use if I see or hear something I shouldn't."

I gulp, my heart now racing. It all sounds like one of his movies, but this is actually my life right now.

Stepping out of his hold, I start looking around, my eyes taking in every inch of the room.

"What are you doing?"

"Nothing." I wave him off.

He laughs, clearly aware of exactly what I'm up to, but indulging me.

I spot a piece of artwork on one side of the room. Looking at it, the frame is a little thicker than what I would ordinarily see at any of the museums or art galleries I've visited, and I know I've found a camera. I spot Sutton's jacket on the nearby chair and grab it.

"I'm just going to hang your jacket so it doesn't crumple," I say loudly, lifting the jacket and placing it over the frame. As I get close, spotting the camera lens, my assumption is proven correct. It's barely visible, but on the angle, it's obvious.

"You're a freak of nature..." Sutton murmurs through a chuckle, grinning brightly at me.

Giving him a wink, my eyes go to the lamp near the bed next, and I walk over to it. I look inside, and sure enough, I find a small mic, the size of my pinky nail. Grabbing it out, I look at him and place my finger against my lips, asking him to be quiet before I take it to the bathroom and flush it down the toilet.

He raises his eyebrow at me. "They probably aren't going to be happy about any of that."

"Probably not. I assume Brigitte will replace it all tomorrow anyway, but at least we have tonight?" I move back toward him, resuming my adoration of his body.

"Really, where the hell did you come from?" He looks at me in awe, head shaking.

I shrug innocently. "I told you. Manhattan."

He barks a laugh before he grabs my waist, pulling me to him. Trailing his fingers down my torso, he teases at the hem of my shirt. Slow, deliberate, like he's savoring every second.

"I'm going to take my time with you tonight." His voice is low, rich with promise, and my breath hitches as he lifts my shirt, slipping it up and over my head. My hair tumbles around my bare shoulders, and I feel the warmth of his gaze fixed on me.

With my stomach fluttering, his fingers brush over the satin of my bra, just barely, and the sensation sends a shiver racing down my spine. I watch his throat work on a swallow, his mouth parting slightly, like he's trying to resist the urge to taste every inch of me.

"That's the one thing we both don't have..." My voice is quieter now. We both know this stolen time won't last.

The moment that whiskey commercial goes live, Whispers will be swarmed with media. He'll have to step into the light, and I'll have to disappear into the shadows. He's the man the world needs to see, and I'm the woman who wants to hide from it all. Like Romeo and Juliet, we're destined to fall, yet unable to stay away from each other.

"But we do have tonight," he says tenderly.

As he unbuttons my jeans, I grip his shoulders, steadying myself, and he slides them down, his knuckles grazing my skin, leaving fire in their wake. I step out of them, standing before him in my matching set, relishing how his gaze darkens, devouring me. I swear it feels like every inch of my body is burning under the weight of it.

He exhales sharply. "We better make it count."

I rise onto my tiptoes, cupping his face, pulling him to me, no hesitation, no doubt. I feel the second his restraint shatters. His mouth crashes onto mine, and his hands grip under my thighs, lifting me effortlessly. I gasp against his lips as my arms wrap around his neck as he steps us over to the bed.

"Sutton!" I squeal as he throws me onto the mattress, quickly chasing me.

"Yes, Charlotte?" I feel his smile on my neck as he kisses across my shoulders. His hands are already on my waist, pulling at my underwear, and he sits up, sliding them down my legs in one swoop.

"I love you," I whisper.

He stalls, his face in complete shock. My heart is thudding, loud in the silence of the room as I wait. He declared his love for me publicly at the diner just yesterday and has reiterated it since. Now, as my words sit between us, I'm not sure what he thinks.

"Say that again." He looks almost unsure, like perhaps he didn't hear me right.

I smile. "I love you, Sutton." I'm cautious, saying them slowly, ensuring he understands. His hand drops to my bare leg, and he smooths it up to my thigh.

"Again," he says huskily.

I giggle, then I snort, and his smile widens.

"I love you."

"Mmm. Again."

"Sutton!" I laugh, and he playfully pinches my side. Holding his face in my hands, I look at him seriously as I say, "I love you. You came barreling into my life when I wasn't looking, completely taking me by surprise. But I can't imagine it any other way now. You're so good to not only me, but my brother, too. I love how you sit at the diner and wait for me, making me smile all day, you spend time with Preston and have helped him more than you know, you embrace my weird and wonderful sustainability projects. You're kind and thoughtful and protective, and being around you makes me happier than I've ever been."

Swallowing roughly, his hand glides up my torso, eyes burning into mine. Placing his hands on the bed, planted on either side of my head, our noses almost touching, he says once more, "Again..." Almost like he's in disbelief.

"I lov—" I don't get to finish. His lips collide with mine, and he kisses away my words. So slowly, so seductively, I almost melt straight into the mattress. With every movement of his lips, I feel the ferocity of his feelings, and as he lowers his body onto mine, his heart thumps against my chest, just as powerfully as my own.

Breathless, he lifts to lean on his elbow, and his fingers trail down the side of my cheek before he gently grabs my neck, lifting my chin to look him in the eye.

"You are the best thing that's ever happened to me. I want you to know that every day." His voice is a mere whisper. It wouldn't matter if there were more bugs in the room; the chances of them hearing that sentence would be nil. I feel every word he says like he's branding it into my flesh with a hot poker.

Lifting my legs, I curl them around his naked hips, pulling him to me.

"And you me." I barely get the words out before he slides into me, and I gasp, the intrusion both delicious and breathtaking in the same moment. He doesn't give me time to settle before he pulls back and thrusts in again.

"Sutton," I choke out as his hips move at the perfect pace, his hand remaining around my jaw, the two of us barely even blinking as we stare into each other's eyes.

Sex with Sutton is like nothing I've experienced before. It's sultry, it's fire, it's addictive. But right now, he holds my gaze on his, telling me he loves me again, like he's giving me every emotion along with his desire, ensuring I feel deep within my bones just how strongly he feels about me.

"I love your pussy too." His jaw tics like he's holding back, our breathing becoming labored with the intensity of this connection.

I moan, "You do?"

"I love everything about you..." He's thrusting harder now, my body jolting with every motion as he grits his teeth.

"Lift your hands above your head," he demands, and I move immediately. My arms lift above my head, where he grabs my wrists with his hands, his face still hovering above mine, his hips working overtime. My legs widen a little more, our skin slapping, and my body starts to tingle.

"Oh yes," I warn through a whimper. My orgasm is coming fast, and I arch my back, wanting to be closer to him.

"Like that... Good girl," he murmurs.

I'm a panting mess, our movements in sync, and I push my head back, my eyes closing.

But he's not having that. "Look at me..."

My eyes ping open, landing right on his.

"Now give me your pretty pussy, Charlotte, and come for me."

I hitch a breath, and with my eyes glued to his, I let go. My body shudders all the way to my toes, and I release a guttural moan as stars fill my vision, the orgasm like nothing I've experienced before.

"Roll over," he says sharply as he lifts off me, and I turn on the mattress, my limbs wobbly. As I do, he grabs my hips, pulling them up before he slides back into me.

"Oh my…" I pant, feeling sensitive as he manhandles me in a way that makes me feel even more wanted.

"That's it, Tinker… Fuck, I love your body. You get so wet for me, baby," he grits out as he thrusts in deeper, sending a shiver through me.

"Sutton…" I hiccup, the feeling too much, my toes curling in the sheets as my hands grip the headboard, white-knuckled.

He moans, low and gruff, as he grabs my shoulders, pulling me up so I'm sitting on him, my back to his chest. His hand runs over my breasts, grabbing my jaw, and turning me to face him as I start to bounce.

"That's it," he says before his lips hit mine. His other hand grips my hips, helping me move up and down, my body slapping onto his. We're both wanton, messy, and sweaty, and I'm so glad I hid that camera.

"Oh God, Sutton," I whimper, feeling another orgasm building, this one from deep within. His hand moves from my hip to my clit, where he circles over and over in time with our thrusts. I've never done this position before. I feel completely open, exposed almost, but with his hands holding me tight, I know I'm safe.

"Yes… Yes…" I pant as I roll my hips on his.

"I love you… I love you so goddamn much…" He pushes his words into my neck, nipping the skin there.

"I love you," I whisper as I take in a deep breath before a silent scream of pleasure rips from my chest. My entire body convulses onto his as he comes with a muffled growl into my neck, slamming into me quickly a few more times before he lets go.

Our movements slow, his hands roaming my body as I slump back against him, completely spent.

Gently, he lifts me off him, laying me down and positioning himself beside me, keeping me close as we just look at each other. Our breathing calms back to normal, sweat still on my brow, and he grins as his forehead rests against mine.

It's perfect. Everything about it.

And in this moment, I hope more than anything that love is going to be enough.

39

SUTTON

I look at the ceiling as Charlotte's naked body drapes over mine. Her head rests on my chest as I absent-mindedly strum her bare arm.

I feel in control. For the first time in what feels like ever, I'm leading my life how I want to. I would prefer to not be on the run from the media, hiding in a mob house and trying to figure out what my next steps have to be. But the past day or so is the first time in a long time that I put myself on the line for something that's important to me. She's important to me.

"I need to tell you something..." I don't stop my hand as it continues to run up and down her arm.

"Hmmmm... did you buy some more forests?" she teases, and I smile into her hair.

"I've been having immunotherapy."

Her body tenses, eyes widening as they look up at me. "Immunotherapy?"

"Hudson has been helping me at the hospital. It's where he injects me with bee venom in the hopes that my toler-ance for bee stings will increase to the point that if I get stung, my reaction will be similar to that of a person who doesn't have an allergy to bees."

"What? I had no idea that was even a thing."

"Yeah, well, I read up on it and thought I'd give it a go. We've had a few sessions now. So far, it's going well. My histamine response has really leveled out. Maybe a few more treatments, and I'll be good to go."

She smiles brightly, relief in her tone. "Seriously?"

I nod, smiling right back. "It's been amazing."

"I was so worried. When you talked about your beehives, I could see the excitement on your face, but I'll admit, I was scared."

"I'll still be careful. But if I wear all the protective clothes and ensure I don't anger the bees when I get them, then maybe in a few months, we can have our own honey."

"That sounds perfect." I can't wait to wake her up with breakfast in bed, maybe some fruit from my orchard and honey from the bees.

Humming, she cuddles closer.

We're quiet for a bit, my hand still rubbing her back, but I can hear her thinking. I'm patient for her to open up to me; she'll do it in her own time.

With a deep breath, she breaks the silence, her voice quiet.

"We're running from my stepmother."

My brow crinkles with curiosity and concern as I kiss the top of her head. "Your stepmother?"

"My full name is Charlotte Titan." *Titan*. It sounds familiar, but I can't put my finger on why.

"My father is Colin Titan, owner of Titan Energy, the biggest oil conglomerate in the country and perhaps the world."

I still. Yes, I know that name. Colin Titan is one of the

richest men in the country. Ruthless in business. I sat next to him at a charity gala once, I think.

"I think I met him once. A charity gala in LA."

She nods. "Sounds about right. He often attends dinners and things. He was a great dad until my mother died. That's when things changed."

They say a mother is the glue that holds a family together, and I believe it wholeheartedly. I see it in my own mom. The quiet strength, the unwavering presence, how she made everything feel whole even in the hardest times.

Charlotte's mother must've been the same. I see it in Charlotte. In the way she moves through the world, instinctively protecting, nurturing, and guiding Preston like it's second nature.

It's not just responsibility, it's like love is woven into every action, a quiet yet undeniable force that holds them both steady.

"Mom died just before college. I worked hard at my degree, enjoyed it. My dad thought I would then step into the family business, and when I didn't, he didn't take it well. I'm sure he thought I was just being an unruly kid. But I have other dreams, and they don't align with drilling for oil. So we became strained, and he submerged himself into work even more. It created distance between us that was never there before.

"Then he met Maribel. She hated Preston and me from day one, and there was nothing we could do that would change that. Over time, Maribel turned my father against us. He was still angry and frustrated with me, so he cut me off, froze my trust funds. I was okay with being cut off. I was determined to make it on my own. But he put the word on the street for no one to hire me. Which meant I had no money and no job prospects. That wasn't enough for Maribel. She was money hungry, wanted his kids gone so she was the only one in his life. The only one who could inherit anything. She decided I was being rebellious and disobedient. I wasn't. But Dad listened to everything she said, and eventually, she locked me out. Out of the house, out of the family..."

My body goes rigid at that. "What do you mean, locked you out?"

"She pushed me out of my family and my home. I stayed with friends for a while, but even that was hard."

"What?" I'm trying to pull the pieces together, wondering how in the world a father could do that to his daughter.

"My father doesn't know the extent in which Maribel changed our home. When Maribel wouldn't let me inside the house to see Preston, I had to sneak through the gates. Chef Luc often disguised me as a bag of dirty laundry or a large box of apples to get me inside. I always hated how small I was, but it was beneficial back then."

I can only shake my head, completely in awe of her as she continues.

"Maribel doesn't have an empathetic bone in her body. She made sure Dad wouldn't see me. I tried. Calls, office visits, nothing. He was never available. She controls everything. She wanted me gone. But then it escalated."

"How so?" I ask, and she shifts so we're face-to-face.

"She locked him in his room. No friends, no sports, no life. Just school and silence. His mental health started to suffer; the light in his eyes was slowly being extinguished. I snuck in at night to see him, but then she caught us."

Oh no. I know where this is going. "What did she do?"

"Gave us an ultimatum. Leave and disappear, or she'd send Preston to military school and destroy Dad with false assault claims, insider trading rumors. She knows how to ruin people."

I nearly balk. "That's insane. Can't you talk to your father?"

"I tried. He wouldn't take my calls. She gave me an hour to leave, or she'd call the police. I didn't wait to see if she was bluffing. Preston would never survive that type of school and those kind of allegations will ruin my father. He's many things and has failed us more than a father should. But he built that business from nothing. He gave my mother a wonderful life, and up until the day she died, he was the best dad ever. I can't let Maribel ruin my brother and my father. So I grabbed Preston, and we ran."

My blood simmers. A ten-year-old locked away like a prisoner? Charlotte cast out like she's nothing? I clench my fists. Maribel's on my shit list. Her father too.

"Sawyer will know what to do," I say, grounding myself.

Charlotte sits up then, expression torn. "I don't want you dragged into this. You've got enough going on."

I shake my head. "You're not alone. Not anymore." I brush her hair back and tuck it behind her ear. She melts into my touch. "We're in this together."

Her breath catches, eyes filling with tears. She sees it now—my choice is already made.

"We've got bigger obstacles than most, but I love you. Whatever it takes to protect Preston, we'll do it."

"Even if I go to jail?" she says, almost a whisper.

"You won't," I assure her.

"Kidnapping is a crime."

"So is abuse. Locking Preston up, cutting you off—that's abuse. Emotional, physical. All of it."

The way she's staring at me, her breaths shallow, her fear is palpable. I want nothing more than to take that away and replace it with safety and comfort and joy. "She's untouchable… She has money. Power."

"So do I, Tinker Bell." I look into her eyes, steady and sure. "And I'll use every bit of it to protect you if they ever try to accuse you of anything other than being a loving sister."

Nodding, tears in her eyes, she exhales heavily and leans against my chest. I hold her close, praying it doesn't come to that.

40

CHARLOTTE

We've lived in unaware bliss here in Provence all week, but the familiar ache of uncertainty sits like a weight on my chest. I've lain by the pool all day, my tan now one that only the sun of the Mediterranean can make. Seeing Preston laughing and swimming and roughhousing with Sutton in the water has been good for my soul. Reminds me of why I've done what I've done. Am I in the wrong for taking him? I don't think so. Even though legally it probably wasn't right, it was right for him. If he was happy at home, I would've gone on to life after college. I would've left him, traveled, gotten a job somewhere else, and just lived how any other woman my age lives.

But that wasn't his story, so it wasn't mine.

My thoughts are interrupted by the garden sprinklers. They come on every day at this time like clockwork. The lawn is vast and green, the jets of water spouting from the ground covering every inch, including the decadent garden beds that are full of lush roses.

Sutton's cell chimes like it has all week. For the most

part, he's ignored it. Looking at the screen, he answers it, talking in low tones. He's trying to prolong the inevitable, but I'm a realist. I might want him to be my forever, but Maribel taught me to never wish for that.

"Whispers is inundated." He throws his cell on the lounge chair next to mine, coming to sit near me, Preston now bobbing and swimming, having a great time on his own.

My stomach sinks. "Oh no." I frown, thinking of poor Rochelle and everyone and the mess we left behind.

"It's a good thing, apparently."

That has me rearing back. "What?"

"Sawyer tells me Rochelle is doing a roaring trade. The bed-and-breakfasts in town have tripled their prices and the out-of-towners are paying. The distillery is going gangbusters. Local shops are doing well. Sawyer says Annabelle has been selling out of soaps. Peter had to put on an extra driver for his taxis, and the Whiteman's Bar is full every night. The only people upset are all the billionaires up on Billionaire Boulevard. But the sheriff has blocked off the road to residents only. So they all get to keep their privacy. Besides, I know most of them, so they'll get over it."

"Wow," is all I can say, completely awed. But it makes sense; the media have to stay and eat somewhere. I just didn't account for the positive effect it would have on the local economy.

"And even better news: Griffin and his team are almost finished on the house. He has three crews there now to try to get it done by the time we get back, or at least soon after that. They're working around the clock." He pauses for a moment, both of us sharing a smile. "Rochelle says she misses you, though."

"I miss her." I miss the small town that took me in, gave

me a safe haven, and loved Preston and me as if we were one of their own.

"I miss her pies..." Sutton says, looking grim, and I laugh.

"There's more to her than just pies."

"I know. She's a hell of a woman," Sutton agrees.

"She reminds me of my mom. All kindhearted, warm, nurturing. She makes me feel connected."

"It's nice that you have her. I think she loves you just as much."

Sutton goes silent, his mind elsewhere for a moment, looking suddenly melancholy.

"You alright?" I reach out, grabbing his hand.

Squeezing my hand, he turns to me. "As happy as I am for Whispers and want to get back to where I've felt so at home, I guess the media have drones everywhere. Everyone wants to see where the celebrity now lives..." His voice drifts off as he looks out at Preston, lips pressed in a tense line. "I've never felt like an animal in a cage like I do right now. The press are intrusive, but I never minded this much. So what if I have a bad hair day or did a walk of shame from somewhere? But now... now I have something to protect, and it feels like it's out of control."

Emotion clogs my throat. I've been so consumed by my own plight, I haven't really considered his privacy. "Do you think it will calm down soon?"

"No. It's not going to calm down until they spot me. I'll probably have to do an interview. Maybe a daytime talk show or something. But I need to give them something. The more elusive I am, the more they want. So I'm going to go back to LA."

A sharp pain zings through my chest. "LA?" Is he leaving

me now? Now that we've fled together, said I love you, and spent a magical week with our heads in the sand?

"I need to pull their attention away from Whispers. Away from you. I need to give them something. Hopefully, pulling the media away from Whispers and back to LA will give you and Preston time to hide back at the cottage without anyone spotting you or knowing who you are. You won't be able to work with Rochelle. Those assholes from the diner are still around, probably waiting to point you out. Although, the sheriff is keeping an eye on them, waiting for them to step out of line just once so he can haul them in and charge them with something."

I take a deep breath, the reality of my new life hitting me like a slap in the face. We didn't press charges against the men who assaulted me. Mainly because we don't need the additional stress and they didn't press charges against Sutton either. Obviously knowing they were in the wrong.

"We'll get you and Preston on Tanner's jet back to Whispers, where Sawyer will take care of you. I'll pop my face out in Paris, make sure I'm seen there, and then jump on a jet to LA. I won't be there long, though, since the Whiteman's launch is going live next week. That's a big night."

I feel momentarily relieved. "I forgot about that with everything happening. I'm excited for you."

"My mom is even flying in. I can't wait for you to meet her." He looks at me and grins, and my eyebrows rise in surprise.

"You want me to meet your mom?"

"Of course. My mom is great, and I already know she'll love you."

While I'm nervous and still don't know how we're going to navigate everything, I feel excited to have a way forward.

I'm not yet sure what the reality of that will be, but we'll work it out.

His thumb rubs the back of my hand in soothing circles as he takes a deep breath. "The whiskey launch at Whiteman's will put me on an entirely new trajectory, as everyone will then know that Whispers is exactly where I've been hiding all this time. I know I just mentioned hiding out at the cottage, but I'm not exaggerating. We'll need to lie low."

"Okay..." I don't know what to say; it all sounds crazy. I know he's doing all of this for me. If I was just a normal girl, I could probably go to LA with him, be seen on his arm, go on dates, and not worry about the media or paparazzi that follow us. But I'm not a normal girl. I'm Charlotte Titan, heiress to the Titan fortune. Not that I'll probably see any of it.

"You'll be safe, since not many locals know that's where you are. No school, no library, and best to stay indoors as much as you can. We'll use the yellow path; I'll come to you or you to me, or we meet in the middle, I don't care, but I can't live without you. The week away in LA without seeing you is going to be enough to kill me."

My heart thuds out of my chest. This next step of our future feels almost insurmountable.

I nod as I try to digest exactly what's going on. The perfect week we've had is now coming to an end.

"I've also called my security team. Jackson is my head of security. I'll be bringing him and a small team back to Whispers with me. I need everyone safe. I need our safety respected, and I want another set of eyes on you and Preston."

Again, I nod. My mind is spinning as I look up at the sky, closing my eyes for a moment.

He clears his throat. "There's something else."

My eyes shoot back to his, not sure I can take much more.

"I had Sawyer look into guardianship for Preston. I told him just what he needed to know." He looks guilt-ridden, and while it makes me anxious to know other people are aware of my secret, I trust him and I trust his brother. I need someone on my side, and I hope they can help.

"My father?" I ask shakily.

He nods. "He knows your father."

I should've known Sawyer would.

"Sawyer's going to start pulling some things together. A contract that gives you custody of your brother, some legal paperwork that you can present to him. He's going to start to build a legal defense, in case it's needed, then we'll be ready without delays." My flight-or-fight starts to flutter, and my breathing quickens.

I don't know what to say without sobbing, so I don't say anything. I remain quiet, my eyes conveying every *thank you* and *I love you* to Sutton as he reaches forward and wipes a stray tear from my cheek.

Reaching over, he lifts me from my chair and sits me in front of him, my back to his chest as he wraps his arms around me. We watch Preston laugh and play, soaking up the sun in each other's embrace until it sets on the horizon. Like the final curtain call to my life.

"Got everything?" I smile at Preston, not because I'm happy, but because I need to ensure he isn't worried.

"Yeah." His voice tells me he's bummed to be leaving.

We're standing with our luggage at the front of the house, watching the same black car approaching that transported us here a week ago. Comical, really. My life could be a TV show with how it's been going lately.

I swallow at seeing Hugo step out. I haven't asked questions. It's not the time and it certainly isn't the place. His grin is wide, a crocodile smile in full effect. I don't like him, and I certainly don't trust him.

"I assume your stay went well." He looks at Sutton and shakes his hand.

"It did. Thank you. If you ever need anything…"

"I will call. Expect it," he says quickly, and I see Sutton's jaw clench.

"The car will take you to the private airstrip a few miles away. There are two jets there, one for you and one for her."

"Thanks, Hugo. I appreciate it, really," Sutton says gratefully, speaking for all of us. I'm not sure what we would've done otherwise.

The sprinklers come on, taking my attention, and I frown.

"You know, you really should swap your irrigation for a slow drip system. It'll probably save about fifty percent of your water consumption year-round. You'll have less runoff and reduce fungal disease of the plants." I look back at Hugo before my eyes widen in shock at what I just said to him. Sutton coughs, in disbelief and humor at my antics.

His stare burns as I wet my lips and try to swallow. "It's just an idea." I can barely breathe. I sure would hate to ever be on his bad side.

Eyes narrowing slightly, he says, "I'll tell my gardener."

He turns then, his body facing me entirely, and I feel Sutton's grip on my hand tighten.

"You're not like your father at all, are you, Charlotte?" My blood turns to ice. I'm not sure why I thought he would have no idea who I was. He's clearly a powerful man.

"No. Not at all," I answer, voice steady. Even on my worst day, that's one fact I'm confident in.

"Good." He nods before slapping Sutton on the shoulder and walking past him, into the house with his men as our luggage is placed in the trunk. My breath whooshes from my lungs, feeling like I just passed a test.

Only a minute later, Preston, Sutton, and I are climbing into the car, and we're on our way.

The drive is quiet, the pain in my chest at being away from Sutton heavy, and before we know it, we're at the airstrip. My palm is sweaty where I've squeezed Sutton's hand so tight, I think I cut off his circulation. As the car pulls up on the tarmac, I see the two jets Hugo mentioned.

"Preston. I love you. Take care of your sister for me." Sutton pulls Preston into a tight hug, and my eyes start to water.

My brother nods, grabbing his bag and stepping out of the car. "Thanks, Sutton. I love you too. And I promise I'll take care of Charlotte."

Sutton looks at me with teary eyes, cups my jaw with his hands, and presses his forehead to mine. I release a trembling breath, feeling his warmth surrounding me, nervous about what's to come.

"I'm sorry for all this. I hate that I have to leave you. I love you. I fucking love you, and I'll be back for you." He kisses me, here in the back seat of a mob car, in the middle of a private airstrip in Provence, and that's when more tears fall.

If I had any subconscious doubts of his love for me, they disappear with this goodbye kiss.

And it's the hardest goodbye I've ever had to make.

41

———

SUTTON

I lifted my head in Paris.

I had a friend give a tip-off to the local media, which led to a frenzy of cameras on the far side of the small private airport where I deplaned from Hugo's jet and reboarded my own jet for the next flight. Even though the large fence kept them out, I still saw their long lenses. Fucking piranhas.

Sawyer sent our jet from Whispers, so of course it was followed online. The gossip is already all over the internet, with my flight path, the type of aircraft I'm in, and a lot of talk about me being alone. They're right. I feel lonely for the first time ever. Not because no one is here with me. But because she isn't.

I left Charlotte hours ago, and I'm already aching to see her again. Now, as the LA skyline comes into view, I look at my cell, seeing the text she sent.

Landed.

No more words. No emojis. Nothing. We agreed to limited communication this week because the media are assholes and they'll no doubt steal my phone or something else untoward. It's frustrating. Frustrating that I can't just be with my girl, take her out, date her, spend time out in the open with her. But for her safety, for her secret to remain just that, I need to play the game. If it wasn't for the media attention and my global fame, I could have her all to myself. That's the downside of being an actor.

But for the first time ever, I'm in complete control of what I'm doing. I've planned this with Sawyer over the past week, down to every last detail. Her safety is paramount, and while I've fucked up a lot of things in my life over the years, she isn't going to be one of them.

I look at the other message on my cell. From Bobby.

Meet you at home.

Bobby has been blowing up my cell and calling or texting almost hourly. He's also harassing Sawyer in Whispers. He flew in like he said he would, and for the week I was away, he hung around Whispers, chasing and calling Sawyer until my brother threatened legal action, and then he went quiet. But he clearly knows I'm heading back to LA, and he's smart enough to know that this is the end of us.

Jackson and my security team are briefed. They're doing regular sweeps of my property, and no one is allowed in. Not the cleaners. Not even Bobby. So if he comes to the house, he'll be turned away. And the media will be all over that. It's long overdue and maybe should be handled differently after ten years of working together, but he brought us to this point because of his own behavior. Did he make me into the superstar I've become? Maybe. But that took a lot of my own blood, sweat, and tears as well.

With the media focusing on Bobby and the breakdown of our relationship, it gives them the leading story that they're drooling for. And then we'll leak our own stories about me taking a career break to reassess management options, which should explain my time in Whispers. Enough so that it will draw everyone away from the small town I've grown to love. Hopefully, any leads of me having a secret family will be thrown to the side as fake news. I'll do anything to protect Charlotte's identity, including using my asshole of an ex-manager to cover it.

Sawyer is putting the final touches on the letter Bobby will receive, severing our partnership, paying him a small fortune as thanks for ten years, and then he'll be permanently out of my life. At the thought of my brother I see his text message.

Eagle is in the nest.

She's at the cottage, safe. I feel unsettled not being with her, trusting Sawyer with the most important person in my life, so he better look after her.

As the jet descends, I wipe my palms on my jeans, my heart pounding, and I try to focus on my persona. It's like acting a part. Sutton Silvers, the movie star, is a completely different character to Sutton Silvers, the man. And I've only just realized. My true self rarely comes out in my day-to-day here in LA. It was exhausting. No wonder I ran to Whispers to hide. I needed it. I was burned-out.

Being back here will be the biggest acting job of my career. Because I don't want to be here. Even seeing the LA skyline gives me hives. *Hives.* I have my beehives all in place at my new home, and I grin to myself, knowing my beekeeping suit and all my tools of the trade are arriving this week. Griffin is going to think I've gone mad.

The jet lands, and with it, I mentally put my mask on. I straighten my shoulders and roll my head, getting into character.

As we pull up on the tarmac, I take off my seat belt and spot Jackson, my head of security, out the window, standing near the car, waiting. He looks refreshed, ready for anything. I guess that'll happen when you have a few months off.

"Good to see you, Sutton."

I shake his hand as I disembark. He's the one person who's been by my side for years. He and Bobby are my two longest employees.

"Miss me?" The Sutton Silvers grin is now in full effect.

"No." He smirks, and I slap his shoulder.

"Mm-hmm. Liar."

Jackson maneuvers us out of the airport and through what can only be described as a barrage of media. They're at least ten deep; you would think I was the fucking King of England or something.

"Shit." I rub my chin as I look out the window, flashes of white almost blinding me, but I keep my face open. I need them to see me. I need them to confirm to the world that I'm in LA.

"They're at the house too. Have been for weeks, but today, the media scrum is thicker than I've ever seen it." Jackson's eyes stay focused on the road. "Even taking time off, I was keeping an eye on your surveillance. It's been pretty much nonstop since you went away."

"Seems like I can't just take a fucking holiday," I grit out.

He shakes his head with a sigh. "Seems not."

Let the games begin.

I STEP off the set of the daytime talk show, my grin wide and fake as hell. The camera flashes almost blind me as I walk across the sidewalk to my waiting car. It's been four days. Four days of running around LA, paps following me, my car being tailed. Four days without my Tinker Bell.

As soon as I slide in the back seat of the car, I'm calling.

"How is she?" I ask before Sawyer has time to answer.

"She's fine. Just like she was two hours ago when you called."

I drop my head back and pull at my hair, the tension building. I don't want to be here. I don't want to do this anymore.

"Preston?"

"Fine too. They've planted some wildflowers at the cottage, and now they're building some type of contraption on their dining table."

I chuckle, already feeling a little better. "What is it?"

"Some solar thermal something-or-other. I have no idea, and it all just looks like junk to me," he grumbles good-naturedly.

My smile is wide. Fuck, I love her.

Then something hits me. "Wait. So, you've been over? You'll be followed, Sawyer." My voice is demanding as panic swirls. Jackson looks up at me in the rearview mirror.

"I took your little path. That's very cute, by the way," he teases me like this isn't a fucking nightmare.

"I can't do it," I say quietly, my usual unflappable facade breaking down.

"What do you mean?"

"I mean, I can't do it. I can't be away from her. Not like this." Heart racing, I look out the window, the familiar LA streets flying by. All I want to do is teleport to her.

"Shall I give her a message? I know you guys can't really talk, but you'll be here in a few days. Tanner and Connor have been busy organizing everything for the launch. It's their biggest yet, thanks to you."

I rub my eyes. At least something good is coming out of all this bullshit.

"Let's fly Mom in early. Let's do a Thanksgiving dinner. For the family," I tell him, just thinking about it now. I could use some quality family time after everything that's been going on..

"Thanksgiving dinner?" Sawyer sounds surprised. We've never really celebrated the holidays much before. Mainly because it was just the three of us growing up, and as we got older, my brother and I were on opposite sides of the country.

"Well, we both have a bigger family now. Whispers is our home."

He huffs a laugh. "Annabelle and the boys will love that. So will Mom," he adds, sounding genuinely happy about it.

"You get Mom there. And tell Charlotte..." I pause, knowing a message from Sawyer isn't going to be enough. "Tell her I'll be home soon." I end the call and lock eyes with Jackson, who's still flicking his gaze from me in the rearview to the road ahead.

"Change of plans?"

"Ready to go to Whispers?" I ask him with a quirked eyebrow.

A grin pulls at his lips. "Sure am."

"Let's get to the jet. I've got a turkey to cook."

He takes a turn, moving us in the direction of the small airport where my jet sits. One quick call to my pilot, and we're leaving LA behind.

For good.

42

CHARLOTTE

I bite my lip as I look over my latest project.

"I'm bored," Preston says, for what feels like the twentieth time today. It's almost dark. The days here while holed up at the cottage drag on longer than any other. Nights without Sutton are even worse. But I need to remain hidden. I can't be seen. I need to keep my brother safe.

"Well, this might be ready to test tomorrow." I offer him a smile, and he looks over it. The mesh of old copper pipes and black tubing are designed to absorb the heat, creating solar heating of sorts.

"Can't we just go to the library?" he whines, and I can't help but chuckle. He never whines. It's actually a normal reaction for a child. The fact that Preston is even doing it is testament to how far he's come. No longer the introverted boy who was locked up and too scared to say and do anything. Too fearful to show his emotions. Now, he's comfortable expressing himself, and for that, I'm thankful.

"You know we can't. Let's just wait for Sutton to come back." My heart is heavy. I miss him. I've never really connected to someone like I have with Sutton. Male or female. Best friends for me were like boyfriends—usually only after my connections, my social presence. Most of which, I shunned. As I got older, I understood that people weren't genuine; they didn't like me for me.

"Do you think it'll work?" Preston looks at my project again, unsure, but one thing about Preston is, he always loves my random inventions.

"I guess we will just have to—" I stop the minute I hear a noise.

I haven't had contact with anyone other than Sawyer. He's walked the path a few times, usually around this time of the day, when the sun starts to lower and the drones are gone.

"Is that Sawyer?" Preston looks out the window.

I jump up, striding over to where Preston's standing and look out as well. My heart thumps, my fear spiking, wondering who's wandering around out there. We can't see anyone. Everything looks just as it should. But then I spot him.

"Sutton!" I gasp, seeing him walking out from serial killer forest. Whipping the door open, I fly outside, my body so full of adrenaline to get to him it should be embarrassing. He looks up at hearing the door creak, his grin taking over his face as I run to him and jump into his arms. I feel like I can breathe for the first time all week. He holds me tightly as my legs wrap around his waist, Preston slamming into both of us and joining our reunion.

"Ahhh, Tinker... I've missed you." His words push into my hair as I tuck my face into his neck.

"I missed you too, so much," I say against him, my heart racing as he slowly lowers me to the ground.

"I just flew in. I couldn't stay away a minute longer." He sounds choked up, and tears streak down my cheeks.

"You came back!" Preston muffles, his face still plastered to Sutton's side.

"Of course I did. I told you I would." Sutton bends down, giving him a big hug before standing and meeting my gaze. He has one arm resting on Preston's shoulder as the other hand cups my cheek, his thumb wiping my tears.

"I want you guys to pack a bag. The house is ready, and I want you both with me."

"It's ready?" I'm surprised. Griffin was working around the clock, but clearly, he worked faster than I was expecting.

"It is. Mom's flying in tomorrow, and we're doing Thanksgiving together. I also have my head of security with me. Jackson will stay in the guesthouse."

"Thanksgiving?" Preston's eyes light up, mine probably doing the same.

"I've never done Thanksgiving lunch before, but how hard can a turkey be, right?" Sutton scruffs Preston's hair, and I grin.

"Any updates on the media?" I look at him in question. Since Preston and I haven't left this place, I have no idea what the town is like now.

"A few paps are still hanging around, but the media thinks I'm still in LA. So we'll be okay for a while."

I look up, seeing the sky clear of drones and not hearing the familiar purr of them in the sky nearby.

He reads my mind, sighing. "Those drones will be back at some point. Once they know I'm here for sure, they'll want to see where I am and why I'm back here."

I swallow roughly. They might as well just ask for a pint of my blood at this point. Wherever he goes, he's going to be followed. If not by media, by fans. Once the new Whiteman's Whiskey launch happens, it'll be crazier.

"Won't they see us?" We're leaving one prison to go to

another, but I would rather be there with him than not. And Preston will probably have way more fun there too.

"No one's going to get to you. I promise. Besides... I have something I want to show you."

I trust Sutton. But my gut feels heavy. And his gaze says it all.

It's going to get worse before it gets better.

43

CHARLOTTE

In awe, I stare at the TV.

"This is the best part," my brother tells me, sitting on the edge of his seat.

"Argh, this is the worst part." Sutton's mom shields her eyes as Sutton flies through the air and wrestles a monster before they both splash into the ocean.

"Oh God, I can't watch." I side with his mom and squeeze my eyes shut, and my brother and Kevin both cheer for Sutton's superhero character on the screen.

"Seriously, this is gross..." Annabelle scrunches her face as she watches Sutton's character fight, and I'm sure there's blood and all sorts of things flying around. I wouldn't know; I can't look at it.

"I much prefer the library..." I say quietly, wincing at the loud noises from all the action playing out.

Sutton's mom looks at me, and we share a smile, because she knows exactly which library I'm talking about.

To say I was stunned when Sutton brought Preston and me here, immediately showing us his library, would be an understatement. He thought of everything; from non-fiction books that Preston might need for school and a vast fiction selection too, lots of environmental and gardening books and, of course, I saw his little stash of beekeeping materials, the ones that seem to grow almost every day.

I know he built it with me in mind. I almost couldn't believe it. He's added cute reading nooks along the windows, a desk where Preston can do his homework, and a really cool ladder that runs across the length of the shelves, which Preston loves swinging from. There's even a fireplace with the comfiest sofa that might as well be a big bed in front of it, covered with pillows and surrounded by end tables that hold snack baskets and a mini fridge of refreshments.

It's perfect. Just like him.

"I'm so glad that Sutton has finally found someone who cares about him. I knew the minute I saw him, by the big bright smile on his face, that his heart is whole. It's a wonderful thing for a mother to see," she whispers to me.

My chest aches in the best way at having her approval. "He's a pretty great guy. You raised him well. I'm lucky to have met him."

Her eyes are full of warmth.

"And to have little Preston with us too. Oh, it's just such a delight to have all these kids around... Although, as much as I love my son, I do prefer my game shows."

I chuckle at that. She's amazing. I can see where Sutton gets his love of life from. She arrived yesterday and was such a breath of fresh air. She took to Preston and me the moment of our introduction, and while I was nervous to meet her, it's clear she has a lot of love for her boys.

"Oh! Love this scene." Sutton walks in from the kitchen, wearing a pink frilly apron, coming to stand behind the sofa where I sit. I look up at him as he squeezes my shoulders.

"Why didn't you tell me it was so anxiety inducing?" I whine playfully, his mom giggling beside us.

"Don't worry, Tinker. I save the day." He winks at me.

"At least I'm not the only one who can't watch it," his mom says, to which Sutton gives her a teasing huff.

"How is it that my two favorite women in my life can't watch me onscreen?"

"Because we love you, that's why. We don't want anyone to harm you," I tell him, and he leans in to press a sweet kiss on my lips. It's quick, just showing his affection, feeling so natural, I don't even care who's around.

When we pull apart, his mom is looking at us both with hearts in her eyes.

"Well, it's the last movie I'll do, so you both can breathe a sigh of relief."

My breath catches, head snapping back to him.

"Last one?" his mom asks with just as much shock in her tone.

"Yep. No more movies for me, Mom. I'm retiring."

"Retiring?" I'm in complete disbelief. How has he not mentioned that before? I was wondering how we would make it all work. But I didn't want to be a woman who demanded his time or forced him into making decisions that he wasn't ready to.

"Yeah, I've been thinking about it for a while. I love it here. I love you, and there's no way in hell I can be away on a movie set for six months of the year without you. Plus, I've hit every goal an actor could. I've won awards, done well for myself. I want to leave on top. So, I'm going to hang up my acting boots. I have a few things coming down the pipeline with Tanner and the distillery that will keep me in the game for a while, but I'm really itching to get the beehives going."

"Are you sure, honey?" his mom asks, her expression

shifting to one that shows she couldn't be happier about all this.

"I am, Mom. I really am. It's time." Once he reassures his mom, he looks back to me. "You going to get tired of having me in Whispers, baby?" His tone is light, not serious, but I answer him anyway.

"Not possible," I say sweetly, then add, "But I might need to keep you out of the kitchen for the major holidays. Is something burning?"

"Shoot!" He jolts, eyes wide, like he forgot all about the meal he was preparing. "I'm not sure turkey chef is my next adventure."

His mom and I laugh as he rushes back to the kitchen, catching Sawyer's attention.

"Is it ready?" he asks, just as Sutton steps back into the room, looking like someone just kicked his puppy. He and Sawyer have been in the kitchen all morning, not wanting any help from their mom, Annabelle, or me.

Sutton sighs. "As ready as it's ever going to be."

"This is... nice." My jaw is sore from chewing another dry piece of turkey, needing to add more cranberry sauce to swallow it.

"Liar." Sutton grins, clearly not taking his lack of cooking skills to heart.

"Well, the beans are lovely, boys," his mom says as she stabs a droopy bean on her fork and pretends it's the most delightful thing she's ever eaten.

"Another liar." Sawyer looks at her cheekily.

"Should we just skip it all and go straight to dessert?"

Annabelle asks the table. "And if we're hungry later, we can throw together some pizza bites?"

"Yes!" all the boys say in unison, and I laugh, just as enthused by that idea as they are. Thanksgiving was never like this for me. Growing up, it was a big day. Chef Luc outdid himself every year. As if Preston knows what I'm thinking, he looks at me, and I nod. *I know, buddy. I miss him too.*

We all clear the table, taking a little break before dessert. His mom hangs out with Noah, Kevin, and Preston as Sawyer and Annabelle wash the dishes in the kitchen. I tried to help but was told to go relax, and since Sutton messed up dinner, his brother didn't want him "breaking any dishes too," which made everyone laugh.

"Here, this might help wash your mouth out." Sutton slides his whiskey glass over to me, where we sit back at the dining table, having some time to ourselves. I've only ever drank whiskey once before, with my dad on my birthday. It seems somewhat serendipitous that I'm now drinking it at what's becoming my rebirth of sorts.

I lift the glass to my lips, and the smell of it burns my nose hairs.

"Whiteman's?" I ask, because I think it's illegal to have any other brand in this town.

His eyes light up as he nods. "The new one. My one."

That makes me smile as I touch the glass to my lips. Sutton watches me carefully as the amber liquid moves to my mouth. I take a sip, just enough to coat my tongue and hold it in my mouth. This is how my father taught me to appreciate whiskey. I swirl it a little, exposing it to my palette before I swallow, savoring the flavors.

"Shit... you even make drinking whiskey sexy, Tinker..." he says gruffly.

I hum, leaning a little closer to him. "It's nice. Smooth. I taste a little honey?"

Smiling, he nods. "Tanner coated the barrels in honey before aging. Makes it very smooth."

"Easy to drink." I nod in agreement.

"That's why, with every sale of a bottle, Tanner is giving ten percent to the Save the Bees charity."

"Save the Bees?" The question leaves me on a breath. I wonder briefly if this man is actually real. He keeps surprising me in ways that leave me astounded.

He grabs my hand. "Yep," he says, popping the *P* and giving me a wink. "My girl loves bees, I love bees, Tanner... likes bees. You know how much reading I've been doing, and I've learned how important they are to pollinate the plants, to make food, so it's a worthy cause, don't you think?" His loving eyes search mine as he brings my hand to his lips, kissing every knuckle.

"Oh my God, you're serious?"

"Yeah. I'm serious. Bee deaths are on the rise."

I have to swallow past the sudden lump in my throat. "I swear, I think my mom brought me straight to you..." My voice breaks as I think of her, and he looks at me meaningfully.

"I think she did too, Tinker. I'll make her proud and treat you like the princess you are every damn day." He has so much conviction in every word, it can't be denied.

"She would've liked you." Even feeling emotional, I grin just thinking about it.

"Oh yeah? My handsome good looks or movie-star smile?" He waggles his eyebrows, making me smile.

"No, your kind heart, your gentle soul, and your protective nature all would've rated high in her book."

"I wish I got to meet her." He pushes my hair behind my ear.

"Me too..." I whisper, then lean in to kiss him, just as Sawyer steps back into the dining room.

"Who wants peanut butter cup cheesecake?" Sawyer calls out, carrying a big chocolate cake to the table, and my eyes widen. Everyone comes rushing back in, taking their seats and passing plates around.

Sutton pulls my chair closer to his, serving me a piece. "I made it just for you."

I melt a little more inside, especially when I take a bite and it's surprisingly delicious.

Listening to the laughter and chatter, everyone full of joy, I know we'll figure things out. Even with so much up in the air and fear still lingering inside me at what's to come, I have people around me who will help us along the way.

For that, I'm thankful.

44

SUTTON

I've turned off my cell. Bobby's calls were becoming problematic. They have been all week, ever since the news broke on social media that I'm leaving LA for good. Now, he's here in Whispers; he's been at the front gate for hours. Demanding that I talk with him, when I prefer to do anything but. The media is out there as well, capturing every angry minute.

"Maybe we just let him in and get it over with." Sawyer rubs his head.

"I can escort him in and out," Jackson adds, the three of us standing in my new kitchen, the appliances shiny, the cabinetry perfect. Thanksgiving lunch went amazingly well, considering how shit the food was—minus the cheesecake, because that was a slam dunk on my part. Mom loves Charlotte, just like I knew she would, and the fact that she now has three instant grandchildren made her smile all day long.

"Fine," I relent as Jackson pushes off the counter and walks out to the gate.

This is long overdue, and it's time to get it over with.

"You don't owe him anything. He profited amazingly well

from you," Sawyer reminds me, and my gaze moves to the family room, where Preston sits with his new tablet in his hands and earphones on, Charlotte working on her solar contraption. They look good in our home. It feels complete with us all here together.

"You want me to hide them?" Sawyer moves toward the family room, and I shake my head.

"No. Bobby won't have a camera. He doesn't know who they are." I take a deep breath, just as I hear the commotion.

"About fucking time, Sutton." Bobby strides in, a man on a mission, his chest puffed out and his face all red.

"Bobby." I nod as Jackson brings him into the kitchen, the hundred yards he walked from the gate clearly too much for him as he breathes heavily.

"Bobby? Bobby? That's all you've got to say after a decade?" he roars, and now he has Charlotte's attention. I see her sit up at the commotion from my peripheral vision, Preston still with his noise-canceling headphones on, completely oblivious.

"It was all outlined clearly in the letter—" Sawyer starts his legal jargon, but Bobby isn't having it.

"Shut up, Sawyer. I don't need to listen to anything you have to say." Bobby stares at me only, never even looking in Sawyer's direction, and I see my brother's hands tighten into fists at his sides.

"You do, actually." My brother steps forward, and I'm wondering what he means.

Bobby tenses. "You going to school me now?"

"Just wondering why you put a naked, underage girl in my brother's bed? Was it meant to get positive press? Did you do it to ruin his career?"

My gaze snaps to Bobby, having not thought of exactly why that happened or who orchestrated it. Sawyer's always had suspicions about my manager, and I've brushed it off. But now, as I look at him, I know my brother's been right all along.

Bobby gives a sadistic grin but remains silent. My stomach curdles that I had someone on my team, someone so close to me, who would put my career on the line like that.

"Or what about the guy who Jackson hit with the car? The one who walked off without a scratch but ended up in hospital with a broken leg. The media ate that up as well. What I can't figure out is why you would set all that up?" Sawyer presses, his voice holding an edge, but Bobby barely shows any remorse.

"Any publicity is good publicity, you know that." He looks me dead in the eye, like the issues he orchestrated were merely speedbumps, not issues that could've completely derailed my career had I stayed in LA. This is what he's become—sneaky, sleezy, underhanded.

I can't even speak as I stare at him, my blood boiling, and I see the moment he relents.

"Fine. I could see you pulling away, alright!" He runs his hands through his hair, releasing a deep huff. "I could tell your heart wasn't really in it, that I was losing you. You're my last client. I needed to continue to make you relevant."

"You did it all to increase media attention?" I frown as things click into place.

"YES!" he yells. "Without you, I'm nothing. So, I tried to make you relevant. I ensured that people were talking about you. I did my job!"

With a clenched jaw, I don't wait any longer to say, "It's over, Bobby."

His head looks like it's about ready to explode as he yells some more. "Over?! OVER?!!"

"It's been ten years, but it's time for me to move on," I say calmly, keeping my cool, and watch as his gaze moves over my shoulder. When I turn to see what he's looking at, Charlotte's standing there. I watch her swallow before she walks closer. I might be protective of her, but she's also protective of me.

"You!" He points at her. "This is all over some fucking piece of pussy?"

I can feel my heart pounding in my ears as I look back at him. "That is your one and only pass you'll get."

"Fuck. She must have a magical fucking cun—" He doesn't get to finish. My fist flies out and hits his jaw, and he's laid out on the new kitchen floor before he can get another word out. Charlotte gasps behind me, Sawyer muttering a "shit," but I step toward Bobby, relishing how he's now bleeding from his nose. Looking down on him, I now see him for the sniveling asshole he is.

"Say it again, Bobby. I fucking dare you," I grit out, my jaw working overtime. Clearly, my quick anger only happens when someone insults my woman. Sawyer and Jackson stand close by, here if I need them. Which I don't.

"You've changed." He slowly stands, grabbing a white handkerchief from his jacket, bringing it to his face.

"I have." I don't deny it.

"I'll charge you with assault."

It's an empty threat. He won't.

"Go ahead."

"Fuck." He's calm now. Knows my mind isn't changing. He knows this is the end.

"Ten fucking years, Silvers." With a shake of his head, he throws his arms up.

"It's been a hell of a ride. But it's now over."

"I can't hear no fat lady yet..." He lets his loose threat

linger before turning and walking to the door, never one to admit defeat, but at least now he'll give my phone a rest. Jackson follows him out, ensuring he leaves the grounds, and Sawyer blows out a breath as my girl comes to my side.

"I guess that was Bobby?" She looks up at me with widened eyes, and while I feel a little heavy for having such a relationship end, it was long overdue.

"It was."

She grabs my hand, inspecting my knuckles. "You alright?" This little pocket rocket looked almost ready to punch Bobby herself, and now she couldn't sound more innocent.

"Never been better. Angiogenesis is already starting." I wink at her.

"I love you," she says with a smile.

I swear my knees buckle nearly every time.

"And I love you," I give her a sweet kiss before she looks between me and my brother and walks back to her copper tubing. I love seeing her working on her projects in our home.

Sawyer wipes his hand down his face. "Well, that went about as well as I suspected."

"At least he understands now."

He looks at me with doubt in his eyes. "Do you think he did? Something tells me Bobby won't go down without a fight."

"What can he do?" I shrug.

"Ruin your career? Make up stories that pull you even further into trouble?"

Sawyer's right; he could. But I'll cross that bridge if it happens.

"I'll just be a professional beekeeper, then."

My brother huffs a laugh, grinning at me.

"Good to have my brother back."

My smile widens to match his. I haven't been myself for years, and finally, I know who I am and what I want.

"Good to be back."

I PULL at my bow tie, already itching to take it off.

"Here, let me." Charlotte steps forward and grabs my tie, undoing it and retying it with clear experience. I'm nervous, not for the launch, hell, I could do that in my sleep. But I'm nervous about leaving her. Almost everyone will be coming with me. Charlotte and Preston are the only ones who aren't. Thank God, Jackson will be here. Otherwise, I'd call the whole thing off.

"What other man have you tied bows for?" My eyes narrow on her, and she giggles, then snorts, and all thoughts of anything else disappear, my love for her expanding even more.

"Just Preston's." She grins, and more than anything, I want her on my arm tonight. But that isn't our story. *Yet.*

"I wish you were coming with me," I tell her softly.

Her eyes meet mine, and I wrap my arms around her waist, keeping her close.

"I know. Me too."

I see it in her eyes. I see her wanting to be with me, sad for missing this milestone. The launch at Whiteman's has already started. Tanner, Connor, and I are making our grand entrance in about half an hour.

"I hear the media are camped out. The commercial is going live across digital and TV at the same time as the launch, so you'll see my face even though I'm not here."

"We'll be watching. Preston is already in front of the TV,

waiting for it."

"I have my cell. Call me if you need me."

"We'll be fine. We have no plans of leaving the sofa," she assures me, pausing with the tie to look into my eyes. I think she can sense my nerves about this.

"Jackson will be here and won't leave the house until I'm back."

"Sutton. Relax. We'll be okay. The gates will lock, and Jackson is here. Preston and I won't move. You'll have all our attention, even if it has to be through a screen." Smiling, she tries to lighten the mood, and I press a kiss to her forehead.

I don't know why I feel agitated. It isn't like I haven't left her before. But I haven't left her side since I got back. We've both been holed up here in my new place, surrounded by the media pack for a few days. Furniture and things arrive every day, her adding her flair with ordering new rugs and cushions, adding a feminine touch to the place, which I love.

"There." She finishes the bow, her hands sliding down my chest, and I look up in the mirror. The tuxedo I'm wearing is molded to my frame. The bow tie she just tied looks perfect, better than I can do myself.

"We need to go!" Sawyer yells from down the hall, but my hands don't want to leave her.

"I'm so proud of you." Her words are a sweet whisper, and my throat constricts. No one has said that to me in a long time, my mom the only one.

"Thank you for that, for everything." I stare right at her. Holding her hand to my chest, I pull her body to me.

"I love you." She lifts up onto her tiptoes, her lips connecting with mine briefly. "Have a great time and celebrate. And we can have our own celebration later."

I hum, already looking forward to getting home and doing just that.

45

CHARLOTTE

Sutton walks out with his brother, slides into the truck, and drives out of the gates. I'm equal parts happy for him and sad that it isn't something that I get to experience at his side.

Looking every inch the billionaire he is, his suit fitted to perfection, his broad shoulders and strong physique one girls swoon over—including me—he'll be the talk of not only the town but the country. This new release of White-man's Whiskey, along with the global release of the new commercial, will have the media buzzing. No doubt, he'll be there all night, fielding questions and smiling for photographers. That's what it's all about. And he needs to play his part. Showcase the whiskey for Tanner and Connor. It's exciting, nerve-racking, and entirely new.

"Can we make popcorn?" Preston asks, the two of us now alone, aside from the security guys who walk around outside.

"Sure. Let me get it. You watch the screen and yell the minute you see the commercial," I tell him, not wanting to miss it. Having already seen snippets from filming day, I know it's going to be amazing.

This new home is incredible, and it's nice to be back in a fully functional kitchen again. I might even have Preston make us his famous *Croque Monsieur* tomorrow; I know Sutton will love it.

Grabbing a bag of popcorn, I throw it in the microwave before I move to the sink and fill up a glass of water. The popping begins immediately, and the kitchen fills with the scent of buttery goodness that can only be achieved by popcorn the minute I open the bag.

"Did I miss anything?" I sit next to Preston on the sofa, the two of us getting comfortable. He immediately dives his hand into the bowl.

"Nothing yet."

The beautiful French doors on the side of the room open, dragging my attention. It's Jackson, Sutton's head of security. Having just met him, I don't know him well. But he always seems grumpy and extremely serious. These security guys are generally all the same. They're working, not relaxing; they have a job to do, and they stay focused.

"Everything alright?" I ask as his eyes roam around the room.

"Everything's fine. Just doing my checks."

I relax as Jackson walks around, ensuring locks are still in place and radioing his team before he leaves again to circle the perimeter.

"He looks so mean..." Preston says, and we giggle, both munching on the popcorn.

I look at my watch, knowing Sutton would've arrived by now and will probably already be working the room. They have lots of media there tonight, plus all the big spenders and key contacts from the city Tanner flew in. It's probably something my dad would ordinarily go to, but I can't imagine him traveling all the way to Whispers for just one night.

I hear a thud outside, and my eyes flick to the French doors.

"Did you hear that?" Preston sits up, his gaze looking in the same direction as mine.

"Yeah… stay here." I jump up and walk tentatively to the glass doors. The night has settled in, and the lights that are usually on in the garden have gone out. "Hmm, lights are out," I tell Preston, and he doesn't say anything.

I turn to look at him and my heart stalls as I see a familiar woman restraining my brother, her hand over his mouth.

My stomach falls to my feet, voice lodging in my throat as someone comes at me from behind.

"No!" I shout as I start to kick and thrash, their hold only tightening with every movement. "What are you doing? Who are you?" I demand as the old guy I recognize from the diner pins my arms behind me.

"Maribel said she'd be a tough one," the woman says, and my blood runs cold. I still, and Preston's eyes widen even more, both of us knowing just how bad this situation is. My shock gives my attacker enough time to secure me and push us out the French doors.

"Help! Help! Jack—" I start to yell, hoping Jackson will hear me, before the old man's hand slaps across my mouth and I continue to twist and thrash with all my might.

"For God's sake." For an older guy, he's pretty strong, but I'm almost out of his arms when I feel a sharp pain in my arm.

Immediately, my body feels off, like I'm falling into a haze. "Ahhh… What…"

"A sedative. Should shut you up for a while," he says as my feet grow heavier.

Then I see Jackson. Hit from behind, his head bleeding, out cold. Preston starts wailing, his mouth then quickly wrapped in cloth, his screams muffled, just as I hear a familiar tune come from the TV inside. I look back quickly, seeing Sutton's face lighting up the screen through the open door behind us. Although, I'm starting to see double.

Looking at Preston, I murmur, "Yellow brick road." He looks at me, his eyes big and round and scared. But we need to at least try to get out of this. Preston nods as he kicks the woman in the shins, and I do the same to the man. It's enough to have their grip slip.

"Run!" Preston turns and runs as I throw an outdoor cushion at the man before I pull the entire outdoor chair out in front of them both. As expected, he runs toward me, swatting the cushion away, but not before he trips and falls, having not seen the chair.

"Fuck!" I hear the woman yell from behind us, Preston and I sprinting.

We dash across the back lawn, straight to our path. I pant, really wishing I did more cardio as my oxygen demand outpaces my supply. My eyesight's fading in and out, my legs weak, but I'm pushing as hard as I can. The cool air feels nice across my hot skin and I see Preston remove his gag, then I stumble.

"Come on, Charlotte. Please, stay with me," Preston pants as he glances behind him, seeing me struggling.

He grabs my arm and pulls me with him, trying to keep us both moving at speed. I can hear footsteps fast approaching, but as we hit the path, the trees offer some coverage to hopefully keep us out of their sight—at least for long enough to do what we need to. And thankfully, Preston and I know the way like the back of our hands.

It's dark, and I trip a little, my vision blurry, but Preston is laser focused. We make it halfway, the little bee box just to my left.

"Sutton." My voice is sluggish as I stop and open the box, pulling out the phone. "Keep going," I tell Preston as I hold the phone like it's my lifeline and dash down the path again.

We make it to the cottage and lock ourselves inside. Grabbing the phone only took a few seconds, but it's enough to have them banging on the door almost immediately. With my heart racing and breaths panting, I lift the phone with shaky hands and hit the button to call Sutton.

We both jolt as a loud thump breaks out across our flimsy door.

"Charlotte..." Preston warns, visibly trembling and stepping back from the door.

"We need a weapon," I say, but my voice comes out slurred, as the bang on the door comes again. I have no doubt this old timber door will splinter in a matter of seconds, and I can barely stand or keep my eyes open. I need someone here to save Preston. I can't let anything happen to him.

The phone rings in my hand as I pray Sutton answers.

"Tinker?" He picks up on the second ring, concern in his voice.

"Sutton... Maribel—" is all I get out before I hear the front door of the cottage crack open, and I drop the phone. Running to the kitchen, I stumble, legs wobbling beneath me. I open the drawers so violently, they fall from the cabinetry, smashing all over the floor.

Preston and I look over everything, seeing my bee clip

shatter more than it already was, and I bend down to grab the large knife from the silverware drawer.

"Preston, get behind me."

He jumps behind me as the couple I served at the diner steps through the door.

"You both need to come with us," the man says, looking angry as he strides in, and Preston backs away, but I stand ready. I've never used a knife like this before. I have no idea if I'm even holding it properly, but I'll do what I have to.

"Who are you and what do you want?" I yell, trying to focus on them, my vision failing me and my voice wonkier by the minute.

"We're here for Maribel. She knew you were here, tracked the call you made to your father. Tut, tut, tut... silly mistake that was," the old guy says as the woman circles around to the side, making me look in two directions and not helping my dizziness.

"All you had to do was stay gone... but lucky for us, she's paying a good sum of money to grab you and ensure you never come back to life again," the woman taunts. I can't believe I thought these people were nice.

I murmur something incomprehensible as the man lunges at me, and Preston throws a chair at him. But he's a big guy. Far outsizing my short five-foot frame, and the chair breaks, shattered against his side.

Again, he lunges at me, grabbing my hair as Preston scurries around, probably looking for something else to defend us. The sting on my scalp burns, and I fling out my arms, still holding the knife, feeling it slice somewhere. The man yells, throwing me to the side, sending me sliding across the floor, seeing bright red now coating his white shirt. When I look up at his face, his scowl turns deadly.

Preston tries to help me, the brave boy he is. I should've

known my little brother wouldn't leave my side. He runs and pushes the woman away, but she doesn't move. Not even an inch. And I know then it's useless. Because she grabs Preston, pulls him to her body, and presses a gun to my little brother's head.

And I can do nothing to stop it. Not as my body gives up on me, the drugs pulling me into darkness.

My time is up.

46

SUTTON

I smile for what feels like the hundredth photo.

"She's safe, at home," Sawyer reminds me as I smile wide again, shaking someone's hand.

The media are everywhere, the distillery restaurant packed. When we aired the commercial, we got a standing ovation and a few wolf whistles. Not to mention, the new whiskey is a huge hit. It's trending on all social media, and print ads roll out starting tomorrow across national newspapers and magazines. The commercial will run for a few weeks before we replace it with a new one. Each made with a large budget, telling the story of the Whiteman's brand and a snippet about the Save the Bees charity. Not only are Tanner and Connor pleased, but their smiles are hard to tame. It's the dream outcome, really, for Tanner, Connor, and me.

"I know," is all I can say, before he goes back to Annabelle.

I'm feeling off. I want Charlotte with me tonight. I want her with me, always. But I know she's home safe. Jackson has checked in. Told us the property is secure, that they're where we left them in the living room. But the commercial went live around the country at the same time as we launched, and I thought I might get a text from her or something.

"Sutton, good to see you." Tyler Grant strides up to me, and the cameras flash.

"Tyler. Long way from home for you here." This business billionaire could probably buy the whole town of Whispers, he's that wealthy.

"Well, I love Tanner's whiskey and wanted to fly out and see what all the fuss is about in this town. I have to say, it's appealing."

"The whiskey or Whispers?" I ask him with a quirked eyebrow.

"Whispers. I'm starting to realize these small towns have a hell of a lot of potential if you find the right one."

I nod, fully understanding that now. "Whispers is pretty special."

"Heard you've built here?"

"Yeah, I'm planning on staying a while." I keep my answers loose, not wanting anyone to know my business, although Tyler is a decent guy.

"Maybe we need to catch up for a drink soon. Good to see you." He slaps my arm as we shake, and I see him move on, his team scuffling behind him, already out the door, probably straight back to his jet.

"Sutton." Tanner walks up, eyes bright, his grumpy side put aside for the evening. "You saw Tyler?"

"He's happy. Likes the whiskey. Likes Whispers." Tanner's keen to work with Tyler—what that looks like, I'm not sure, but there's certainly a lot of money in this room tonight. I spot another guy I know over in the corner. He owns a family winery in Northern California. They make a great wine, one I think Tinker might like, so I make a mental note to say hello. Maybe I can take her out to California to taste a couple; it could be a beautiful weekend trip when everything settles down.

"Good." Tanner grabs my shoulder, giving me a squeeze just as a journalist approaches, grinning at me before a microphone is put in front of my face.

"Sutton, tell me, you've been asked before to be the face of many brands and many products, but you haven't done that until now. What is it about Whiteman's Whiskey that has you putting your name to it?"

"Whiteman's isn't just whiskey; it's heritage in a glass. Every drop carries the craftsmanship of generations, and if I can be a small part of sharing that story, that's a legacy worth raising a glass to." I nod at her and feel Tanner beaming by my side. I swear, if there isn't a box of this release on my doorstep tomorrow morning, he'll be woken up with a call.

The journalist turns to him. "Tanner, how did you know Sutton Silvers was the right man to be the face of your whiskey?"

"I could've picked anyone, but Sutton gets it. He knows Whiteman's Whiskey isn't about trends; it's about tradition, about craftsmanship, about taking your time. About family. That's why he's here tonight, and that's why there was never another choice." Tanner squeezes my shoulder again. We've hit a gold mine working together, and this is just the beginning.

"And Sutton, there's no woman on your arm tonight. Is that a sign for all the ladies that you're still single?" There's a cheeky, flirty glint to her eye. She's pushing the boundaries and knows it.

My answer is instant and without hesitation. "No. I'm not single. I'm very much taken."

She looks shocked, and Tanner coughs, but I can't play the part any longer. I'm not single, and I want the world to know. I just hope it doesn't paint a larger bullseye on our lives.

"Anyone we know?" she asks.

I grin because I can't help it. Every time I think of Charlotte, I smile.

"No. And no more questions. You got your scoop."

She nods, her excitement palpable, knowing I just handed her the leading story that she'll now break to the world.

"Sutton. There're some people here I want you to meet." Tanner turns slightly as a familiar couple stands before me, and my jaw tightens.

"Colin Titan and his new wife, Maribel. Colin is a longtime lover of my whiskey." Tanner beams, having no idea he's just shit on my life. I look at Charlotte's father with barely contained anger. Then my eyes move to her stepmother, and my lip almost curls in a sneer. Standing there, all polished, not a hair out of place. Diamonds dazzling around her neck, her lips plump, her hair frozen solid in place with so much hairspray you could start a wildfire.

"Pleasure to meet you." Her father extends his hand, and I take in a breath.

"Pleasure is all mine." I grip his hand tight.

"So you like Whiteman's Whiskey?" My throat tightens around every word, trying to sound normal and pleasant.

"Yeah, well, it has sentimental value to me." He nods, suddenly looking a little solemn.

My brow pinches. "Sentimental value?" I ask as Tanner turns away, talking to someone else close by.

"I only open a bottle of Whiteman's on special occasions. The last time was with my daughter for her twenty-first birthday." As the word "daughter" leaves his lips, his face falls, dripping with sadness.

I frown. "Oh, did she like it?" I watch him closely as he answers, trying to get a gauge on it all.

His smile is small as he gets lost in his memories. "Yeah, not a lot, but a little. She was my shining star, my baby girl. I came tonight to remember her. She and my son have been missing for months." The raw pain in his eyes isn't something you can fake.

Fuck, my chest hurts.

Before I can tell him that I'm sorry or that I hope he can reunite with them soon—something someone would say who *doesn't* know where his kids are—Maribel speaks up.

"Oh, I've told you, you need to move on," his new wife basically scolds him, slapping his upper arm with her bejeweled fingers, albeit with a little chuckle, like it's all in good humor. I'm not sure what she finds funny.

"Move on?" I tilt my head her way, and she looks at me, a small smile on her face. Sly, almost like a fox.

"Yes, move on. We need to start traveling. Forget about them."

"Forget about them?" both Colin and I say in unison before looking at each other. I see it then with undeniable certainty, the immense sadness in his eyes. Deep remorse for losing them. I know for sure he'll want them back, want them in his lives. But then Maribel speaks.

"Nothing but trouble. They left. We can't find them. They're ungrateful," she says flippantly.

"I never lose hope that they'll come back." He gives me a forced smile. "So I bought one of Tanner's finest bottles tonight, one I can keep to open with my daughter when I see her again."

"What would you do if they turned up tomorrow?" I ask him, but I watch her. Her eyes burn holes into me; she might as well be throwing flames.

"I would give up everything to have them back. I haven't been a great father. Not for a few years anyway. I have my faults. But I'll make it up to them," he admits. I want to dig deeper, see what he might say about Preston, but Maribel interjects once again.

"Well, they don't want to be found. We've looked everywhere. Even in the deepest forests," Maribel says, and something about the way she says it has me looking back at her with intensity.

"Forests?" I bite out, jaw clenched tight as my heart stutters.

"Yeah, you know, there are little cottages hidden all among those types of places. I've left no stone unturned."

My phone rings, and I pull it out, hands shaking as I see the number.

"Excuse me," I say to them and hold up the phone.

"We need to get going. Pleasure to meet you," Colin says politely, and I watch them turn to leave as I pick up the call.

"Tinker?" I breathe out, already worried.

"Sutton... Maribel..." is all I hear, her voice sounding slurred and breathless before the line goes dead.

I stand in shock for a second. My feet unmoving, my heart rate escalating. She sounds off. Something is wrong, wrong, wrong. I look at my cell again, like it can tell me something more, and then I realize she called from the satellite phone and I start to fully panic.

"What is it?" Sawyer's right at my side. I look up and

around, feverishly scanning the crowd for the couple who were just here a moment ago.

"Where are they?" I demand, starting to gather interest from the people around me, but I don't care.

"Who?" Tanner asks as he strides over.

"Where's Colin Titan?" My head whips from side to side, and finally, I spot Colin and Maribel as they're walking out the door.

"Hey!" I shout, dodging waiters as I stomp through the crowd, almost bowling over the wine guy I wanted to talk to in my rush to chase them down.

"Fuck!" I hiss as I see them now outside, almost to their car, and I start to sprint, my brother following, my security team on our heels.

"Stop! Don't leave!" I yell again, my heart lurching from my chest as the party continues inside. I feel nothing as the cold night air hits my face, my eyes blazing on the one woman I know can tell me something.

"I said stop!" I catch them just before they get to their waiting car. Colin pauses and spins around to look at me as I see Maribel pushing him to get in the car.

"What have you done?" I seethe at her, and she pauses, her body tensing for a moment. Then she takes a step forward, and for a split second, her smile gets bigger, before she feigns mock shock.

"I don't know what you're talking about," she says, her voice sickly sweet.

"Sutton?" Sawyer looks at me like I've lost my mind.

"What's going on?" Colin asks, his eyes bouncing between me and his wife, on guard.

"I know where your daughter is, Colin. And Preston," I tell him, knowing he isn't the enemy. He might be guilty of being a shit father, but he isn't guilty of any harm to them.

Maribel's eyes widen, dropping her facade, not thinking I would talk about it so openly. Not realizing her little plan is about to unravel.

"You do?" He stands ten feet taller, looking at me with interest as Maribel starts glancing around for an escape. Only, there's nowhere to run.

"Yeah, but you know what? So does your wife here. Go on. Tell him, Maribel. Tell him all about how you abused Preston. Tell him all about how you blackmailed Charlotte to leave so you wouldn't go to the press about Colin and ruin his reputation. Ruin his business. Tell him that his only daughter, his baby girl, fled with her brother in the middle of the night, out of fear that you were going to hurt them and bring their father down, all so you could get his money. Tell him that she left to save him," I seethe, and a few people nearby gather, but I don't falter.

"What?" Colin looks stunned, like his whole world just brightened and crumbled at the same time. Sawyer grabs my security team, who all subtly position themselves around us, blocking them in and blocking the media out. There's nowhere she can go, nowhere she can hide.

"That's nonsense," she scoffs.

"What the fuck is he talking about, Maribel?" Colin's raised voice captures attention of those around us, and my heart races so fast my hands shake.

"He's talking nonsense. He's probably high on drugs or something..." She's stuttering now.

"You're both coming with me, and I swear, you better hope they're alive when we get there." I look over her shoulder and nod to my security team, who all crowd behind her and Charlotte's father.

"Alive? Where are they? What's happening?" Colin yells in confusion.

"Let me go!" Maribel screams as my team grab her by the upper arms. "Colin! Tell them to let me go!"

Colin pales as he watches the woman he married start screaming and kicking.

"What the hell have you done?" he asks her, voice gruff, anger vibrating around his body. He's a smart man. It's all clear to him now, even if he doesn't have the evidence.

"He's lying. He's an actor. Why would you believe anything he has to say?!" she screeches, but I have little time to hear.

"Go. Connor and I will finish up. We'll come over as soon as we can." Tanner practically pushes us to some waiting trucks nearby. Colin, Sawyer, and I jump in one, my security team taking a screaming Maribel in the other, and we drive off to my place. Adrenaline surges through my body as I'm forced to sit still, desperate to get to Charlotte and Preston.

"What happened?" Sawyer barks as he starts to drive.

"Will someone tell me what the hell is going on?" Colin demands, as Sawyer drives like a madman out of Distillery Drive and straight to Billionaire Boulevard.

"I'm in love with your daughter. She and Preston now live with me. Your wife is a fucking psychopath who abused your kids while you had your head so far up your fucking ass you couldn't see straight! That's what the hell is going on!" I shout. None of this would have happened if he was a better father. If he got his shit together after his wife died. Although, I do have sympathy, because if anything happens to Charlotte, I know it would end me too.

His head rears back as he sucks in a sharp breath. "They're here? In Whispers?"

"Yes. And we're going to them now." I have to take a breath before continuing, too keyed up to think straight.

"Charlotte called on the satellite phone. She didn't sound right, and the call dropped before she could tell me what was happening. That fucking Maribel... I know she has something to do with this; Charlotte said her name, and that's the last thing she said."

"Oh my God..." Colin mutters, beside himself.

Sawyer's serious gaze flicks to me as he pulls into my driveway, my security men surrounding the house. My blood runs cold as I jump out of the truck and see Jackson instructing the team, all of them running in every direction.

"Boss," is all he says, and I notice he looks like he's running ragged.

"What happened? Where's Charlotte?" My words trip over each other as I approach him, out of breath just from nerves.

He swallows roughly. "Gone."

My world moves on its axis.

"Gone?" I stall, and then I see the large gash on his head and blood pouring down his cheek.

"A man and a woman came in, and we think they got through the side entrance. The locks were cut. Got me when I wasn't looking."

"Fuck!" I scream, hitting the front of the truck so hard, I'm surprised the airbags don't deploy.

A moment later, my security team pulls up, Maribel in tow. As they take her out of the car, I shout, "Where is she! Tell me what you did to her!"

"It's too late... The job will be done..." She has a satisfying smirk on her face, one that has Colin turning even more ashen.

"What did you do?" He looks at Maribel like he's seeing a ghost. When she doesn't respond, anger takes over any bewilderment as he stalks up to her and screams in her face. "What did you do!"

This seems to take her by surprise, because for the first time since I met her, the smart-ass smile falters.

"Security footage?" Sawyer asks Jackson.

"No footage. Camera was out."

I growl, tugging at my hair. "What do you mean, it was out?" I'm so angry. I could tear this security team to shreds.

"They cut the wires. This was planned and planned well." Jackson looks around, on high alert before all our eyes lock on Maribel once more.

"I swear to God, Maribel, if my kids die because of something you did, I will fucking end you..." Colin's words have bite, and I know that he means them.

"Jackson," I murmur, nodding at Maribel. "Get information from her any way you know how."

"On it." He grabs Maribel by the arms, and she starts to shriek, her screams loud in the dark night, ranting obscenities filtering through the air as he drags her away.

"Jesus Christ." Sawyer rubs his face, looking just as panic-stricken as I do.

Feeling like I'm about to lose my mind, I take a breath and focus, thinking through what I know and trying to be rational like Charlotte would be in this kind of situation. And like the final piece clicking into place, I know exactly where to go. She called me from the satellite phone, meaning she was in the forest, and Maribel mentioned "forests" like she knew exactly where to find her.

"She's at the cottage." I'm already running, my heart thumping, and I hear Sawyer and the others following me, albeit much slower as they don't know the terrain. Sprinting along my path, each second feels like it could be life or death. With my girl and my new little brother on my mind, I move faster, lungs burning and legs pumping. Seeing the cottage up ahead, I slow my stride, only to take in what's happening. My blood turns cold at the front door off its hinges, and that has me speeding up again.

"Fuck." Sawyer rushes in behind me as I burst through the open door, and we survey the damage. A broken chair, the door shattered, drawers in the kitchen strewn all over the floor. I pull in air quickly, my heart racing and stomach twisting, but I'm quiet as I look around. Stepping toward the kitchen, a bright-yellow sparkle catches my eye, and my feet pause when I see it. Her original bee clip. The one I know she was keeping for sentimental value. I swallow roughly as I bend down, careful to pick up every piece.

"Her clip..." her father says, fear in his voice as he looks at it in my hand. Any hesitations he may have had that his kids weren't here diminish in that instant.

"There's blood," my brother says from a few feet away.

I stand quickly and turn, following Sawyer's gaze, seeing blood on the floor. I don't know if it's hers, but it's fresh, and it isn't a lot. My anger builds, my terror at where they could be battling it.

Pushing that aside, I stay focused and walk down the hall, each step quiet, not knowing what we might find, or who. The others follow, keeping their eyes peeled.

At the end of the hall, it's deathly silent, almost eerily so. As I approach her room, I look back at my security team, and they nod, ready to jump to action. I open her bedroom door, and there, in the middle of the room, are Charlotte and Preston. Tied together, back-to-back, both their mouths covered. Preston looks scared, wide-eyed, but Charlotte is slumped.

"Tinker!" My heart lurches at finding them overwhelming, but I'm frightened at seeing her lifeless. I run to her, eager to touch her. Eager to have her in my arms, where I know she'll be safe.

"Found them." I hear on a radio and stride to where they are, Colin and I both furiously untying the ropes. The two of us thinking of nothing else but saving the two people we love more than anything.

"Sawyer. Paramedics!" I yell to my brother, who's already on the phone.

"It's alright, Preston. We're here. We're all here. You're fine," I tell the boy who looks with teary eyes at me, then his dad, shock evident.

"Preston!" Colin says through a sob as he pulls his son in tight, and I watch Preston fall into his embrace. The small boy missed his dad more than he ever let on.

I pull Charlotte to my chest, cradling her, her body dead weight, her skin pale.

"Tinker... Tinker, wake up." I panic at her not responding, my voice getting choked up. Laying her on the ground, I shake her shoulders, trying to rouse her. "Please, baby. Wake up. I need you."

"They drugged her." Preston catches my attention, as his dad still holds him tight, both of them crying. I can't imagine how he's feeling. He was sitting with her this whole time while she was unconscious, not knowing if she's okay.

"Tinker!" I say, louder this time, shaking her shoulders, my life hanging by a thread. But then she moans.

"Stop yelling..." Her voice is faint, but it's there. I pant, slumping over, trembling as I touch her face.

"Hey, Tinker... thought I lost you for a moment there..." I tell her softly as tears wet my cheeks, the room around us still in a frenzy. I brush the hair from her face, looking her over. Her skin is pale, but I see her pulse thrumming in her neck, which is all I need to confirm I'm not dreaming.

"Hmmmmm..." is all she musters.

"Look at me, baby... Open your pretty eyes for me."

I sense her dad watching, but I don't care.

"Sutton..." She says my name, and her eyes flutter a little before closing again.

"Found the suspects. Caught them on foot. Bringing them in now." I hear the call over a radio as I see the blue and red lights coat the bedroom walls. I pull her close and sag with relief to the floor.

47

CHARLOTTE

I lie in the bed, staring at the bodies next to me, scared to move in case they wake. I've been looking at them for about twenty minutes now. Sutton's sitting right by my bedside and Preston is curled in his lap. They look cute together, the two of them clutching my hand.

Then I turn my head and look back at my father. He hasn't moved the whole time I've been watching. Sitting on the seat across the room, head hung low, staring at the floor. I've heard him cry. I've heard him whimper. It's like the grief of losing Mom all over again.

My foot tingles, so I wiggle my toes a little, and his head shoots up. His bloodshot eyes meet mine, and for a full minute, we just stare at each other. The silence is overwhelming.

"I thought I lost you…" His voice cracks, and a tear runs down his cheek. "Tell me I haven't."

I swallow, my eyes watering. My heart feels like it's ripping in two. But he's my dad.

"Maribel?" My words whisper across the room to him as his jaw clenches.

"With police. I can't believe it... I can't believe any of it." He shakes his head, rubbing a hand down his face. The oil tycoon looks broken.

"You weren't there for us..." I keep my features schooled, my jaw set, but my resolve is crumbling. I just want my dad back. The one who left when Mom died.

"I wasn't a good father. You deserved better. Much better."

I take a shaky breath, letting him continue.

"But I want to try again. I lost your mother. I can't lose you and Preston too. I will do whatever it takes. Whatever it takes. I promise you." I see the determination in his eyes, his love for us shining through. There's a lot of work to be done. My trust in him is completely shattered, but I know he was dealing with his own grief demons, Maribel taking advantage of all that.

I swallow roughly and give him a small nod.

"I love you, Dad..." I can barely get out the words as he rushes to me. Scooping me up tight, holding me close, just like he used to.

"I love you too, sweetie. God, I can't believe I almost lost you. Lost Preston... I'll never let anyone harm you again. Ever again. You're both my everything." He grips me tight, and I wince a little, my muscles sore, but I hold him back just as tightly. I can't stop the tears, and I feel my hair growing wet from where his face is buried.

"You're awake?" Preston's voice is groggy and Dad pulls back slightly as we both look at my brother.

"Come here, you," I tell him, and he dives in, the three of us hugging. It feels so nice. So good to be back with our father. It won't all be erased, and it'll take time. But I know he loves us.

"Hey, buddy. We're alright. We'll be alright," I whisper to my brother, hearing him cry.

I look over Preston's shoulders and see Sutton sitting up, watching it all. *I love you,* I mouth to him, my heart full.

"I love you too, Tinker." The sound of Sutton's deep voice has my father pulling back, all four of us wiping our eyes.

"Tinker..." Sutton comes closer, and my dad is silent, giving us room as I turn, looking at the man who does have all my trust. "Hey, baby... How do you feel?" he croons, sitting forward as his hand comes to my face, caressing me so softly I barely feel it.

"Like I have a hangover without the fun of a party."

"The liver metabolizes the drugs, and it takes time for the body to clear it, rehydrate, and restore normal brain function."

I grin at hearing the small tidbit.

"Well, that's what Hudson said..." He looks sheepish, even though his eyes canvass me, still searching for any other signs of distress.

"Maribel's gone. Sheriff took her. Williamstown police are involved. She has clear ties to the two people who grabbed you guys," Sutton explains, and Preston's hands tighten around me.

"Who were they?" My brain is starting to connect as visions of the older couple from the diner come back to me.

"Her brother and his wife." My dad scoffs, shaking his head. "She wanted you and Preston gone. She wanted to be the only family tie to me. She did it for money. It was all about the money." He looks and sounds disgusted. Disgusted with her and her behavior, but also with himself for the poor choices he made. "I can't believe it. I just can't believe any of it."

"We got to you just in time. They were both amateurs.

They left you and Preston tied together while they went to find their getaway car. Got lost in serial killer forest while trying to find their way out. My team found them pretty quickly."

"They got caught by the forest?" I can't help but chuckle at that fact.

"Yeah... looks like you, me, and Preston are the only ones who know our way around those woods. And our little call box came in handy too."

"It was your good idea to put it there... See? You are resourceful," I tell him as my hand clutches his, and he squeezes it back before lifting it to his lips and kissing my knuckles.

"I was so scared, Tinker..." Vulnerability shines through as his eyes get a little glassy.

"Me too," I whisper to him, holding his gaze, my love for this man expanding.

"Me three..." Preston murmurs.

I hold him close, brushing back the hair off his forehead as his eyes meet mine. "I'm sorry you had to go through that alone when I blacked out. You must have been so scared."

"It's okay. They didn't do anything else. Just tied us up and left. I was mostly scared about if you were going to wake up, but I kept watching you breathe. I knew Sutton would show up and save us."

Another tear trails down my cheek as we both look at Sutton.

"Always, buddy. You can always count on me," he says, swallowing past more emotions.

"Looks like you've all made a little life for yourself here in Whispers..." Dad stands at the end of my bed, watching all three of us with a softened look in his eyes.

"We have." Sutton nods, protectiveness coming to the surface.

"You've been taking care of my kids… when I couldn't…" My dad pauses, shaking his head, but Sutton doesn't let him stumble as he stands, walking toward him.

"I fell in love with your daughter the moment I saw her. And I fall more and more in love with her every second of every day. She's incredible, and Preston is like a little brother to me. We've started building a life here, one where they are safe, loved, and cared for," Sutton says as my father turns to face him.

"I can see that. And I thank you for everything. For loving them."

He nods in understanding, but then says, "I don't need thanks. I just need them. And here in Whispers, I'll make sure they're happy." Sutton smiles, but I know he's stamping his authority.

My dad looks at where Preston and I are, clinging to each other and watching the two men we love talk. He nods at me, and I nod back. A silent conversation that this is where we want to stay.

"Well, looks like I'll be doing a lot of traveling to Whispers, then, doesn't it?" He holds out his hand for Sutton to shake, and Preston and I both tense, waiting to see what Sutton does.

"You're always welcome in Whispers." Sutton takes his hand, and they shake, and I blow out a breath and feel Preston sag in my arms.

It'll take a while, but I know we'll be okay. And we won't be leaving Whispers.

48

SUTTON

"You need to calm down. You're walking around like you have a bee stuck up your pants." Sawyer watches me as I pace the kitchen. While my beehives are doing well, I still make sure I'm never near the hives without layers of protection. Something he finds extremely comical.

"I feel more nervous now than I have before any movie." I can't keep still.

The house is full of all the people I love. Family, both old and new, and I look out the window, seeing everyone sitting outside on the patio, under the heaters, the cool night feeling crisp, but we welcome it.

My eyes roam over Rochelle, the sheriff, my mom, the kids, and then Annabelle before they rest on Colin Titan. He's been staying in Whispers for a little while. Trying to reconnect with his kids, rebuilding the trust he severely damaged. My team are watching every move he makes, but deep down, I know he's a good man. He was broken, living in a state of grief once his wife died and unable to get out of it. Pulling away from his kids and drowning himself in his work, thinking a new wife could manage things.

Now he and his kids are going to therapy, both together and individually, and Preston and Charlotte haven't left Whispers. Haven't left my side. There's still work to be done, but I see the bonds between them strengthening every day.

I had Jackson investigate everyone and everything. He worked with the police and helped build the case against Maribel, who's looking at serving a long time behind bars. I'm forever grateful to him, and he and his small team now reside in Whispers here with me as well. The media are still prolific. There's always a group waiting outside my gates, so his team keeps them at bay.

When everything first happened, Colin brought in every big gun possible. I thought I had connections, but Colin is almost like the president. And my team is amazing, but his is like a whole department, dedicated to the safety and well-being of his family. One he probably should've used much earlier to prevent all this from happening.

But then I wouldn't have met Charlotte.

Thinking of her, my eyes settle on the woman who's my complete other half. She must sense me watching her because she looks up at me, catching my eye mid-laugh at something my mom says, her beautiful blue eyes glistening.

One of the first things I did when we all got home was fly in a hairdresser. She and Preston were locked in the bathroom for hours, and when they came out, I got to see the real her. Her hair is a beautiful strawberry blond, and while she needed a few treatments to get it back to its natural state, I'm glad she now just gets to be her.

"Is it big enough?"

Sawyer snorts at my question. "You can see that fucking thing from Mars."

We look at the ring in the box in my hand. An ethically sourced diamond set with recycled platinum. Making it strong, classic, and perfect for my Tinker.

"Boys, we need some more drinks out there." Colin walks into the kitchen, and I close the box. Sawyer looks at me and nods before leaving the room.

"Colin." Like he can sense my tone, he pauses and gives me his full attention.

"There's still a lot we all need to work through, and a lot of trust still needs to be built, but I wouldn't be the man my mom raised me to be if I didn't ask your permission. So..."

His eyes widen.

"Can I have your permission to ask Charlotte to marry me?"

He blinks a few times, then swallows, and then tears start to form in his eyes. I think I took him by surprise.

"Of course. I would be blessed for her to marry a man like you, Sutton. And I thank you for giving me the opportunity to have this moment with you. For her." He offers me a handshake, and I take it, sealing his approval. Formalizing the commitment that we both make to his daughter.

"Thank you." I smile, feeling like everything is now in motion. "Okay, go back to enjoying yourself. I'll be out in a few minutes."

"Will do. Your mom likes these fruity drinks... says they taste like cordial." He grabs a few bottles from the fridge, and I frown. He and my mom sure do get along well, and as I watch him scurry back outside and take his seat next to her, my mom beams at him.

I put the ring box in my pocket and walk outside, my hands shaking. This is the most real and most important thing I've ever done. I know it will cause ripples around the world, as the media are going to whip into a frenzy, but I don't care about any of that. I just want her with me forever.

"If I can get everyone's attention…" I step up to Charlotte's side, and the table quiets as everyone looks at me. I catch Sawyer's eyes; my older brother looks proud and gives me a small nod in encouragement. Then I look at Charlotte, her face free of stress, watching me so adoringly, I almost crumble. God, how did I get so lucky to meet her?

"Charlotte… I've watched you fight for your brother, for your future, for your peace. You've faced storms that would've broken most people, and you did it with grace, grit, and that fire in your eyes that I fell in love with the moment I saw you." I pause, my throat feeling tight.

"You and I met like kismet. Who would've thought that here, in this small, quiet town, you from Manhattan and me from Hollywood, would have ever met. But we did. You saw me as a man, not a movie star. I saw you as the diner girl, not the heiress. And we've come together in what I know is by far the most extraordinary love story. Not scripted, not staged, just raw, real, and beautifully ours. You challenged me, grounded me, made me laugh when I forgot how. And every day since, I've woken up knowing that no spotlight, no red carpet, no award could ever compare to the way you look at me when I bring you your favorite peanut butter cups."

The table murmurs a small laugh as Charlotte's eyes water, her love shining up at me. Grabbing her hand, I get down on one knee in front of her, and I feel everyone hold their breath.

"So, in front of everyone who matters, our family and friends, I want to ask you… Will you marry me?"

My heart pauses. Candles flicker around us, the sun setting in the distance. The crickets chirping is the only sound as I look into her eyes and wait.

Luckily, she doesn't make me wait long. A smile takes over her face as tears fall down her cheeks.

"It would be my honor to be your wife. Yes, Sutton. Yes, I will marry you." She barely gets out the words before I scoop her up, lifting her out of her chair and pulling her to me.

Everyone cheers, claps, and glasses clink as I kiss my girl, sealing our deal before I put her back on the ground and slide the ring on her finger.

And just like that, I've found my new family, my new home. My new forever.

EPILOGUE - CHARLOTTE

I stretch down and touch my toes, exhaling long and deep.

"That's it. Release the muscles before you come back up and we get onto our mats for five minutes of meditation." Daisy's tranquil voice carries across the room as we all get settled, lying face up on the mats as she turns down the lights.

I'm now a regular at the yoga community nights, and I do a few other paid classes as well. It's been nice to spend time doing the activities I love, and it's a great way to get rid of any stress.

"Breathe in two, three, four, and out, two, three, four..." Her voice gets softer and softer until we're all lying in the darkened room, no sounds but a soft, soothing melody of wind pipes playing in the background.

My eyes are closed, and I breathe deep, but I can't quiet my mind. I wonder briefly if Connor will start snoring again, like he did last week, and I roll my lips at the memory.

If I knew my life would work out like it has, then I

would've made my way to Whispers with Preston much sooner. I'm now working full time at the distillery as their Sustainability Officer, and I love it. Tanner and Connor are great bosses, and they've given me a big budget to work with, their commitment toward a sustainable business one I admire. I'm flying to LA to speak at a sustainability conference next week, and I can't wait. My career is thriving.

I had to give up the diner. It was something that I didn't want to do, but Rochelle and I remain close. All of us are always there in our booth at the back of the diner, grabbing dinner or a cupcake after school when we can.

I see Dad often. He stepped down as the CEO of Titan Energy but remains on the board. He put forward a motion to expand on the very small environmental department Titan has and often asks my view on things. While we still have a way to go to get back to the happy family we once were, he's purchased a place here in Whispers to be closer to Preston and me, and we get to spend time with him almost every other week. He's committed to being a present father, and stepping away from the family business is a big part of that.

Preston is going from strength to strength. He's put his name down to play baseball next season, and his grades continue to impress me. After scoring an A-plus on his Benjamin Franklin project, Sutton now sits with him every night after school to do homework. Sometimes, it's hard to see who's teaching who, but it's cute, and I know they both love it.

"Let the breath carry your thoughts..." Daisy's voice cuts in, her melody starting to bring people back around.

My thoughts continue to wander, thinking about the vast array of wildflowers that now bloom around the cottage. I spend a lot of time there, tinkering with my projects while

Sutton hikes around the forest and checks on his bees. We still haven't found any dead bodies, but we know the soil is good because the flowers are spreading amazingly well and my apple tree is looking like it's going to provide a great harvest.

"And as we come back to ourselves, think of the one thing that makes you smile..." Daisy sits up, and after just a few more minutes of meditation, people move around, the class now over. But before I move, I do what I always do and think of Sutton. The man who's by my side every day and in my bed every night. The man I never expected, but the one who continues to show up for me anyway.

When I grin and open my eyes, looking at the door, there he is, standing there, watching. Waiting for me like he does after every class. Still in his baseball hat and white t-shirt, he holds up another book he has purchased on bees, and I laugh as I gather my things to meet him.

"What are you doing?" I walk straight into his arms, and he holds me tight. To outsiders, we look like we haven't seen each other in weeks, not merely an hour since he dropped me off.

"I saw this at the homeware shop. Evelyn told me she got it in just for me." He grins proudly, and I laugh, then snort, thinking about all the ladies who almost run over themselves to cater to the celebrity who now lives in their town.

"Oh, heads-up," he says quickly as we push through the doors to walk out to the truck. I hear it then. The familiar click of cameras that now follow our every move.

When Sutton and I first came out, it was a whirlwind. We ignored it all, mostly because I was still cementing my relationship with my father, and we were all focused on ensuring Preston was looked after and had everything he needed. After a while, attention died down, almost completely.

Then when he proposed, the media swirled back into town and haven't really left.

"Sutton, give us a smile."

"Sutton, when are you coming back to LA?"

"Charlotte, Titan Energy share price has skyrocketed. Do you have any comment?" Sutton moves us through the few waiting media quickly and gets us into his truck.

"Vultures." He starts to drive. We're both used to it, but neither of us love it.

"Where are we going?" I look out at the beautiful town we now call home, knowing we are going in the wrong direction.

"I want to check on the wedding prep."

I grin, loving how he's organizing the entire thing. I've been so busy in my new role with Whiteman's that when we both decided we wanted a quick engagement, he put his hand up to plan.

"I can't believe it's only a week away!" I look at the diamond on my finger, seeing it sparkle.

"Mmmm. Can't wait." He grabs my hand, bringing it to his lips as he turns down the now familiar road. "It's going to look amazing," he assures me as we turn up the gravel driveway and already see trucks and cars parked everywhere.

"Security's already here?" I ask as we jump out and start to walk hand in hand.

"I have them positioned around the perimeter."

I look at the cottage that we've refurbished and smile when I see the second apple tree growing well.

"Rochelle and Tanner are going to set up the food and bar here. Valet will grab the cars and take them up to

Billionaire Boulevard, out of the way," he starts explaining, and butterflies flutter through my chest.

"I have to say, I never thought I would ever get married in a place we call serial killer forest."

Sutton's grin is wicked when I chuckle.

"Yeah, your father wasn't pleased. But this is us, Tinker..." He stops walking and stands in front of me, pressing a soft kiss to my lips.

"It is, isn't it?" I beam up at him, excitement at becoming Mrs. Sutton Silvers building even more.

"He also wasn't pleased with the honeymoon destination..." Sutton murmurs, and I laugh.

"I can't imagine why," I say sarcastically, already dreaming about lying in that pool at Dragonfly in the South of France.

"Actually, while we're on the topic of parents... is there anything going on with your dad and my mom?" Sutton's frown is enough to tell me he wouldn't be happy if there was.

I roll my lips. They get along well, and truth be told, I have no idea if anything is going on, but they're friends, and it's nice to see. They're lonely, and I'm happy they have some company.

"I don't know... but look..." I point to his arm, where a large bumblebee sits. "They follow you everywhere."

He huffs a laugh. "I'm a real-life pied piper." We watch it carefully before it flies off.

"So, you really ready to get hitched this weekend?" He steps closer, our hands dropping so he can encase my waist, and I grip on to his shoulders.

"I can't wait."

"Neither can I, Tinker... Neither can I..." His lips hit mine, and as we stand in serial killer forest, I know that my life turned out pretty good. All thanks to my mom and her love of bees. And even my dad, because without him, I never would've known Whispers existed.

WANT to know who buys the first jar of Sutton Silvers honey?

Grab the FREE bonus epilogue HERE

ALSO BY SAMANTHA SKYE

Are you ready for Griffin?

GRIFFIN

I came to Whispers to start over. Just me, my baby, and a bakery that smells like second chances.

No more judgmental glances. No more family who treated me like a stain they couldn't scrub out. Just flour, sugar, and the quiet hope that I can build a life worth living.

I didn't expect Griffin Patterson.

Grumpy, gorgeous, and maddeningly closed off, he's the town's most elusive billionaire and the man who built homes for the rich but never made one for himself.

He sees me. Not just the bump or the baggage, but the woman underneath. And when he looks at me like I'm the only thing that's ever made sense, I forget how to breathe.

But trust isn't something I can afford. My past has taught me to be wary of everyone. Even if the grumpy builder says he's ready to fight for something real.

I just hope he knows what it costs.

GRIFFIN - Click HERE to grab your copy!

ALSO BY SAMANTHA SKYE

The Billionaires of Whispers

Tanner

Hudson

Connor

Sawyer

Sutton

Griffin

SCROOGE: A Billionaire Christmas Story

Under The Mistletoe: A Billionaire Christmas Story

The Baltimore Boys

The Charming Billionaire

The Arrogant Billionaire

The Damaged Billionaire

The Secret Billionaire

The Bossy Billionaire

The Billionaire Babe

Men Of New York

My Legacy

My Destiny

My Fight

My Chance

ABOUT THE AUTHOR

Samantha Skye is an international bestselling author. A country kid turned city slicker, she writes spicy and suspenseful contemporary romance novels that leave you hot under the collar and on the edge of your seat.

Samantha lives in Melbourne, Australia and when she's not plotting her next novel, she can be found travelling, drinking margaritas and enjoying a sunset or a stargaze somewhere.

To join in the conversation join Skye's The Limit Facebook group here;

https://www.facebook.com/groups/skyesthelimitbooks